THE BEST AMERICAN

NONREQUIRED
READING
2006

THE BEST AMERICAN

NONREQUIRED
READING

2006

■

EDITED BY

DAVE EGGERS

INTRODUCTION BY

MATT GROENING

HOUGHTON MIFFLIN COMPANY
BOSTON • NEW YORK
2006

Visit our Web site: www.houghtonmifflinbooks.com.

ISSN: 1539-316x
ISBN-13: 978-0-618-57050-8   ISBN-10: 0-618-57050-0
ISBN-13: 978-0-618-57051-5 (pbk.)   ISBN-10: 0-618-57051-9 (pbk.)

Printed in the United States of America

Book design by Robert Overholtzer

MP 10 9 8 7 6 5 4 3 2 1

CONTENTS

INTRODUCTION

LATE AT NIGHT, when all sober people are asleep, I'm probably slouching in bed, all Tivo'd out, reading something like *The Insanity of Normality*, by Arno Gruen. Or a P. G. Wodehouse novel. Or another Isaac Bashevis Singer short story in the three-volume Library of America edition. Or maybe I'm squinting at the latest Acme Novelty Library comic book by Chris Ware. Whatever it is, the next morning I'm another bleary guy with dark circles under his eyes muttering about being late for work in the back of the line at Starbucks.

I'm also the guy not dancing at the happening party on Saturday night. Instead, I've scuttled over to the corner of the den with my head tilted, running my eyes down each shelf of books, looking for titles I've never heard of. Back at home, my dining room table is so stacked with books and magazines and newspapers and scripts and storyboards and comics and mail-order catalogs that I'm forced to tap out this little introduction on my kitchen table, which right now has on it — lemme count — four books, two daily papers, and the latest issue of the *New York Times Book Review*. My bathroom has a couple dozen books next to the toilet, and my bedroom is piled so high with books that I fear it's erotic only to me.

Sometimes I think I have a slight problem. Then I remember most of my friends are also readingly obsessed. It's a struggle for our kind to send flowers on Valentine's Day instead of a book. We think all librarians are hot. When we read one of those newspaper articles about some mad old coot found dead in his apartment, crushed by thousands of books, we think to ourselves, *How romantic.* We not only slow down at every used-book store, we slam on the brakes and make illegal U-turns. We haunt those musty old stores so often that sometimes we run into actual copies of books we once owned, and greet them like long-lost pets.

A few years back, in a sleazy used-book store in Hollywood, I found one of my favorite books, G. Legman's demented *Rationale of the Dirty Joke,* and discovered that the very copy I had grabbed was one I had given as a gift a few years before. I bought the book, crossed out "Merry Xmas 1997" in my dedication, wrote in the current year, and gave it to the same ex-girlfriend that Valentine's Day.

My obsessive love of reading began before I could read at all. As a wee tyke I remember being entranced by my older brother Mark's 1950s-era Little Lulu, Donald Duck, and *Mad* comic books.

"You know how much you like looking at those pictures?" Mark asked me. "Well, when you can read the words in the balloons, it's a zillion times funnier."

In the first grade, my eager smile faded when I was handed my preliminary reading book. That first primer had no words in it, just pictures, and kindly Mrs. Hoover sat with us and cruelly went through the whole thing, illustration by illustration, acquainting us with the utterly lame Dick and Jane and baby Sally and dog Spot and kitten Puff. Finally we got our hands on the first real book, and to this day I still get a thrill out of the word "Look!"

But the real sensation that year was the very first word I learned that actually had some meat to it, a word I had to figure out and puzzle over before unlocking its linguistic secret. The word stumped me at first, because when Mrs. Hoover said to sound it out, I couldn't figure out exactly what that letter combo was supposed to be.

"Tuh," I said.

"Try again, Matty."

"Tuh-huh."

"Try again."

"Tuh-hee. Tuh-hee."

"You're getting there. Sound it out."

"Thuh-huh. Thuh. Thuh?"

"That's right! You got it!"

"Thuh? Thuh? Thuh!"

And that's how I learned to read the word "the."

My budding bibliomania was helped along by a family obsessed by books and words. My grandmother called my dad Homer, after the Greek poet, and likewise my uncle Victor Hugo Groening was named after some French dude. My mom emphasized precision in English, and to this day I have it drilled into my brain that it's not "groom," it's "bridegroom," and that cheerleaders shake their "pom-pons," not their "pom-poms" (which are 40-millimeter antiaircraft guns).

A few years later, through a tragic preadolescent miscalculation, I joined the Boy Scouts, and before I knew what hit me I was on a twelve-day, sixty-five-mile summer trek with sweaty burros in New Mexico. Five days out, I was so crazy with book deprivation that I pounced on a piece of wrinkled, yellowing newspaper in the brush after a nine-mile hike and read every single classified ad on that page.

By that time I was reading stories of bad boys, such as *Tom Sawyer* and *Huckleberry Finn,* and the fictional diaries of Henry A. Shute, including *The Real Diary of a Real Boy.* Then, of course, I discovered the great, funny, sad, messed-up *Catcher in the Rye,* which, next to *Catch-22,* was just about my favorite book in the world. I've often thought that if I ever write a novel, I'll sneak the word "catch" into the title, just so I'll be in good company.

In high school I was a lonely, self-conscious smartass just like everyone else, but I was determined to change my luck. So I used to casually carry around a copy of Germaine Greer's *The Female Eunuch,* praying that a cute feminist girl would see how cool I was, overlook my teenage mustache, and ask me out on a date.

Didn't work.

Typical response: "What's that?"

(Hopes up.) "*The Female Eunuch.*"

"Ewwwwww."

(Crushed.)

In my junior year I had an English teacher who hated me more than usual for a teacher. I admit that technically I was a bit of a goofball, but I did do the required reading, and I was one of the few kids in this class of dunderheads who had bothered to pay attention to the crucial branch-shaking scene in *A Separate Peace*. But no matter how much I raised my hand and blurted out the answers before being called on and generally ran circles around the rest of the dorks, Mrs. T would cut me no slack, and she kept finding good reasons to give me lousy grades.

So we're reading *Death of a Salesman,* and I point out that Willie Loman is a pun (low man, get it?), and Mrs. T tells me to quit being a smart aleck. I realize my grades are going downhill fast, so I get the bright idea to write to Arthur Miller himself and maybe, just maybe, get a reply from the great man and let Mrs. T deal with them apples.

So I write a plaintive letter in cursive, on paper ripped from my notebook, telling Arthur Miller of the teacher who hated my guts and how life was unfair, and was Willie Loman based on anyone you met in real life and please write back soon because I need to get a good grade in this horrible class.

Three weeks later I get a typed postcard back from Arthur Miller! He writes that Willie Loman was based not on any one individual but on the sum total of everything he had experienced in life up to that moment, and concludes: "I'm sorry to hear about your horrible class. Best wishes, Arthur Miller."

Dilemma!

I'm sorry to hear about your horrible class.

How was I going to finesse this?

So in class that very day, we're assigned an essay on *Death of a Salesman* and I hatch my brilliant scheme. I make up a *fake* letter to Arthur Miller! In which I talk about what a wonderful teacher Mrs. T is. The only problem, I write in my bogus letter, is that when we perform scenes from the play, it suffers because we are all such *horrible* actors.

As I smirk to myself at my audacity, the bell rings that ends the class, and Mrs. T cries "Pencils down!" while I'm finishing the last sentence of the essay.

"One more sentence!" I say, scribbling away.

"I said pencils down now!" Mrs. T replies. "If you don't stop writing immediately, I'll give you an F."

In retrospect, I really should have put my pencil down.

Instead, I keep writing, and say, perhaps too cockily, "I think you'll change your mind when you read my essay."

A few seconds later I hand her my paper, and without looking up from her desk, she mutters, "F." The next day she drops my paper into my hands and indeed she is correct: I have received an F.

I thereupon went berserk, ran to the counselor's office, tried to transfer out of that crazy old bat's class, got turned down, threatened to drop out of school, and was finally almost cajoled into writing a final paper so I wouldn't flunk, because flunking meant I would be forced to repeat the same class the following year with Mrs. T.

That night I began making plans to run away and live in a seedy apartment in a big city near a major university, and I started compiling a list of one thousand books I would read in lieu of going to college. The list was cobbled together from every recommended-reading list I could find, but in the end I only read the novels about disobedient kids: Thomas Bailey Aldrich's *Story of a Bad Boy*, Booth Tarkington's *Penrod* and *Penrod and Sam*, and Don Robertson's *The Greatest Thing Since Sliced Bread*.

I ended up buckling under to Mrs. T and over the weekend cranked out a thirty-eight-page paper on the poetry of James Dickey, the author of *Deliverance*. Mrs. T gave me a D−, and as I walked out of her classroom for the last time, she called out that *Deliverance* was "a novel of perversion."

I immediately went to the downtown library and checked out *Deliverance*.

That's when I started burrowing into books about education, such as *How Children Learn* and *How Children Fail* and *Teaching as a Subversive Activity*, and got inspired to go to Evergreen State College in Olympia, Washington, then a brand-new progressive college with no grades. No grades! Every creative weirdo in the Pacific Northwest was jammed into the dorms, and I was in heaven.

I moved to L.A. after graduation and worked a series of lousy, degrading jobs that provided fuel for my subtly titled comic strip *Life in Hell*, which I have been drawing weekly for the past twenty-six years.

I made photocopies at a copy shop and ended up copying stuff for everyone from Frank Zappa to Twiggy, along with manuscripts by the great rock critic Richard Meltzer and Hubert Selby, Jr., author of the chilling, classic novel *Last Exit to Brooklyn.* Inspired by Tom Wolfe, beatnik critic Seymour Krim, and every funny writer I could lay my hands on from James Thurber to Roy Blount, Jr., I started cranking out my own little articles and cartoons for local publications, and then I got a book deal and then I got a TV show and then I got very busy.

Even though there's not time enough in the day to fulfill all my pressing obligations, I am still finding new ways to obsess over books and reading.

I decided in 1999 to plow through the great books of the twentieth century, chronologically, and here in mid-2006 I have finished H. G. Wells's *Love and Mr. Lewisham;* Jack London's first collection of short stories, *The Son of the Wolf;* Theodore Dreiser's *Sister Carrie;* L. Frank Baum's *Wizard of Oz;* and Sigmund Freud's *Interpretation of Dreams,* all published in the year 1900. At this rate I should be finished with the great works of the previous century sometime in the next three hundred years.

Then there's *The New Yorker,* now available in complete form on several annoying CDs. These too I'm plowing through chronologically, and after a year I am almost done with 1925, the first year of *The New Yorker's* existence. I've been reading jazzy quips about Charlie Chaplin, Prohibition, and the Scopes Monkey Trial. The most intriguing thing from 1925 so far is an ad for a Ring Lardner book, *What of It?*

And of course we mustn't forget the book obsessive's treasure trove of books about books: the reading guides, the long lists, the shortlists, the book blogs, and the reading journals. I have collected a few dozen book guides, ranging from the squaresville *How to Read a Book,* by Mortimer Adler, to the breezy *Read 'Em and Weep: My Favorite Novels,* by Barry Gifford. My favorite is Martin Seymour-Smith's *Guide to Modern World Literature.* He seems to have read every novel in every language, and has a pretty cranky opinion about almost all of them.

I try to surprise myself by reading outside the genres I usually gravitate to. Fed up with the repugnant current political scene, I decided to bury my sorrow through biographies of all the American presidents. Currently I'm reading *1776*, *Washington's Crossing*, and *His Excellency, George Washington*, so I have a ways to go. And at a beach house a couple summers ago I found a tattered copy of *The Best Sports Writing of 1947*, which contained "Lethal Lightning," a great article about Joe Louis by Jimmy Cannon, and now I'm thinking I gotta read more sports books. And recently I discovered the weird, outsidery pulp fiction of Harry Stephen Keeler, the author of such intriguing titles as *The Man with the Magic Eardrums*, *The Riddle of the Traveling Skull*, *The Case of the Transposed Legs*, and *Y. Cheung, Business Detective*.

And I still want to read all of Dickens, Wodehouse, Twain, Pynchon, Patrick O'Brian, and John le Carré — one of these days.

You've gotten this far, so you're probably as messed up as I am about reading. Let me conclude with a list that will keep you up late at night when you're supposed to be sleeping or making love: *Wolf Whistle*, by Lewis Nordan; *You Play the Red and the Black Comes Up*, by Eric Knight; *Dog of the South*, by Charles Portis; *The Fan Man*, by William Kotzwinkle; *The Curious Incident of the Dog in the Night-Time*, by Mark Haddon; and short stories by Steve Almond, Bernard Malamud, Flannery O'Connor, Matthew Klam, and Shalom Auslander. And don't forget the pieces in this very anthology. They're not too shabby either.

MATT GROENING

FOR THIS YEAR'S EDITION of *The Best American Nonrequired Reading*, we wanted to expand the scope of the book to include shorter pieces, and fragments of stories, and transcripts, screenplays, television scripts — lots of things that we hadn't included before. Our publisher readily agreed, and so you'll see that this year's edition is far more eclectic in form than previous editions. Along the way to making the book, we also came across a variety of things that didn't fit neatly anywhere, but which we felt should be included, so we conceived this section, which is a loose Best American roundup of notable words and sentences from 2005. It is, like this book in general, obviously and completely incomplete, but might be interesting nevertheless. We start, as would only be natural, with *The Onion*.

Best American Fake Headlines

FROM *The Onion*

1. U.S. Children Still Traumatized One Year after Seeing a Partially Exposed Breast on TV
2. Doctor Unable to Hide His Excitement from Patient with Ultra-Rare Disease

3. Breathalyzer Big Hit at Cop Party
4. Hilary Duff's Number One Fan Tasered
5. Latest Bin Laden Videotape Wishes America a "Crappy Valentine's Day"
6. Cocky Pope-Hopeful Ready to Make Some Changes Around Vatican
7. Neverland Ranch Investigators Discover Corpse of Real Michael Jackson
8. Evangelical Scientists Refute Gravity with New "Intelligent Falling" Theory
9. Fritolaysia Cuts Off Chiplomatic Relations with Snakistan
10. CIA Realizes It's Been Using Black Highlighters All These Years
11. Bush to Appoint Someone to Be in Charge of Country
12. Rest of U2 Perfectly Fine with Africans Starving
13. Bush Braces as Cindy Sheehan's Other Son Drowns in New Orleans
14. Area Baby Doesn't Have Any Friends
15. Google Announces Plan to Destroy All Information It Can't Index
16. Bush Nominates First-Trimester Fetus to Supreme Court
17. Activist Judge Cancels Christmas
18. Cases of Glitter Lung on the Rise among Elementary School Art Teachers
19. ESPN Courts Female Viewers with "World's Emotionally Strongest Man" Competition
20. Bob Marley Rises from Grave to Free Frat Boys from Bonds of Oppression
21. 133 Dead as Delta Cancels Flight in Midair
22. U.S. Troops Draw Up Own Exit Strategy
23. Rove Implicated in Santa Identity Leak
24. Chicago's Shedd Aquarium Admits Panda Exhibit a Ghastly Mistake

25. Blacks, Whites Put Differences Aside, Work Together to Make Better Burger
26. Study: Watching Fewer Than Four Hours of TV a Day Impairs Ability to Ridicule Pop Culture
27. Protest One Person Short of Success
28. 180 Trillion Leisure Hours Lost to Work in 2004
29. Bloodless Coup a Real Letdown
30. "Tony's Law" Would Require Marijuana Users to Inform Interested Neighbors
31. America Still Searching for Funniest Home Video
32. Cost of Living Now Outweighs Benefits
33. Report: U.S. Foreign Policy Hurting American Students' Chances of Getting Laid Abroad
34. Scientology Losing Ground to New Fictionology
35. Bush Challenges America to Produce the Perfect Romantic Comedy by 2009
36. Date Disastrously Bypasses Physical Intimacy, Goes Straight to Emotional Intimacy
37. Bush Vows to Eliminate U.S. Dependence on Oil by 4920
38. Police Search of Backpack Yields Explosive Bestseller
39. Rumsfeld Makes Surprise Visit to Wife's Vagina
40. Genie Grants Scalia Strict-Constructionist Interpretation of Wish
41. Report: 92 Percent of Souls in Hell There on Drug Charges
42. Philandering String Theorist Can Explain Everything
43. NASA Chief under Fire for Personal Shuttle Use
44. Terrorist Has No Idea What to Do with All This Plutonium
45. Mythbusters Team Struck Down by Zeus
46. Suicide Bomber Killed En Route by Car Bomb

Best American *Daily Show* Exchange on the Anniversary of Watergate

FROM *The Daily Show with Jon Stewart*

JON STEWART: For more on these revelations, we turn now to senior scandal historian Stephen Colbert. Stephen?

STEPHEN COLBERT: *(emerging from shadow)* Jon.

JON: Stephen, is that you? It's a little dark.

STEPHEN: Oh, one sec, Jon. *(reaches up, screws in bulb)* That's better. Sorry 'bout that. Jon, for those of us who covered Watergate, the revelation that W. Mark —

JON: Wait, you covered Watergate? You must have been —

STEPHEN: I was eight, Jon, and full of piss and vinegar. I was a cub reporter with the old UPI syndicate. Hell of a summer. I'll never forget the bustle in the newsroom, the smell of the cherry blossoms . . . banging Helen Thomas in the shadow of the Washington Monument. My parents thought I was at fat camp. Anyway, for those of us who covered Watergate, the revelation of Deep Throat's identity brings back a lot of happy memories.

JON: Happy? Stephen, Watergate is considered to be the death of our national innocence.

STEPHEN: Yes, that wonderful time when our nation's innocence was still alive to be killed.

JON: What do you think the legacy of Watergate is?

STEPHEN: It's twofold, Jon. For the media, the legacy of Watergate was an oppositional culture in which the press went to any lengths to catch the government committing crimes. For the government, Watergate left them with a real sense that they should stop recording their conversations about all the crimes they were committing. And, of course, it was the first time the suffix "gate" really caught on as a way to denote the truly serious nature of a scandal.

JON: Stephen, no. Actually, the "gate" comes from the name of the hotel, the Watergate. That was the first time that suffix was even used.

STEPHEN: No, Jon. If you'll remember, there was Bay of Pigs–gate, Teapot Dome–gate, Slavery-gate — shameful chapter.

JON: Those actually came well before, Stephen. They weren't referred to in that way.

STEPHEN: Yeah, the "gate" thing didn't really stick till Watergate. Been with us ever since.

JON: Stephen, could the press break a story like Watergate today?

STEPHEN: Not without the tapes. They don't have the credibility. And today's politicians are very good about a lot, leaving hard evidence. Everything becomes a "he said, she said." Is this globe warming, or are you wearing too many layers? Was Terry Schiavo in a vegetative state, or was she a Pilates class away from joining the cast of *Stomp*?

JON: So the reality is, the media couldn't break Watergate today.

STEPHEN: Correct, Jon. It lacks the credibility.

JON: The media?

STEPHEN: No. Reality.

Best American Ringing Defeat of Religion Masquerading as Science

FROM *Kitzmiller v. Dover*

On December 14, 2004, eleven parents of ninth-graders in Dover, Pennsylvania, brought suit against the local school board for violating their children's First Amendment rights. This was the case of Kitzmiller v. Dover. *Four weeks earlier, the school board legislated a new policy requiring teachers to read the following statement:*

> The Pennsylvania Academic Standards require students to learn about Darwin's Theory of Evolution and eventually to take a standardized test of which evolution is a part.
>
> Because Darwin's Theory is a theory, it continues to be tested as new evidence is discovered. The Theory is not a fact. Gaps in the Theory exist for which there is no evidence. A theory is defined as a well-tested

explanation that unifies a broad range of observations. Intelligent Design is an explanation of the origin of life that differs from Darwin's view. The reference book, *Of Pandas and People,* is available for students who might be interested in gaining an understanding of what Intelligent Design actually involves.

With respect to any theory, students are encouraged to keep an open mind. The school leaves the discussion of the Origins of Life to individual students and their families. As a Standards-driven district, class instruction focuses upon preparing students to achieve proficiency on Standards-based assessments.

From the Transcript of Proceedings, November 4, 2005

Attorney Erich Rothschild offered pro bono services to the parents, and Patrick Gillen represented the school board. This exchange occurred as the trial reached its end. Judge John Jones III presided.

THE COURT: Fundamentally, it was my distinct and rare privilege and honor to sit through this extended trial. I know that this case is important to the parties. I'm extremely cognizant of that. This case has not ended for me and hard work lies ahead. And as I said in my dialogue with counsel, I will endeavor to render a decision as promptly as I can, applying the law to the facts as I find them. I assure you of that, and I assure you that I will do my duty in doing so. Counsel, do you have anything further before we adjourn these proceedings? From the plaintiffs?

MR. ROTHSCHILD: No, Your Honor. Thank you.

THE COURT: From the defendants?

MR. GILLEN: Your Honor, I have one question, and that's this: By my reckoning, this is the 40th day since the trial began and tonight will be the 40th night, and I would like to know if you did that on purpose.

THE COURT: Mr. Gillen, that is an interesting coincidence, but it was not by design. *(laughter and applause)* With that, I declare the trial portion of this extended case adjourned.

The conclusion of Judge John Jones III, December 20, 2005

The following is an excerpt of Judge Jones's ruling in favor of the plaintiffs:

The proper application of both the endorsement and *Lemon* tests to the facts of this case makes it abundantly clear that the Board's ID [intelligent design] Policy violates the Establishment Clause. In making this determination, we have addressed the seminal question of whether ID is science. We have concluded that it is not, and moreover that ID cannot uncouple itself from its creationist, and thus religious, antecedents.

Both Defendants and many of the leading proponents of ID make a bedrock assumption which is utterly false. Their presupposition is that evolutionary theory is antithetical to a belief in the existence of a supreme being and to religion in general. Repeatedly in this trial, Plaintiffs' scientific experts testified that the theory of evolution represents good science, is overwhelmingly accepted by the scientific community, and that it in no way conflicts with, nor does it deny, the existence of a divine creator.

To be sure, Darwin's theory of evolution is imperfect. However, the fact that a scientific theory cannot yet render an explanation on every point should not be used as a pretext to thrust an untestable alternative hypothesis grounded in religion into the science classroom or to misrepresent well-established scientific propositions.

The citizens of the Dover area were poorly served by the members of the Board who voted for the ID Policy. It is ironic that several of these individuals, who so staunchly and proudly touted their religious convictions in public, would time and again lie to cover their tracks and disguise the real purpose behind the ID Policy.

With that said, we do not question that many of the leading advocates of ID have bona fide and deeply held beliefs which drive their scholarly endeavors. Nor do we controvert that ID should continue to be studied, debated, and discussed. As stated, our conclusion today is that it is unconstitutional to teach ID as an alternative to evolution in a public school science classroom.

Those who disagree with our holding will likely mark it as the product of an activist judge. If so, they will have erred as this is manifestly not an activist Court. Rather, this case came to us as the result of the activism of an ill-informed faction on a school board, aided by a national public interest law firm eager to find a constitutional test case on ID, who in combination drove the Board to adopt an imprudent and ultimately unconstitutional policy. The breathtaking inanity of the Board's decision is evident when considered against the factual backdrop which has now been fully revealed through this trial. The students, parents, and teachers of the Dover Area School District deserved better than to be dragged into this legal maelstrom, with its resulting utter waste of monetary and personal resources. To preserve the separation of church and state mandated by the Establishment Clause of the First Amendment to the United States Constitution, and Art. I, §3 of the Pennsylvania Constitution, we will enter an order permanently enjoining Defendants from maintaining the ID Policy in any school within the Dover Area School District, from requiring teachers to denigrate or disparage the scientific theory of evolution, and from requiring teachers to refer to a religious, alternative theory known as ID. We will also issue a declaratory judgment that Plaintiffs' rights under the Constitutions of the United States and the Commonwealth of Pennsylvania have been violated by Defendants' actions. Defendants' actions in violation of Plaintiffs' civil rights as guaranteed to them by the Constitution of the United States and 42 U.S.C. §1983 subject Defendants to liability with respect to injunctive and declaratory relief, but also for nominal damages and the reasonable value of Plaintiffs' attorneys' services and costs incurred in vindicating Plaintiffs' constitutional rights.

Best American Answers to the Question "What Do You Believe Is True Even Though You Cannot Prove It?"

Each year, the Edge Foundation (www.edge.org) poses one question to elite scientists and leading intellectuals from around the world. This year it asked "What do you believe is true even though you cannot prove it?" of 120 scientists. Here are selected excerpts:

CARLO ROVELLI, physicist, Institut Universitaire de France and Université de la Méditerranée; author of *Quantum Gravity*

I am convinced, but cannot prove, that time does not exist.

I mean that I am convinced that there is a consistent way of thinking about nature that makes no use of the notions of space and time at the fundamental level. And that this way of thinking will turn out to be the useful and convincing one.

I think that the notions of space and time will turn out to be useful only within some approximation. They are similar to a notion like "the surface of the water," which loses meaning when we describe the dynamics of the individual atoms forming water and air: if we look at it on a very small scale, there isn't really any actual surface down there. I am convinced space and time are like the surface of the water: convenient macroscopic approximations, flimsy but illusory and insufficient screens that our mind uses to organize reality.

In particular, I am convinced that time is an artifact of the approximation in which we disregard the large majority of the degrees of freedom of reality. Thus "time" is just the reflection of our ignorance.

I am also convinced, but cannot prove, that there are no objects, but only relations. By this I mean that I am convinced that there is a consistent way of thinking about nature that refers only to interactions between systems and not to states of or changes in individual systems. I am convinced that this way of thinking of nature will end up to be the useful and natural one in physics.

Beliefs that one cannot prove are often wrong, as proven by the fact that this Edge list contains contradictory beliefs. But they are essential in science and often healthy. Here is a good example from twenty-five centuries ago. Socrates, in Plato's *Phaedon*, says: "[It] seems to me very hard to prove, and I think I wouldn't be able to prove it . . . but I am convinced . . . that the earth is spherical."

Finally, I am also convinced, but cannot prove, that we humans have an instinct to collaborate, and that we have rational reasons for collaborating. I am convinced that ultimately this rationality and this instinct of collaboration will prevail over the shortsighted egoistic and aggressive instinct that produces exploitation and war. Rationality and the instinct of collaboration have already given us large regions and long periods of peace and prosperity. Ultimately, they will lead us to a planet without countries, without wars, without patriotism, without religions, without poverty, where we will be able to share the world. Actually, maybe I am not sure I truly believe that I believe this, but I do want to believe that I believe this.

DAVID BUSS, psychologist, University of Texas, Austin; author of *The Evolution of Desire*

True love.

I've spent two decades of my professional life studying human mating. In that time, I've documented phenomena ranging from what men and women desire in a mate to the most diabolical forms of sexual treachery. I've discovered the astonishingly creative ways in which men and women deceive and manipulate each other. I've studied mate poachers, obsessed stalkers, sexual predators, and spouse murderers. But throughout this exploration of the dark dimensions of human mating, I've remained unwavering in my belief in true love.

While love is common, true love is rare, and I believe that few people are fortunate enough to experience it. The roads of regular love are well traveled and their markers are well understood by many — the mesmerizing attraction, the ideational obsession, the sexual afterglow, the profound self-sacrifice, and the desire to combine DNA. But true love takes its own course through uncharted territory. It knows no fences, has no barriers or boundaries. It's difficult to define, eludes modern measurement, and seems scientifically woolly. But I know true love exists. I just can't prove it.

TOM STANDAGE, technology editor, the *Economist*

I believe that the radiation emitted by mobile phones is harmless.

Mobile phones seem to me to be the latest example of what has become a familiar pattern: anecdotal evidence suggests that a technology might be harmful, and however many studies fail to find evidence of harm, there are always calls for more research.

The underlying problem, of course, is the impossibility of proving a negative. During the fuss over genetically modified crops in Europe, there were repeated calls for proof that genetic-modification technology was safe. Similarly, in the aftermath of the mad-cow-disease scare in Britain, scientists were repeatedly asked for proof that beef was safe to eat. But you cannot prove that something has no effect: absence of evidence is not evidence of absence. All you can do is look for evidence of harm. If you don't find it, you can look again. If you still fail to find it, the question is still open: "lack of evidence of harm" means both "safe as far as we can tell" and "we still don't know if it's safe or not." Scientists are often unfairly accused of logic-chopping when they point this out.

I expect mobile phones will turn out to be merely the latest in a long line of technologies that have raised health concerns that subsequently turned out to be unwarranted. Back in the nineteenth century, long before fears were raised over power lines and PC monitor emissions, telegraph wires were accused of affecting the weather, and railway travel was believed to cause nervous disorders.

The irony is that since my belief that mobile phones are safe is based on a historical analysis, I am on no firmer ground scientifically than those who believe mobile phones are harmful. Still, I believe they are safe, though I can't prove it.

MARTIN E. P. SELIGMAN, psychologist, University of Pennsylvania; author of *Authentic Happiness*

The rotten-to-the-core assumption about human nature, espoused so widely in the social sciences and the humanities, is wrong.

This premise had its origin in the religious dogma of original sin and was dragged into the secular twentieth century by Freud, reinforced by two world wars, the Great Depression, the cold war, and genocides too numerous to list. The premise holds that virtue, nobility, meaning, and positive human motivation generally are reducible to, parasitic upon, and compensations for what is really authentic about human nature: selfishness, greed, indifference, corruption, and savagery. The only reason that I am sitting in front of this computer typing away, rather than running out to rape and kill, is that I am "compensated": zipped up and successfully defending myself against these fundamental underlying impulses.

In spite of its widespread acceptance in the religious and academic world, there is not a shred of evidence, not an iota of data, that compels us to believe that nobility and virtue are somehow derived from negative motivation. On the contrary, I believe that evolution has favored both positive and negative traits, and many niches have selected for morality, cooperation, altruism, and goodness, just as many have also selected for murder, theft, self-seeking, and terrorism.

More plausible than the rotten-to-the-core theory of human nature is the dual-aspect theory in which the strengths and the virtues are just as basic to human nature as the negative traits: that negative motivation and emotion have been selected for by zero-sum-game survival struggles, while virtue and positive emotion have been selected for by positive-sum-game sexual selection. These two overarching systems sit side by side in our central nervous system, ready to be activated by privation and thwarting, on the one hand, and by abundance and the prospect of success on the other.

SUSAN BLACKMORE, psychologist, visiting lecturer, University of the West of England, Bristol; author of *The Meme Machine*

It is possible to live happily and morally without believing in free will.

As Samuel Johnson said, "All theory is against the freedom of the will; all experience is for it." With recent developments in neuroscience and theories of consciousness, theory is even more against it than it was in his time, more than two hundred years ago. So I long ago set about to systematically change the experience. I now have no feeling of acting with free will, although the feeling took many years to ebb away.

But what happens? People say I'm lying! They say it's impossible, and so I must be deluding myself to preserve my theory. And what can I do or say to challenge them? I have no idea, other than to suggest that other people try the exercise, demanding as it is.

When the feeling is gone, decisions just happen with no sense of anyone making them, but then a new question arises: Will the decisions be morally acceptable? Here I have made a great leap of faith (or the memes and genes and the world have done so). It seems that when people throw out the illusion of an inner self who acts, as many mystics and Buddhist practitioners have done, they generally do behave in ways that we think of as moral or good. So perhaps giving up free will is not as dangerous as it sounds. But this too I cannot prove.

As for giving up the sense of an inner conscious self altogether, this is much harder. I just keep on seeming to exist. But though I cannot prove it, I think it is true that I don't.

ALISON GOPNIK, psychologist, University of California, Berkeley; coauthor of *The Scientist in the Crib*

I believe, but cannot prove, that babies and young children are more conscious, more vividly aware, of their external world and internal life than adults are.

I believe this because there is strong evidence for a functional tradeoff with development. Young children are much better than adults at learning new things and flexibly changing what they think about the world. On the other hand, they are much worse at using their knowledge to act in a swift, efficient, and automatic way. They can learn three languages at once, but they can't tie their shoelaces.

This tradeoff makes sense from an evolutionary perspective. Our species relies more on learning than any other and has a longer childhood than any other. Human childhood is a protected period in which we are free to learn without being forced to act. There is even some neurological evidence for this. Young children have substantially more neural connections than adults — more potential to put different kinds of information together. With experience, some connections are strengthened and many others disappear entirely. As neuroscientists say, we gain conductive efficiency but lose plasticity.

What does this have to do with consciousness? Consider the experiences we adults associate with these two kinds of functions. When we know how to do something really well and efficiently, we typically lose, or at least reduce, our conscious awareness of that action. We literally don't see the familiar houses and streets on the well-worn route home, although of course in some functional sense we must be visually taking them in. In contrast, as adults, when we are faced with the unfamiliar, when we fall in love with someone new, or when we travel to a new place, our consciousness of what is around us and inside us suddenly becomes far more vivid and intense. In fact, we are willing to spend lots of money and expend lots of emotional energy for those few intensely alive days in Paris or Beijing, which we will remember long after months of everyday life have vanished.

Similarly, as adults, when we need to learn something new — say, when we learn to skydive, or work out a new scientific idea, or even deal with a new computer — we become vividly, even painfully conscious of what we are doing; we need, as we say, to pay attention. As we become expert, we need less and less attention, and we experience the actual movements and thoughts and keystrokes less and less. We sometimes say that adults are better at paying attention than children, but really we mean just the opposite. Adults are better at *not* paying attention. They're better at screening out everything else and restricting their consciousness to a single focus. Again, there is a certain amount of brain evidence for this. Some brain areas, like the dorsolateral prefrontal cortex, consistently light up for adults when they are deeply engaged in learning something new. But for more everyday tasks, these areas light up much less. For children, though the pattern is different, these areas light up even for mundane tasks.

I think that for babies every day is first love in Paris. Every wobbly step is skydiving, every game of hide-and-seek is Einstein in 1905.

The astute reader will note that this is just the opposite of what Dan Dennett believes but cannot prove. And this brings me to a second thing I believe but cannot prove: the problem of capital-C Consciousness will disappear in psychology, just as the problem of Life disappeared in biology. Instead we'll develop much more complex, fine-grained, and theoretically driven accounts of the connections between particular types of phenomenological experience and particular functional and neurological phenomena. The vividness and intensity of our attentive awareness, for example, may be completely divorced from our experience of a constant first-person "I." Babies may be more conscious in one way and less in the other. The consciousness of pain may be entirely different from the consciousness of red, which may be entirely different from the babbling stream of Joyce and Woolf.

STEPHEN KOSSLYN, psychologist, Harvard University; author of *Wet Mind*

Mental processes: an out-of-body existence?

These days, it seems obvious that the mind arises from the brain, not the heart, liver, or some other organ. In fact, I have gone so far as to claim that "the mind is what the brain does." But this notion does not preclude an unconventional idea: your mind may arise not simply from your own brain, but in part from the brains of other people.

This idea rests on three key observations.

The first is that our brains are limited, and so we use crutches to supplement and extend our abilities. For example, try to multiply 756 by 312 in your head. Difficult, right? You would be happier with a pencil and a piece of paper — or better yet, an electronic calculator. These devices serve as prosthetic systems, making up for cognitive deficiencies (just as a wooden leg would make up for a physical deficiency).

The second observation is that the major prosthetic system we use is other people. We set up what I call social prosthetic systems (SPSs) in which we rely on others to extend our reasoning abilities and to help us regulate and constructively employ our emotions. A good marriage may arise in part because two people can serve as effective SPSs for each other.

The third observation is that a key element of serving as an SPS is learning how best to help someone. Others who function as your SPSs adapt to your particular needs, desires, and predilections. And the act of learning changes the brain. By becoming your SPS, a person literally lends you part of his or her brain!

In short, parts of other people's brains come to serve as extensions of your own brain. And if the mind is "what the brain does," then your mind in fact arises from the activity of not only your own brain, but those of your SPSs.

This idea has many implications, ranging from the reasons why we behave in certain ways toward others to the foundations of ethics and religion. One could even argue that when your body dies, part of your mind may survive. But before getting into such dark and dusty corners, it would be nice to have a firm footing — to collect evidence that these speculations are really worth taking seriously.

PAUL STEINHARDT, Albert Einstein Professor of Physics, Princeton University

I believe that our universe is not accidental, but I cannot prove it.

Historically, most physicists have shared this point of view. For centuries, most of us have believed that the universe is governed by a simple set of physical laws that are the same everywhere, and that these laws derive from a simple unified theory.

In the past few years, however, an increasing number of my respected colleagues have become enamored of the anthropic principle: the idea that there is an enormous multiplicity of universes with widely different physical properties, and the properties of our particular observable universe arose by pure accident. The only special feature of our universe is that its properties are compatible with the evolution of intelligent life. The change in attitude is motivated in part by the failure, so far, to find a unified theory that predicts our universe as the unique possibility. According to some recent calculations, the current best hope for a unified theory — superstring theory — allows an exponentially large number of different universes, most of which look nothing like our own. String theorists have turned to the anthropic principle for salvation.

I view this as an act of desperation. I don't have much patience for the anthropic principle. I think the concept is at heart nonscientific. A proper scientific theory is based on testable assumptions and is judged by its predictive power. The anthropic principle makes a huge number of assumptions — regarding the existence of multiple universes, a random creation process, probability distributions that determine the likelihood of different features, and so on — none of which are testable because they entail hypothetical regions of spacetime that are forever beyond the reach of observation. As for predictions, there are very few, if any. In the case of string theory, the principle is invoked only to explain known observations, not to predict new ones. (In other versions of the anthropic principle, where predictions are made, the predictions have proven to be wrong. Some physicists cite the recent evidence for a cosmological constant as having been anticipated by anthropic argument; however, the observed value does not agree with the anthropically predicted value.)

I find the desperation especially unwarranted because I see no evidence that our universe arose by a random process. Quite the contrary, recent observations and experiments suggest that our universe is extremely simple. The distribution of matter and energy is remarkably uniform. The hierarchy of complex structures, ranging from galaxy clusters to subnuclear particles, can all be described in terms of a few dozen elementary constituents and less than a handful of forces, all related by simple symmetries. A simple universe demands a simple explanation. Why do we need to postulate an infinite number of universes with all sorts of different properties just to explain our one?

Of course my colleagues and I are eager for further reductionism. But I view the current failure of string theory to find a unique universe as a sign that our understanding of string theory is still immature (or perhaps that string theory is wrong). Decades from now, I hope that physicists will be pursuing once again their dreams of a truly scientific "final theory" and will look back at the current anthropic craze as millennial madness.

ROBERT R. PROVINE, psychologist and neuroscientist, University of Maryland; author of *Laughter*

Human behavior is unconsciously controlled.

Until proven otherwise, why not assume that consciousness does not play a role in human behavior? Although it may seem radical on first hearing, this is actually the conservative position that makes the fewest assumptions. The null position is an antidote to "philosopher's disease," the inappropriate attribution of rational, conscious control over processes that may be irrational and unconscious. The argument here is not that we lack consciousness, but that we overestimate the conscious control of behavior. I believe this statement to be true. But proving it is a challenge, because it's difficult to think about consciousness. We are misled by an inner voice that generates a reasonable but often fallacious narrative and explanation of our actions. That the beam of conscious awareness that illuminates our actions is "on" only part of the time further complicates the task. Since we are not conscious of our state of unconsciousness, we vastly overestimate the amount of time that we are aware of our own actions, whatever their cause.

My thinking about unconscious control was shaped by my field studies of the primitive play vocalization of laughter. When I asked people to explain why they laughed in a particular situation, they would concoct some reasonable fiction about the cause of their behavior: "someone did something funny," "it was something she said," "I wanted to put her at ease." Observations of social context showed that such explanations were usually wrong. In clinical settings, such post hoc misattributions would be termed "confabulations," honest but flawed attempts to explain one's actions.

Subjects also incorrectly presumed that laughing is a choice and under conscious control, a reason for their confident, if bogus, explanations of their behavior. But laughing is not a matter of speaking "ha-ha," as we would choose a word in speech. When challenged to laugh on command, most subjects could not do so. In certain, usually playful social contexts, laughter simply happens. However, this lack of voluntary control does not preclude a lawful pattern of behavior. Laughter appears at those places where punctuation would appear in a transcription of a conversation — laughter seldom interrupts the phrase structure of speech. We may say, "I have to go now — ha-ha," but rarely, "I have to — ha-ha — go now." This punctuation effect is highly reliable and requires the coordination of laughing with the linguistic structure of speech, yet it is performed without the conscious awareness of the speaker. Other airway maneuvers such as breathing and coughing punctuate speech and are performed without the speaker's awareness.

The discovery of lawful but unconsciously controlled laughter produced by people who could not accurately explain their actions led me to consider the generality of this situation to other kinds of behavior. Do we go through life listening to an inner voice that provides similar confabulations about the causes of our actions? Are essential details of the neurological process governing human behavior inaccessible to introspection? Can the question of animal consciousness be stood on its head and treated in a more parsimonious manner? Instead of considering whether other animals are conscious, or have a different or lesser consciousness than our own, should we question if our behavior is under no more conscious control than theirs? The complex social order of bees, ants, and termites documents what can be achieved with little, if any, conscious control as we think of it. Is machine consciousness possible or even desirable? Is intelligent behavior a sign of conscious control? What kinds of tasks require consciousness? Answering these questions requires an often counterintuitive approach to the role, evolution, and development of consciousness.

Best American Excerpt from a Military Blog

FROM *A Soldier's Thoughts* (Misoldierthoughts.blogspot.com)

Zachary Scott-Singley, the author of this blog, was a sergeant in the 3rd Infantry Division, stationed in Tikrit, Iraq.

April 29, 2005 — Memories of Death

THERE IS GOOD out there even though at times it all seems bleak. There is also death. How many have dealt in death? Some would call it murder. Well, I have a confession to make, my platoon and I have had over 192 confirmed kills during our first deployment here (during the war on our way to capture Baghdad). We targeted people and then they just disappeared. Why? They were going to kill me. I had my orders and they had theirs. We were mortal enemies because we were told that we were. There are some who would tell me to not think about what I had to do, or it will drive you insane.

For me, however, I can't help but think about it. They were men like me. Some of them were even conscripted into military service. What made them fight? Were they more scared of their leader than of us? What has become of their families? How could I forget or not think about all that I have done? Should I wash my hands of it all like Pontius Pilate? I think not. My choices have been made, my actions irreversible. So live I will, for we were the victors, right? The ones who survived. It is our victory, and our burden to carry, and I bear it with pride and with the greatest of remorse. Do you think that there is a special place in hell for people like me? Or will God judge me to have been a man of honor and duty?

When they told us how many we had killed my first thought was pride. Pride for such a high number. How does one feel pride for killing? Two years later and my thoughts are changed, transformed if you will. Those were just numbers so long ago when I first heard them. Now, however, I know that they were men with families like mine. It is crazy that we humans can be so destructive. There are people out there lining up to become martyrs, to kill themselves in order to kill others, and yet you still have people who fight tooth and nail to live for just one more minute longer. We are an oxymoron, humanity that is. What makes someone look down the sights of a rifle to take aim on a fellow human being? What does it take to pull the trigger? I have done those things. I have done them and would do it again if it meant returning to my wife and children again. Some of you may think that I am a beast and you are probably right. I am. I will kill, I will take aim and fire, I will call fire upon you from afar with rockets and bombs or anything I can get my hands on if it means that I will see my family one more time.

But, I will also choose to dwell on and live with my choices. I chose to enlist as a soldier. My time has been served and now it is becoming overtime, but I won't just run away. As much as I would love to just be done (and rightly so now that I have been involuntarily extended). One thing is all I ask of you. I ask that you not judge me. Let me be my own judge, for my judgment is harsher than any you could give me anyway. For I will always have those memories to remind me of what I have done and what I am. Please know that I pray for peace every day, that and to see my family again.

May 4, 2005 — It Was Still Dark . . .

It was still dark. I got dressed in that darkness. When I was ready I grabbed an MRE (meal ready to eat) and got in the truck. I was going to go line the truck up in preparation for the raid we were about to go on. The targets were three houses where RPG attacks had come from a few days prior. Sitting there in that darkness listening to the briefing on how we were to execute the mission, I let my mind wander from the briefing and said a prayer. "Just one more day, God, let me live one more day and we will go from there . . ." It was the same prayer I said every day because every day I did the same thing. I left the base. With a small team I would go out each day on different missions. I was their translator.

There were different people to meet each day. There were some who would kill you if they could. They would look at you and you could see the hate in their eyes. I also met with people who would have given me everything they owned. People that were so thankful to us because we had rid them of Saddam. Well, this day was not really much different from all those other days so far. After the briefing we all got into our assigned seats and convoyed out to the raid site. I was to go in directly after the military police that would clear the building.

The raid began without a hitch. Inside one of the courtyards of one of the houses, talking to an Iraqi woman, checking to see if her story correlated with what the detained men had said, I heard gunfire. It was automatic gunfire. Ducking next to the stone wall I yelled at the woman to get inside her house, and when the gunfire stopped I peeked my head around the front gate. I saw a soldier amongst the others who was pulling rear security by our vehicles. This soldier I saw was still aiming his M249 (a fully automatic belt-fed machine gun) at a black truck off in the distance. His was the weapon I had heard.

I ran up near his position and overheard the captain in charge of the raid asking what had happened and why had this soldier opened fire. The soldier kept his weapon aimed and answered that he was sure he had seen a man holding an AK-47 in the back of the black truck. I was amongst the four (along with the soldier who had fired on the black truck) who had been selected to go and see what was up with that truck.

We were out of breath when we got to the gun truck nearest to the black civilian truck (a gun truck is a HUMMWV, sometimes called a Hummer by civilians, with a .50-caliber machine gun on its roof). There was a group of four Iraqis walking towards us from the black truck. They were carrying a body. When I saw this I ran forward and began to speak (in Arabic) to the man holding the body but I couldn't say a word.

There right in front of me in the arms of one of the men I saw a small boy (no more than three years old). His head was cocked back at the wrong angle and there was blood. So much blood. How could all that blood be from that small boy? I heard crying too. All of the Iraqi men standing there were crying and sobbing and asking me WHY? Someone behind me started screaming for a medic. It was the young soldier (around my age) who had fired his weapon. He screamed and screamed for a medic until his voice was hoarse and a medic came just to tell us what I already knew. The boy was dead. I was so numb.

I stood there looking at that little child, someone's child (just like mine), and seeing how red the clean white shirt of the man holding the boy was turning. It was then that I realized that I had been speaking to them, speaking in a voice that sounded so very far away. I heard my voice telling them (in Arabic) how sorry we were. My mouth was saying this but all my mind could focus on was the hole in the child's head. The white shirt covered in bright red blood. Every color was so bright. There were other colors too. The glistening white pieces of the child's skull still splattered on that so very white shirt. I couldn't stop looking at them even as I continued telling them how sorry we were.

I can still see it all to this very day. The raid was over, there were no weapons to be found, and we had accomplished nothing except killing a child of some unknowing mother. Not wanting to leave yet, I stayed as long as I could, talking to the man holding the child. I couldn't leave because I needed to know who they were. I wanted to remember. The man was the brother of the child's father. He was the boy's uncle, and he was watching him for his father who had gone to the market. They were carpenters and the soldier who had fired upon the truck had seen someone holding a piece of wood and standing in the truck bed.

Before I left to go back to our base I saw the young soldier who had killed the boy. His eyes were unfocused and he was just standing there, staring off into the distance. My hand went to my canteen and I took a drink of water. That soldier looked so lost, so I offered him a drink from my canteen. In a hoarse voice he quietly thanked me and then gave me such a thankful look, like I had given him gold.

Later that day those of us who had been selected to go inspect the black truck were filling reports out about what we had witnessed for the investigation. The captain who had led the raid entered the room we were in and you could see that he was angry. He said, "Well this is just great! Now we have to go and give that family bags of money to shut them up." I wanted to kill him. I sat there trembling with my rage. Some family had just lost their beautiful baby boy and this man, this COMMISSIONED OFFICER in the United States Army is worried about trying to pay off the family's grief and sorrow. He must not have been a father, otherwise he would know that money doesn't even come close . . . I wanted to use my bare hands to kill him, but instead I just sat there and waited until the investigating officer called me into his office.

To this day I still think about that raid, that family, that boy. I wonder if they are making attacks on us now. I would be. If someone took the life of my son or my daughter nothing other than my own death would stop me from killing that person. I still cry too. I cry when the memory hits me. I cry when I think of how very far away I am from my family who needs me. I am not there just like the boy's father wasn't there. I pray every day for my family's safety and just that I was with them. I have served my time, I have my nightmares, I have enough blood on my hands. My contract with the Army has been involuntarily extended. I am not asking for medicine to help with the nightmares or for anything else, only that the Army would have held true to the contract I signed and let me be a father, a husband, a daddy again.

May 29, 2005 — My Thoughts on Monsters

There is a place where the skies are blue, the water is clean, and life is good. This place cannot be found where I am at. Over here almost every single morning begins with violence, explosions, and people being killed. Over here the locals can't make enough money because it is so unsafe to be out and working. Over here things are different. Down is often up and up isn't down but sideways. In Iraq there are some who want only to see their children grow up, to grow old with their loved ones.

There are also monsters here. "Monsters?" you say. "Those can't be real." I tell you that they are. I have seen with my own eyes that they are. The worst part is that they look just like people. They aren't, though. They think that the way to do things is to violently end their lives. Most of the time they end up destroying and devastating those regular people who love their families. People who work honestly, those who have hearts. The monsters, however, are hard to spot because like I said, they look like regular people.

I have spoken with these monsters, seen their eyes. I wonder how you can fit so much hate in there. Maybe that is why they blow themselves up. They just can't contain all that hate . . .

Want to know what it is like to be one? I have come close before. Close, because I wanted to kill so badly, to destroy those same monsters, but I realized something. You are only a monster if you let yourself become one.

So now I dream not about monsters but about that place. It is so very far away that it doesn't seem like it is real anymore. That place is called home. I just hope that I make it back there.

June 17, 2005 — Sticks and Stones but Words Can Never Hurt

I can't stop thinking about what a major said to me the other day: "The whole country of Iraq, every man, woman, and child . . . Kill every one of them and it still won't be worth one American's life."

Perhaps this is why we won't win here, because so many feel that the life of an Iraqi doesn't even register when compared to that of an American. This kind of mindset permeates the thoughts of many of the soldiers here in Iraq.

So often I hear, "I gotta go f— guard Hajji!" from the soldiers assigned the duty of watching over the Iraqi workers who are working on our base. Another thing I hear so very often is, "I'm gonna go shoot me some Hajji." The soldiers who say these things speak as if the Iraqi people were some kind of animal to be hunted. You might tell me that terrorists are nothing more than animals to be hunted but if you look at the statistics most of those killed are civilians not foreign fighters.

It is time to wake up and realize that there are more important things than the Michael Jackson trial. There are things like the value of a human life or the value of an *entire* nation that has been kicked so many times by tyrants that it may look downtrodden and useless but under it all there is the beauty of LIFE.

October 27, 2005 — Our Walk Through Life

What is the human condition? Here in Iraq we fight terrorists and insurgents. We give them names (hajji, towelhead, raghead) to peel away their humanity. We focus only on the horrible things that have happened so that we can bring ourselves to kill, but in doing so we too become changed. No longer do we fit in when we get home. We become outsiders and misfits amongst our own families and distance ourselves as others too distance themselves from us.

Alone, it becomes easier with time to be that way. You can't let others know the things you have done because they would never understand and it would only serve to make us even more alone.

We must build as well; we become so proficient at building that we could be engineers. Walls are our specialty, so we build them thick and high around ourselves. These walls shut out all the pain and hurt we feel when others can't seem to understand why we are the way we are, or when they judge and condemn us as if they were God himself. The walls don't just keep those things out, but they serve to keep so much in as well. All of it, the guilt, the pain, and the fears we have can be kept deep inside where nobody will have to see them except ourselves.

That is OK though, because from there we can learn one last and important skill, that of the beast tamer. Like a monster everything we keep inside locked away can take on a mind of its own, creating even more pain. Some of us fall apart at this point, hitting the ground so hard that we decide we cannot get up. And so it ends.

The rest of us learn tricks to keep that beast inside so that nobody will ever have to see how much of a monster we have become. In doing so we can continue our walk through life. That is the soldier's cost of war, and it is ours to bear alone until the end.

Best American Epigraph Wherein a Contemporary Writer Quotes a Great Writer Who Died in 2005

FROM *Saturday*, by Ian McEwan

FOR INSTANCE? Well, for instance, what it means to be a man. In a city. In a century. In transition. In a mass. Transformed by science. Under organized power. Subject to tremendous controls. In a condition caused by mechanization. After the late failure of radical hopes. In a society that was no community and devalued the person. Owing to the multiplied power of numbers which made the self negligible. Which spent military billions against foreign enemies but would not pay for order at home. Which permitted savagery and barbarism in its own great cities. At the same time, the pressure of human millions who have discovered what concerted efforts and thoughts can do. As megatons of water shape organisms on the ocean floor. As tides polish stones. As winds hollow cliffs. The beautiful supermachinery opening a new life for innumerable mankind. Would you deny them the right to exist? Would you ask them to labor and go hungry while you yourself enjoyed old-fashioned Values? You — you yourself are a child of this mass and a brother to all the rest. Or else an ingrate, dilettante, idiot. There, Herzog, thought Herzog, since you ask for the instance, is the way it runs.

— Saul Bellow, *Herzog,* 1964

Best American First Sentences of Novels of 2005

NADEEM ASLAM, *Maps for Lost Lovers*
"Shamas stands in the open door and watches the earth, the magnet that it is, pulling snowflakes out of the sky towards itself."

PAUL AUSTER, *The Brooklyn Follies*
"I was looking for a quiet place to die."

DEAN BAKOPOULOS, *Please Don't Come Back from the Moon*
"When I was sixteen, my father went to the moon."

JOHN BANVILLE, *The Sea*
"They departed, the gods, on the day of the strange tide."

JULIAN BARNES, *Arthur & George*
"A child wants to see."

JOHN BARTH, *Where Three Roads Meet*
"If and when he ever gets his narrative shit together, Will Chase might tell the Story of the Three Floods more or less like this — freely changing names, roles, settings, and any other elements large or small as his by-then-more-seasoned muse sees fit, neither to protect the innocent nor to shield the blamable, but simply to make the tale more tellworthy."

AIMEE BENDER, *Willful Creatures*
"Ten men go to ten doctors."

MACKENZIE BEZOS, *The Testing of Luther Albright*
"The year I lost my wife and son, my son performed nine separate tests of my character."

GERALDINE BROOKS, *March*
"This is what I write to her: The clouds tonight embossed the sky."

KALISHA BUCKHANON, *Upstate*
"Dear Natasha, Baby, the first thing I need to know from you is do you believe I killed my father?"

JUDY BUDNITZ, *Nice Big American Baby*
"There was a woman who had seven sons and was happy."

PHILIP CAPUTO, *Acts of Faith*
"On a hot night in Lokichokio, as a generator thumps in the distance and katydids cling like thin winged leaves to the lightbulb overhead, he tells his visitor that there is no difference between God and the Devil in Africa."

CHARLES CHADWICK, *It's All Right Now*
"For a while the houses on either side of us were empty."

J. M. COETZEE, *Slow Man*
"The blow catches him from the right, sharp and surprising and painful, like a bolt of electricity, lifting him off the bicycle."

ELLEN COONEY, *A Private Hotel for Gentle Ladies*
"Charlotte Heath was in such a hurry to get to her husband, it took her a while to notice the absence of her bells."

DENNIS COOPER, *God Jr.*
"I work for a company called the Little Evening Out."

ROBERT COOVER, *A Child Again*
"Puff that mighty dragon: where is he?"

DOUGLAS COUPLAND, *Eleanor Rigby*
"I had always thought that a person born blind and given sight later on in life through the miracles of modern medicine would feel reborn."

MITCH CULLIN, *A Slight Trick of the Mind*
"Upon arriving from his travels abroad, he entered his stone-built farmhouse on a summer's afternoon, leaving the luggage by the front door for his housekeeper to manage."

MICHAEL CUNNINGHAM, *Specimen Days*

"Walt said that the dead turned the grass, but there was no grass where they'd buried Simon."

TRINIE DALTON, *Wide Eyed*

"We were performing a play about this maggot on our kitchen floor who grew until he was squishing out the windows, suffocating us and all those who came into the Ranch House."

FRANK DELANEY, *Ireland*

"Wonderfully, it was the boy who saw him first."

E. L. DOCTOROW, *The March*

"At five in the morning someone banging on the door and shouting, her husband, John, leaping out of bed, grabbing his rifle, and Roscoe at the same time roused from the back house, his bare feet pounding: Mattie hurriedly pulled on her robe, her mind prepared for the alarm of war, but her heart stricken that it would finally have come, and down the stairs she flew to see through the open door in the lamplight, at the steps of the portico, the two horses, steam rising from their flanks, their heads lifting, their eyes wild, the driver a young darkie with rounded shoulders, showing stolid patience even in this, and the woman standing in her carriage no one but her aunt Letitia Pettibone of McDonough, her elderly face drawn in anguish, her hair a straggled mess, this woman of such fine grooming, this dowager who practically ruled the season in Atlanta standing up in the equipage like some hag of doom, which indeed she would prove to be."

BRET EASTON ELLIS, *Lunar Park*

"You do an awfully good impression of yourself."

LOUISE ERDRICH, *The Painted Drum*

"Leaving the child cemetery with its plain hand-lettered sign and stones carved into the weathered shapes of lambs and angels, I am lost in my thoughts and pause too long where the cemetery road meets the two-lane highway."

STEVE ERICKSON, *Our Ecstatic Days*

"Sometimes I'm paralyzed by my love for him."

DIANA EVANS, *26a*
"Before they were born, Georgia and Bessi experienced a moment of indecision."

KAREN FISHER, *A Sudden Country*
"He carried his girl tied to his front, the trapsack on his back, the rifle balanced like a yoke along his shoulders."

JONATHAN SAFRAN FOER, *Extremely Loud and Incredibly Close*
"What about a teakettle?"

SESSHU FOSTER, *Atomik Aztex*
"I am Zenzontli, keeper of the House of Darkness of the Aztex, and I am getting fucked in the head and I think I like it."

NEIL GAIMAN, *Anansi Boys*
"It begins, as most things begin, with a song."

MARY GAITSKILL, *Veronica*
"When I was young, my mother read me a story about a wicked little girl."

GREGORY GALLAWAY, *As Simple As Snow*
"Anna Cayne had moved here in August, just before our sophomore year in high school, but by February she had, one by one, killed everyone in town."

AMITAV GHOSH, *The Hungry Tide*
"Kanai spotted her the moment he stepped onto the crowded platform: he was deceived neither by her close-cropped black hair nor by her clothes, which were those of a teenage boy — loose cotton pants and an oversized white shirt."

MARY GORDON, *Pearl*
"We may as well begin with the ride home."

MO HAYDER, *The Devil of Nanking*
"To those who fight and rage against superstition, I say only this: why?"

KAUI HART HEMMINGS, *House of Thieves*
"The sun is shining, mynah birds are hopping, palm trees are swaying, so what."

NICK HORNBY, *A Long Way Down*
"Can I explain why I wanted to jump off the top of a tower block?"

C. J. HRIBAL, *The Company Car*
"There are times on this drive when I have been tempted to turn to Dorie and shout, 'Our parents have been dead for years! Our father died while piloting a La-Z-Boy into oblivion, the remote still warm in his fingers! Our mother died in her bedroom; her last whispered words being "More! More!" That's what happened to our parents! Not this! Not this!'"

UZODINMA IWEALA, *Beasts of No Nation*
"It is starting like this."

NICOLE KRAUSS, *The History of Love*
"When they write my obituary."

PETER LEFCOURT, *The Manhattan Beach Project*
"Three years, nine months and twenty-four days after winning an Academy Award for producing the best picture of the year, Charlie Berns was sitting on a folding chair in a second-floor room at the Brentwood Unitarian Church Annex listening to a woman with smeared lipstick and a bad postnasal drip tell him, and the other thirteen people in the room, that she had just charged $1,496 worth of cashmere sweaters on a VISA card she had received in the mail and failed to destroy."

RABINDRANATH MAHARAJ, *A Perfect Pledge*
"On the evening the baby was delivered by Mullai, the village midwife, a chain-smoking dwarf who smelled of roasted almonds, cumin, and cucumber stems, Narpat, who was fifty-five years old, had given up the idea of fathering a son, was sitting cross-legged in the kitchen methodically compiling one of his lists: ginger, saffron, coconut jelly, and *sikya* fig, a small banana found in all the birdcages in the village."

GABRIEL GARCÍA MÁRQUEZ, *Memories of My Melancholy Whores*
"The year I turned ninety, I wanted to give myself the gift of a night of wild love with an adolescent virgin."

CORMAC MCCARTHY, *No Country for Old Men*
"I sent one boy to the gaschamber at Huntsville."

IAN MCEWAN, *Saturday*
"Some hours before dawn Henry Perowne, a neurosurgeon, wakes to find himself already in motion, pushing back the covers from a sitting position, and then rising to his feet."

JAMES MEEK, *The People's Act of Love*
"When Kyrill Ivonovich Samarin was twelve, years before he would catch, among the scent of textbooks and cologne in a girl's satchel, the distinct odor of dynamite, he demanded that his uncle let him change his second name."

MICHAEL MEJIA, *Forgetfulness*
"The eye, acquiring cyclopean proportions when seen reversely through the magnifying glass before it, is not still."

STEPHENIE MEYER, *Twilight*
"I'd never given much thought to how I would die — though I'd had reason enough in the last few months — but even if I had, I would not have imagined it like this."

LYDIA MILLET, *Oh Pure and Radiant Heart*
"In the middle of the twentieth century three men were charged with the task of removing the tension between minute and vast things."

RICK MOODY, *The Diviners*
"Rosa Elisabetta Meandro, in insubstantial light, entrails in flames."

HARUKI MURAKAMI, *Kafka on the Shore*
"'So you're all set for money, then?' the boy named Crow asks in his typical sluggish voice."

ARTURO PÉREZ-REVERTE, *Purity of Blood*
"That day there were bullfights in the Plaza Mayor, but Constable Martín Saldaña's festive fire had been doused."

SALVADOR PLASCENCIA, *The People of Paper*
"She was made after the time of ribs and mud."

FRANCINE PROSE, *A Changed Man*
"Olan pulls into the parking garage, braced for the Rican attendant with the *cojones* big enough to make a point of wondering what this rusted hunk of Chevy pickup junk is doing in Jag-u-ar City."

SALMAN RUSHDIE, *Shalimar the Clown*
"At twenty-four the ambassador's daughter slept badly through the warm, unsurprising nights."

ALBERT SÁNCHEZ PIÑOL, *Cold Skin*
"We are never very far from those we hate."

GEORGE SAUNDERS, *The Brief and Frightening Reign of Phil*
"It's one thing to be a small country, but the country of Inner Horner was so small only one Inner Hornerite at a time could fit inside, and the other six Inner Hornerites had to wait their turns to live in their own country while standing very timidly in the surrounding country of Outer Horner."

JOANNA SCOTT, *Liberation*
"She remembers shoes shuffling, hiccup of her mother's stifled sneeze, water trickling down a pipe, soft breathing, whispers like pages of a newspaper blowing across a deserted piazza, the neighbor's dog barking in the field, grunt of a curse, click of her teeth on her thumbnail, rattling of rain or water boiling or bicycle wheels turning, creak of a chair as whoever had been leaning back replanted his front legs on the floor, crackling of gunfire across the harbor or maybe someone had thrown a fistful of pebbles in the air, 'ssss' in place of *stai zitta*, 'ssss' in place of *silenzio*, strike of a match, her uncle clearing his throat, three quick coughs, suck of a cigarette, murmur of prayer."

DANA ADAM SHAPIRO, *The Every Boy*
"For his fifth birthday Henry got two presents that would come to shape his soul."

CARL SHUKER, *The Method Actors*
"The young historian sits at his desk high above Tokyo on the day he disappears."

CURTIS SITTENFELD, *Prep*
"I think that everything, or at least the part of everything that happened to me, started with the Roman architecture mix-up."

JULIA SLAVIN, *Carnivore Diet*
"My years were the cartoon's best, and I'm not bragging."

CHRISTOPHER SORRENTINO, *Trance*
"Here's a red and white VW van, parked and baking in the sun on this clear and warm May day, and the young woman seated in the front passenger seat, the van's sole occupant, stirs uncomfortably, her clothes sticking to her, her scalp roasting under the towering Afro wig she wears."

ALI SMITH, *The Accidental*
"My mother began me one evening in 1968 on a table in the cafe of the town's only cinema."

ZADIE SMITH, *On Beauty*
"One may as well begin with Jerome's e-mails to his father:"

RENÉ STEINKE, *Holy Skirts*
"Elsa had never been like the other girls she knew, modest and squeamish about their bodies."

AMY TAN, *Saving Fish from Drowning*
"It was not my fault."

COLM TOIBIN, *The Master*
"Sometimes in the night he dreamed about the dead — familiar faces and the others, half-forgotten ones, fleetingly summoned up."

SCOTT TUROW, *Ordinary Heroes*
"All parents keep secrets from their children."

LUIS ALBERTO URREA, *The Hummingbird's Daughter*
"On the cool October morning when Cayetana Chavez brought her baby to light, it was the start of that season in Sinaloa when the humid torments of summer finally gave way to breezes and falling leaves, and small red birds skittered through the corrals, and the dogs grew new coats."

WILLIAM T. VOLLMANN, *Europe Central*
"A squat black telephone, I mean an octopus, the god of our Signal Corps, owns a recess in Berlin (more probably Moscow, which one German general has named the core of the enemy's whole being)."

Best American New Words and Phrases

FROM *The Oxford Dictionary of English, Revised Second Edition*

beatbox • *verb*   imitate the sounds of a drum machine with the voice.

boo2 • *noun* (U.S. informal)   a person's boyfriend or girlfriend.

chip and PIN • *noun*   a way of paying for goods by debit or credit card whereby one enters one's personal identification number in an electronic device rather than signing a slip.

chugger • *noun* (informal)   a person who approaches passers-by in the street asking for donations or subscriptions to a particular charity.

chupacabra • *noun*   an animal said to exist in parts of Central America, where it supposedly attacks animals, especially goats.

clueful • *adjective* (informal)   having knowledge or understanding of something; well informed.

cockapoo • *noun*   a dog that is a crossbreed of an American cocker spaniel and a miniature poodle.

cold-cock • *verb* (N. Amer. informal)   knock (someone) out, typically with a blow to the head.

demographic • *noun*   a particular sector of a population.

desi (also **deshi**) • *noun* a person of Indian, Pakistani, or Bangladeshi birth or descent who lives abroad.

down-low • *noun* (in phrase **on the down-low**) (chiefly black slang) **1.** on the quiet; in secret. **2.** (of a man) concealing his homosexual tendencies.

dramedy • *noun (pl.* **dramedies**) a television programme or film in which the comic elements derive mainly from character and plot development.

eighty-six • *verb* (N. Amer. informal) reject, discard, or destroy.

enrobe • *verb* coat (an item of food) in chocolate, a sauce, etc.

Europop • *noun* pop music from continental Europe with simple melodies and lyrics, often sung in English.

fanboy • *noun* (informal) a male fan, especially one who is obsessive about comics, music, film, or science fiction.

flatline • *verb* fail to increase; remain static.

flippy • *adjective* (of a skirt) flared and relatively short, so as to flick up as the wearer walks.

floss • *verb* (black slang) behave in a flamboyant manner; show off.

'fro • *noun (pl.* **'fros**) an Afro hairstyle or a frizzy or bushy hairstyle resembling one.

geocaching • *noun* a form of treasure hunt using GPS, in which an item is hidden somewhere in the world and its coordinates posted on the Internet, so that GPS users can locate it.

Greek god • *noun* (informal) an extremely handsome man.

greige • *noun* a colour between beige and grey.

guided imagery • *noun* a method of relaxation which concentrates the mind on positive images in an attempt to reduce pain, stress, etc.

Hinglish • *noun* (informal) a blend of Hindi and English, in particular a variety of English used by speakers of Hindi, characterized by frequent use of Hindi vocabulary or constructions.

jilbab • *noun* a full-length outer garment, traditionally covering the head and hands, worn in public by some Muslim women.

labradoodle • *noun* a dog of a breed developed as a cross between a Labrador retriever and a poodle.

leverage • *verb* use (something) to maximum advantage.

-licious • *combining form*   forming adjectives denoting someone or something delightful or extremely attractive: *babelicious.*

nanoscale • *adjective*   on a scale of 10^{-9} meter; having or involving dimensions of less than 100 nanometers.

offshoring • *noun*   the practice of basing some of a company's processes or services overseas, so as to take advantage of lower costs.

overdog • *noun* (informal)   a person who is successful or dominant in their field.

phishing • *noun*   the fraudulent practice of sending e-mails purporting to be from reputable companies in order to induce individuals to reveal personal information, such as passwords and credit card numbers, online.

picturize (also **picturise**) • *verb*   adapt (a story or screenplay) into a film.

podcast • *noun*   a digital recording of a radio broadcast or similar programme, made available on the Internet for downloading to a personal audio player.

props • *noun* (black slang)   due respect.

retail politics • *plural noun* (U.S.)   a style of political campaigning in which the candidate attends local events in order to target voters on a small-scale or individual basis.

rock up • *verb*   arrive; turn up.

sing-jay • *noun*   a DJ who raps and sings as part of their performance.

smackdown • *noun* (informal, chiefly U.S.)   1. a bitter contest or confrontation. 2. a decisive or humiliating defeat or setback.

spendy • *adjective* (informal, chiefly U.S.)   1. costing a great deal; expensive. 2. spending a great deal of money; extravagant.

step change • *noun* (in business or politics)   a significant change in policy or attitude, especially one that results in an improvement or increase.

supersize • *adjective*   larger than average or standard sizes; extremely large. • *verb* [often as *adj.*] (**supersized**)   greatly increase the size of.

supertaster • *noun*   a person who has more taste buds than normal and is very sensitive to particular tastes.

tag • *noun*   a nickname or other identifying mark written as the signature of a graffiti artist • *verb* (of a graffiti artist) write their tag on a surface.

throwdown • *noun* (informal) a performance by or competition between DJs, rappers, or similar artistes.

twofer • *noun* (N. Amer. informal) an item or offer that comprises two items but is sold for the price of one.

ur- • *combining form* denoting someone or something regarded as embodying the basic or intrinsic qualities of a particular class or type: *ur-thespians Patrick Stewart and Ian McKellan.*

vermicomposting • *noun* the use of earthworms to convert organic waste into fertilizer.

vibe • *verb* (informal) 1. enjoy oneself by listening to or dancing to popular music. 2. get on; have a good relationship. 3. transmit or give out (a feeling or atmosphere).

wife-beater • *noun* (U.S. informal) a man's sleeveless vest or T-shirt.

wiki • *noun* a website or database developed collaboratively by a community of users, allowing any user to add and edit content.

Best American New Band Names

A MILLION BILLION, The Age of Rockets, The Alarms, Ambulette, American Minor, Arctic Monkeys, Assbaboons of Venus, The Asshole Two, The Audition, The Automatic, Babyshambles, Band of Horses, Beaten Awake, Birdmonster, Birthday Suits, Black Mountain, Bloc Party, The Blue Van, The Botticellis, The Boy Least Likely To, The Bravery, Brazilian Girls, Bullet for My Valentine, Calling All Monsters, Caribou, Cherry Monroe, Chooglin', Clap Your Hands Say Yeah, The Classic Crime, The Click 5, Clor, Cunninlynguists, Dead 60s, The Deaf, Death from Above 1979, Departure, Discover America, Early Man, Edan, Editors, Engineers, Envy and Other Sins, Ergoism, Final Fantasy, The Fold, Forward, Russia!, The Fray, The Go! Team, God Damn Doo Wop Band, Goodnight Gracie, Gospel, Hawk Nelson, I

Love You but I've Chosen Darkness, I Will Kill You Fucker, Jack's Mannequin, Jonezetta, Kill the Vultures, Komakino, Let's Get Out of This Terrible Sandwich Shop, Libido Funk Circus, Lords, Low Red Land, Magic Marker Karate Co., The Magic Numbers, Manuok, Maximo Park, Morning Runner, Negative for Francis, New Roman Times, Nine Black Alps, Olivia the Band, The Paddingtons, Panda & Angel, Panic! at the Disco, Pissed Jeans, Public Display of Funk, The Raconteurs, The Rakes, Run Kid Run, Stellar Kart, Sugarland, Tapes 'n' Tapes, Terminal, Tiger Bear Wolf, Tiny Hawks, Voxtrot, Waking Ashland, We Start Fires, Well Hungarians, When Rocky Beat the Russian, Wolf Parade, Wolfmother

Best American Things to Know about Chuck Norris

FROM *Chuck Norris Facts* (www.chucknorrisfacts.com)

- Chuck Norris created the hole in the ozone layer "to get a better look at the sun."
- When Chuck Norris claps, the lights always turn on. Even if he doesn't have a Clapper.
- Chuck Norris's family crest is a picture of a barracuda eating Neil Armstrong.
- Chuck Norris doesn't read books. He stares them down until he gets the information he wants.
- Chuck Norris does not sleep. He waits.
- Chuck Norris is currently suing NBC, claiming Law and Order are trademarked names for his left and right legs.
- Chuck Norris is the reason why Waldo is hiding.
- Chuck Norris counted to infinity — twice.
- There is no chin behind Chuck Norris's beard. There is only another fist.
- Chuck Norris's hand is the only hand that can beat a royal flush.

- There are no races, only countries, of people Chuck Norris has beaten to different shades of black and blue.
- When Chuck Norris falls in water, Chuck Norris doesn't get wet. Water gets Chuck Norris.
- Chuck Norris's house has no doors, only walls that he walks through.
- Chuck Norris doesn't actually write books. The words assemble themselves out of fear.
- The grass is always greener on the other side, unless Chuck Norris has been there. In that case the grass is most likely soaked in blood and tears.
- Chuck Norris has twelve moons. One of those moons is Earth.
- Chuck Norris grinds his coffee with his teeth and boils the water with his rage.
- Chuck Norris played Russian roulette with a fully loaded gun and won.
- Chuck Norris does not style his hair. It lies perfectly in place out of sheer terror.
- Chuck Norris is the only person in the world who can actually e-mail a roundhouse kick.
- Chuck Norris destroyed the Periodic Table because Chuck Norris only recognizes the element of surprise.
- It is believed dinosaurs are extinct because of a giant meteor. That's true if you want to call Chuck Norris a giant meteor.
- Chuck Norris doesn't wear a watch. He decides what time it is.
- When Chuck Norris does division, there are no remainders.
- Staring at Chuck Norris for extended periods of time without proper eye protection will cause blindness and possibly foot-size bruises on the face.
- Chuck Norris never has to wax his skis because they're always slick with blood.
- Two wrongs don't make a right. Unless you're Chuck Norris. Then two wrongs make a roundhouse kick to the face.
- When Chuck Norris wants an egg, he cracks open a chicken.
- Chuck Norris doesn't have blood. He is filled with magma.
- Chuck Norris once rode a nine-foot grizzly bear through an automatic car wash instead of taking a shower.

- Chuck Norris has to use a stunt double when he does crying scenes.
- Chuck Norris can get blackjack with just one card.

Best American Things
to Know about Hoboes

The following is an excerpt from The Areas of My Expertise *by John Hodgman. The information given in the book is questionable.*

THEY CALLED IT the War to End All Wars. They called it the London Fire and the Trail of Tears. But they were all wrong. It was called the Great Depression, and the hoboes saw it coming.

1929, October. Black Thursday. The 24th day of October, 1929: the day the stock market crashed, instantly wiping out $30 billion in stock value. Soon after, the Bank of the United States would collapse, trapping all inside, many of them orphans. From his hover-yacht in the Caspian Sea, President Hoover reassured the panicked nation that only foreigners and the mentally feeble would suffer. But the damage was too great. After a decade of high-flying prosperity, the United States' economy fell to earth and began tunneling to an awful volcanic core of despair, food riots, cloying folk songs, and lava. By March, 250,000 apple sellers would crowd the streets of Manhattan, desperately refusing to sell any other kind of fruit. But apples and sellers alike were easy picking . . . for the hoboes.

There had been hoboes in the United States since there had been trains and liquor, which is to say: always. But by 1930, an estimated two million broken souls had taken to the wandering life, hopping boxcars, picking up work where they could find it, and drinking, drinking, drinking. When Prohibition reigned, the hoboes knew of secret stills and hidden lakes of moonshine. It made them strong and willful, and it made them blind and disfigured, and it spurred them to sing strange guttural songs in croaking voices that haunted the American night.

In many ways, they were a nation unto themselves. They had their own currency in the form of "hobo nickels" — the ordinary buffalo nickels onto which they would intricately carve new words and images, changing the Indian head to a picture of a hobo or changing the buffalo into a large hairy man wearing a cloak and fake horns. Another common craft was lint-knitting, using scraps of wool fuzz from pilled sweaters to make new sweaters, which they would then attempt to sell door to door. They had their own flag, which was identical to the flag of Barbados (this was either a coincidence or a deliberate effort to confuse).

And they devised a secret language of signs and scrawls used to alert their passing brethren to danger or opportunity. A crucifix chalked on the side of a house meant that religious talk would get you a free meal inside. A picture of a cat meant "a kind woman lives here." But intersecting circles warned that the local sheriff carried throwing stars, while twin W's meant a mean dog slept in the yard and would rise on two legs and whisper secrets if you slept in the bushes. On some alley walls in whistle-stop towns you might find a cryptic translation of the complete text of *Tristram Shandy*, as that was the hobo's favorite novel. And a picture of an H with sunrays around it meant that the hour had come: it was time to overthrow the government of the United States.

When in the spring of 1932 great masses of unemployed veterans descended upon Washington to urge the passing of the Bonus Bill, hoboes came with them. Under the leadership of Joey Stink-Eye Smiles, they infiltrated the White House, pocketing sandwiches and replacing Secretary of the Treasury Ogden Mills with one of their own, Hobo Joe Junkpan. And across the country they began a coordinated reign of terror: soiling featherbeds, salting the cornfields, and dancing manic, heavy-footed jigs on parlor floors while ordinary citizens looked on in horror. In Kansas City, a hobo declared himself Duke of All the West and began demanding tithes. They wanted cheep beer and warm hats. They wanted bent nails and pieces of string. They demanded half barrels of swallowfeather sauce, and no one knew what they were talking about.

At his inauguration in 1933, a new, crippled president named Roosevelt addressed the nervous crowd: "The people of the United States have not failed. In their need, they have registered a mandate that they want direct, vigorous action. And so I will kill all the hoboes, and together we will gnaw on their bones." It was time for a comprehensive Hobo Eradication Plan called "The New Deal."

The president acted swiftly. He established the Civilian Conservation and Hobo Fighting Corps. He took the country off the gold standard, denying the hoboes the use of their precious teeth. The Works Progress Administration was created largely as a cover for Walker Evans, photographer by day, hobo hunter by night. He had only one target: Joey Stink-Eye Smiles. But Smiles was slippery, twice eluding the photographer's poisoned darts before disappearing into a ditch or a shrub. Now it was war. The hoboes retaliated by sneaking up behind the White House and whistling very loudly. They wrote confusing, illiterate editorials. And they summoned giant dust storms that stalked the land, eroding topsoil and swallowing small towns whole.

Finally the president knew there was only one way to end the hoboes' march across the blighted land: polio. Alone in his secret White House lab, Roosevelt created a concentrated serum of the dreaded disease that would be placed in the nation's water supply by the Tennessee Valley Authority. According to his contemporaries, Roosevelt was tortured by this decision. He knew that a certain number of non-hobo citizens would spend the rest of their lives in iron lungs as a result his actions, but it would finally put a stop to the wandering people — starting at their feet and ending at their waists.

But then came Pearl Harbor. Some say Roosevelt knew the Japanese would attack that infamous December 7th. The truth is, he didn't. But the hoboes did. And as the tragic war that followed put a final end to the Great Depression, so too did it put an end to the hobo war. As quickly as they had come, the hoboes mysteriously disappeared. No one knows where they went, or why. Some say they found patriotism in their hearts, joining the war against a common enemy. Others say they went to the stars or to another dimension. And still others say they live on today, moving quietly from town to town, preparing for the time when their great chicken-bone and moonshine empire will rise again. Is it possible? No, because historians agree that they almost certainly went to the stars.

But if you live near a railway track and listen as the train passes, it is almost as if you can still hear them singing — the dark and lonely wind of history still blowing from their rotted lungs.

Though the hoboes are gone, there are those who still admire their lifestyle of unworried rambling and crusty pants. I do not understand these people and I cannot stop them. But I can insist that if you do decide to take to the rails, you should choose for yourself a proper hobo moniker. Here are seven hundred more known historical hoboes whose names you can steal. You should not feel guilty about this. If they were still at large, they would steal *your* name without hesitation. If they could manage it, they'd steal your reflection from the mirror and sell it to the still surface of a moonlit pond. And then they would drain the pond out of spite.

If you wish, you may append your hobo name with "Jr.," "II," or "fils," after the custom of the more honorable hoboes, bearing in mind that the more honorable hoboes tended to be strangled on sight.

You may also use these names if you are having a child. It does not necessarily mean that they will become hoboes!

1. Stewbuilder Dennis
2. Cholly the Yegg
3. Holden the Expert Dreamtwister
4. The Rza
5. Jack Skunk
6. Jack Skunk Fils
7. Lord Dan X. Still-Standing
8. Marlon Fitz-fancy
9. Bazino Bazino, The Kid Whose Hair Is On Fire
10. Whispering-Lies McGruder
11. Nit Louse
12. Dan'l Dinsmore Tackadoo
13. Hobo Zero
14. The Silver Jacket Man
15. No-Shoulders Smalltooth Jones
16. Sistery Brothery Nabob
17. Name Withheld
18. Staniel the Spaniel
19. Frederick Bannister, the Tree Surgeon
20. Tarnose Cohen
21. Mr. Wilson Fancypants
22. Floyd Dangle
23. Shane Stoopback
24. Wicked Paul Fourteen-Toes
25. Normal-Faced Olaf
26. Tearbaby Hannity Stoop
27. The Damned Swede
28. Pierre Tin-Hat
29. Ol' Barb Stab-You-Quick
30. Mr. Whist
31. James Fenimore Cooper
32. Twistback John, the Scoliosis Sufferer
33. Sweet Daddy Champagne
34. Senator Cletus Scoffpossum
35. Horus, the Bird-Headed Fool
36. 50-Tooth Slim
37. Monk, the Monkey Man (which is to say: "the Man")
38. Thad the Bunter
39. Balloonpopper Chillingsworth
40. All-but-Dissertation Tucker Dummychuck
41. Finnish Jim

42. Flemish Jim
43. Foreign Tomas, the Strangetalker
44. Roadhouse Ogilvy and Sons
45. Jokestealer John Selden
46. Giancarlo, Master of the Metal Trapeze
47. Dr. Bill Stain-Chin, the Boxcar Medic
48. Boxcar Ted
49. Boxcar Mick
50. Boxcars [sic] Timothy Twin
51. Boxcar Jones, the Boxcar Benjamin Disraeli
52. Boxcar Aldous Huxley
53. JR Lintstockings
54. Gila Monster, Jr.
55. Irontrousers the Strong
56. "X," the Anonymous Man or Woman
57. Orphaned Reynaldo, the Child with Haunting Eyes (while there were children hoboes, Reynaldo took this name when he was 45; prior to this, he was known as . . .)
58. Reynaldo Reynaldoson, Who Will One Day Kill His Father
59. Thoughtless Harry Hsu
60. Clinical Psychiatrist Hugo Rivera
61. Peter Ox-Hands
62. Ponytail Douglas Winthrop
63. Lil' Jonny Songbird, the Songbird-Eater
64. King Snake: the Eternal Mystery
65. Ghostly Nose Silvie
66. Fonzie
67. DiCapa the Hound
68. Beef-or-Chicken Bob Nubbins
69. Honest Amelia Dirt
70. Slow-Motion Jones
71. Canadian Football Pete
72. Meep Meep, the Italian Tailor
73. Jonathan William Coulton, the Colchester Kid
74. Maria the Pumpkin-Patch Crooner
75. Bix Shmix
76. Vice President Garrett Hobart
77. Stun Gun Jones
78. Prostate Davey
79. Flea Stick
80. Niles Butterball, the Frozen Turkey
81. Todd Four-Flush
82. Stick-Legs McOhio
83. The Unanswered Question of Timothy
84. Mickey the Assistant Manager
85. Guesstimate Jones
86. Goofus
87. Gallant
88. Sir Roundbelly DeDelight
89. Newton Fig
90. Chicken Nugget Will
91. Parlor Peter, the Sneak Thief
92. Ovid
93. Bathsheba Ditz
94. Alan Pockmark, Esq.
95. Lolly Hoot Holler
96. Von Skump
97. Lonnie Choke
98. Chisolm Chesthair
99. Freak Le Freak, the Freakster
100. Rex Spangler, the Bedazzler
101. Randall Mouth-Harp
102. Chrysler LeBaron
103. The Fishin' Physician
104. Persuasive Frederick
105. Celestial Stubbs
106. Teary-Eyed Fingal
107. Mairah Nix
108. Cthulhu Carl
109. Del Folksy-Beard
110. No-Banjo Burnes
111. Chainmail Giles Godfrey
112. Lois "Charles" Ladyfinger
113. Plausible Zane Scarrey
114. Huckle Smothered
115. MmmmmDandy Dundee
116. Mountain-Humper Edgar Ames
117. Spasmodic Hilary
118. Doc Aquatic
119. Molly Bewigged
120. Cincinnati O'Gurk
121. Metuchen O'Sullivan
122. Cherry Hill O'Manley
123. Cheesequake O'Lennox
124. Booper O'Montauk
125. Zaxxon Galaxian
126. Drinky Drunky Thom, the Drunk

127. Terry Gross
128. Spooky Night Spooky-Day
129. Zipgun Gloucester Gluck
130. Human Hair Frum
131. Sherlock-Holmes-Hat Carl III
132. Patrick Intergalactic
133. Ambidextrous Stang
134. Yum-Yum Sinclair Snowballeater
135. Ponzi-Scheme Jeremiah Ponzi
136. Toodles Strunk
137. Monkeybars Matthew Manx
138. Pineneedle-Jacket Jericho Fop
139. Robert the Tot
140. Robert the Child-Size
141. Robert the Minuscule
142. Robert the Wee
143. Robert Fits-in-a-Case
144. Robert Eats-for-Free
145. Robert Is-He-an-Elf? (The seven Silk brothers, all named Robert, were also known for their small stature and predictable bitterness.)
146. Dennis Big-Ear Fox
147. Jethro the Pagan
148. Asterix the Gaul
149. Black Bolt, King of the Inhumans
150. Strictly Local Henry Bobtail
151. Manny the High-Ranking Mason
152. Fry-Pan Jim Fry
153. Slo-Mo Deuteronomy
154. Half-Bearded Mark
155. Knee-Brace Kenny
156. Morris the Personal Trainer
157. Thundertwine
158. Cleats Onionpocket
159. Deformed Abe
160. Trainwhistle Abejundio
161. David No-Ears
162. Achilles Snail-Hair the Buddha
163. Frog-Eatin' Lou
164. Admiral's Club Wilbur
165. Max Meatboots the First-Class Lounger
166. Dora the Explorer
167. Ms. Mary Manx, the Tailless Cat
168. Free-Peanuts Doug
169. Steve the Human Tunneler
170. Redball Charlie Dickens
171. Twink the Reading-Room Snoozer
172. Microfiche Roy, the Side-Scroller
173. McGurk, Who May Be Found by the Card Catalogue
174. Booster D'Souza
175. Commodore Sixty-Four
176. Moped Enid, the Mopedist
177. Lamont the Junkman
178. Fast-Neck Nell
179. Bill Never-Uses-a-Cookbook
180. Bee-Beard
181. Lil' Max Meatboots
182. The Personal Secretary to Jed
183. Dee Snider
184. Sausage Patty
185. Desert Locust
186. Gummy Miles
187. Gyppo Moot, the Enigma Machine
188. Ol' Stiffpants
189. Skywise the Sexual Elf
190. Craine T. Eyebrow-Smeller
191. Lonely Heiney Alan Meister
192. Shakey Aitch the Boneyard Concierge
193. Woody Damn
194. Alatar
195. Pallando
196. Saltfish Bunyan
197. Poor, Poor, Poor Charlie Short
198. Venomous Byron
199. Five-Chambered-Stomach Mort St. John
200. Gravybelly Dunstan
201. Extra-Skin Dave
202. Beanbag-Chair Bill
203. Grant Sharpnails, the Scratcher
204. Tommy Lice-Comb
205. "Medicated Shampoo" Jonah Jump
206. General Woundwort, the Giant Rabbit
207. Genius L. Cravat, the Gentleman
208. Giant Bat Wings Roland
209. Nick Nolte
210. Salty Salty Friday
211. Fatman and the Creature (note: there was no creature)

212. Cecelia Graveside
213. Hoosegow Earl French
214. Stymie Stonewrist
215. Roadrunner "Meep Meep" Fabong
216. Bruised-Rib Johansson, the Beefer
217. Joachim Bat-in-Hair
218. Food-Eating Micah
219. Rubbery Dmitry, the Mad Monk
220. Honey Bunches of Donald
221. Crispy Morton
222. Feminine Forearms Rosengarten
223. Two-Headed Mike Hoover
224. Manny Stillwaggon, the Man with the Handlebar Eyebrows
225. Bean-Hoarder Newt
226. Texas Emil
227. The Moor of Venice
228. Averroes Nix
229. Human Hair Blanket Morris Burnes
230. Canadian Paul Tough
231. Crooner Sy
232. Manuel Pants-Too-High
233. Sylvia Patience Hidden-Forks
234. Sung, the Land Pirate
235. Opie, the Boston Bum
236. Hard-Flossing Hope Peak
237. Stingo the Bandana Origami Prodigy
238. Franklin Ape and His Inner Ear Infection
239. Questionable-Judgment Theodore Stomachbrace
240. Thermos H. Christ
241. Sir Mix-a-Lot
242. The Nine Doctor Whos
243. Lord Winston Two-Monocles
244. The Freewheelin' Barry Sin
245. Diego the Spark-Spitter
246. American Citizen Zane Pain
247. Abraham, the Secret Collector of Decorative China
248. Linty Sullivan, the Lint-Collector
249. Socks Monster
250. Ma Churchill
251. Pappy Churchill
252. The Young Churchill

253. The Young Churchill's Hated Bride
254. Churchill-Lover Phineas Redfish
255. Crispus T. Muzzlewitt
256. Stain-Sucker Duncan
257. Dick the Candy Dandy
258. Albuterol Inhaler Preston McWeak
259. Longtime Listener, First-Time Caller
260. Mastiff Mama
261. Tennessee Ernie Dietz
262. Sharkey, the Secret Cop
263. Gooseberry Johnson, Head Brain of the Hobosphere
264. Weekend-Circular Deborah
265. Marcus Chickenstock
266. Stunted Newton
267. Magnus Shortwave
268. U.S. Fool
269. Manatee the Railyard Toreador
270. Utah Manfred Succor-Munt
271. Laura Delite
272. Edwin Winnipeg
273. Eyepatch Reese Andiron
274. Tom False-Lips Real-Teeth
275. Fabulon Darkness
276. Cricket-Eating Charles Digges
277. Pally McAffable, Everybody's Friend
278. Sully Straightjacket
279. Half-Dollar Funk Nelson
280. Whitman Sampler
281. Chili-Mix Wilma Bensen
282. Sting, the Glowing Blade
283. Professor Challenger
284. Lil' Shorty Longhorn
285. Rumpshaker Phil
286. Swing State Myron
287. Alistair Crowley, the Devil
288. Gutthrower Sy Salt
289. Sweetback Barney, the Dilettante
290. The Car-Knocker Killer
291. The Chamberlain
292. The Emperor
293. The Ritual-Master
294. The Garthim-Master
295. The Scientist
296. The Gourmand
297. The Slave-Master

298. The Treasurer
299. The Scroll Keeper
300. The Ornamentalist
301. Captain Slick-Talk
302. Sackfist, the Tapdancing Trombo
303. Souvenir-Selling Mlodinow
304. Blind Buck and "Woozy," the Invisible Seeing-Eye Dog
305. Roundhouse Farter
306. Red Ball Pnutz
307. Fake Cockney Accent Alan Strippe
308. Air and Whiskey Dale McGlue
309. Johnny RC Airplane
310. Narcotic Morgan Suds
311. Sir Frances Drank
312. Mahayana Mike
313. Miniyana Geoffrey
314. Three-Bean Otz
315. Maury the Monsoon
316. Czech Czarlie Czill
317. Sssssssssssssssss, the Hisser
318. Thanatos Koch
319. Henry Eatsmelts
320. Modem-Sniffer Gunderson
321. Half-Albino Alejandro
322. Gluttonous-Slim
323. Ragweed-Allergic Matt
324. Amorous Luminous Dirk
325. Moray Eel Ken Elmer
326. The Railbender
327. Antonio the Ombudsman
328. Karl Solenoid IV
329. Czar King Rex the Glorious Leader
330. Andy Bunkum
331. Plastic-Moustache Mortimer Tall
332. Samuel Gel Insole
333. Lemuel Gel Insole
334. Amanda Until
335. Crispy Whiskery
336. Robert Louis Stephenson, the Pirate
337. Hobo Overload
338. Leopard Print Steven Kane
339. Astonishing Shaun Eyelash
340. Billy Creak Knees
341. Owlie
342. Anwar, the Bionic
343. Reasonably Priced Motel Reese Unger
344. Fibery Dana
345. Cranberry Sauce Oppenheimer
346. Nancified Frederick
347. The Loon
348. Itinerant Jane
349. Holy Hannah Hottentot-Smythe
350. Fleabottle Boone
351. Amazin' Jack Caroo
352. Stupefying P, the Riddle-Maker
353. Todd Flaky-Palms
354. Waspwaist Fritz
355. Judge Roughneck
356. Slam Dance Dooze
357. Mariah Duckface, the Beaked Woman
358. Count Mesmerize
359. Sonny-Boy Oedipus Acre
360. Pick Mama Susan Xavier
361. Chelsea Bacon
362. Archie Axe
363. Sally Hoot-Hoot
364. Mr. Pendleton
365. Saves-Receipts Dave
366. Sir Walter British
367. Elmer, the Crankscout
368. Golden Neck
369. Marinated Alex Pons
370. El Boot
371. Shapeshifting Demon
372. Jeremiah Tip Top
373. Amanda CeeCee Strobelight
374. Irving Alva Edison, Inventor of the Hobophone
375. Leather Apron
376. Lead Apron
377. Foil Apron
378. Burnt Goathead
379. Saint Sorryass
380. Overly Familiar Fung
381. Chalmers, the Bridge Champ
382. Elephantine McMoot
383. Neekerbeeker Perry Toenz
384. Teattime BB Stiles
385. Coalie T
386. Hubbel "I Predicted Lindy Hop" Deerblind
387. Hubie Hewitt, the Broadway Legend

388. Huge Crybaby McWeepy
389. Poo-Knickers Elias
390. Elffriend Weingarten
391. Forktongue Nigel Fork
392. Woodeye Apfel
393. Hairlip Mikhail
394. Solid First Draft Patton Taylor
395. Prettynickels, the Lamb
396. Not-Only But-Also Pete
397. Penthief Hickock
398. La Grande Mel
399. Applebee O'Bennigan McFridays
400. Lardy Jerry Lardo
401. Low-Carb Aleks Stovepipe
402. Hugo Stares
403. Eldred Splinters
404. Oliver, the Train-Oyster
405. Pring, Ultralord of the Hobo Jungle
406. Utz, the Crab Chip
407. Salt-and-Pepper Chest
408. Beverly Hills Buntz
409. Mississippi Barry Phlegm
410. Matter-Eater Brad
411. 49-State Apthorp, the Alaska-Phobe
412. New Hampshire Todd
413. "Taxachusetts" Glenn
414. Hydrocephalic Jones
415. Vermont "Greenmountain Boy" Phil Marijuana
416. Alaska Mick the Crabber
417. Arizona Ludwig
418. California Ainsley Shortpants
419. Collegeboy Brainiac, the Hobo Einstein
420. Dr. Zizmor
421. Silas Swollentoe
422. Slimneck Holden Fop
423. Aspiring Jaster
424. Illinois Obama
425. Sammy Austere
426. New Mexico Anselm Turquoise-Eater
427. Caboose-Fouling Ferris Ntz
428. Prayerful Stan, the Bent-Knee Yahoo
429. Four-Fisted Jock Socko
430. Buttery-Cheeks Anton

431. Shadow ("Blinky") Preston
432. Godigisel the Vandal
433. Gunderic Godigiselson
434. Panzo the Spiral-Cut Ham
435. Smoke-Collecting Reg
436. Hot Gnome Jimmy Jackson
437. Pontius Cornsilk-Heart
438. Sanford Who Lacks Fingerprints
439. Treesap-Covered N. Magruder
440. Thor Hammserkold, the Mexican
441. Bingo-Balls Nick Chintz
442. Bleedingtoe the Barefoot 'Bo
443. Hondo "Whatever That Lizard Is That Walks on Water"
444. Salami Sunshine
445. Fourteen-Bindlestick Frank
446. Oregon Brucie Shunt
447. Pirandello, the Many-Bearded
448. Quinn and His Quaker Oats Box Drum
449. Fatneck Runt
450. my-e-hobo.com
451. Somersaulting Mike Spitz
452. Bo 'Bo
453. Abelard "Sunken Treasure" Lowtrousers
454. Colin, That Cheerful Fuck
455. Battling Joe Frickinfrack
456. Monsieur Dookie, the Francophonic
457. Happy Horace Noosemaker
458. Hieronymous Crosseyes
459. Crumbjacket Timmy
460. Overload-the-Dishwasher Mac
461. Rhythmic Clyde Hopp
462. Microbrew Stymie
463. El Caballo, the Spanish Steed
464. Lee Burned-Beyond-Recognition
465. Hollering Martin Mandible
466. Damien Pitchfork, the Freightyard Satan
467. Handformed Hamburger Clarence West
468. Dr. Nobel Dynamite
469. Pickled-Noggin Nettles
470. Mischievous Craig
471. Baldy Lutz, the Amityville Horror
472. Ashen Merle Buzzard
473. Frypan Nonstick McGee
474. Singleminded Hubbard

475. Maryland Sol Saynomore
476. Baked Salmon Salad Finn
477. Unshakably Morose Flo
478. Fr. Christian Irish, the Deep-Fat Friar
479. Smokestack-Hugger Jools Nygaard
480. Fossilwise Opie Fingernail
481. Tab-Collar Dix
482. George Slay, the Duck Throttler
483. Eldon Waxhat, the Waterproof Man
484. Timely Clayton, the Human Wristwatch (so named not because of his punctuality, but because one arm was significantly shorter than the other)
485. Both Dakotas Dave
486. Duke Jeremiah Choo-Choo
487. Transistorized Maximillian, the Hobo Cyborg
488. Gravelbed Gavin Astor
489. Pantless, Sockless, Shoeless Buster Bareass
490. Alternate-Dimension Bela Boost
491. Atlas Flatshoulders
492. Scurvied Leo Falsebreath
493. Toby Anchovy, the Canned Man
494. Mad Max
495. The Goose
496. Not the Goose
497. Mister Torso, the Legless Wonder
498. Jedediah Dryasdust
499. Loving Vincent Hugsalot
500. The Rambling, Rambling Boris Wander
501. Business-Class Klaus Riel
502. Emergency Exit Aisle Gustav Nook
503. Unnervingly Candid Nicky Thain
504. Snoops Lightstep Trenchcoat, the Hobo PI
505. William Carlos Williams
506. Beef Grease Porter Dripchin
507. Exoskeleton Chester Fields
508. Roth IRA Romeo Leeds, the Well Prepared
509. Bum-Smiter Phillip
510. Bum-Hating Virgil Hate-Bum
511. Thor the Bum-Hammer
512. Bum-Tolerant Brendan Sleek
513. Most Agree: It's Kilpatrick
514. The Beloved Dale Thankyounote
515. Unpronounceable
516. Thad Malfeasance
517. Chiseltooth Muck Manly
518. Amsterdam Jocko
519. Sinister Leonard Longhair
520. Beery Clive the Eunuch
521. Chaim the Squirrelkeeper
522. Nightblind and Colorblind, the Blind Twins
523. Milosz the Anarchist Puppeteer
524. Jimmy "New Man" Neandertal
525. Lonnie Pina Colada
526. Washington State Amy Swipe
527. Gopher-State Sam, the Minnesota Man
528. Candle-Eyed Sally
529. Packrat Red and his Cart o' Sad Crap
530. Trixie of the East
531. Trixie of the West
532. Fine-Nipple Tom Bazoo
533. The Friends of Reginald McHate Society
534. Oregon Perry Hashpipe
535. Bold 'n' Zesty Brad
536. Mermaid Betty Scales
537. Spotted Dick
538. Shanty Queen Elizabeth Regina
539. Nichols Crackknuckle
540. Stew Socksarewarm
541. Huge-Calves Dwight
542. A-Number-1
543. N-Number-13
544. Arthur Moonlight
545. Andrea Clarke, the Human Shark
546. Monkey's-Paw Patterson
547. Myron Biscuitspear, the Dumpster Archeologist
548. Ollie Ebonsquirrel
549. The Classic Brett Martin
550. Douglas, the Future of Hoboing
551. Ironbelly Norton
552. Dilly Shinguards
553. Rufus Caboose
554. Rear Admiral JF Grease Pencil

555. King Cotton
556. Prince Hal Oystershuck, the Royal Shucker
557. Unconditional Gavin
558. Squirrelcloak
559. Idaho Woody Harrelson
560. Jane the Boxcar Beekeeper
561. Aaron Three-Shirts
562. Paste-Smeller Luke
563. Lowly Highley
564. Elihu Skinpockets
565. Marian May Wyomingsong
566. Stitches the Railyard Sutureman
567. Klonopin Clyde
568. Benny Twenty-Squirrels
569. Chickeny-Flavored Remy Bunk
570. Juicepockets Thomas Moone
571. Eustace Feetbeer
572. Amnesiac Jared Stringy
573. Shagrat, Orc of the Ozarks
574. Billy Butterfly Net
575. Ammonia Cocktail Jones
576. Norma Shinynickels
577. Jonathan Crouton
578. Antigone Spit
579. El Top-Hat Swindlefingers
580. PomPom the Texas Dancing Dog
581. Gin-Bucket Greg
582. Yuri Trimble, the Alien Pod-Person
583. South Carolina Sarah Lardblood
584. Bloody-Stool LaSalle
585. Pith-Helmet Andy
586. Self-Taught-Guitarist Edmund
587. Don Tomasino di Shit-the-Bed
588. Markansas
589. Neckfat JK Trestle
590. Pansy Overpass
591. Ralph Raclette Cornichon, Hobo of the Mountains
592. Montana Nbdego Tch!k
593. Unbearably Oenophilic Ned
594. Jonas Tugboy, Professional Masturbator
595. Cinderfella Dana Dane
596. Kerosene-Soaked Tom
597. Black-Bottle Priam
598. Pinprick Butell
599. Stool-Sample Frank
600. Iowa Noam Chomsky

601. Etienne, Roi of the Rapier
602. Amesy Squirrelstomper, the Chipmunk Preferrer
603. Ned Gravelshirt
604. NPR Willard Hotz, the Soothing-Voiced
605. Amen to Polly Fud
606. Constantly Sobbing Forrester
607. Maine-iac Leonid
608. Magnetized James
609. Hobo Jake Jerrold, Representing the Whole Mid-Atlantic Region
610. Jiminy Sinner
611. Pamela Chickeneggs (i.e., Hobo Caviar)
612. Chuck McKindred: Not So Holy, But Very Moley
613. Q the Quantum Man
614. Salad-Fork Ron
615. Warbling Timmy Tin Voice and His Voicebox
616. Ambassador Roasting Pan
617. Warren Smazell, Founder of Hobotics®
618. Ventriloquism Jimmy and "Madam," the Talking Bean Can
619. Nosepicker Rick Pick
620. The Black Squirrel Fairy
621. Alabama Edsel Brainquake
622. Kid Silverhair, the Man of Indeterminate Age
623. Catscratch Tremont Nude
624. Bill Jaundice
625. Sugarhouse Morris the Sapper
626. Nutrition-Shake Emery
627. Nicknameless Norris Shine
628. Stinging Polly Papercuts
629. Deke Hidden Hornets' Nest
630. The Wisconsin Scourge
631. Brendan Headbristles
632. His Excellency Nooney Sockjelly
633. Whistling Anus Mecham, Le Petomaine
634. Talmidge, the Bactine Bearer
635. Tailstump Gunther, the Vestigial Man
636. The Hon. Charlie Weed-Farmer
637. Philatelist Joey Licks
638. Old Pliny Dance-for-Ham
639. Rheumy Sven

640. Wormy Glenn and Nootka the Flatworm
641. Hidalgo, the Devil Stick Artiste
642. The Fucky from Kentucky
643. Prince Bert in Exile, the Man in the Foil Mask
644. Siderodromophobic Billy
645. Antlered Calvin
646. Cambridge Massachusetts Claude
647. Cyrus the Persian Sturgeon
648. Kneepants Erasmus, the Humanist
649. Little Gavin Spittle
650. Tar-tongue Godfrey Strange
651. Honeypalms Gordon Lips
652. Luke "the Lifestyle" Dammmers
653. Simon Squirrelskin
654. Scabpicker Sandy Rump
655. Chicken Butt, Five Cents a Cut
656. Wise Solomon Babysplitter
657. Telekinetic Dave B.
658. Telekinetic Dave F.
659. Whiskeyblood Willie Sot
660. Unger and his Duststorm Bride
661. Zachary Goatflirter
662. "La Grippe"
663. Uranus John, the Star-Traveler
664. Accusin' Tim Dunn
665. Tennessee Linthelmet
666. The Unformed Twin of Tennessee Linthelmet
667. Turkeyballs Paco
668. Andre the Indianapolist
669. Wally Dregs, the Newfoundland Screech
670. Flaky Mike Psoriasis
671. Hell's Own Breath Hinkley
672. Gerald Chapcheeks
673. Acid-Saliva Curly Stokes
674. Oklahoma Stilgar
675. Rocky Shitstain Mankowicz
676. Rocky Shitstain Mankowicz Part II, the Quickening
677. Professor Ω
678. Sanitized-for-Your-Protection Eddie Summers
679. Jan, the Jager-Meister
680. Big-Tipper Silas Fake-Nickel
681. Anaerobic Eben Stiles
682. Replicant Wemberly Plastiskin and his Clockwork Squrrel "Toothy"
683. Harry Coughblood
684. Aesop Bedroll, the Fluffy Pillow Man
685. Widow-Kisser Roger
686. Experimental Hobo Infiltration Droid "41-K"
687. Baron Bayonet, the Bull-Sticker
688. Mikey Gluesniff
689. Bell's-Palsy Brennan
690. Chiptooth Berman, the Bottle Biter
691. Undertaker Robert, the Lint-Coffin Weaver
692. Betty, the Exorcist
693. Tittytwister Blake Horrid
694. Mallory Many-Bruises
695. Mad or Sad Judd (no one can tell)
696. Troglodytic Amory Funt
697. Smokehouse "Frankie" Jowl-Poker
698. Utility-Belt Deana
699. The Unshakable Will of Wade Terps
700. Trainwhistle Ernie Roosevelt, the President's Long-Lost Brother

II

CAT BOHANNON

■

Shipwreck

FROM *The Georgia Review*

And the Devil bubbled below the keel: "It's human, but is it Art?"
— RUDYARD KIPLING

KATRIN LIES IN FRONT of me, face-down and covered in plastic. A
Chinese man in his twenties moves back the film to expose her hand
and carves a little slit down her thumb. Moving quickly, he peels the
skin back with tweezers and a scalpel, and I can see the thick flesh at
the heel of the palm. A thin layer of fat as yellow as the fruit of a
mango sits on a membrane above the muscle, and with a quick cut
and pull it cleaves cleanly away. He flicks the globule of fat into a little
metal bowl. Within a few minutes, the hand is skinned enough that I
can see a strip of ligament running from a fingertip to the wrist. She
might have been a typist — the ligament is thick and developed, as if
she relied on it. She might have been a writer. A journalist. A pianist.

Katrin is destined to be a part of Body Worlds — a set of exhibitions
traveling through Europe and Asia, for which human corpses are
made into mummies called "plastinates." Unlike the mummies of
Egypt, however, these plastinates are perfectly preserved. Through a
complicated process, the fluids in the body are replaced with a polymer. Thus a body can look much as it did upon death, hypotheti-
cally for thousands of years. Standing in the dissection hall in north-
eastern China, watching Katrin's hand being flayed, I notice the
fingerprints peel off the pads of each finger in quick slips. Dr. Gunther von Hagens, a German anatomist, invented plastination in 1979
and immediately began taking volunteers — people willing to have
their bodies plastinated after death. Katrin was one such volunteer.

The worker holds up a fingerprint for me, transparent by the light of the window. Here in Dalian, Plastination City processes hundreds of bodies each year.

A few weeks ago, my brother e-mailed me from London with a picture of his new girlfriend and a hyperlink: www.bodyworlds. com. He was heading to China to write an article for *Science* magazine, and wondered if I wouldn't like to come along as a "poet in residence." (He's always concocting ways for me to tag along — if I weren't busy finishing grad school, in a few months I'd be on a ship in the Indian Ocean, trying to harpoon a sperm whale. Ya-hey, Ahab.) Having never been to Asia, and curious about China's frenzied pursuit of capitalism in the "new economic zone" of Dalian, I immediately agreed to go. I didn't check the link he'd sent me for another week. That's when I saw a child's head made entirely of plastinated veins.

They'd pumped resins through the circulatory system of the young body and then dipped the whole thing in acid — only the blood vessels were left. It looks like a faint red cloud of a child. A whisper and hush. I immediately checked out a copy of *Grey's Anatomy* and snagged a plane ticket on the cheap. When you go scuba diving, you fall into the water headfirst and backward. I think this was something like that.

A worker slides a scalpel under the lip of Katrin's thumbnail and pulls.

Body Worlds is "anatomical art," a tradition started in the Middle Ages when artists such as Andreas Vesalius and Michelangelo explored the aesthetics of anatomy. Dead bodies were depicted as partially flayed nudes, gracefully presenting their own organs. This tradition has long since fallen out of fashion, and anatomy has been relegated to anatomical museums, featuring jars of floating organs or virtual-reality tours of body systems. Now, as if walking out of history, von Hagens has taken the Renaissance nudes and brought them to life. But *his* nudes actually *are* nudes — every body on display was once a living, breathing individual. This has shocked the people coming to the London exhibition. Unlike the Renaissance audience, accustomed to plagues, public hangings, and vivisections, we rarely encounter death in person.

Dr. von Hagens is away in South Korea, at a new exhibition in Seoul. So, armed with a notepad, a translator, and Christine — the very press-shy manager of Plastination City, a tall blond northern German with somewhat menacing teeth — I find myself here in the dissection hallway around midmorning, and embark on a journey in which I will see more dead bodies than I have ever seen in my life. My brother is off pursuing photos. I tuck my stomach into a tight little corner and order it to keep quiet.

The Body Worlds Web site keeps a running tally: before I left California, the wait to get into the London exhibit (in a warehouse on the outskirts of town) was around two hours. To date, more than 13.5 million people have gone through the doors. But why are we coming? What do we want from Katrin? All she has to offer is muscle and teeth, the white hair of nerves, the swollen sack of the heart — the shipwreck of her body. Yet there's no lack of interest in her. Thousands of people have walked through row after row of corpses in a peculiar hush, like a procession in a church. To try to find out why we keep going to these exhibitions, I need to know just what kind of art this is. If these were simple nudes, I wouldn't need to travel halfway across the planet. The nude is familiar territory, with a pedigree going back thousands of years, written in stone and patina. But these are not simulacra. Can a dead human body be a piece of art "about" the human body?

I look down at death for answers. One worker begins stripping the skin from Katrin's calf. Watching feels a little like staring down from a great precipice — a dizziness and exhilaration and the simultaneous desire to jump and to run back to the car. As the shin bone hovers behind fat and membranes, as a caterpillar shows through its chrysalis, I scramble back to what I know about art. Artists have used parts of the body in their work before — urine and blood, for instance. Spit. Artists have used animal bones in their art, even. But no one's taken an entire *human* body and turned it into raw material.

It's been said that every work of art has a subject. One might say that Picasso's *Guernica* is about the horror of war, or that Monet's *Jardin de Giverny* is about the beauty of peace. Even Duchamp's ubiquitous urinal had a subject — the piece was about art and intent. Watching the skin gradually peeling off Katrin's extremities like the skin of a fruit, I know that the subject of these pieces must have something to do with the body. But I'm not sure that the subject of a sculpture can be itself. Michelangelo's *David* certainly isn't "about" marble. So it seems unlikely that the subject of von Hagens's cadavers is the nude. If these are indeed artworks, what is their subject? When asked, Dr. von Hagens has answered mysteriously, "The body is the ship of the soul."

A man scrapes tissue off his gloved finger on the side of the metal table. The workers joke with one another in Chinese. I know they're joking because they're laughing. I don't speak a whiff of Chinese. I don't ask my translator because people should be allowed to go about their business without always explaining it to the American. This feels suspiciously like reading Pound's *Cantos*.

When asked about the aim of his exhibitions, Dr. von Hagens has said humans "reveal their individuality not only through the visible exterior, but also through the interior of their bodies, as each one is distinctly different. Position, size, shape, and structure of skeleton, muscles, nerves, and organs determine our face within." But then, in these exhibitions, he purposefully changes the position and structure of these bodies to *reveal* something — we normally can't see organs through a wall of muscle, so he cuts a window in the muscle. There are buckets of spare organs across the room — is the "face within" still the same face without its nose or eyes? What if the face were rearranged like a Picasso? And what of this face belongs to the conscious individual that once resided in the body — the "ship" that carries us? His metaphors feel slippy. I've come to Dalian, a port town on the north rim of the Yellow Sea, to find out what happens when a human body becomes a work of art, and what that art could possibly be *about*.

While we stand around Katrin's corpse, Christine begins rattling off the four steps of plastination. "First the bodies are dissected, to remove the skin and fatty layers." The metal bowls positioned around the table are filling with yellow fat. I notice one worker has a bowl perched in the hollow below Katrin's pubic bone. The fat wobbles with each addition. "After dissection, the bodies are further defatted in acetone. Once the body is done in defatting, it is impregnated with polymer." The bowl in Katrin's crotch leans worriedly to the left. "For the final step, the bodies are positioned in various gestures and given a gas cure to harden the polymer." The worker moves the bowl down between Katrin's knees. I look back up at Christine. "The tour will follow these steps, in order, so that you will see bodies at each stage of the process." She smiles, looking for recognition.

I tuck my notepad into my jacket. "Yes. That sounds lovely."

Plastination City is composed of two drab concrete buildings and two bunkers, high up on a hill in Dalian's new technology park. The tour begins in the dissection hall. At the far end, two men insert mung beans into the fissures of human skulls, which they will water until the skull cracks along its fault lines. Winter light filters in through the blinds. Stretching back in double rows from the skulls, there are more than a dozen tables like the one Katrin is on. Around each table, two or three workers hunch over tendons and ligaments, each carving according to Dr. von Hagens's vision. It reminds me of descriptions I've read of Warhol's "factory." Except, of course, this artist is a scientist and a millionaire. That's a bit different. And his "materials" were once living, breathing, conscious people.

A girl in her twenties is cutting the fat from Katrin's Achilles tendon in short, clever strokes, palms as small as a pocket mirror. Through the film, I can see Katrin's ear, delicately molded, like seeing an iris in a freezer bag. Her hair is gone. In my pocket, I finger my comb.

Moving to another table, bearing a heavyset man with a butterflied thigh, I ask our translator if there is one set process to these dissections, or if it differs from body to body.

"According to what Gunter wants, they will dissect the body, usually taking off the skin and fatty layer and bringing out details of the musculature or skeleton, according to what will be the focus of the masterpiece." Behind us, a man in his early thirties is trimming the fat from Katrin's left thigh, which flies pointedly into a little metal bowl set aside for scraps. I make it a point not to stand near the bowls.

After a few minutes of walking among the bodies and buckets of extra organs, the tour moves to the Dehydration room. Once she has been trimmed for up to eight weeks in Dissection, Katrin will be moved here. The bodies are stored in pure acetone in large metal vats. A window looks out on a wintering hill, where scrub clings hopelessly to dust and gravel. The smell of acetone is overpowering when the lid opens, like a tub of nail polish remover.

The translator helps another worker open a vat of human parts. I see lungs, brains, various organs, and strangely, a single pair of feet sunk in a clear stringent pool. The worker standing next to me delicately holds his nose.

He closes the vat, and my tour moves to the Defatting room across the hall. The stench is overpowering. It's not a rotting smell, as there is no decomposition here. The room has to be at ambient temperature so that the acetone can dissolve the remaining fats from the flesh. Katrin will stay in one of these vats for a month or so. She'll need to be turned frequently, so the defatting is even. A man floats face-down in the vat, his heels at a rigid angle. I know in a few hours they will turn him, his nose grazing the surface of the liquid. The windows in this room look out on an industrial park. The tour shuffles quickly on.

As we walk, I scribble in my notebook. Nothing about the process thus far seems particularly artful. It may take a lot of skill, but nothing beyond creative anatomy. I think of one of the more famous plastinates from the exhibitions: a man holding his own skin. On the skin (which looks like a sad, wrinkled balloon) one can see the calluses on the soles of his feet. His arm is raised, and his face looks curiously proud. Anatomical displays are not supposed to have an expression. And why should they? Science has no need for gesture. The standard anatomical museum keeps death in a safe white room; its only purpose is education. But we all know we have calluses on our feet. Works of art usually serve a further purpose: they illuminate some aspect of the human experience.

Dr. von Hagens has been roundly criticized by British ethicists and anatomists alike. Some call him the "Disney of Death" (and here I am at Epcot Center). Despite a creeping nausea, I find myself on von Hagens's side — thus far I've seen very little that's controversial. Yes, burial and cremation and ritual; all in all we've found a very neat scaffolding for death. But there is also medicine and poetic license, and there's nothing wrong with donating one's body willfully, right? My driver's license says I'm donating my organs, even my eyes (myopic as they are, hazel, with that yellow ring around the pupil).

There are large freezers in the hallway as we make our way to the stairs. I'm guessing they're not full of pies.

We arrive upstairs at the Plastination room, where Katrin will go immediately after her defatting. After the stench of acetone, I feel a little flimsy, sort of stretched out. I lean against another silicone-filled vat for support. There is a body lying face-up on an operating table, covered in Saran Wrap and some kind of goo the color of Pepto-Bismol. A steady drip from the table hits the grated floor and oozes through the spaces. Three men and one woman hold long syringes, injecting liquid silicone into the muscles. Two feet point toward me, their skin removed, and I can see the thick strap of muscle that runs under the bones, up the heel to the ankle. The muscle has strings of viscous pink connecting it to the table, and I can't help but think of the feet of dancers, incredibly strong but hopelessly mangled. My toes sweat in their winter socks.

My translator goes into some technical details about the vat I'm leaning on. I move aside and hop from one foot to another. Two men with plastic gloves assist Christine while the translator moves what looks like a timer. I ask her what it's for. "Impregnation. This one's done cooking in about twenty hours."

A plate glass window separates the contents of the vat from open air. The inside is kept under vacuum so the silicone boils cold. A fat bubble pops near my arm. It strikes me as odd that a wooden two-by-four floats on the surface. Before I can ask, the translator tells me it's weighting down the body.

I suddenly realize there is a corpse hidden within this liquid. It's been stewing under there for weeks, while the acetone bubbles away from the flesh and the silicone seeps in. The liquid is candy pink, like cheap bubblegum, Pepto-Bismol. Pokémon pink. Katrin will boil in this vat for two to three months.

I'm feeling lightheaded and swimmy. I can see the precipice stretching before me, and pebbles below my feet. From far away, a voice says, "After Plastination, the bodies are moved to Positioning. Shall we go there now?"

I try to locate the voice. I stare at Christine's teeth. I thumb the pages of my notebook and say, "Yes. Yes. That would be lovely."

I step on my own foot to snap out of it. I button up my jacket as we walk out of the room, and I hope Christine hasn't noticed that I nearly fainted. But she must get a lot of that. We go down the stairs and move outside and cross over to Bunker 2. When Katrin is taken here, she will be carried on a gurney by two workers over a gravel driveway in the springtime China air, covered in plastic and secured with a strap. I pull my scarf more tightly around my neck, gulping for oxygen just south of Siberia. The sky is an improbable blue.

We hurry through the cold into Bunker 2, and the door closes with a little click behind us. I desperately hope this room will provide me with answers. So far, all I've seen is death and how to stop decay. I still haven't seen a hint of art. I peek around Christine's shoulder and survey the premises. To my left, three workers are planting colored flags in a cross section of body, sliced (I'm told) by a giant saw through either side of the man's nose down through his feet — about two inches of a man, lengthwise. The workers mumble to each other in Chinese. They look like heads of state muttering over the division of colonies — a red flag for the pancreas, France gets Congo. A blue-pinned flag through a testicle, South Africa. I scan over to my right. Although I'm beginning to become desensitized to the macabre, I'm startled to find a camel dominating the room.

The beast is huge, and it stands on a platform, which further dwarfs the anatomists working in the bunker. It's been sliced two times in precise increments through the head and neck, such that the eyes are on slabs of camel head separated from the center slab, which has the nose, parts of the tongue, and the sinuses. Much as Leonardo da Vinci showed a diagram of the human body in motion — the famous sketch in which the man, located in a sphere, has multiple arms shown in different positions — what they've done is taken these three slabs and fanned them out vertically. The effect is to see the far inside of the head at the top, at a standard elevation. Then the middle slab dips a bit down from the other, and finally the near slab, with its lips and eyelashes, is all the way down toward the ground, as if it were grazing on desert scrub. In this way, I can see the physical movement, like snapshots, of a camel grazing, while also seeing the mechanisms that make it possible — the incisors, the throat, the tongue, the massive nose and sinus cavities, the striated muscle of the neck. It's highly educational, but I am also made to feel as if the camel were alive and I just happened to have x-ray vision. They've added black marbles behind the eyelids, which reflect the lashes and our faces in a convex mirror. Wildflowers have been stuffed into its open stomach. Clearly, this isn't the work of purists or simple anatomists. This room is a workshop for artists.

As I move closer to the near slice of the camel's head, watching my own face distort in the glass eye, I feel less than certain that I'm seeing the "face within" that Dr. von Hagens described. "I would reach the limit of good taste," Dr. von Hagens once admitted, "if I carved a vase from a lung, filled it with water, and placed a daisy in it. Or if I fashioned a carnival mask from a stomach." And yet here, with this camel before me (whose stomach had the side wall punched out and serves as a vase for dried wildflowers), I realize the line between good taste and bad taste blurs, as does the line between science and art. Sure, the camel might eat wildflowers (there's a shortage in the Sahara, but camels certainly would eat them if the opportunity presented itself). But the flowers are artfully arranged, as one might find in a vase. While von Hagens argues that using the body tissue as one might use clay would be inexcusable, these pieces *aren't* representative of how the body *actually* appears under the skin; it's how the body appears according to Dr. von Hagens's imagination, coupled with a good deal of intent. If we have a face within, this German does make it a bit of a carnival. Maybe this camel wouldn't be out of place in New Orleans.

As we drift between clusters of activity, the translator describes the final step in plastination. When Katrin arrives, she will be assigned a small group of workers who will "position" her as Dr. von Hagens has ordered. They will move her bones, trim her muscle (pulling strings out, if need be, to emphasize striation), and give her face expression. All this will work to choreograph her final gesture. Depending on the complexity of the work, she could be here anywhere from three months to a year or more. Little string after little string. Like choreography. Like practicing for piano recitals. But only one performance, and only one piece left to perform. Forever.

The bunker is massive, with at least two dozen workers hovering around stations scattered throughout the room. Many pieces are strung from wires hung from mobile frames, which suspend the body and give it form. For instance, behind the camel sits "The Philosopher," his arms hovering over a table of invisible work, wires hooked into his shoulders to determine the posture. The flesh has been cut away from his back, revealing nerves of the spinal structure. A baby camel stands in the far right corner. To my left, workers flick excess material into silver bowls from a corpse on a metal gurney. (I again avoid the bowls.)

About five feet from the adult camel, two men sit hunched over one of Dr. von Hagens's sculptures. From the ceiling, a single arm dangles from two wires, severed at the shoulder, pointing downward with a yellow fingernail. Our translator introduces one of the men as Zhou Shouli, the senior worker in Plastination City. She tells me he can speak authoritatively on just about anything that occurs here in Positioning.

Zhou Shouli is working on an "exploded elbow." Like any devoted nerd's, his eyes light up when I show genuine interest in his work. He draws me in closer and shows how they pulled the bones of the joint apart in order to demonstrate the particular muscles that hold the structure together. It's rather like being shown the parts of an engine: here's a cam, here's a shaft. When I ask what the overall purpose is, however, he points toward a trunk of nerves that moves from the shoulder down through the elbow, fanning out into smaller nerves once it reaches the wrist. The nerves (which look like tangled white hair) have been pulled away from the hand and drape gently over the side of the ring finger. Marriage of muscle and electrical patterns. I catch myself pointing at my own forearm as I talk to Zhou, demonstrating the line of nerves from the wrist to the elbow. I picture the skin folding away from my finger, like Katrin's hand back in Dissection, exposing the bones and veins and wet muscle. I start to get dizzy again, and try to ignore it.

The gesture of the hand Zhou is working on is much like Adam's on the ceiling of the Sistine Chapel. Three fingers are curled very gently away, and the extended finger isn't rigid, but rather moves in a gentler arc toward the polished concrete floor. A muted reflection in the tile points back upward. This isn't the natural repose of a hand, so I have to presume it was "positioned" this way. Another mark of the artist.

I ask him which piece is his favorite, and he smiles and thinks for a moment. He says his favorite work is called "Standing Beauty" and consists of a pregnant woman standing with one hand in front of her belly and another sweeping to the side. The stomach has been cut away, exposing the layers of the abdomen and the fetus within the womb. He says it is as if she were "asking someone to protect her child." It isn't the most complicated piece, as one might expect an anatomist to choose. It isn't particularly instructive, or at least no more instructive than the other pregnant body in the exhibition, which is shown in a reclining position — "Reclining Beauty" — and was criticized for seeming sexualized. Rather, he says that he loves "Standing Beauty" simply "because of the gesture."

On a hunch, I ask Zhou if he loves the piece because of the art of it. He gets excited and says rapidly, "Yes. The art. The gesture. It is more subtle than the other, but it is more artful." He calls the work a "masterpiece."

Despite the simplicity of her posture, he'd worked on "Standing Beauty" for eighteen months. More complicated plastinates can take much longer. There's no prescribed gestation period. Like any artwork, it's done when it's done.

We let Zhou get back to his work, which seems intensive. We walk casually through the room, looking over the shoulders of the workers, trying not to get in the way. We pass "The Philosopher," the camel, and many, many others, all attentively serviced by the workers. One woman wipes more silicone on a forearm — it's imperative that the bodies stay wet until they are cured.

My attention is drawn to the back of the room, where a large chalkboard announces something important-looking in Chinese. My translator says it's mostly announcements for the company. Like posting boards in universities, its edges are aflurry with fliers. On the chalkboard itself are two free-form sketches of human figures done in the style of Picasso. The faces are a geometry of lines, the arms are mismatched lengths, the feet aren't discernible. I wonder if they know that Picasso often said that his portraits were attempting to show "how the model really looks." I wonder if they find themselves, in the heavy hours of the workshop, thinking that they are making portraits of individuals, using the bodies they've left behind. If Katrin were to become "The Philosopher," would she be a portrait of how she must have looked when she engaged in logic? Sitting at the table, then, notes strewn in front of her, a dichotomy of nerves. Writing a treatise on the metaphysics of magnets. The pull and repel. Desire.

Near the chalkboard there is a worker pulling strings of muscle from a female pelvis. He gestures to us to come closer, and then points at the muscles wrapped around her hips. He says something to the translator and smiles broadly.

She laughs and says to me, "He says she was very strong."

"Who?"

"The woman. He says she must have been very strong."

I'm baffled. The body is only the pelvis, lopped off above the hips and below midthigh. She? She was very strong? Even headless, without even a portion of a face or a mummified brain, does this piece make its sculptor wonder about the individual?

"How can you tell?"

He draws a line in the air with his finger above the muscles. It seems the musculature is more developed than in the average woman. They can also tell her age, just by the pelvis. Anatomists are magicians with mirrors and saws. How old is Katrin, I wonder. Thirty? Twenty? Forty-five? I'm self-conscious of the calendar between my hips. Does it know when I will die?

If the skin hadn't been removed, then Body Worlds would be a kind of Madame Tussauds wax museum in the flesh. But there's no way to recognize these individuals. According to von Hagens's wishes, all records of the individual are destroyed before display. So can any connection remain between the audience and the people who once occupied these grotesque forms?

I feel I'm about to crack the code. If bodies truly are "the ship of the soul," as Dr. von Hagens says, then what happens to the ship once the passenger has left? Wouldn't we find evidence of the passage? If a body is a ship, then wouldn't we find some remnants of the individual in the depths of its ballasts? Or, if nothing else, wouldn't we desire to know where it has been, the line of its journey? Some mark of salt on its skin? And if we were lost and came upon a ship that seemed to be pointed toward our destination, wouldn't we at least look through the wreckage for its log and compass?

When Katrin is finally positioned, she will be given a gas cure. This will solidify the resins in her body and make a permanence of her final gesture. As the camel is such a large piece, it's being left in Positioning to continue drying. So it isn't done. Wanting to see a recently finished product, I ask if they have any here in Dalian. The translator rushes off with a doctor, looking excited. The doctor opens a metal drawer in a cabinet I hadn't noticed before and withdraws a large, wrapped package. She promptly unwraps it and holds it up for me to look at.

The translator smiles and says blithely, "Smoker's lungs."

I'm floored. The lungs are perfectly shaped, like folded wings drawn by a cubist. But what draws me to them is their color. They look something like freshly mined ore — thin ribbons of green and metallic black run across their surface in chaotic patterns, as iron veins will run in rock. Working up my courage, I brush the left lung. It feels like rigid Styrofoam. I ask the translator if they've added color anywhere in the process.

"No, this is the color. Tar deposits."

I've already seen pictures of smokers' lungs. They were used to scare kids away from smoking. But these lungs, plastinated, are both gorgeous and ominous. They have their own message. They're not telling me "Don't smoke or you'll regret it." Instead, when I'm holding these pieces, I imagine the lung filling and filling with smoke. I imagine the smoke coloring the tissue with metals and tar. I imagine the mouth inhaling the smoke, and the mouth turning to speak to an unknown listener. I hear coughing and laughter. As I turn the lung over in my hands, I listen to a message spoken in an unfamiliar language — a language made of breath and blood and finality. And what's most unexpected, and sends my stomach reeling, is that the message isn't von Hagens's. I'm hearing ghosts.

As I hand over the lung and walk back out into the shocking cold, I come to a decision. This story is not von Hagens's or China's or even mine. It belongs to these bodies. These pieces *are* portraits, of a kind, in that they carry remnants of the individual who once lived inside them. Whatever Dr. von Hagens's intentions, they are a kind of monument, the way a shipwreck, once discovered by divers, is a testament to both its cargo and its journey into the sea. And when the audience comes diving, we're looking for something. The reason everyone's so quiet in the exhibitions is not simply out of respect. What saves Body Worlds from being a carnival of the grotesque — a Disney World of Death — is *our* intention. We are coming for answers. What is living? What dying? We want answers from the flesh. When we come to the Body Worlds exhibitions, we are listening for the dead.

In a room in Dalian, a body I named Katrin lies on a metal table, her feet pointed toward the window, her hands skinless and cupped. She can't tell me where she came from. She can't tell me about the boat she took here, carrying hundreds of other donated bodies in metal vats from Germany, through the Mediterranean, past Egypt, and down a canal into the Bitter Lakes and finally the widening bay. She can't lift her fingers to draw a map on a piece of paper. If I were to ask her, she would simply stare at the faint red glow of the back of her eyelids, her neck in a delicate arc, her lips stuck together in the blue rose of nothing. Below her toe, where under the nail a cube of sand lies stranded, a worker uses a scalpel to ease the skin back and down. I look past her body, out the window to an industrial park, and down toward the sea. But that ship is gone.

■

Nadia

FROM *One Story*

OUR FRIEND JOEL got one of those mail-order brides. It was all perfectly legitimate: he made some calls, looked through the catalogs,
comparison-shopped. He filled out the forms without lying about his
income or his height. Where it asked "Marital status?" he wrote "Divorced!" and "When she left me I threw my ring into the sea."

"That's so romantic," we all said when he did it. "No it wasn't, it was
stupid," he said. "I could have sold that ring for a lot of money." We
insisted, "No, it's very romantic."

"Do you think?"

"Any woman would want you now," we said as we put on bathing
suits and diving masks and headed down to the beach.

I'll call her Nadia. That was not her name, but I'll call her that to
protect her identity. She came from a place where that was necessary. "Nadia" brings up images of Russian gymnasts. Or is it Roma-
nian? Bulgarian? She had the sad ancient eyes, the strained-back hair,
the small knotty muscles. The real Nadia, the famous Nadia, I forget
what she did exactly — I have vague memories of her winning a gold
medal with a grievous wound, a broken bone, a burst appendix. I
think she defected. I picture her running across a no man's land between her country and ours, dressed in her leotard and bare feet,
sprinting across a barren minefield where tangles of barbed wire roll
about like tumbleweed and bullets rain down and bounce on the
ground like hail.

But our Nadia, Joel's Nadia, came wrapped as if to prevent break-
age, in a puffy quilted coat that covered her head to foot. She kept the
hood up, the strings drawn tight, so all we could see was her snout

poking out. She must have been cold when she first came; she stood in his apartment and wouldn't take it off, and then went and leaned against the radiator. We were all there to welcome her, we had come bringing beer and wine and flavored vodkas: orange, pepper, vanilla.

It was an old-fashioned radiator and her coat must have been made of some cheap synthetic because it melted to the metal. When she tried to step away and found she couldn't, she moved in a jerky panicked way that was strangely endearing. Joel tried to help her out of the coat but she wouldn't let him; she jerked and flailed until the coat ripped open and the filling spilled out. It wasn't down, it was like some kind of packing material, polystyrene peanuts or shredded paper.

It reminded me — a few months earlier I'd ordered some dishes, and when they came in the mail I found they'd been packed in popcorn, real popcorn. Some companies do that now, I've been told, because it's biodegradable, more environment-friendly. I took out the dishes and wondered if I should eat all that popcorn, but it seemed unsanitary. It might have touched something, I don't know, at the plant: dust, mouse droppings, the dirty hands of some factory worker. So I threw it away, this big box of popcorn. I still think about it. Probably that box could have fed Nadia's whole family for a week.

Joel and Nadia had written to each other, their letters filtered and garbled by interpreters. They described themselves — hair, eyes, height, weight, preferences in food, drink, animals, colors, recreation. She could speak English but not write it; they had a few phone conversations. What could they possibly have talked about? What did she say? It was enough to make him pay the money, buy the ticket, sign the papers to bring her over the ocean.

These days, ever since her arrival, Joel looked happy. He had a sheen. Someone had cleaned the waxy buildup from his ears. We asked if she was different from the women here, if she had a way of walking, an extra flap of skin, a special smell. Did she smell of cigarettes, patchouli, foreign sewers, unbathedness?

"I think she has some extra bones in her spine," he said. "She seems to have a lot of them. Like a string of beads. A rosary."

We'd seen more of her by then, up close, coatless. Her hair was bright red, black at the roots, which gave her head the look of a tarnished penny.

"Tell us *something* about her," we said. He closed his eyes. "When I take off her shirt," he said, "her breasts jump right into my hands, asking to be touched."

He opened his eyes to see how we took that.

"Her nipples crinkle up," he said, "like dried fruit. Apricots."

"She has orange nipples?"

We'd always insisted that Joel be completely open with us, tell us everything and anything he would tell a male friend. How could we advise him unless he told us the truth? Utter frankness, we told him, was the basis of any mature friendship between men and women. He often seemed to be trying to test this theory, prove us wrong. "Frankness will be the death of any good relationship," he'd say.

Joel was what we called a teddy-bear type, meaning he was large and hairy and gentle. He had a short soft beard all around his mouth so you could not see any lips. Hair grew in two bristly patches on the back of his neck. His fingertips were blunt and square, his eyes set far back in his head so that they were hard to read. His knees were knobby and full of personality, almost like two pudgy faces. In fact, he sometimes drew faces on them to amuse his soccer team, or us. Some of us had been in love with him once, but that was long past. Friendship was more important than any illusions of romance.

Nadia did not smile much. At first we thought it was because she was unhappy. Later she began smirking in an awful closed-lipped way so we thought she didn't like us. It took us a while to understand that it was a smile. Eventually we discovered the reason: her teeth were amazing, gray and almost translucent, evidence of some vitamin deficiency. When she spoke, air whistled through them, giving her a charming lisp.

She spoke English well enough, with a singsong lilting accent that lifted the end of every word. So that each word sounded as if it ended with a curlicue, a kite tail, a question mark.

She trilled certain consonants. "Lovely," she said, and trilled the *v*. Trilled the *v!* Have you ever heard that before? She must have had some extra ridges on her tongue.

She burst into tears at unpredictable times. She needed her own bedroom, so he cleared out his home office for her. We saw her bed, the child-size cot.

We began to suspect that he had done it all purely out of kindness, that he had wanted to rescue someone and give her a better home, a new life. He wanted to be a savior, not a husband. "Why didn't he just adopt a child, then?" we asked each other.

I thought maybe *I* should adopt a child. I ought to have one of my own — people are always looking at me and saying "childbearing hips" as if it's a compliment. But then I think of the rabbit my sister had as a pet when we were little girls. I remember holding him tightly to my chest until he stopped kicking. I was keeping him warm, but when I let go he was limp. We put him back in the cage for our father to find. I still dream of white fur, one sticky pink eye. I worry I might do the same to a baby. I could adopt a bigger one, a toddler. Not too sickly. But what if it doesn't understand English?

Of course you want to help, but what can you do? We did what we could. We gave money to feed overseas orphans, money for artificial limbs and eye operations. We volunteered at local schools, we brought meals to housebound invalids once a month, we passed out leaflets on street corners. A friend of mine who volunteers by escorting women past protesters at abortion clinics has invited me to join her, but it's never a good day for me. We recycle. We get angry and self-righteous about what we see on the news. When I see a homeless person on the street, I give whatever's in my pocket.

It's not enough. But what can you do? What can you do?

Joel had a friend, Malcolm, he was always promising to introduce us to. Malcolm worked for a global humanitarian organization. We saw him on television occasionally, reporting from some war-torn, decimated, or drought-stricken place, hospital beds in the background, people missing feet with flies clustered on their eyes, potbellied children washing their heads in what looks like a cesspool. Malcolm was balding but handsome in a weather-beaten, cowboy way. His earnest face made you want to reach for your wallet. "That guy, he can relief-effort me anytime," we'd say to Joel. But we hadn't met him yet. We were beginning to suspect he existed only inside the box and was not allowed out.

As for Nadia. "Where's she from exactly?" we asked Joel.

"A bad place," he said, frowning. "Her village is right in the middle of contested territory, every week a new name. Don't ask her about it. It makes her sad."

"All right," we said, but privately we wondered at his protecting her feelings like that. No one *we* knew had ever stopped talking about something because it made *us* sad. No one. Not even Joel. Was it because we were fat happy Americans, incapable of real sadness? Was it because he thought we had no feelings, or because he thought we were strong enough to bear sadness? Unlike poor delicate Nadia with her pink-rimmed eyes, Nadia who bought her clothes in the children's department because she had no hips. She said she did it because the clothes were sturdier, better quality, would last longer.

Last longer? How much longer will she need green corduroy overalls or narrow jeans with unicorns embroidered on the back pockets? How much longer before her hips swell and her legs thicken and her collarbone stops sticking out in that unbecoming way?

Her legs are not like American legs; they are pieces of string, flimsy and boneless.

"We'll take her shopping," we told Joel. "We'll show her the ropes."

"She's doing just fine," he said. "I'll take her."

I said, "You should be careful. I've heard, people like her, the first time they go to an American supermarket, they have seizures or pass out."

"Why?" he said.

"They just can't take it," I said. "They're not used to it. The . . . the *abundance* or something. Overstimulation."

"Thanks for the heads-up," he said, but he wasn't looking at me. Nadia stood at the other end of the room, before a window, so that sunlight set her hair afire and shone right through her pink translucent ears. Her ankles were crossed, her arms folded, a cigarette hung from her fingers. The skin on her face, her arms, was so milky white her ears didn't seem to belong to her. Around her, people moved in shadows.

"Do you know," he said, "she lets me hold her hand. In public? Just walking down the street? All the time."

He was beginning to talk like her, question marks in the wrong places.

"I love her," he said in a stupid way. He was talking like one of his moony students. There was something black floating in his drink, next to the ice cube, and he didn't even notice.

"How do you hold hands?" I said. "Like this?"

"Well, no," he said. "Usually I take her by the wrist. Or grab her thumb. But she doesn't pull away. She lets me. She likes it."

"Like this?" I said. "Or like *this?*"

"Not exactly," he said. "Her wrist is so little, my fingers go right around . . . Like this, see, only hers are even smaller. I can hold them both in one hand."

His palm was the same, still warm and damp, fingers long and blunt-tipped, hair on the backs. The hair almost hid the new wedding ring. There were bulgy things in the breast pockets of his shirt. The toe of my shoe was almost touching the toe of his. I wondered if she would look up and see us holding hands like this.

But she didn't. She was absorbed in her cigarette, her halo of sunlight.

Joel was a high school teacher. He loved kids. People always said that about him, first thing: "He loves kids." "Such a nice guy." We had always thought it was a wonderful thing about him. It meant he was caring, he was generous, he was nurturing, he was fun. He would be a terrific father. He taught chemistry, he coached the soccer team. He had won the Teacher of the Year plaque three times. Kids came to him in tears — they trusted him that much — and he'd let them cry through a box of Kleenex and keep his mouth shut and the classroom door open, and then hand them over to the proper counselor or police officer or health care worker. There had never been a bit of trouble. Not with the girls, not with anyone. He had perfected the art of the friendly distance, the arm's-length intimacy. We had always known a girlfriend or wife would never have reason to worry about cheerleaders or teen temptresses. Joel was better than that.

At least, we had never suspected anything of him until he brought home this child bride who must have weighed half of what he did, who sometimes wore her hair in two long braids. Then we had to wonder. Before, we liked to hear him talk about his students. Now there was something off about it, a sour note. "My kids," he would say. "I love those kids. Do you know what they did? Stephanie Riser and Ashley Mink? Listen —" And we would listen, but there was something tainting it now, a thin black thread.

"Don't you think she's a little too young?" we said.

"Nadia? No! She's thirty-three."

"No!" we said.

"Yes," he said, looking pleased.

"She must be lying," we said. "She can't be."

"It's right on her papers," he said.

"As if that proves anything," we said. But we said it nicely.

They bought a house together. What does that mean? *He* bought the house. It was his money. She contributed nothing. What did she do with herself all day? "She makes me happy," Joel said.

Her?

"She's trained as a doctor," he said. "She has to pass a test before she can practice here."

"What kind of doctor?"

"It's a source of great frustration. She has to relearn things she studied years ago, chemistry, anatomy, in a new language. You should see the size of these books."

"Are you going to have children?" we asked him.

"Of course," he said.

But there was no sign of them. So we kept asking.

"Of course," he said.

"Later."

"Maybe."

"I don't know."

Of course we were really asking something else. We wondered if she had her own bedroom in the new house. But of course we couldn't ask.

"He seems frustrated," we told each other. "Yes, definitely. Bottled up."

One of our old friends was chosen to be on a televised game show. We had a party to watch her and invited Joel and Nadia. We screamed when we saw her, taking her place among flashing lights and boldly punching her buzzer. But by the third question, a sweaty sheen had broken out above her upper lip. She faltered, mumbled, and in seconds she had disappeared forever. It was hard to work up any kind of real feeling — it was just dots on a screen. Only a game.

Joel seemed distracted. Nadia stared at the wall and then got up to use the bathroom.

"You have no idea what she's been through," Joel said, apropos of nothing. "You have no idea."

Which is unfair; we have all known suffering, we have all known loss. Certainly I have, and Joel should have known that better than anyone.

The sun going behind clouds, trees creaking in the wind. The house Joel bought was all windows, making it easier for the weather to force its mood upon them. That's how I explain the gloom. It was a sunless winter. She decorated the house herself, she did everything backward: hung rugs on the walls, stood dishes on their rims on the shelves, set table lamps on the floor, left the windows bare but hung curtains round the beds. She used a lot of red for someone so lacking in color.

Whenever we visited now she'd be listening to her own music. She'd found a station, way at one end of the AM dial, that played her type of thing. She'd play it for us if we asked her, to be polite. Horns and bells, nasal voices, songs like sobbing. More often she'd listen to it on the headphones he'd given her, and he'd talk to us. It was easier this way. She sat among us with a blissful look on her face, and we could talk about her without worrying about her overhearing us.

We saw her country on the news sometimes. Shaky camera, people running. Trucks. Shouting. Crowds of people pulling at each other. Are they using black-and-white film, or is everything gray there? She refused to watch.

"Is she afraid she'll see someone she knows? Does she want to block it all out? Does she still have family back there?"

"I don't know," Joel would say. We could no longer tell when he was lying.

"She doesn't talk about her family?"

"No."

"Maybe she's angry at them. Maybe they sold her to the mail-order people and took the money."

"Maybe," he said, in the way that meant he was not listening at all.

We could not get the picture out of our heads: Nadia ripped from the arms of . . . someone. By someone. That part is hazy. We see the hands reaching out, Nadia crying silently. Women with kerchiefs on their heads weeping, men with huge mustaches looking stern, children hugging her knees. Nadia's chin upraised, throat exposed, martyr-light in her eyes. Her shabby relations counting the money and raising their hands to the heavens in thanks, the starving children already stuffing their mouths with bread. It would make a nice painting, Nadia standing among shadows and grubby faces with a shaft of light falling on her, the way it always does no matter where she stands.

Then again. Maybe we've seen too many movies. "How do we know her family got the money?" I said. "Maybe *she* came here to get rich. Maybe *she's* the gold digger. Maybe she thought high school teachers make a lot of money."

I thought he'd be more willing to talk about it alone, without the others. I left work in the afternoon and went to his high school. I found him grading papers with a student sitting on his desk. She was sucking on a lollipop, swinging her legs. She looked like a twenty-five-year-old pretending to be fifteen, her tiny rear just inches from Joel's pen (purple — he said red was too harsh). She knocked her heels against the desk and he looked up.

"To what do I owe this . . . ," he said. He took off his glasses and pinched the inside corners of his eyes. Heavy indentations marked the sides of his nose. His fingers left purply smudges. Ink and exhaustion had bruised his face like a boxer's. The classroom had the sweaty-gym-socks-and-hormones smell of all high schools. On top of that there was an aggressively floral smell that was coming off the girl and a stale, musty, old-man sort of smell that, I realized, was coming from Joel.

"Sondra," he said, "go wait for your bus outside."

"Okay Mr. J," she said, and slowly got up and fixed her skirt and sauntered out. Her bare thighs had left two misty marks on the desk.

"I don't think it's appropriate," I said, tracing them with my finger.

"You have to know how to handle these kids," he said. "Sometimes they're just trying to get your goat, and the best thing to do is ignore them." He wrote an X on a student's paper, then scribbled over the X, then circled it, then wrote "sorry" in the margin.

"I still think —"

"They'll get bored in five minutes and do something else. Half these kids have ADD. They have the attention span of a fly."

"I wanted to talk to you about —"

"What? What was that?" He'd gone back to his grading.

If you looked at those few square inches of skin on the nape of his neck, the backs of his ears, you could almost imagine little-boy Joel. A vulnerable angle, looking down at his hunched shoulders and thinning hair. On the desk in front of him, next to a jar full of pens and highlighters, was a tiny snapshot of Nadia set in an oval ceramic frame. The picture was too small and blurry to make out her face. A gesture, that's all it was, having that photo there, nothing more. Joel's hands stopped moving. A flush moved along his scalp. He waited.

It's not a good time, I said, or thought, and left.

Clearly he was upset. I was worried. We were all worried about Joel. His clothes were limp. He drooped. He yawned constantly. "Is it Nadia?" we said. At first he ignored us. We kept asking. Finally he nodded.

Just at we thought. She was abusing him, demanding things, running him ragged. We knew she had it in her. It's the quiet, shy ones who are the hardest inside. And Joel was too kind; of course he would give in to her. All she had to do was find his sensitive spots, pinch him there. *We* knew where they were. She could probably find them. They were not hard to find.

But no, he said, it wasn't like that at all. "She's sad," he said. "About something. She won't tell me. It's killing me to see her so miserable."

We worried. Why shouldn't we? He was our friend. We'd known him for a long time. Long enough to see changes in him, long enough to still see the face of younger-Joel embedded in the flesh of older-Joel. We had known him when his pores were small, his hair thick, and his body an inverted triangle rather than a pear. Of course we worried. We had a right to.

Joel was lucky to have us. Men need female friends; they need our clear-sightedness, our intuition. And certainly women need male friends as well. The ideal male friend is one you've slept with at some point in the past — that way there's no curiosity, no wondering to taint the friendship.

Joel would not do it. He was too kind to deal with her. We took it upon ourselves. On a day when we knew he was coaching "his kids" at a soccer match, we went to the house. Nadia let us in, offered to make tea. She seemed no more dejected than usual. She was wearing enormous furry slippers shaped like bunnies, her narrow ankles plunged deep in their bellies. Perhaps she was accustomed to wearing dead animals on her feet. She shuffled across the floor, raising a foot to show us. "Funny, no?" she said.

Funny. No.

We sat her down and gave her a talking-to. She kicked off the slippers and sat cross-legged on the sofa, and we gathered around her, holding her hands, knees, shoulders, and got right to it.

"Why are you making Joel unhappy?" we asked her.

"I don't," she said. "I make him tea, I make him dinner, I make his bed. I don't make him unhappy."

"What's the trouble," we asked her. "Are you homesick?"

The end of her nose was turning pink. It was easier than we'd expected.

"You can tell us," we said. "Tell us anything. Need a shoulder to cry on? A hand to hold? Let it out. Have a good cry." She kept her head still but her eyes darted back and forth.

"What about children?" we asked. "Don't you want children?"

"We want children."

"Joel wants children."

"Joel wants children."

"But you don't."

"No . . ."

"You can't?"

"No!"

"Are you trying?"

"Yes."

"But you don't want to have a child?"

"I *have* child!" she said. She twisted away from us and went to take the teakettle off the stove. We wanted to press further, but we thought she'd said enough. By the time she returned with cups and spoons and the teapot on a tray, we were gathered at the door, ready to leave. She carried the tray so easily, she must have had some waitressing experience in her past, we agreed as we headed up the street. We must have imagined the shatter and skid of china somewhere in the dark house behind us.

Of course we told Joel, and he got it all out of her. In his gentle, imploring way. Nadia had a twelve-year-old daughter back in . . . wherever it was. (I looked it up — one of those places with the devious names that sound nothing like they're spelled.) Joel told her over and over, he told us over and over, that she shouldn't have kept it from him, that of course he would welcome her daughter as his own.

Outside of Nadia's hearing, he hissed that he was furious with us, with what he termed our interfering. Interfering! We'd done it for his own good. For the good of both of them. Frankness, we reminded him, was the basis of any good relationship.

We thought he would want to know what kind of woman his wife really was. How could she do such a thing? Leave her own daughter behind?

Joel didn't mention — though we suspected he brooded over — the fact that a daughter meant there was a father. Dead? An ex-husband? A current husband? A boyfriend past or present? All men are jealous. Even men like Joel. They don't get jealous the same way women do, but they get jealous all the same.

"We're going to bring her over," he told us.

"Who? You?"

"Nadia can't go . . . She won't be able to get out again. I'm going."

"By yourself?"

"Malcolm can help, maybe," he said.

"What are you going to do, just go over there and snatch the kid?"

"There must be a legal way to do it," he said. "And if not . . ."

Joel had never been the type to make threats; we were almost inclined to laugh. But now look at him, pounding his fist into his hand, throwing back his shoulders, glaring as if looking for a fight. She had changed him, she *had* been riding him after all, but in a more insidious way than we'd suspected. She must have sulked and whined and prodded and provoked him into charging back to her backwoods hometown to rescue her brat. Her daughter, whom we imagined as a miniature, even more doll-like version of Nadia.

We still didn't believe it. Out of those girls' size-twelve hips? Such a tight squeeze. We pictured a blue and dented baby amid gray hospital linen.

Her body — too ungenerous to nurture anything: husband, child. Not like ours. Me, I stand in front of the mirror sometimes, squeezing hard enough to leave pink fingerprints. I imagine people taking bites, here and here and here. I could feed a family of five for a week.

Perhaps Joel's resoluteness had something to do with the phantom father — perhaps out of jealousy, or out of chivalry, he wanted to track the man down, see him face to face. And then what? We liked the idea of it, Joel as hero-avenger, toting the twelve-year-old under his arm and staring down a dark-faced stranger. But we couldn't quite make it work. The picture in our heads looked like Joel manhandling one of his students, getting too rough on the kickball field, overstepping the bounds of discipline. Setting himself up for a lawsuit. The "He's such a nice guy" refrain would be replaced with "But he *seemed* like such a nice guy."

We thought Joel was all bluster, but he did it. He made plans, he bought tickets. Had to get special permission, made shady arrangements. Bought six pairs of Nikes, a dozen pairs of blue jeans. "Gifts." How did he know what size to get? Sunglasses and a money pouch that strapped around his waist.

I went by the house when he was packing, to lend him my kit of outlet adapters. So many different configurations of prongs and holes. Neither of us knew which he would need.

"Take them all," I said. My hands were overflowing. We were alone in the bedroom, suitcase splayed over the bed. I said, "It doesn't bother you? That she has a child? That she loved someone else? Maybe she still thinks about him."

"She left, didn't she?" he said. "Everyone deserves a second chance." He was using the voice he used with his students, brightly chiding.

"Second chance?" I said. "Everyone?"

He walked to the other side of the bed and very studiously folded a T-shirt into a perfect square. "You know, what do I need all these plugs for, anyway? A hair dryer? An electric razor?" He tugged at his beard, just in case I didn't get it. "Thanks, but no thanks."

I passed Nadia in the hallway. "Tea?" she said.

"What?" I said. "What? Enunciate, please."

He went. And left Nadia behind. In the drafty house. Which seemed colder than ever in the spring chill. We visited her again, we kept her company in twos and threes, we watched television with her while she listened to her earphones. We noticed bruises on her arms, on her ribs once when she was taking off her sweater and her undershirt rode up. Splotches like handprints. We didn't ask. We figured she was anemic. It would make sense: she must have grown up malnourished. I've heard about people like that; they bruise so easily that sitting in a chair leaves them black-and-blue. You can bruise them by breathing on them.

We didn't know what Joel was doing over there. He probably didn't call Nadia either. She showed us a picture of her daughter, but it was an old Polaroid and too faded for us to make out the features. A bleached ghost, with a cat clearly visible in the darkened doorway beyond. The cat's eyes were red. The ghost's shoes were untied. Surely, if it was her daughter, she would have tied them before taking the picture. Later we heard that Joel had been befriending journalists, bribing locals, sneaking into places he wasn't supposed to be.

Of course we saw it on the news, the ugly things that were happening over there. But we didn't really think that Joel was in the midst of it. There's a small part of me that wonders if what we see on the news isn't real, if it's fabricated, reenacted. I swear it's the same shabby group of refugees each time, the same line of tanks, the same bandaged heads, even the same flies. Same barbed-wire fences, same hand-dug grave and sloppily wrapped corpse. Same corn-fed private telling the camera he can't wait to get home to his baby daughter. Same concluding shot of a child's toy crushed in a soldier's muddy bootprint. It's as if all the TV stations are borrowing the same bunch of actors.

Oh, I don't *really* think that. I know those things are really happening. I mean, I know now.

We might never have found out what happened — Joel would never have told us — if a photojournalist hadn't been there and snapped a picture. And so Joel had to explain — we read the quotes in the news-papers. He explained how he (and Malcolm, the mysterious Malcolm) had talked to people, who sent them to a particular neighborhood, where they'd seen the girl on a deserted street and thought she was the right one. Something about the shape of a hand, the tentative, up-on-the-toes walk. The translucent ears. I don't know. He wasn't think-ing, he said; he just rushed out and grabbed her and then the shoot-ing started.

He said he didn't know about the snipers on the rooftops. He said he thought the street was deserted. He didn't realize people were hiding behind locked doors and boarded windows, waiting in their homes, afraid to go out. He didn't know that only children were sent out to do errands, because a child, being smaller, might have a better chance of dodging bullets. They might not shoot a child.

He said that when he ran out into the street he only wanted to bring the girl home, and when the shooting started he only wanted to pro-tect her. He said he was trying to keep her out of the line of fire, trying to block the bullets. But it's clear from the photograph, in which he's looking to one side and gripping to his chest a bundle of hair and dress and dangling legs, that he's using her body to shield his own.

We saw the photograph, read about it. There's a dark wet spot on the little girl's back. You can see Joel's wedding ring, you can see how bushy his beard's grown. He's wearing a hat we'd never seen before, and though the eyes are a smudge you can see his mouth hanging open, slack, completely unmoored.

We wanted to tell Nadia, couldn't tell Nadia. It wasn't really our place, we decided. We lacked the vocabulary. I doubt Joel called her. What would he say? She found out somehow. I suppose there were people she could call, family, friends. I suppose she's not as alone as she seems.

He came back eventually. Came back to the States, that is. He didn't come to see any of us. We heard he returned without the daughter. Was that because he didn't find her? Or was *that* her, the girl in the photograph? It couldn't be. We told each other that, most likely, he had found the girl, and she'd taken one look at this huge foreign-talk-ing man and decided to stay where she was. Probably she's happier with her father, we told each other. Probably she has a whole family of her own. We pictured a father who was a counterpoint to Joel: small, graceful, clean-shaven, stouthearted.

Joel avoided us. Fine. We didn't want to know what he'd brought back with him. Infection. Those diseases they have over there. Odorous invasions of the skin and digestive tract, diseases of neglect. The ones the travel books warn you about.

I wonder what that's like. There have been times when I'm sure I'm dying — when my heart flutters in the middle of the night for no reason, when a loneliness or craving is so strong it nauseates me — but of course I'm not. I wonder if living close to the edge of desperation like that makes you feel more alive. It's a cliché, I know, but most clichés have a core of truth, don't they? One time I tried to ask Nadia about it — whether she'd felt more alive back there in her homeland with death all around. She didn't seem to understand the question. She didn't see a difference between there and here. As if for her it was all the same: life was perilous everywhere, a teetering tightrope walk from one minute to the next.

We wondered what would happen to Joel and Nadia. Surely they couldn't go on together? How could he explain it? Even if it wasn't her daughter, how could he have done such a thing? She wouldn't be able to stay with him. How could she? She might even go back. Maybe she'd realize that her kind of people demand a kind of heroism that she won't find here.

We felt certain Joel wouldn't have hidden behind the bodies of *our* hypothetical daughters. He would have taken a bullet, rather. We all knew this. Nadia and her kind were different, they counted less. They were one degree closer to being objects, to his mind. He might deny it, but actions speak louder, don't they? In moments of panic, the true self comes to the surface.

And *she* had abandoned her own daughter. How could they stay together, knowing these ugly truths about each other? So much for frankness.

To be rid of Nadia. Hadn't that been the intent all along? No one wanted to say it outright, but I would. Yes, it was. But now the prospect of a solitary Joel was no longer appetizing. We knew that, despite the avoidance, Joel was in need of our friendship, our pity. Probably for the first time. But now we didn't feel like giving it to him; we wanted to lavish it on someone more worthy.

Suddenly, we didn't want Nadia to leave. "Have you seen Nadia?" we asked each other. "He doesn't let her out," we said. "He's holding her hostage in that miserable house."

We organized a rescue mission. "We'll break the door down if we have to," we said. Of course we didn't have to. Joel opened the door with bowed head. "Where is she?" we said, pushing our way in. We were momentarily distracted; Joel looked like he might tolerate, for once might even welcome, a hug or a kiss on the cheek. We steeled ourselves and pressed on.

"Nadia," we said, "do you want some tea? Tea? Are you warm enough? Can we make you a sandwich?"

She was sitting before the fireplace, orange light warming her face like sunlight. She looked ageless, beautiful and sorrowful, a classical sculpture. I looked at her and thought, Devastating. I will never in my life look like that. It was both a disappointment and a relief.

"I never asked him to go," she said, twisting her hair in her fingers. "I miss her, but my daughter, she is happy with her father and father's new wife. But Joel, he sees I am sad, so he tries to bring her to me anyway. He thinks he can make her come."

Joel had never told us that part of the story.

We surrounded her, touched her gently. We tried to tell her our plans for her. How we were ready to embrace her, shield her, take her in. We wanted to give her the sense of security she'd never had, had never known existed. Nadia could not always follow the gist of the conversation. But we knew she was listening, we knew she understood. We wanted to have with her what she had had with women at home. The unspoken female kinship. I could picture it. Women cooking together, sewing together, braiding each other's hair. Napping with their heads on each other's shoulders and laps. Gathered around beds, wiping each other's foreheads, murmuring encouragement. Birth, death, all the same. Gathered around a candlelit bed. Sewing a swaddling cloth, sewing a shroud. I think they go to public bathhouses, dunk in cold pools, then sit in the steam. All the women together, young ones, pregnant ones, old ones with drooping breasts.

Sharing the towels, the moist wooden benches. They have no concep-
tion of embarrassment. They rub a gray paste into their hair to dye it
red. The longer they leave it in, the redder it gets. They beat each other
with hazel branches — I hear it's good for the skin.

"You're safe now," I told her slowly and clearly. "No more tightrope."

We wanted to live with her. At least until our cycles became syn-
chronized, until our secrets were the same.

The more we talked, the more we realized we had nothing to offer,
nothing that compared to the female utopia she'd once known. The
desire rose in us not to keep her here but to let her go home — and
take us along.

"You miss your daughter, don't you," we said. "You're jealous of
her stepmother, aren't you." For the first time her eyes snapped into
focus.

Joel came into the room then, shooed us away like chickens.

We came back in shifts, bringing soup, sweaters, flowers, children's books — to help her learn English, we thought. I don't know
how to cook — I emptied canned soup into a pot — but it's the thought
that counts.

We tried to be like her. We drank her vodka, listened to her music.
We drank more, and danced and threw our glasses in the fireplace. She fell asleep while we sang along with the incomprehensible
lyrics and clapped our hands before falling into giddy heaps on the
floor.

Nadia took to her bed. We told Joel it was female trouble, that he
should stay away and let us handle it.

"Are you pregnant?" we asked her.

"Maybe," she said carelessly, sucking on a cigarette. The ashtray beside her bed was overflowing. The skin around her eyes was creased
and crumpled with a hundred tiny wrinkles. Her hair lay over her
shoulders, spread over the pillow. The hair, I thought, that's what
makes her look so young. If she had a sensible cut she'd look like
everybody else.

She seemed to get weaker and weaker, day by day. We plied her with
pills: extra-strength, fast-acting, non-drowsy, maximum-strength,
weapons-grade, the strongest medicine you can buy without a pre-

scription. None of it seemed to do any good. Joel gave her a Chinese checkers game, and she used the pills as game pieces.

"She is a doctor, you know," Joel said one day, materializing out of a dark hallway as we were leaving. "She knows how to take care of herself."

"But she's not doing it," we said. "She's letting herself go. And you're not taking care of her."

His old-man hands fumbled with his sweater. He'd missed too many classes and had been given an unpaid leave of absence. We saw him once or twice strolling past the high school, staring longingly at his former students, trying to engage them in conversation on their way in or out. You could see what he'd eventually turn into.

"You shouldn't smoke," we told her, gently but firmly. "It's bad for the baby."

"You would take away the one thing that gives me pleasure?" she said, smiling an ironic smile. She did this sometimes, said something so sarcastic and knowing that she seemed infinitely older and wiser than any of us. We were shocked to see a gap in her smile. One of her teeth — a canine — had fallen out.

I sometimes thought that if I could just be alone with her, we might be able to have a real conversation. But the others were always there, chattering, squawking, plumping pillows, humming over her, stroking her forehead, doing their best Florence Nightingale imitations. I wasn't like them. I had never been. I wasn't sure she could see that.

She seemed to be growing hotter and hotter, more and more translucent, a mere glow; I was sure one day we'd come in to find an invisible shape, a warm vapor humping up the blankets. We had to stop her. We had to save her.

"Take her to the emergency room," one of us said.

"No," I said. "She doesn't want modern medicine. What she needs is an old-fashioned cure."

The others clucked in surprise. But they liked the idea, I could tell. We discussed the various cures and remedies our grandmothers had dosed us with. We talked of slimy poultices, hideous potions, onions and garlic rubbed on the chest, ointments made from fish eyes, immersion in tea, in tomato soup, in ice water.

"When my grandmother had a fever, she'd go swim naked in the river," I said. "Even in the middle of winter. She swore by it."

The others looked at me suspiciously. But they nodded their heads. Something about the plan seemed appropriate, seemed right, like something they had seen in an old yellowed photograph or in a television documentary. The image of Nadia, pink-nosed, sodden, wrapped in an enormous, scratchy gray blanket, shivering in our arms, luminously grateful — this picture appealed to all of us.

There was still snow on the ground. "Good, good," we told each other. "Nice and cold." We bundled Nadia into the car — "I am all right, I am OK," she insisted, shrugging off our helping hands. We were quiet during the cramped drive, our breaths steaming up the windows as if the car were full of frantically necking teenagers.

The riverbank. I was disappointed, it was not as scenic as I remembered. Deserted picnic tables lumped with snow. Cars whizzing past on the nearby overpass. Bare skeletal trees against a low smothering sky. Everything in shades of black and gray. Like Nadia's home, I realized. Perfect.

The river — mucky banks, thick black water with chunks of ice floating in it.

She tottered from the car on thin unsteady legs. We reached out to help her. She shook us off. We smiled indulgently. She was like a cartoon of endearing gangliness, a human version of Bambi.

"Take in that breeze," we said encouragingly. "Breathe it in. Aaah. Bracing," we said. "Take big cleansing breaths. Like this."

She looked at us quizzically, the sleeves of Joel's shirt pulled down to cover her hands, a cigarette protruding from one of them.

"She needs to feel the water," someone said.

"Just dunk her feet."

"A splash on her face."

"Get her shoes off."

"What you are doing?" Nadia said.

"It's for your own good," we said. "We're only trying to help." We got her down to the water. She was not cooperating, but not really resisting either. We pulled off her flimsy ballet-type shoes, her crocheted socks. Why did she look so confused? Hadn't she done this before? Or seen it done to others? I could swear I read it in a book, saw it on an educational program, the women in their shawls and kerchiefs dunking a fever-stricken child in ice-cold water in a rhythmic ritual, the child in a nightshirt with thin bone-white feet just like Nadia's. There's singing or chanting, something, old men rubbing their bare chests with snow.

"Here," we said, holding her arms, nudging her forward into the water. She shrieked, lifted her knees to her chest so that she hung suspended in our grip. "Again," we said. "No," she said, twisting. She struck someone in the nose, there was a curse, a spray of blood. She kicked me and I fell to my hands and knees, covered in muck, my new trousers, the stain would never come out.

"You ungrateful —" someone shouted.

"We're only trying to —"

"— ignorant little —"

"— think you're so special —"

"— and *this* is how you thank us?"

Nadia stood knee-deep in water, cigarette held high above her head. The others were crowded on the bank, blocking her path, so she started backing away. She waded slowly, seemingly unaware of the cold, as the others shouted accusations and encouragement.

Then an undercurrent swept her off her feet and carried her downstream. It happened so swiftly, it was like an amusement park ride, Nadia down and then bobbing back up, spinning like a paper doll, trailing streaming hair. Just like that, she was gone.

Once we couldn't see her, it was like it hadn't happened. It was as if I'd closed my eyes and asked myself, I wonder what Nadia would look like spinning down the river, ah, yes, *that's* what it would look like, and then opened my eyes again.

We looked at one another.

"We killed her," someone said. There were nervous giggles. The words sounded absurd.

"We have to call the police," someone said.

"I can't," I said. "I have to get home. Get these clothes off."

"This was all your idea," someone said.

I admit, I would have left right then if I could have. But we'd all come in the same car.

"It was an accident."

"It doesn't look like one."

"I can't be involved in this," I said.

"Why?"

"Well," I said. "You know how Joel and I . . . how we used to . . . people might think I had a motive. They'd think I *wanted* to get rid of her."

"That's no reason."

I looked at them all and wondered, not for the first time, how many of them had slept with Joel too. We stared at one another, our breaths puffing white in the air.

What happened next is something I'd rather not dwell on. Someone lunged at someone else, hoping to snatch the car keys and make a run for it. Someone pushed someone else, someone tripped, someone kicked someone else in the mouth. Someone's purse got thrown in the river, and soon there were five purses sailing down the current. Someone particularly bloodthirsty tore an earring from someone else's ear. There were punches, kicks, scratching. Someone picked up a broken bottle. It was a brawl, a melee, mayhem. We surprised ourselves, and not in a good way. Surprised by the extent of the viciousness we had all harbored for each other. We had all suspected it was there, but never in our worst paranoid nightmares had we expected there to be so much of it.

And I think I was most surprised by pain. I was surprised by how much it *hurt*. There was nothing heroic or dramatic about it. I thought pain is supposed to bring clarity, as if a jolt to the nerve endings should reveal the meaning of life. Instead all it does is make you more conscious of your body, how rickety it is, how vulnerable. It gave me an appreciation for the padded living I had always despised.

There was the momentary satisfaction of doing something you had longed to do for years — "I could kill her," you think twice a day, listening to her whining on the phone — followed immediately by disappointment, the dirty, undignified, shameful reality.

They found Nadia four miles downstream, washed up against a bridge piling. I saw her on the news, the pink nose and gray blanket, just as I'd envisioned. They were calling it a miracle: she'd spent minutes submerged, but the coldness of the water slowed down her body's processes, kept her from drowning.

"Clever Nadia," I said.

I wondered what she would tell people, would tell Joel. I felt strangely immune, as if she could not reach me. Now that she'd entered the television world, she'd be trapped there forever.

I say I felt immune, but really I felt more that I was at an impasse. I was waiting, waiting. I had no idea what would happen next.

But as I said, it was oddly satisfying to see Nadia on the television screen. It was as if she was back where she belonged, as if she could change the channel and zap herself home, to the shouting, the running, the bombs falling, the tanks stirring up clouds of dust. Or, alternately, jump into a sunny sitcom, a dazzling toothpaste commercial, a heavy-breathing pornographic movie.

A reporter grasped her shoulder and shook her, holding a microphone to her face. "What was it like?" he asked. "Did you have a near-death experience?"

"Near-death experience?" she repeated. Her blue lips strained into a smile. "I have been having one of these for years. I am having it right now."

GUY DELISLE

■

Pyongyang: A Journey
in North Korea

THE ULTRA-SECRETIVE Communist dynasty of North Korea recently
opened its doors, somewhat, to foreign investment. Guy Delisle was
sent to the country's capital to work with a French animation company subcontracting in Pyongyang. Accompanied at all times by government "guides," Delisle was able to record his impressions of life
— and the daily deification of Kim Jong Il — in possibly the least free
nation on earth.

THERE'S A BANNER ON EVERY BUILDING, A PORTRAIT ON EVERY WALL, A PIN ON EVERY CHEST.

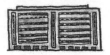

THAT'S A LOT. I SHOULD TRY COUNTING THE NUMBER OF EFFIGIES OF THE DEAR LEADER THAT I COME ACROSS IN A DAY.

LET'S SEE,... A SERIES OF PAINTINGS IN THE LOBBY DEPICT ORDERS GIVEN BY GENERAL KIM JONG-IL (WHO IN FACT NEVER SERVED IN THE ARMY).

AS A STUDENT, HE APPARENTLY PUBLISHED NO LESS THAN 1,200 WORKS, INCLUDING A NUMBER OF SPECIALIZED MILITARY TREATISES.

AND IN HIS FIRST GOLF GAME, HE HIT 11 HOLES-IN-ONE.

WHEREVER YOU LOOK, YOU SEE PAINTED OR SCULPTED AVATARS OF THE "PERFECT MIND" IN THE FORM OF A RED FLOWER: THE KIMJONGILIA.

THE WALL OF ONE OF THE RESTAURANTS DEPICTS MOUNT PAEKTU, THE HIGHEST PEAK IN KOREA, WHERE THE PRODIGIOUS SON IS SAID TO HAVE BEEN BORN UNDER A DOUBLE RAINBOW AND A SHINING STAR.*

* IN FACT, HE WAS BORN SOMEWHERE IN SIBERIA.

ON THE FAÇADE OF KIM JONG-IL UNIVERSITY, THERE'S A PORTRAIT OF KIM JONG-IL.

ADD TO THAT THE PORTRAITS IN EVERY ROOM, THE BADGES AND THE COMMENTS I HEAR AT WORK.

NOTHING IS IMPOSSIBLE WITH THE GUIDANCE OF KIM JONG-IL...

SURE...

HEY, MAYBE WE COULD GIVE HIM A CALL SO HE CAN TELL US WHAT TO DO ABOUT EPISODE 3?

AND OF COURSE "WE SHALL BE FAITHFUL FROM GENERATION TO GENERATION", OUR LOVELY ASSISTANT'S FAVORITE TUNE.

CLICK! CENSORED!

SORRY, BUT ALL THIS PROPAGANDA COULD HAVE A BAD INFLUENCE ON ME.

AND LASTLY, ON EVERY FLOOR THERE'S A LITTLE BOOK OF THE DEAR LEADER'S THOUGHTS, HANDWRITTEN AND UPDATED EVERY MONTH.

YUP... I THINK THAT PRETTY MUCH SUMS IT UP.

AFTER MAKING MY LIST, I HAD A DEEPLY TROUBLING EXPERIENCE.

WALKING PAST MY ASSISTANT'S DESK...

I COULD HAVE SWORN I SAW KIM JONG-IL'S FACE IN THE MIRROR IN- STEAD OF MY OWN.

?!

INTRIGUED, I STEPPED BACK TO DISPEL THE CRAZY NOTION I'D HAD.

TO MY DISMAY, THE HORRI- FYING TRUTH STARED BACK AT ME!

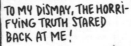

NO!

IT WAS ONLY AFTER MY PULSE SETTLED THAT I REALIZED WHAT HAD CAUSED THE ILLUSION.

MIRROR

KIM&KIM

ME

HA HA... WHAT A JOKE!

27 28 29 30 31...

I'VE GOTTA GET OUTTA HERE.

SORRY TO SAY, GUYS... BUT YOUR OPERA ISN'T COMING ALONG TOO FAST...

SOMETIMES, WHEN I'M FED UP, I STOP BY THE BACKGROUND DEPARTMENT TO SEE DAVID.

YOU DO THIS.

THIS.

AND THIS.

I'VE NEVER SEEN ANYONE QUICKER ON PHOTOSHOP... IT'S LIKE HE'S ON FAST FORWARD.

THIS.

THIS.

THIS.

AND WHAT'RE THE MASKS FOR?

THIS.

THIS.

AND THIS.

AH!

HE GETS TO INTERACT WITH A LOT OF PEOPLE.

THERE'S ONE GUY WITH A CAP WHO ALWAYS HANGS OUT AROUND THE STUDIO. I'VE BEEN TOLD HE'S A DIRECTOR, BUT I DOUBT IT.

TO KEEP FROM WEARING OUT THEIR HEMS, THE BOYS WALK AROUND LIKE THIS:

AND WHEN IT'S HOT, THEY ALSO DO THIS:

LOOKING GOOD!

THE GIRLS ARE ON THE CUTTING EDGE OF FASHION TOO...

SKIRTS ARE WORN OVER THE KNEES, AND SHIRTS BUTTONED ALL THE WAY.

IT DOESN'T GET MORE DECOLLETÉ THAN THIS.

AND MANY WEAR SOCKS OVER THEIR NYLONS. MMM...

THIS WEEK'S NEW ARRIVAL AT THE SEK IS HENRI.

HE'S A PRODUCER FOR LAFABRIQUE, A STUDIO IN A REMOTE CORNER OF FRANCE WHERE I WORKED AGES AGO.

SO, EVEN THE SMALL FRY ARE COMING TO NORTH KOREA!

IT'S AN ANIMATION WHO'S WHO!

I GET TO HAVE LUNCH AT HIS HOTEL, THE KORYO.

IT'S NO BETTER THAN OURS.

THE KORYO IS FAMOUS FOR ITS CAFE, WHERE WEAPONS CONTRACTS ARE NEGOTIATED WITH FOREIGN DELEGATIONS. WEAPONS ARE THE REGIME'S PRIMARY TRADE ASSET.

NICE VIEW!

MY GUIDE IS WAITING AT THE EXIT. I HAD FORGOTTEN OUR EXCURSION TO THE DIPLOMATIC STORE.

THE WEEKLY PILGRIMAGE TO THE ONLY LOCAL SANCTUARY DEDICATED TO CONSUMERISM...

AND AN OPPORTUNITY TO BUY A LITTLE GIFT FOR MY HOSTS.

CLOPES OR GNÔLE?

HELLO BRIDGET... IT'S ME... HURRY OVER! A SHIPMENT OF MANGOES JUST CAME IN!

THE THRILLING LIFE OF A DIPLOMAT'S WIFE.

ONE THING THAT STRIKES YOU AFTER WEEKS OF LOOKING AT THE IMMACULATE STREETS OF PYONGYANG IS THE COMPLETE ABSENCE OF HANDICAPPED PEOPLE.

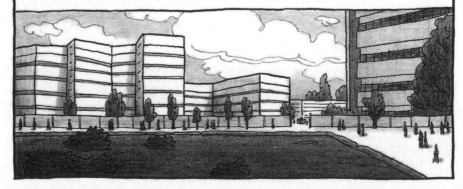

EVEN MORE SURPRISING IS THE ANSWER I GET WHEN I WONDER ALOUD ABOUT THIS...

ON AVERAGE, 7 TO 10% OF THE POPULATION ...

THERE ARE NONE... WE'RE A VERY HOMOGENOUS NATION. ALL NORTH KOREANS ARE BORN STRONG, INTELLIGENT AND HEALTHY.

AND FROM THE WAY HE SAYS IT, I THINK HE BELIEVES IT.

TO WHAT EXTENT CAN A MIND BE MANIPULATED? WE'LL PROBABLY GET SOME IDEA WHEN THE COUNTRY EVENTUALLY OPENS UP OR COLLAPSES.

SINCE THE FIRST DAY OF MY STAY, I'VE BEEN ASKING FOR A BIKE TO RIDE AROUND ON.

AND THE BIKE?

BECAUSE THEY FIRST CLAIMED THAT ANYTHING WAS POSSIBLE, I KEEP AT IT.

WHEN? TOMORROW?

OF COURSE I KNOW I'LL NEVER GET ONE, BUT I'D LIKE AN HONEST ANSWER. INSTEAD, IT'S BECOME A KIND OF JOKE.

ANY NEWS ABOUT MY BIKE?

HA HA HA HA !

IT'S LIKE THE SERIES OF OUTINGS WE'LL NEVER GO ON...

THE KIM IL-SUNG MEMORIAL WITH ITS SHOESHINE MACHINE.

THE MUSEUM OF FINE ARTS, WHERE 80% OF THE PAINTINGS DEPICT KIM AND KIM.

AND THE DEMILITARIZED ZONE...

WHAT ABOUT THE DMZ?

WE'D BETTER WAIT. THE ATMOSPHERE HAS BEEN TENSE SINCE W. BUSH'S ELECTION. IF SOUTHERN SOLDIERS SEE A FOREIGNER ON OUR SIDE, THEY MIGHT FEEL PROVOKED AND SHOOT, AND THAT COULD SPARK CONFLICT.

SPARK CONFLICT...

AND WHAT ELSE...

SOME SUGAR WITH THAT?

IN THE AFTERNOONS, RICHARD OFTEN STOPS BY FOR A NESCAFÉ BREAK ON OUR FLOOR. IT'S AN OPPORTUNITY FOR THE REST OF US TO HEAR THE LATEST NEWS, SINCE HE'S THE ONLY ONE WITH CABLE IN HIS HOTEL...

WELL, KIM JONG-IL'S SON, THE ONE WHO LIVES IN SWITZERLAND, GOT CAUGHT ENTERING JAPAN WITH A FALSE PASSPORT... THEY SAY HE WASN'T SPYING, HE JUST WANTED TO VISIT TOKYO DISNEYLAND! HA HA!

AND THE DEAR LEADER IS PLANNING A VISIT TO PUTIN IN HIS ARMORED TRAIN.

YOU FIND OUT MORE ABOUT THE COUNTRY FROM OUTSIDE THAN INSIDE. PEOPLE HERE DON'T EVEN KNOW THEIR DEAR LEADER HAS CHILDREN.

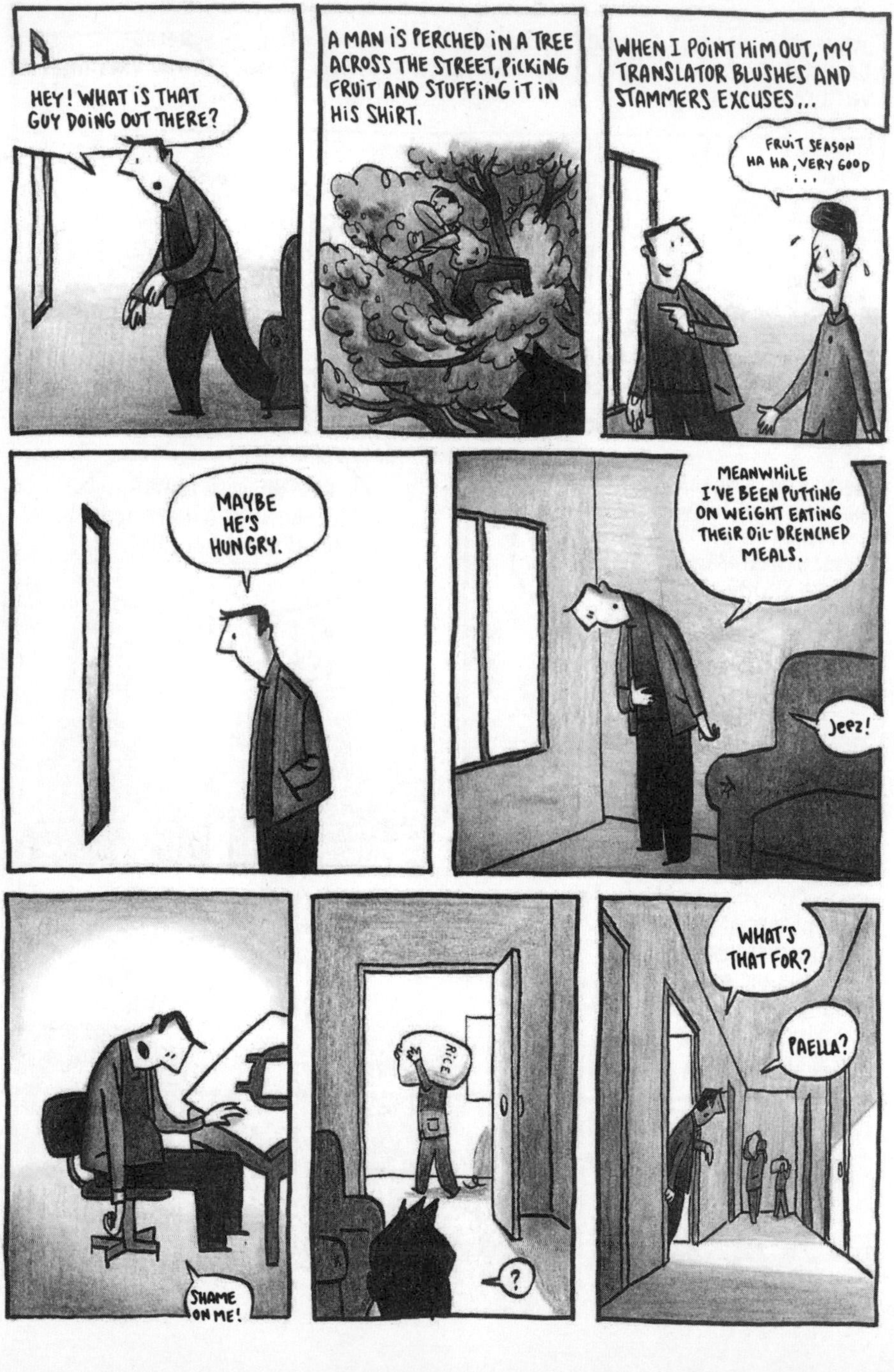
HEY! WHAT IS THAT GUY DOING OUT THERE?
A MAN IS PERCHED IN A TREE ACROSS THE STREET, PICKING FRUIT AND STUFFING IT IN HIS SHIRT.
WHEN I POINT HIM OUT, MY TRANSLATOR BLUSHES AND STAMMERS EXCUSES...
FRUIT SEASON HA HA, VERY GOOD ...
MAYBE HE'S HUNGRY.
MEANWHILE I'VE BEEN PUTTING ON WEIGHT EATING THEIR OIL-DRENCHED MEALS.
Jeez!
SHAME ON ME!
RICE
?
WHAT'S THAT FOR?
PAELLA?

THEY'RE STORING BAGS OF RICE ...

I WONDER WHY?

MISTER GUY?

MM?

WOULD YOU LIKE TO SEE A TAEKWONDO DEMONSTRATION?

SURE.

WE FIND OURSELVES IN A HUGE SPORTS FACILITY THAT HOUSES A STADIUM AND 10 GYMS, INCLUDING THE TAEKWONDO HALL BUILT IN 1992.

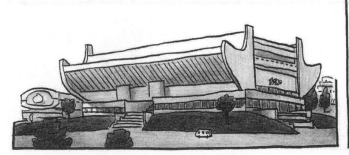

CAPTAIN SIN HAS COME ALONG.

CAPTAIN SIN YOU'RE OUR HERO

THE FAÇADE FEATURES A GOLD-PLATED REPRODUCTION OF CALLIGRAPHY BY KIM JONG-IL.

HMM NICE!

INSIDE, A GUIDE BOMBARDS US WITH STATISTICS ABOUT THE ARCHITECTURE WHILE TAKING US THROUGH ONE HUGE HALL AFTER ANOTHER.

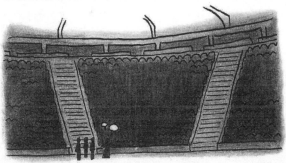

BUT I GET THE FEELING THERE WON'T BE A TAEKWONDO DEMONSTRATION: THERE ISN'T A SINGLE ATHLETE IN SIGHT.

WHAT ABOUT THE DEMO? IS IT STILL ON?

UNFORTUNATELY THE ATHLETES HAVE LEFT TO TRAIN IN THE NORTH. IT'S TOO HOT HERE... THEY'LL BE BETTER OFF WHERE IT'S COOLER.

I SEE...

TRAINING IN THE RICE PADDIES, I BET.

BUT IT WASN'T A TOTAL LOSS. WE STOPPED BY ANOTHER SPORTS FACILITY THAT WAS MUCH MORE ENTERTAINING.

FOR THE PRICE OF ONE WON PER BALL, YOU CAN PRACTICE SHARP-SHOOTING WITH OLD RUSSIAN PISTOLS.

GO AHEAD.

I DON'T KNOW.

YOU FIRST!

NEVER HAVING BEEN IN THE MILITARY, I HAVE NO IDEA WHAT THE RIGHT POSITION IS. INSTINCTIVELY, I PLAY IT LIKE CORTO MALTESE.

MY COMRADES HAVE THE ADVANTAGE OF A FEW YEARS OF MILITARY TRAINING.

BUT THAT DOESN'T STOP ME FROM GETTING THE HIGHEST SCORE. HA HA!

YES!

CAPTAIN GUY HE'S OUR POWER MAGNIFIED!

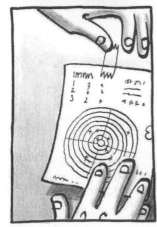

NO!

IT'S FORBIDDEN TO TACK ANYTHING ELSE ONTO A PORTRAIT WALL.

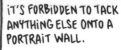

OH!

TOM DOWNEY

■

The Insurgent's Tale

FROM *Rolling Stone*

KHALID HAD BEEN IN IRAQ for only a few weeks, but he was already sick of the place. It wasn't the missions that bothered him. He was fighting alongside a small group of Saudis, and they were consummate professionals when it came to jihad, completely focused on the lightning-fast attacks they staged each day on the foreign invaders. The ambushes usually lasted no more than five or ten minutes, but Khalid reveled in the chance to hit the streets and fire off his AK-47 at the American soldiers and their allies, four grenades strapped to his waist so he could kill himself if captured.

After the attacks, however, Khalid and the other fighters were confined to safe houses in Mosul and Haditha — dark, dank places with no hot water or electricity. The biggest problem was the Iraqis, the very people he was there to help. Sometimes it seemed as though there were double agents everywhere, checking him out on the street, trying to overhear him speaking the Yemeni dialect that would betray him as a foreigner, all so they could pick up their cell phones and call in the Americans, maybe even collect a reward. That made this jihad more dangerous and unpredictable than the other wars Khalid had fought in — Afghanistan, Bosnia, Somalia, places where they were often treated like heroes. When they weren't out on missions in Iraq, he and the Saudis were forced to stay in the safe house, the shades pulled down, with only a well-thumbed copy of the Koran and five prayer sessions a day to break the monotony.

Abu Musab al-Zarqawi was a pillar of strength to the insurgents. Khalid knew him from a decade and a half ago, when they were fighting the Soviets and their proxies in Afghanistan. But now, meeting al-

Zarqawi in Mosul, he was amazed at the changes in his old comrade. Back then al-Zarqawi was an ordinary foot soldier like Khalid. Now, flanked by two bodyguards and barking orders with fiery determination, he was the most wanted man in Iraq, an Islamic militant with a $25 million price on his head. He had been hailed by Sheikh Osama bin Laden himself as "the prince of Al Qaeda in Iraq," but al-Zarqawi still had time for a word with someone from the old days. He and Khalid chatted for a few minutes, recalling their time together in Afghanistan, before al-Zarqawi rushed off to make arrangements with an ally in Kurdistan to try to send some insurgents off to Iraq's northern mountains to fight.

That was more than two years ago, when the insurgency had been looking for fighters like Khalid, veteran soldiers who could be relied on to attack foreign troops with skill and precision. Now, back in Yemen, Khalid heard that they were looking for suicide bombers only. He would watch kids he knew signing up to go to Iraq, unaware that they were being recruited to kill themselves. It made Khalid glad he wasn't in Iraq anymore. Not that he had anything against that kind of mission — it was a noble calling — but he thought that a person willing to fight and die should know what he was meant to do before he left home.

At thirty-two, Khalid was beginning to have serious reservations about the course of the insurgency in Iraq. *They are overkilling there.* Fighting foreign soldiers was one thing — he had been doing it all of his adult life. But did his faith really sanction killing civilians in their own country? *The blood of people is too cheap.* Fifteen years in the jihad, fighting in five foreign wars, imprisoned in England and Yemen, enduring the death of a close friend on a mission in Iraq — enough. The cost was just too high. Although he was proud of all the fighting he had done in the past, Khalid wanted to settle down to an ordinary life as a father, husband, and son. He was a soldier fighting a war. *But what if the war had no end?*

Khalid, who agreed to recount the story of his jihad on the condition that his identity not be revealed, is a Yemeni from the ancient city of Sanaa in northern Yemen. The country is one of the most lawless and drug-addicted places in the world. Despite a recent government crackdown, hand grenades are laid out alongside fresh produce at street-side markets, and sources estimate that there are at least ten million guns in circulation, in a country with a population of twenty million.

Social life revolves around qat, a leafy, reddish-green plant that contains amphetamine-like substances. Eighty percent of adult men in Yemen chew regularly, and important political and business decisions are routinely made in the *mafraj*, a room in many homes specially designed for chewing sessions. The leaf combines the talkative affability of pot with the drive of speed. First comes euphoria and intense sociability — not ponderous, marijuana-induced ramblings but a deep appreciation of the flow of conversation. In this stage, five hours can pass in what seems like ten minutes. Next comes reflective quiet — a comfortable silence descends as people look inward, contemplating the contents of their minds. The final stage is depression and insomnia — it's not uncommon to see solitary cloaked figures roaming the streets at night, waiting for the effects of the drug to pass. On average, Yemeni men spend about a third of their income on qat, and commerce in the leaf accounts for a third of the nation's gross national product.

I met Khalid at a qat chew in the *mafraj* of a friend. The room was hot and stuffy, the way chewers like it, and each man in the room was identically posed: left knee up and right arm resting on a cushion. Cold bottles of "Canada" — the Yemeni term for water, based on the market dominance of Canada Dry — were distributed all around. The room was clean, but people were already beginning to litter the floor with leaves or stalks too thick or firm to chew. After a few hours, the middle of the room would be blanketed with a thick green carpet of discarded qat.

Qat sessions usually begin with a raucous flow of conversation. But Khalid was quiet, smiling at jokes, carefully pruning his stalks, venturing little. When he finally spoke, he told me that he had just been let out of a Yemeni prison. I asked him why.

"I was arrested as a terrorist," he told me in English, with a trace of a working-class British accent.

Late one night, he went on, an undercover anti-terrorism squad had dragged him away from his family's home in a comfortable, middle-class neighborhood of Sanaa. He was locked up and questioned repeatedly by Yemeni police in the presence of American agents. To curry favor with the Bush administration, Yemen's president, Ali Abdullah Salih, has arrested hundreds of suspected terrorists, imprisoning almost everyone who returns to Yemen with a Syrian or Iranian stamp in their passport — prima facie evidence that they fought in Iraq. Khalid was released after thirty days when a family friend posted a large bond to ensure that he would stay out of trouble.

At this point, a friend at the qat chew hissed at Khalid in Arabic: "Why are you telling him this? Don't talk about these things."

"I have nothing to hide," Khalid told him. He then proceeded to recount the extraordinary story of his fifteen years fighting as a foot soldier in the jihad. Although it is impossible to independently corroborate every detail of his tale, other Yemenis confirmed Khalid's long, frequent absences from Yemen, his presence at training camps in Afghanistan, and his imprisonment in Yemen by the anti-terrorism police. His passport contains entry stamps to Syria that match the dates he said he had gone to Iraq, and the account he gave of his arrest in England mirrors one reported by police there around the same time. Moreover, the details Khalid gave of fighting in relatively obscure battles in Bosnia, Somalia, and Afghanistan match events that actually took place. In the broad strokes of his story, at least, he appears to be telling the truth.

Khalid is not an ultraorthodox, unbending Muslim. Although he meets to chew qat wearing his Yemeni dress cut midcalf, in the style of an Islamic purist, he also wears button-down shirts and European hiking boots. He has lived in England for years and has befriended Westerners. Slight and handsome, he has the quiet charisma and modesty of the guy who is elected class president based on his low-key appeal. In short, he is not the kind of enemy we have been led to believe we are fighting. He harbors some of the same doubts that our own soldiers have about what brought them to fight and, perhaps, to die, in a place so far from home. To hear a polite and thoughtful man talk casually about his friends in Al Qaeda is to have the whole enterprise reduced to a more fragile, human scale. It is to see this war for what it is: a battle between men filled with contradictions, inconsistencies, and weaknesses, not a mythic struggle between our supermen and their ghosts.

Khalid's jihad began with a videotape he viewed at a mosque in Sanaa in 1989. He can still remember the anger he felt when, at the age of sixteen, he watched that footage of Muslim brothers and sisters being slaughtered in Afghanistan. A friend of his had died fighting there — a martyr promised the rewards of paradise. Khalid didn't think much about his own decision to follow his friend into battle; it was the natural, instinctive thing to do. He had seen what the Russians were doing to the brothers, as Khalid calls his fellow soldiers in the holy war. His best friend had stood up to them and died. Now it was his turn.

Yemen is pious and militant, and it has supplied many thousands of the young men who have filled the front lines of jihad, fighting for their faith from Afghanistan to Iraq. The country is the ancestral home of bin Laden, whose father was a one-eyed Yemeni dockworker, and among the few people successfully prosecuted by the Bush administration on terrorism charges were the "Lackawanna Six," Yemeni Americans from Buffalo, New York, convicted of attending an Al Qaeda training camp in Afghanistan, and Sheikh al-Moayad, a cleric from Sanaa convicted of conspiring to support terrorism.

There was nothing in Khalid's childhood to suggest that he would wind up joining the jihad. His father was a moderate Muslim with a steady job as a civil servant in the Yemeni government. Khalid worried that he wouldn't be able to get a passport or leave the country without his father's permission. But the recruiters for the Afghan war were acting with the support of the Yemeni government, and within a few weeks, whether or not his father liked it, Khalid had a brand-new passport stamped with a visa for Pakistan.

The final hitch was that a close relative of Khalid's worked at the Sanaa Airport. Khalid feared that an airport clerk might recognize him and alert his family. The recruiters got around that by driving him directly onto the tarmac. Khalid climbed aboard the plane to Pakistan without even passing through immigration.

The reality of jihad, Khalid quickly discovered, was very different from the images presented on the videotape. When he finally made it into Afghanistan, he spent his first night near the front. That evening, a soldier who had been killed was brought back for burial by the mujahideen. Khalid didn't know the man, but seeing his body terrified him. "I'm scared," he told a friend. "I just want to go home."

"Everybody feels like that at first," his friend said. "But soon you won't be scared."

Khalid fought in Afghanistan for two years. He learned to use his weapon, to fight, and to pray with the precision and punctuality of the Salafis, the Islamic purists who were driving the holy war. It was a harder, less forgiving kind of Islam than he had known in Yemen, but its rigidity gave him the strength and discipline he needed to survive as a homesick kid at war in a foreign land. He had arrived in Afghanistan at a pivotal moment. The war against the Soviets was giving birth to a new breed of Arab fighters known as "Afghan Arabs." It was there that the seed of allegiance was planted for the thousands of young men who had flocked to the mountains of the Hindu Kush to help fight the communists. Afghanistan represented the birth of the global struggle. By helping defeat a superpower, the jihadists showed the world the power of Islam. And in the decade that followed, they would spread that war to the rest of the world.

In 1993, after Khalid had returned home from Afghanistan, he began to hear about a war in Europe where Christians were slaughtering Muslims. Stirred by the stories, he went to join the fighting in Bosnia. Again, as in Afghanistan, he was on the side the world viewed as the good guys — the Bosnian Muslims who were the victims of relentless "ethnic cleansing" at the hands of the Serbian nationalists led by Slobodan Milosević. The combat was much more intense than the action he had seen in Afghanistan, where the Soviets used superior firepower to bomb them from a distance. In Bosnia, the enemy was right in front of you, and you had to kill or be killed each day. Khalid fought alongside a group called the Green Berets, named not after the American Special Forces but after the color of Islam.

One day, after a year at war in Bosnia, Khalid was on the front line between Tuzla and Zenica, battling Serbian snipers who were shooting into Muslim villages from a nearby mountain. Suddenly, he came face to face with a Serb. The Serb got the jump, firing seven bullets into Khalid's stomach. Bundled up in heavy winter clothing, Khalid at first couldn't even tell how badly he was hit. When he started to peel off the layers around his stomach, part of his guts leaked out into his hands. He stuffed whatever he could back in and lay down on the ground. When a Saudi brother managed to drag Khalid beyond the reach of the Serb snipers, it took three injections of morphine to quiet his screaming. "You must be a heavy drinker," said the medic from Bahrain who administered the shots.

"No," Khalid said. "I chew qat." The medic, who had never heard of the plant, thought Khalid was hallucinating.

It took hours to carry Khalid down the mine-covered trail. When he finally arrived at a triage area at the base of the mountain, he was put with a group of those too far gone to save and left to die.

Soon after, the medic who had given Khalid the morphine arrived and began searching for his patient. He found Khalid lying among the rows of the dead and ordered a Bosnian army helicopter to speed Khalid to a hospital, where he woke up in pre-op. For six months he lived off an IV tube, his intestines hanging outside his body in a sterilized bag. He shrank to skin and bones — under seventy-five pounds — until he looked like "an African famine victim." The hunger was so intense, he would claw at his own stomach.

On his way to Saudi Arabia for further surgery, Khalid stopped home in Yemen. When he arrived at the airport in a wheelchair, his father slapped him across the face. "This is all your doing — tell Sheikh Zindani to help you now," he said, referring to a firebrand cleric who had urged Khalid to go to Bosnia. But Khalid received a warmer welcome in Saudi Arabia, where people from all over the country visited him in the hospital, leaving gifts of flowers, perfume, and money for a man they considered a hero.

It took Khalid several years to recover from his wounds. In 1996, he joined a group of Arab fighters going to Kosovo, where Christian Serbs were once again menacing a Muslim minority. By the time he arrived, however, the Serbs had already sealed off the country, making it impossible for him to enter. Unable to join the jihad, Khalid decided to move to England, where many of the brothers had settled. England is the home of one of the largest concentrations of Yemenis in the world; parts of Yemen were long ruled by the British, and thousands of Khalid's countrymen have settled there. When Khalid arrived, he went to see a Palestinian cleric he knew, who helped connect him to the Yemeni community. Khalid settled down to work at a corner store, chewing qat all day while manning the register. The leaf is legal in England, and Khalid's store stocked and sold qat to Yemenis in the neighborhood.

Khalid was twenty-three. For the past seven years, he had been fighting in battles all over the world. He had never been on a date, never kissed a girl, never really talked to a female who wasn't a close relation. So he did what many a lonely guy does when he's stuck in a city he doesn't know very well: he fell for the waitress at the coffee shop.

She was of Irish descent, and she smiled every time she brought him his coffee. Khalid went to a Yemeni friend and explained his quandary: he was in love, but he didn't know what to say.

"No problem," the friend told him. "I'll ask her out for you."

The waitress was receptive but confused. "I like him," she told the friend. "But why doesn't he just talk to me himself?"

Things were rocky from the start. On the first date, she wanted to go to a disco, but Khalid refused. Outside a restaurant, he grew angry when a passing man looked at her. "What are you going to do if I walk on the street with you?" she asked. "Fight everybody in the city?"

A couple of dates later came the gifts: three bottles of pricey perfume and a ring — *the* ring. He could barely get the words out in English: "I want to marry you."

"Marry me?" She was surprised, amused even. "What's my name?"

"It's hard for me to remember it," he stuttered.

He gave her a week to decide. His gallantry must have won her over, because they were married within a month.

Right after that, the misery began. Khalid tried to control her and force her to wear the *hijab*, the headscarf worn by devout Muslim women. Their arguments were so loud that neighbors knocked on the door and banged on the walls. He realized the way he treated her was wrong, but he didn't know any other way. They separated, and Khalid got a British passport out of the marriage.

Khalid returned to the only life he knew. This time, his destination was Somalia, where a radical Muslim faction was attempting to impose strict Islamic law, known as *sharia*, on the entire country. Posing as a Red Crescent worker, Khalid bribed a pilot to fly him from Nairobi to the Somali town of Luuq, where he delivered $40,000 in cash to a Somali warlord allied with the Islamic faction. The money was from Arab backers, mostly Saudis, who were using their disposable income to influence the many conflicts that plagued Africa and the Middle East. Their cash not only advanced the cause of Islam — it also bought allies who might help the struggle in the future.

There were forty Arab fighters in Luuq helping to fight the Ethiopian army, which regularly attacked from across the border. The longer Khalid stayed, the more dire conditions grew. At times the insurgents survived only by eating pure sugar. The brothers eventually organized a counterattack and retook the city. Khalid fought for two days straight, until he and his men ran out of ammunition. Reduced to throwing stones, most of the Arab and Somali fighters were killed. At one point the few remaining survivors were so desperate, they started to dig their own graves.

Khalid escaped, badly shaken but alive, with neither the money nor the means to get home. What do you do when you're on jihad, all the money's run out, and you just want to leave? For Khalid and his remaining men, their only chance was to try to get a piece of the forty grand that Khalid had already delivered to the warlord.

"I can't help you," the Somali leader told him. "We need all that money for our fight."

Khalid wasn't a high school debater, he was a holy warrior, so he did what came naturally: he put a loaded gun to the man's head. "I'll kill you or you'll help us get out of here," he said. "We brought you forty thousand dollars. Now you need to help us." The warlord was convinced. Khalid and his fellow insurgents eventually escaped to Yemen by crossing the Gulf of Aden on a dhow packed with goats.

When Khalid finally arrived home, his father was furious. "What the hell happened to you?" he demanded. "Where did you come from?" To calm him down, Khalid promised to stop fighting and start a normal life.

But whenever the call came, he answered. In 1999, Khalid traveled to Tbilisi, in Georgia, and tried to get into Chechnya, where the Russian army was slaughtering Muslims. But many mujahideen, he learned, had died trying to walk across the mountains to Chechnya. Khalid was willing to die fighting for his cause, a gun in his hand, but freezing to death on a mountaintop was no way for a soldier to give up his life. He headed back to England, returning to his job as a clerk at the corner store, chewing qat to keep himself alert, always on the lookout for the next opportunity.

In 2001, he got a call from Afghanistan. The brothers wanted him there.

When Khalid arrived in Afghanistan early that year, the Taliban had unified most of the country under the strict banner of *sharia* law. The ragtag bands of foreign jihadists who had fought the communists were gone. In their place was a sophisticated network of training camps run by Al Qaeda. This was a new age of jihad, a well-organized, well-financed struggle led by Osama bin Laden. Jihad, Khalid discovered, had been institutionalized.

At first, Khalid ran a sort of hostel in Mashhad, deep in the rugged Iranian frontier. The six-hundred-mile border between Iran and Afghanistan is difficult to police because of its steep mountains and many trails, and Al Qaeda was taking advantage of the covert passageways, sheltering jihadists at Khalid's hostel before sending them over the mountains into Afghanistan.

That summer, on a trip into Afghanistan, Khalid met bin Laden at the leader's camp near Kandahar. They talked about the course of jihad and the situation in Yemen, a country for which bin Laden had a special fondness — his father and one of his wives were born there, and Yemen had always supplied some of the best and bravest mujahideen, men bin Laden relied on as his most trusted fighters and bodyguards. Khalid thought jihad should be extended to Yemen, but bin Laden disagreed, saying it would stretch his forces too thin. "There is no justice in Yemen," he told Khalid, "but we can't fight there now."

By the summer of 2001, there was a palpable feeling in the camps that something big was about to happen. Around that time, Khalid ran into an old friend from his days in Bosnia: Khalid Sheikh Mohammed, a Pakistani who had risen to prominence as an operational chief of Al Qaeda. Mohammed asked Khalid to volunteer for a mission to the United States or Europe — his British passport would enable him to slip in and out of a Western country. But Khalid refused. He was willing to fight foreign soldiers invading Arab lands, but he wasn't ready to take the war to America or Europe.

On September 11, Khalid was near Kabul when a Libyan cleric announced that the World Trade Center had been destroyed. Everyone in the camp exploded in jubilation — the mood was exhilarating, insane, like Mecca at the height of the hajj. As Khalid remembers it, it was the moment when everything changed. The mujahideen had struck a blow against the West that would never be forgotten. And in the process, they had made themselves the target of the world's only remaining superpower.

When the United States invaded Afghanistan, Khalid saw his most intense fighting in and around Khost. Even with help from a local sheikh, the foreign fighters couldn't do much against the American onslaught. One night, Khalid was sleeping in a car near Khost with three other fighters. When he woke up and walked away to relieve himself, the car was blown to bits. Khalid later helped to bury a body he believed to be the wife of Ayman al-Zawahiri, bin Laden's second in command. The woman had been killed in a school where many Al Qaeda families had sought shelter from the American bombings.

After a few weeks, as the relentless bombing continued, a message arrived from bin Laden: any mujahideen who could still travel should return to their home countries. There was no point in dying in Afghanistan. "There was no way to fight a decent war there with the Americans," Khalid recalled. "We hardly ever saw a soldier to fire at." Though the Bush administration believed it had routed the Islamic forces, the mujahideen, in fact, had beat a strategic retreat. American commanders, reluctant to expose ground troops to danger, had relied on a strategy of bombing from above that allowed many Al Qaeda members to slip away, ready and willing to fight again another day.

In late 2001, Sheikh Mohammed, the Al Qaeda operational chief, ordered Khalid to guide a group of fifty women and children to safety in Iran, over the same mountains he had crossed to enter Afghanistan. "You know the route," Mohammed said. "Take some families with you." He gave Khalid thousands of dollars to pay for Afghan guides and to take care of the Iranian border guards.

The journey to Iran took two weeks. They trekked across high mountains — a string of women and children wandering through a remote corner of the world, eating dates, plants, and whatever animals they could kill along the way. When they reached Iran, pro-

Taliban allies were waiting to shuttle them to safety. For weeks after the trip, Khalid's shoulders ached from carrying so many children on his back.

In the years before September 11, Khalid and his fellow mujahideen could move around the world with relative ease — creating fake passports, bribing border police, claiming that they were Iraqi dissidents fleeing the tyranny of Saddam Hussein. Immigration officials were a nuisance, but there was always a way around them. Now, returning to England from Afghanistan in 2002, Khalid discovered that even a real British passport couldn't protect him from scrutiny. When he changed planes in Abu Dhabi, the police stopped him, suspecting that his passport was fake. A well-dressed supervisor came out to question him. "What's Marks and Spencer?" the man asked.

"A big British department store," Khalid said. "Look, I'm a British citizen, from Yemen. I'm Shiite. Why would I want to go and help the Taliban? They hate Shiites. I was on a pilgrimage to holy places in Iran." After a few hours they let him go, and he boarded a plane to London.

At Heathrow, he was detained again. British officials asked for his luggage and he told them he had only hand baggage. Strike one. They examined his ticket: one-way from Tehran. Strike two. As he sat on a hard bench in a glass-paneled interrogation room, deathly afraid, he could see officials leafing through his passport in the next room. They kept coming back to one page — a page that had been doctored in Afghanistan to remove a Pakistani visa. He claimed he had accidentally left it in his pants and then ironed them, but they didn't buy it. Strike three. At midnight the agents handcuffed him, shoved him in the back seat of an unmarked car, and took him to a maximum-security detention facility.

They questioned him for five days. As the interrogation continued, however, Khalid came to see that he was safer in England, protected by the country's due-process laws, than many of his brothers detained by the Americans in Afghanistan. Realizing that the police had nothing on him, he denied everything. They finally let him go, unable to hold him without further evidence.

The incident communicated something important to Khalid: the jihadi's life had changed after 9/11. Not long ago he could travel all over the world with impunity; now they were hassling him at Heathrow just because he was flying in from Tehran on a one-way ticket with a piece of hand luggage.

Khalid lived quietly in England for a year and a half, working at the corner shop and praying at a local mosque. Around that time, he befriended a fellow Yemeni who would come to share his passion for jihad: Wa'il al Dhaleai, who was well known in England as a leading tae kwon do instructor and Olympic hopeful.

In 2003, when the United States invaded Iraq, it was clear to Khalid where he would next do battle. Getting into Iraq from Syria was no more difficult than dressing up like a farmer and walking across the border with phony papers in the middle of the night. But the fighting was a different story. In the early stages of the war, there weren't many foreign fighters like Khalid in Iraq; the bulk of the insurgency was comprised of native-born Sunnis who simply wanted to drive the Americans from their country. They welcomed the foreigners — they weren't in a position to be choosy — but they weren't interested in jihad's broader goal of imposing Islamic law on Iraq.

Khalid quickly discovered that it was impossible to blend in — Iraqis tend to be bigger than Yemenis, and their body language and dialect are hard to imitate. Shiites were especially quick to report foreign Sunnis to the authorities. Khalid and his Arab brothers had the same problem as the American forces they were fighting: they didn't know which Iraqis they could trust.

Most of the foreign fighters in Iraq were very young. At thirty-two, Khalid felt like an old man. Stuck in their safe houses, the mujahideen had to rely on Iraqi insurgents to report on the movement of American convoys, scouting for an opening that would allow them to attack. Months after President Bush declared "mission accomplished" in Iraq, Khalid was ambushing U.S. forces in the northern city of Mosul. Around the same time, Saddam Hussein's sons died in a fierce gun battle there. That October, Khalid's friend Wa'il also died, fighting the Americans in the town of Ramadi.

After three months in Iraq, Khalid returned to England through Syria. But jihad seemed to shadow him everywhere. One evening, after returning home from work, Khalid heard a helicopter overhead. Seconds later the police kicked in the door, handcuffed him, and arrested him on suspicion of terrorism. People on his block couldn't believe that the friendly guy who sat behind the counter at their corner store was an Al Qaeda fighter.

The agents interrogated Khalid about his past. They knew he'd been in Syria. Business, he explained. They knew he'd been detained in 2002 after returning to England from Iran. Shiite pilgrimage. I've never been in Afghanistan. I don't want to go. They knew there were Yemeni fighters being held in Guantánamo who said Khalid had recruited them to train in Afghanistan. Liars. They knew he had spoken on his cell phone to Wa'il, shortly before his friend had died in Iraq. Just a chat.

After Khalid spent a week in prison they let him out, just as they always did. They didn't have enough evidence to keep him. When he was released, his next-door neighbors, mostly white Britons, were there to welcome him home. "I might doubt my own son," one old man said, "but I'll always believe Khalid." Most of the Yemenis and other Muslims who had been Khalid's friends had deserted him when he was arrested, fearing for their own safety. When he saw his British neighbors standing by him, Khalid couldn't help bawling.

After the arrest, Khalid returned to Iraq for two more months in 2004, in part to honor the memory of Wa'il. Living in safe houses, he once again went out on raids against the Americans. The heaviest fighting he saw was in Al Qa'im, where thirty Arabs and more than a hundred Iraqis fought for a week against the Americans. Khalid saw seven brothers killed, mostly from Syria and Saudi Arabia. He believed the insurgents killed about ten soldiers from the other side. By this time, however, the nature of the insurgency had changed. Al-Zarqawi had succeeded, for the moment, in taking over the homegrown resistance. Many of Saddam's former secret police and Republican Guard were now integrated into cells with jihadists like Khalid. The leadership of Al Qaeda had financial resources and strategic expertise that the Iraqis lacked, and the foreign fighters were more willing to die than the local Sunnis — and more willing to kill civilians.

Disturbed by the killings, Khalid began to rethink the role of jihad in his life. Would his faith really justify killing his British neighbors in their own country? Would he ever be able to live a normal life? Hearing about Yemenis he knew who had disappeared into the gulag at Guantánamo, he feared he could end up in prison for life, a fate he considered worse than death.

The doubts intensified after he returned home to Yemen and was arrested earlier this year. "Enough is enough," his father implored. "It's time to settle down and stop this stuff." After Khalid was released from prison, he and a group of other Afghan Arabs — the blanket term for those who fought or trained in Afghanistan — were summoned to a meeting with Ali Abdullah Salih, the president of Yemen, who was trying to contain the jihadists. In private, Salih called them "my sons" and said he had been pressured by the Bush administration to crack down on them. He also did something seldom acknowledged in the war on terror: he offered to pay them off to stop fighting.

"We will help you get jobs, get married," Salih told the men. "Write down your name and what you want."

Khalid didn't take the money, but he was tempted by the offer. He wanted out of jihad. On a trip back to England in late 2004, he had proposed to a Muslim woman he met through friends. In August, his fiancée and her family visited him in Yemen. He was visibly excited about the prospect of settling down and starting a family. He and his betrothed would go on heavily chaperoned picnics to a park outside Sanaa with their extended families, or visit the home of a close relative. They have never been alone together, and he has never seen her face.

But Khalid can see no way to escape from his past. Like many veterans, he looks back on his years of fighting with nostalgia — the thrill of battle, the feeling of brotherhood, the steadfast devotion to a cause. But on some days, it feels as if he has no place in the world. He lives in Sanaa, but it no longer seems like home. Every few days he walks down to a storefront calling center and phones his brother in England. He doubts he can ever go back to the life he knew there. He often visited the mosques frequented by the London bombers, and he fears police will arrest him if he tries to return. But if he stays in Yemen, the brothers will keep trying to draw him back into the struggle.

These days, when they come over to his house and try to rally him for a mission to Iraq or Sudan, Khalid looks bored and says that he can't go anywhere now, that it would put his family in Yemen at risk. Even his fiancée's younger brother tried to enlist his aid to join the insurgency in Iraq. Khalid told him he couldn't help. He doesn't want any part of the fighting, but uncertainty might be seen as betrayal. So he keeps silent, and waits, and imagines the day when the war, and all that comes with it, will finally end.

GIPI

■

The Innocents

FROM *Wish You Were Here*

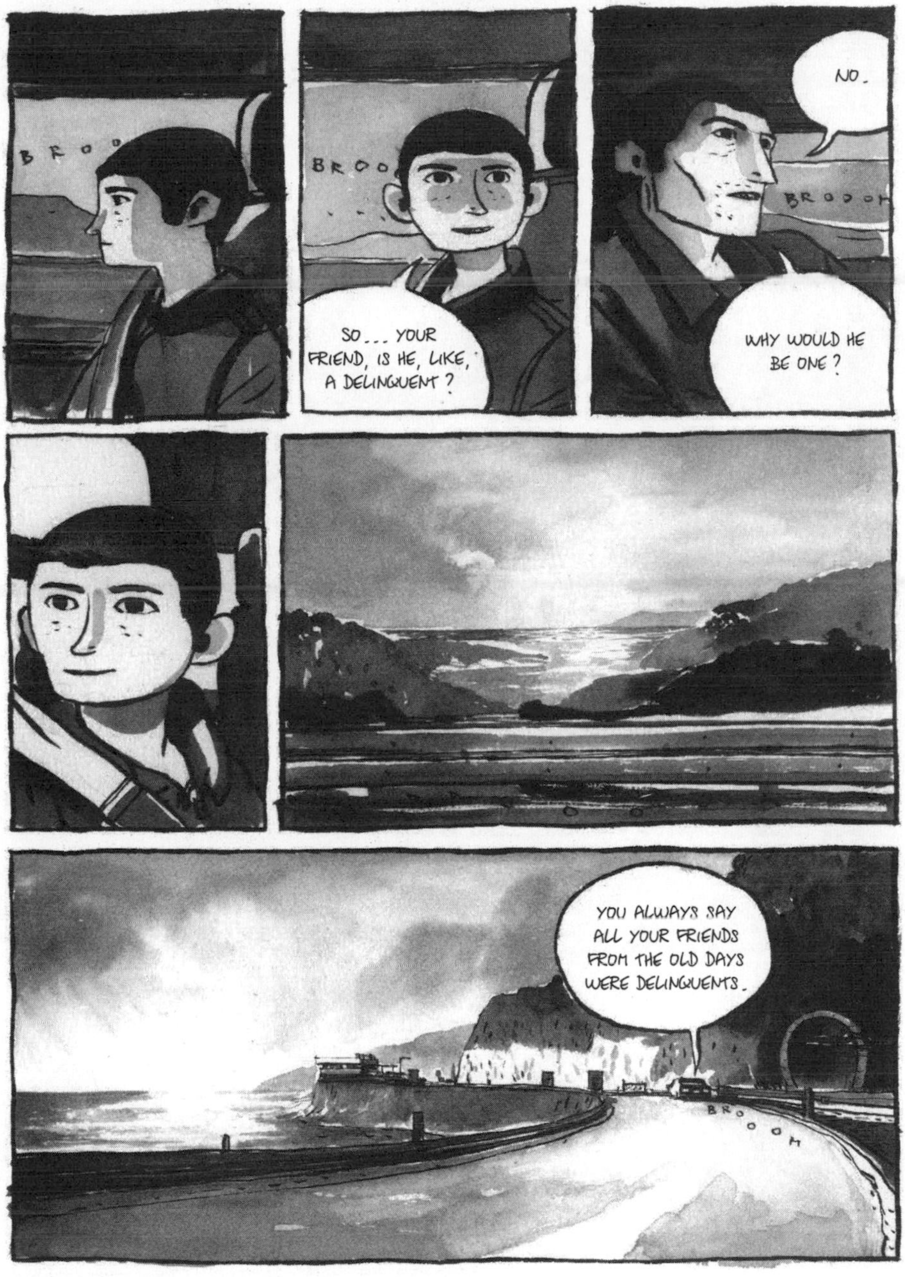
BROO
BROO
SO... YOUR FRIEND, IS HE, LIKE, A DELINQUENT?
NO.
BROOM
WHY WOULD HE BE ONE?
YOU ALWAYS SAY ALL YOUR FRIENDS FROM THE OLD DAYS WERE DELINQUENTS.
BROOOM

DID HE GO TO PRISON TOO ?
HE WENT TO PRISON, BUT HE'S NOT A DELINQUENT.
HE WAS INNOCENT.
REALLY ?
YES.
ARE ALL YOUR FRIENDS WHO WENT TO PRISON INNOCENT ?

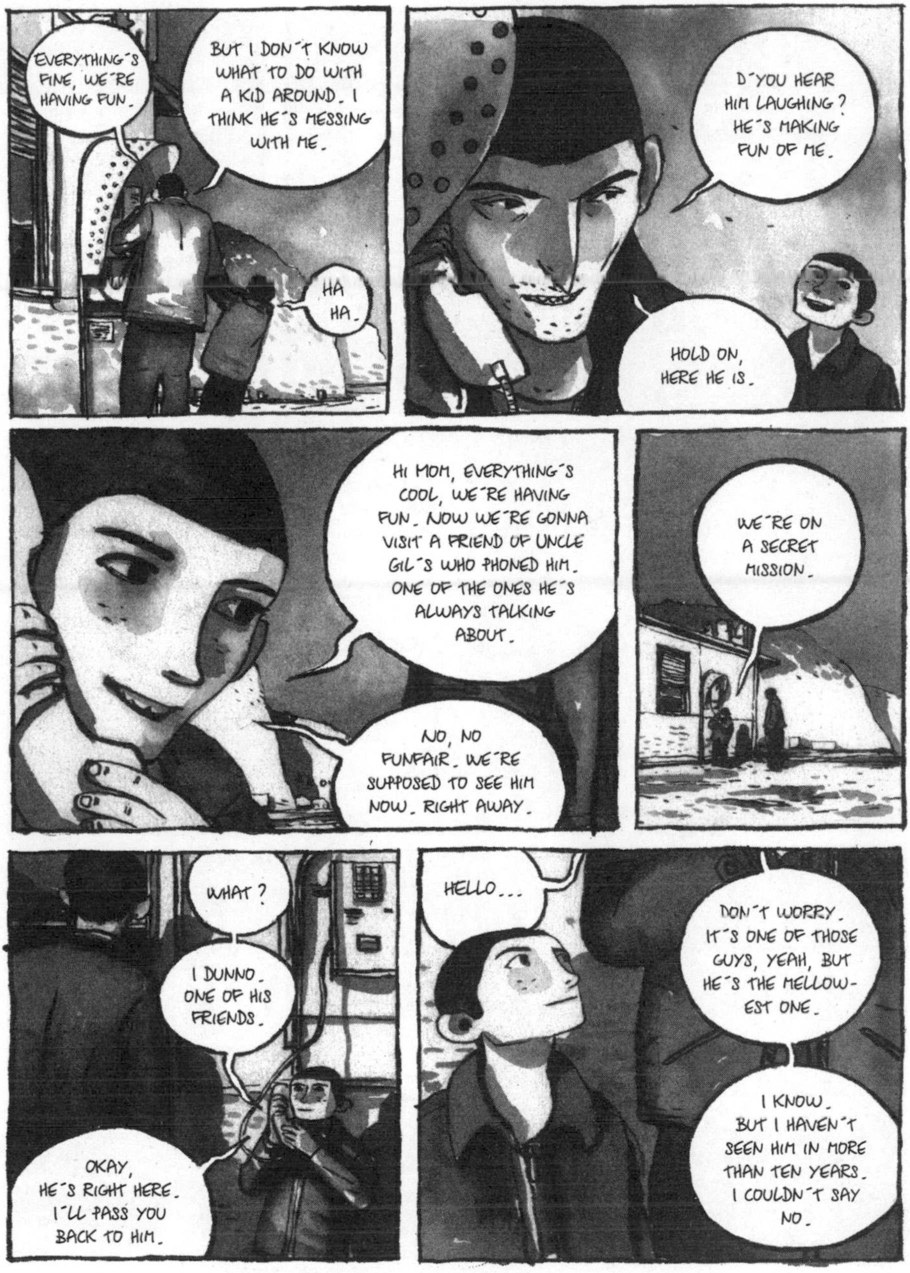
EVERYTHING´S FINE, WE´RE HAVING FUN.
BUT I DON´T KNOW WHAT TO DO WITH A KID AROUND. I THINK HE´S MESSING WITH ME.
HA HA.
D´YOU HEAR HIM LAUGHING? HE´S MAKING FUN OF ME.
HOLD ON, HERE HE IS.
HI MOM, EVERYTHING´S COOL, WE´RE HAVING FUN. NOW WE´RE GONNA VISIT A FRIEND OF UNCLE GIL´S WHO PHONED HIM. ONE OF THE ONES HE´S ALWAYS TALKING ABOUT.
NO, NO FUNFAIR. WE´RE SUPPOSED TO SEE HIM NOW. RIGHT AWAY.
WE´RE ON A SECRET MISSION.
WHAT?
I DUNNO. ONE OF HIS FRIENDS.
OKAY, HE´S RIGHT HERE. I´LL PASS YOU BACK TO HIM.
HELLO...
DON´T WORRY. IT´S ONE OF THOSE GUYS, YEAH, BUT HE´S THE MELLOW-EST ONE.
I KNOW. BUT I HAVEN´T SEEN HIM IN MORE THAN TEN YEARS. I COULDN´T SAY NO.

AND ANDREA?

ANDREA WILL MEET A PERSON A LITTLE BIT DIFFERENT FROM THE ONES HE'S USUALLY AROUND. DON'T WORRY.

HE'S NOT AN IDIOT.

BLEH BLEH.

I'M A SHMARTY!

CUT IT OUT, YOU SPAZ.

I AIN'T NO IDJIT.

BLEH BLEH *GIGGLE*

IT WAS SUPPOSED TO BE A SECRET MISSION. DO YOU KNOW WHAT A SECRET IS?

WATCH OUT FOR THE CARS.

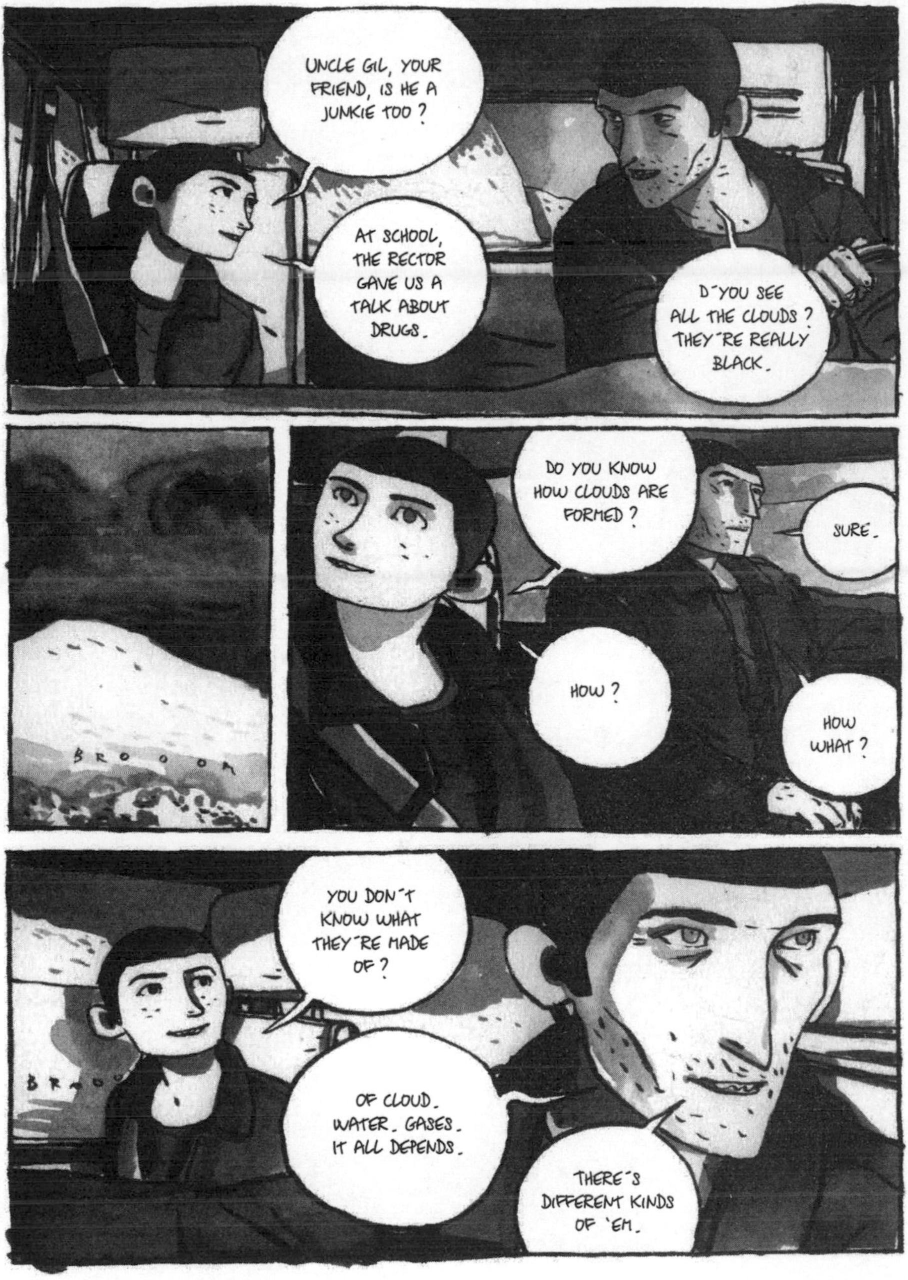
UNCLE GIL, YOUR FRIEND, IS HE A JUNKIE TOO ?
AT SCHOOL, THE RECTOR GAVE US A TALK ABOUT DRUGS.
D'YOU SEE ALL THE CLOUDS ? THEY'RE REALLY BLACK.
BROOOM
DO YOU KNOW HOW CLOUDS ARE FORMED ?
SURE.
HOW ?
HOW WHAT ?
YOU DON'T KNOW WHAT THEY'RE MADE OF ?
BRO
OF CLOUD. WATER. GASES. IT ALL DEPENDS.
THERE'S DIFFERENT KINDS OF 'EM.

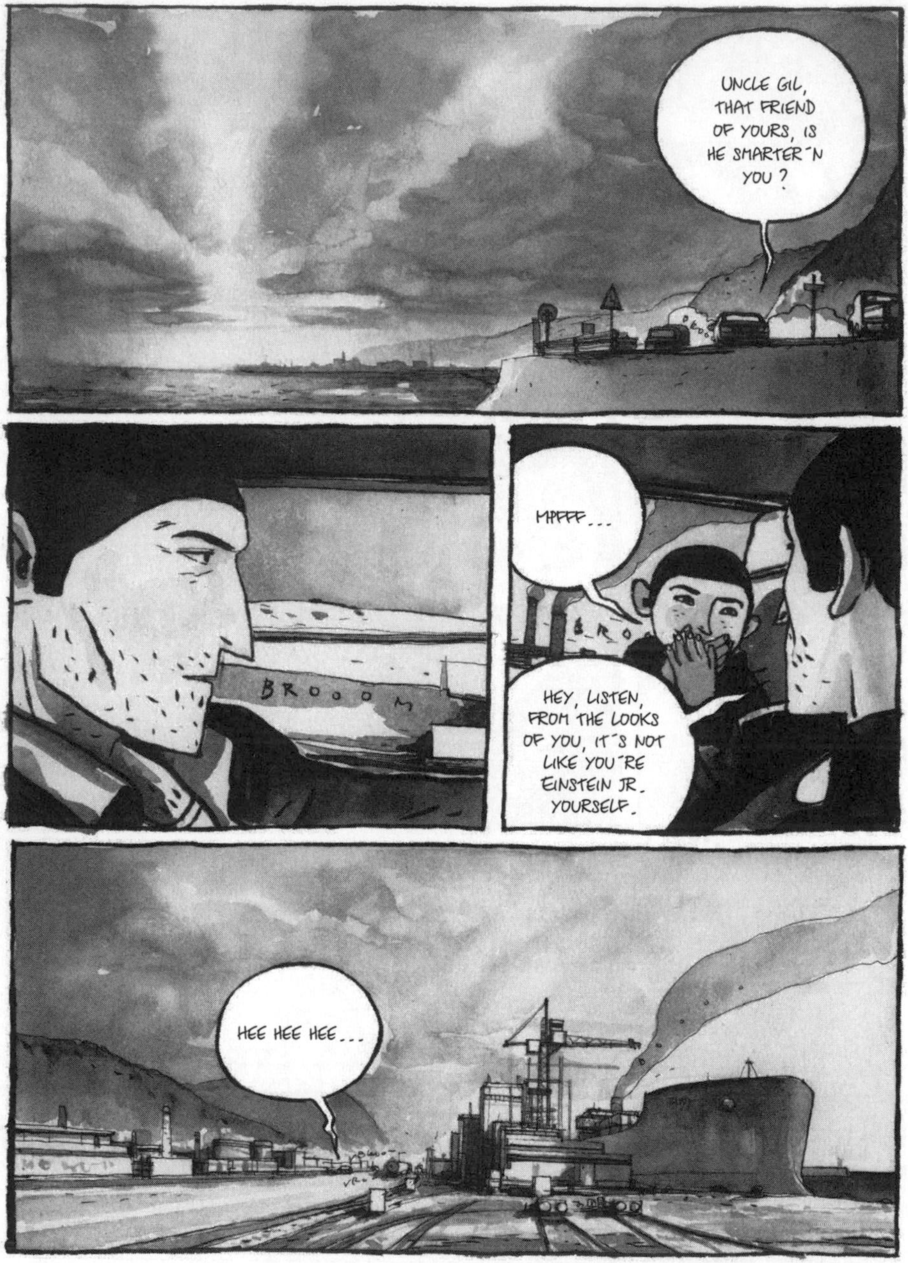
UNCLE GIL, THAT FRIEND OF YOURS, IS HE SMARTER'N YOU?
BROOOM
MPFFF...
HEY, LISTEN, FROM THE LOOKS OF YOU, IT'S NOT LIKE YOU'RE EINSTEIN JR. YOURSELF.
HEE HEE HEE...

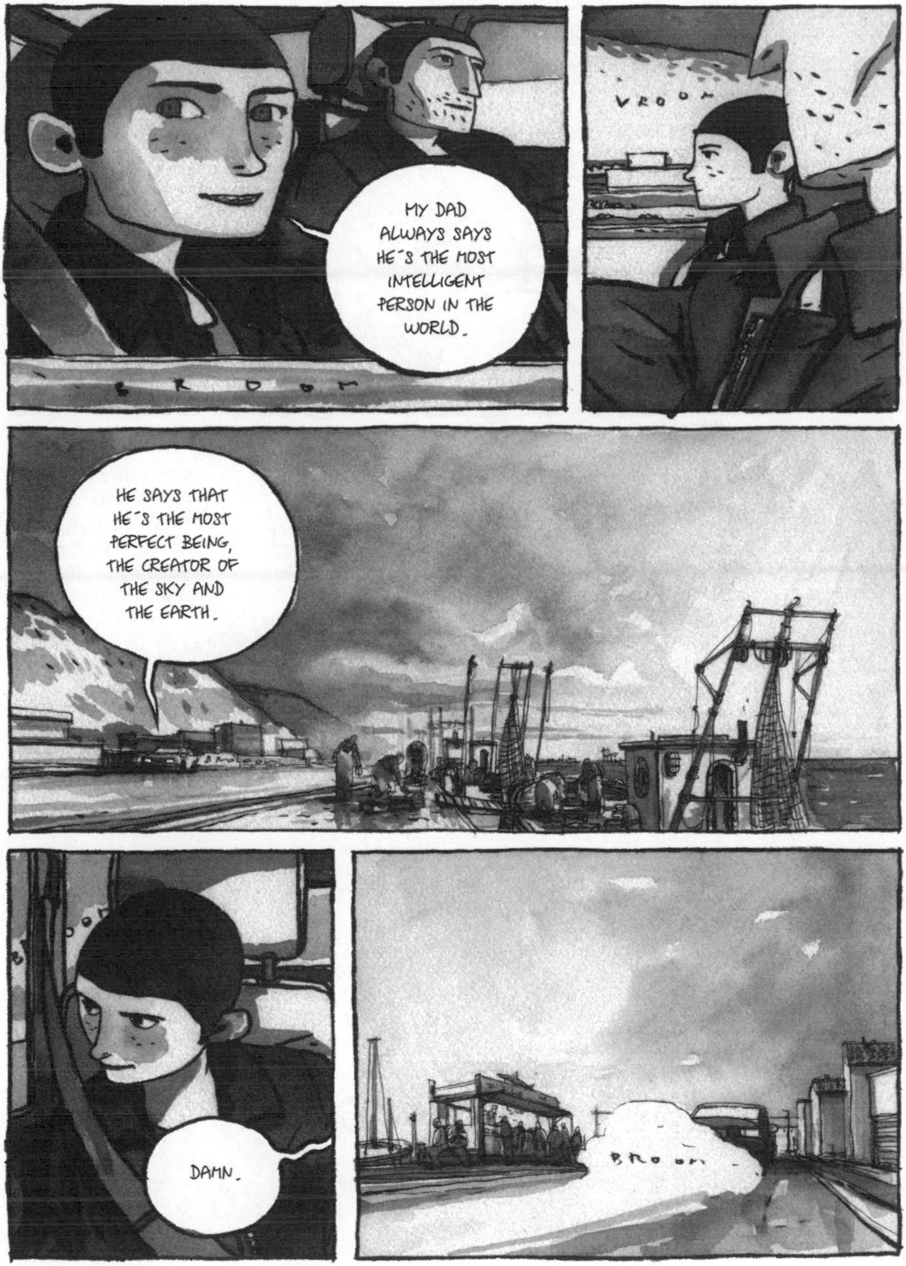
MY DAD ALWAYS SAYS HE´S THE MOST INTELLIGENT PERSON IN THE WORLD.
VROOM
HE SAYS THAT HE´S THE MOST PERFECT BEING, THE CREATOR OF THE SKY AND THE EARTH.
DAMN.
BROOM

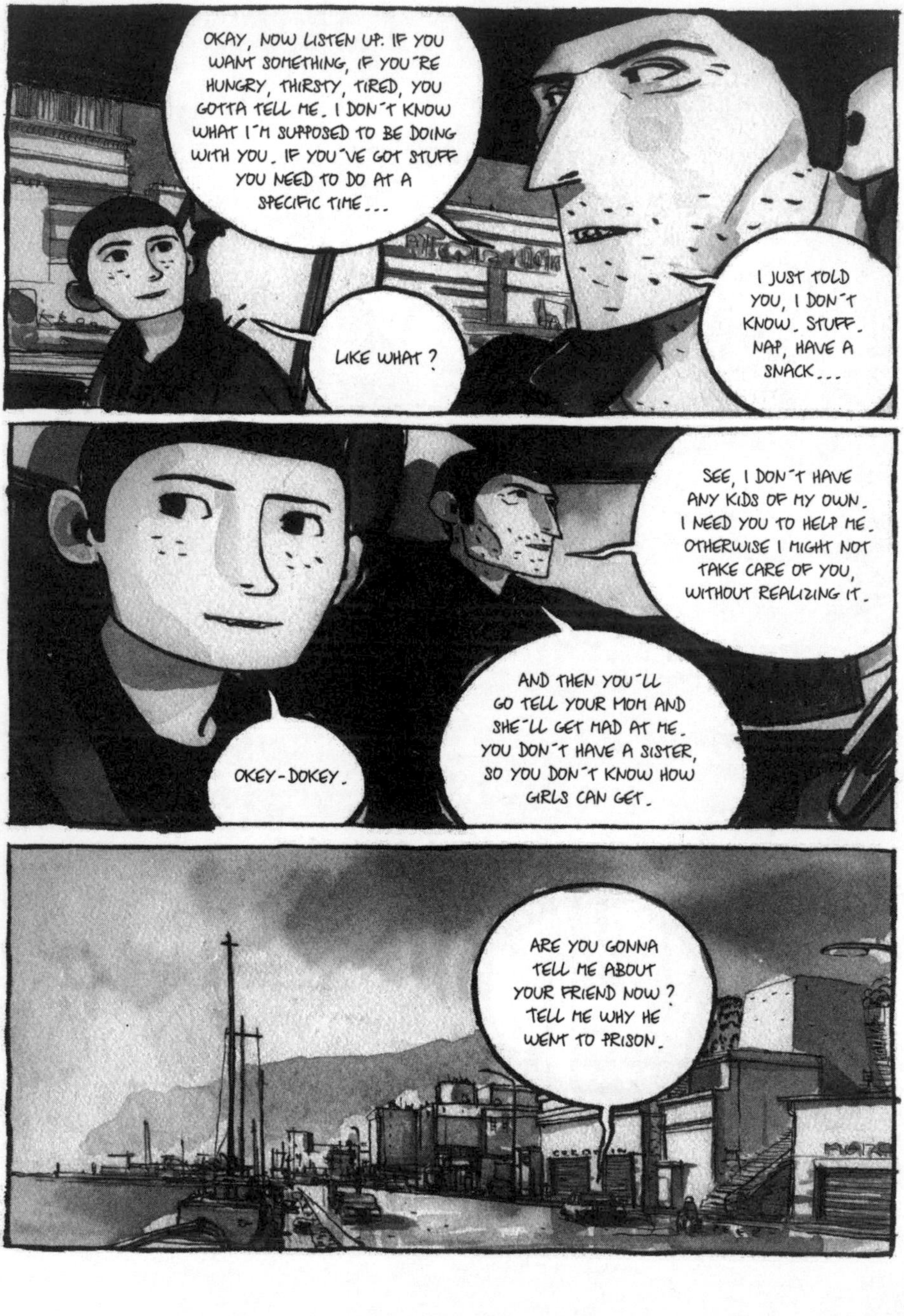
OKAY, NOW LISTEN UP: IF YOU WANT SOMETHING, IF YOU'RE HUNGRY, THIRSTY, TIRED, YOU GOTTA TELL ME. I DON'T KNOW WHAT I'M SUPPOSED TO BE DOING WITH YOU. IF YOU'VE GOT STUFF YOU NEED TO DO AT A SPECIFIC TIME...
LIKE WHAT?
I JUST TOLD YOU, I DON'T KNOW. STUFF. NAP, HAVE A SNACK...
SEE, I DON'T HAVE ANY KIDS OF MY OWN. I NEED YOU TO HELP ME. OTHERWISE I MIGHT NOT TAKE CARE OF YOU, WITHOUT REALIZING IT.
OKEY-DOKEY.
AND THEN YOU'LL GO TELL YOUR MOM AND SHE'LL GET MAD AT ME. YOU DON'T HAVE A SISTER, SO YOU DON'T KNOW HOW GIRLS CAN GET.
ARE YOU GONNA TELL ME ABOUT YOUR FRIEND NOW? TELL ME WHY HE WENT TO PRISON.

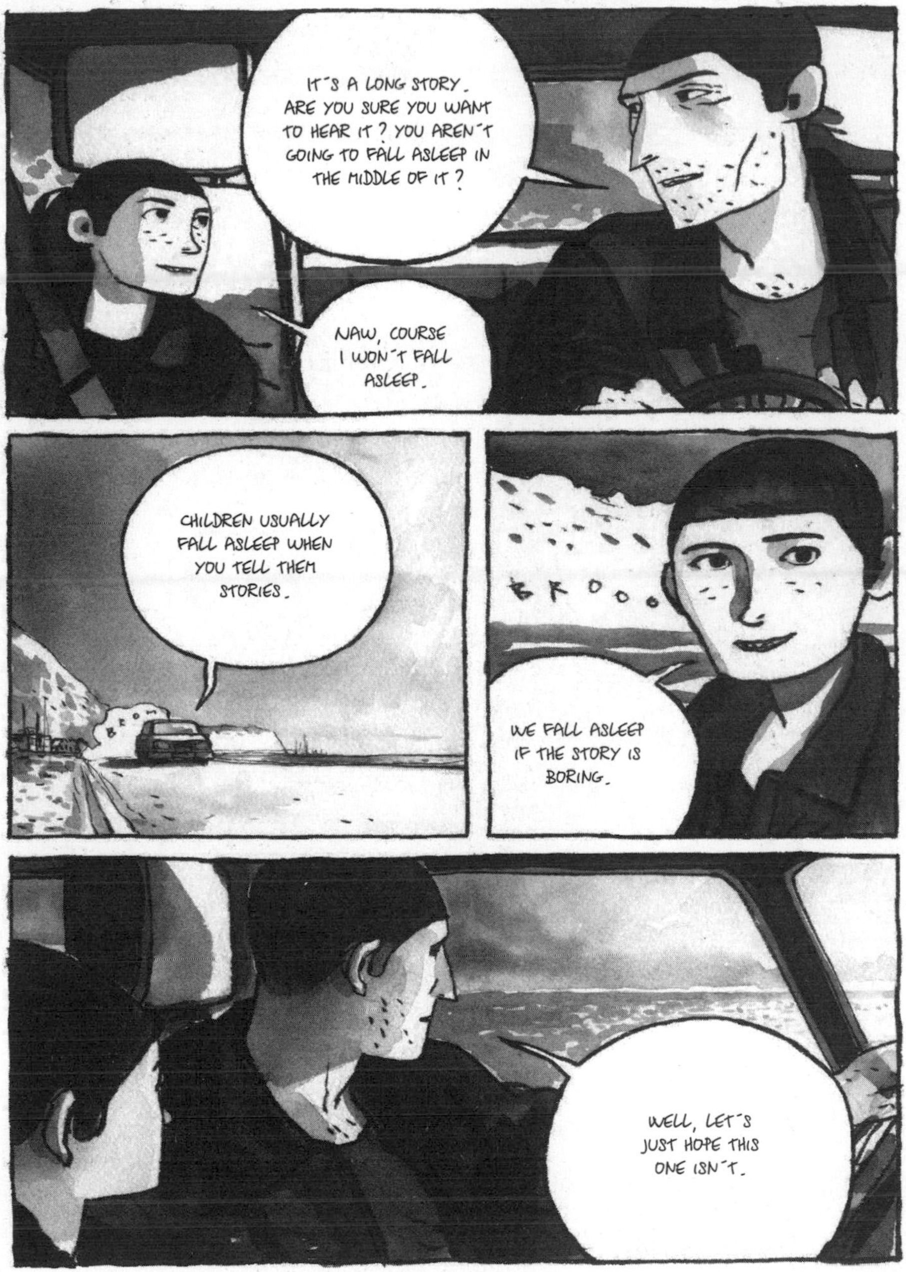
IT'S A LONG STORY. ARE YOU SURE YOU WANT TO HEAR IT? YOU AREN'T GOING TO FALL ASLEEP IN THE MIDDLE OF IT?
NAW, COURSE I WON'T FALL ASLEEP.
CHILDREN USUALLY FALL ASLEEP WHEN YOU TELL THEM STORIES.
BROOOO
WE FALL ASLEEP IF THE STORY IS BORING.
WELL, LET'S JUST HOPE THIS ONE ISN'T.

WHEN WE WERE YOUNG, ME AND MY PALS WERE ALWAYS HANGING OUT IN THE STREETS.
THERE WAS A WHOLE GANG OF US.

THAT'S ME,
THERE.

THIS ONE'S
VALERIO.

THIS FRIEND OF MINE, VALERIO,
WAS A NICE KID, AND A FUNNY
ONE, TOO. NOT A MEAN BONE IN
HIS BODY. HE WAS MELLOW.
PROBABLY THE MELLOWEST OF
ALL OF US.

SO WE MADE FUN OF HIM,
WE TOLD HIM HE COULD'VE
BEEN THE RECTOR'S SON.
HE PRETENDED LIKE HE
WAS MAD AND WE'D PLAY
KICK-ASS.

AARH!

OOHH!

HA HA HA

ONE DAY, TWO NEW COPS SHOWED UP IN THE NEIGHBORHOOD. THEY
CAME FROM THE CAPITAL, THE ANTI-TERRORIST SQUAD. WE HAD NO
IDEA WHY THEY'D SENT THEM OUR WAY, DOWN HERE IN THE STICKS,
WHERE NOTHING EVER HAPPENED.

HI.

WHEN I SAY HELLO
IT'S WITH MY FIST,
THAT OK WITH YOU?

THEY IMMEDIATELY STARTED PICKING ON US. FOR NO REASON.

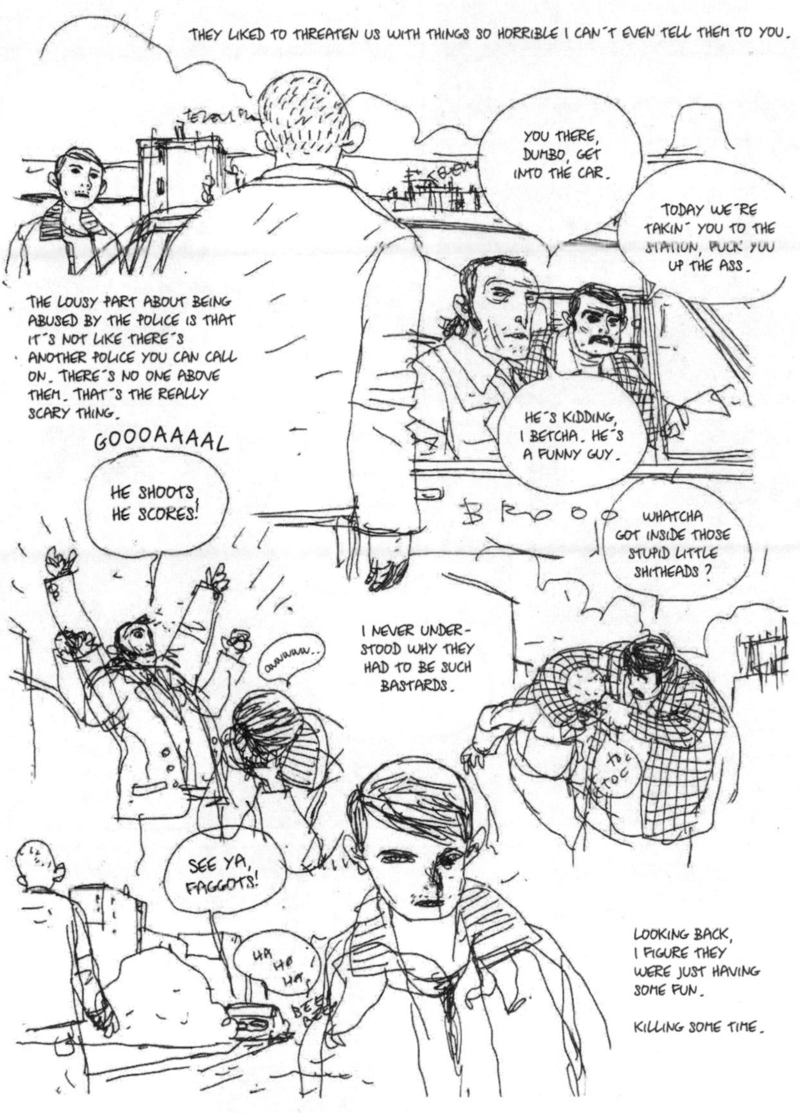
THEY LIKED TO THREATEN US WITH THINGS SO HORRIBLE I CAN´T EVEN TELL THEM TO YOU.
YOU THERE, DUMBO, GET INTO THE CAR.
TODAY WE´RE TAKIN´ YOU TO THE STATION, FUCK YOU UP THE ASS.
THE LOUSY PART ABOUT BEING ABUSED BY THE POLICE IS THAT IT´S NOT LIKE THERE´S ANOTHER POLICE YOU CAN CALL ON. THERE´S NO ONE ABOVE THEM. THAT´S THE REALLY SCARY THING.
HE´S KIDDING, I BETCHA. HE´S A FUNNY GUY.
GOOOAAAAL
HE SHOOTS, HE SCORES!
BROOO
WHATCHA GOT INSIDE THOSE STUPID LITTLE SHITHEADS?
I NEVER UNDERSTOOD WHY THEY HAD TO BE SUCH BASTARDS.
TOC TOC
SEE YA, FAGGOTS!
HA HO HA
LOOKING BACK, I FIGURE THEY WERE JUST HAVING SOME FUN.
KILLING SOME TIME.

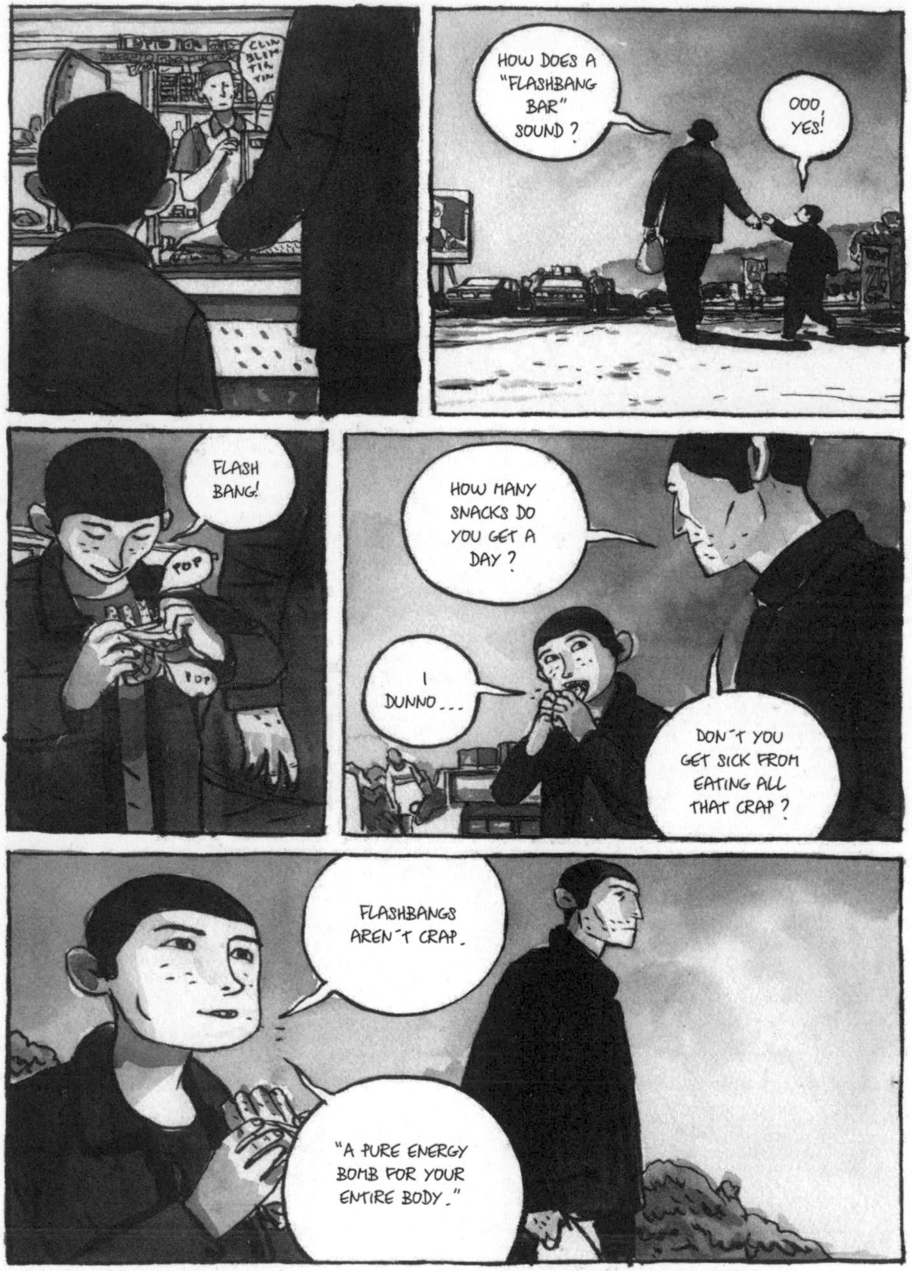
CLIN BLIM TIN TIN
HOW DOES A "FLASHBANG BAR" SOUND?
OOO, YES!
FLASH BANG!
POP
POP
HOW MANY SNACKS DO YOU GET A DAY?
I DUNNO...
DON'T YOU GET SICK FROM EATING ALL THAT CRAP?
FLASHBANGS AREN'T CRAP.
"A PURE ENERGY BOMB FOR YOUR ENTIRE BODY."

UNCLE GIL, THIS FRIEND OF YOURS WE'RE SEEING, IS HE NICE?

YEAH, HE'S NICE.

AT LEAST, HE WAS WHEN HE WAS YOUNG. I HAVEN'T SEEN HIM IN A LONG TIME.

HE MUST HAVE CHANGED.

WHAT WITH ALL THE STUFF HE WENT THROUGH.

WILL YOU TELL ME ABOUT THAT TOO?

MMMMMM... COCO-BANANA FLASHBANG.

COCO-BANANA FLASHBANGS ARE WICKED GOOD, AREN'T THEY?

"A PURE ENERGY BOMB FOR YOUR ENTIRE BODY."

ANYWAY, APRIL IS HERE. IN THE CAPITAL, THE TERRORISTS SHOOT AT A POLICE COMMISSIONER. THEY KILL HIM, FOR REAL.

WE HAVE NO CLUE. WE HAVEN'T EVEN SEEN THE NEWS ON TV. BUT THE TWO COPS ARE IN A BAD MOOD AND THEY'RE TRYING TO BLOW OFF STEAM ANY WHICH WAY THEY CAN. HERE IN THE STICKS, THERE AREN'T ANY TERRORISTS. THERE'S JUST US.

ME AND VALERIO, WE'RE SMOKING OURSELVES SOME SPANISH CIGARETTES WHEN THEY SHOW UP.

TODAY WE AIN'T KIDDING AROUND.

THEY ASK US SOME QUESTIONS. WE DON'T KNOW WHAT TO ANSWER. VALERIO SAYS SOMETHING THEY DON'T LIKE (I DON'T REMEMBER WHAT). THEY TAKE HIM WITH THEM, KEEP HIM AT THE STATION ALL NIGHT.

THE FOLLOWING MORNING, HE'S A DIFFERENT PERSON.

HE NEVER TALKS ABOUT IT, BUT HE TAKES IT OUT ON EVERYONE.

YOU BOXERS, YOU'RE ALL FAGS.

HE STARTS GETTING INTO FIGHTS FOR NO REASON.

IT GETS SO IT'S DANGEROUS JUST TO WALK DOWN THE STREET WITH HIM...

ON HIS ACCOUNT, WE ALL GET IN TROUBLE ALL SUMMER LONG.

EVERYONE STARTS AVOIDING HIM.

WHERE YOU GOIN', GUYS?

HE STRUTS AROUND WITH A SWITCHBLADE KNIFE, WITH A BLADE YAY LONG. IT'S OBVIOUS HE'S DYING TO USE IT ON SOMEONE.

ONE AFTERNOON WE'RE IN THE STREET.

THE TWO COPS SHOW UP.

HE'S GOT HIS KNIFE IN HIS JEANS POCKET.

THE TWO COPS DON'T HAVE A CLUE. THEY MAKE HIM GET INTO THE CAR. THEY TAKE HIM WITH THEM.

THEY'VE GOT ANOTHER NIGHT OF FUN PLANNED.

THEY THREATEN HIM. HE DOESN'T PUT UP ANY RESISTANCE. HE LOSES IT AND STABS ONE OF THEM IN THE SHOULDER. HE'S ARRESTED, SENTENCED. IN THOSE YEARS, BECAUSE OF THE TERRORISM, THERE ARE SPECIAL LAWS, REALLY HARSH ONES. VALERIO IS SENTENCED TO TWELVE YEARS FOR ATTEMPTED MURDER.

AND THEN WE NEVER SAW EACH OTHER AGAIN. I MOVED TO A DIFFERENT TOWN.

HOW COULD I HAVE VISITED HIM IN PRISON?

AND ANYWAY, I DON'T THINK THEY WOULD HAVE LET ME SEE HIM.

IT'S ONLY THE FAMILY THAT'S ALLOWED IN TO SEE PRISONERS, ISN'T THAT RIGHT?

UNCLE GIL...

THAT KINDA STUFF, I DON'T KNOW ANYTHING ABOUT...

BROOM
BROOM

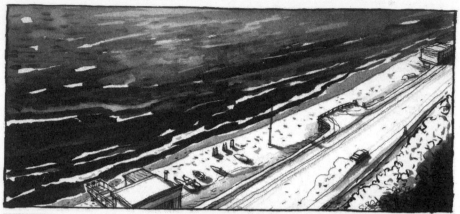

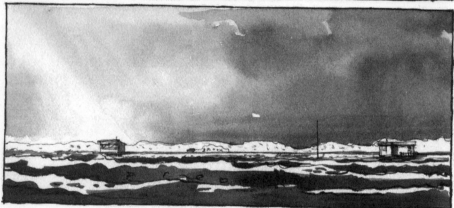

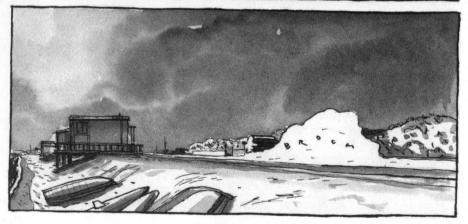

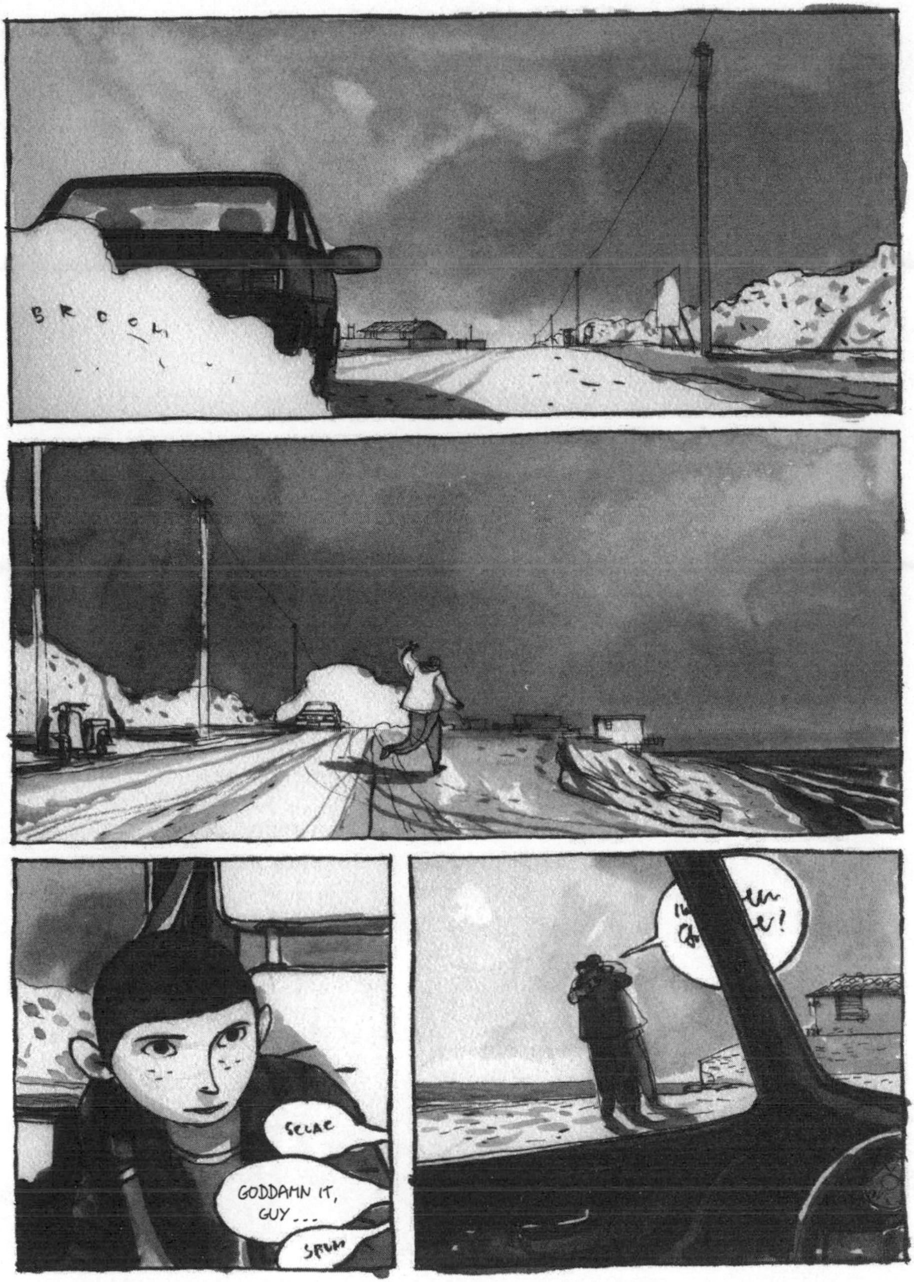
BROOM
SCLAC
GODDAMN IT, GUY...
SPUM

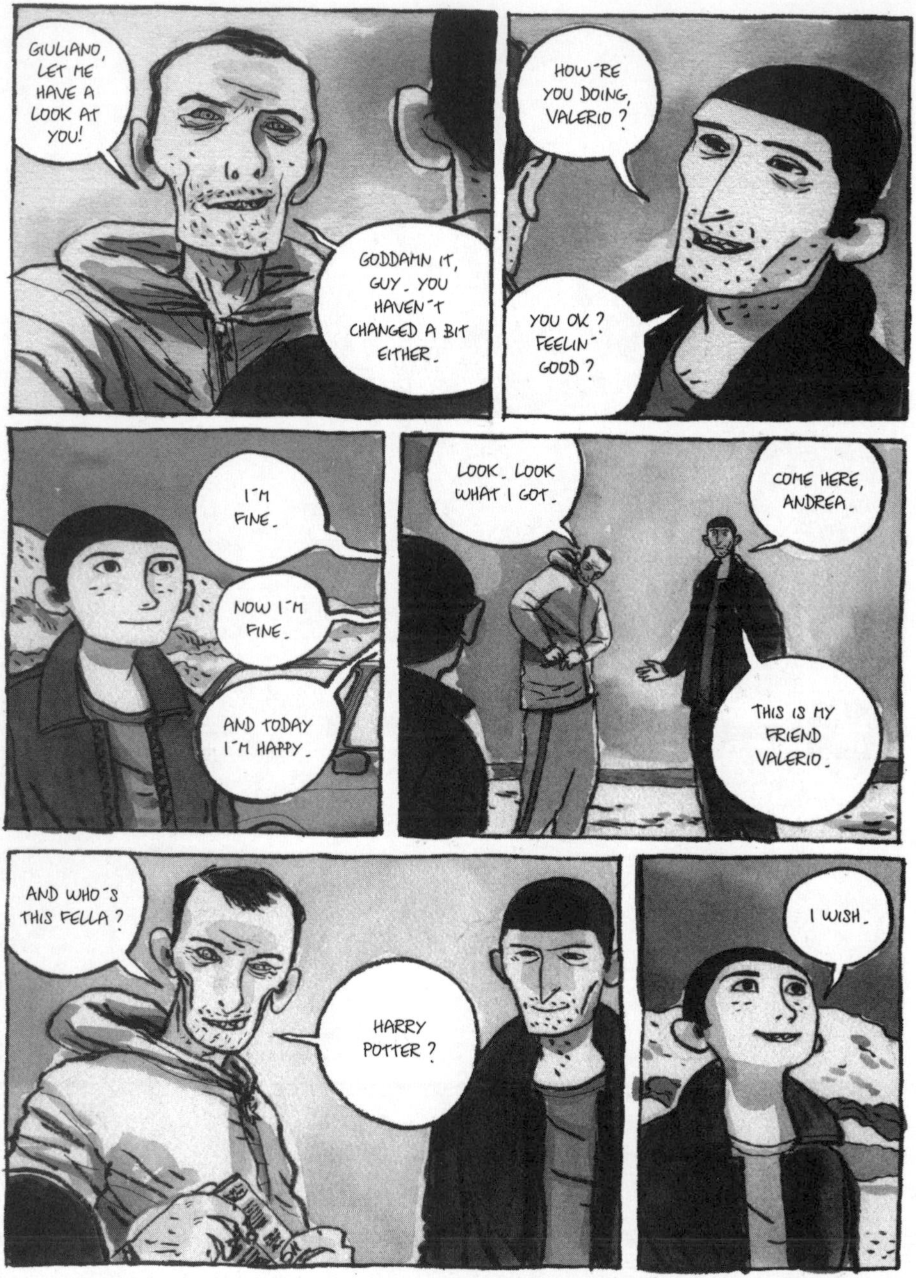
GIULIANO, LET ME HAVE A LOOK AT YOU!
GODDAMN IT, GUY. YOU HAVEN'T CHANGED A BIT EITHER.
HOW'RE YOU DOING, VALERIO?
YOU OK? FEELIN' GOOD?
I'M FINE.
NOW I'M FINE.
AND TODAY I'M HAPPY.
LOOK. LOOK WHAT I GOT.
COME HERE, ANDREA.
THIS IS MY FRIEND VALERIO.
AND WHO'S THIS FELLA?
HARRY POTTER?
I WISH.

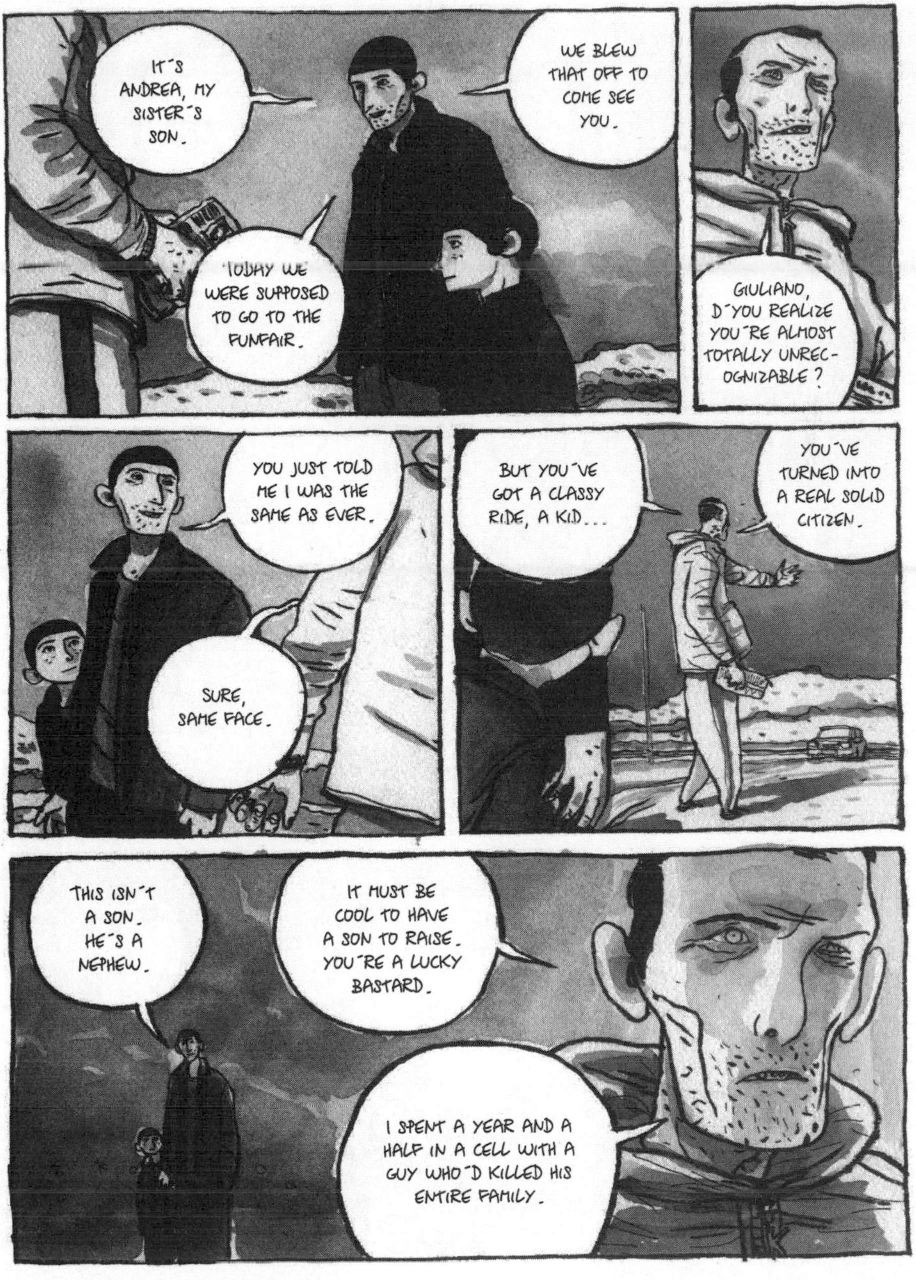
IT'S ANDREA, MY SISTER'S SON.
WE BLEW THAT OFF TO COME SEE YOU.
TODAY WE WERE SUPPOSED TO GO TO THE FUNFAIR.
GIULIANO, D'YOU REALIZE YOU'RE ALMOST TOTALLY UNREC-OGNIZABLE?
YOU JUST TOLD ME I WAS THE SAME AS EVER.
SURE, SAME FACE.
BUT YOU'VE GOT A CLASSY RIDE, A KID...
YOU'VE TURNED INTO A REAL SOLID CITIZEN.
THIS ISN'T A SON. HE'S A NEPHEW.
IT MUST BE COOL TO HAVE A SON TO RAISE. YOU'RE A LUCKY BASTARD.
I SPENT A YEAR AND A HALF IN A CELL WITH A GUY WHO'D KILLED HIS ENTIRE FAMILY.

HIS WIFE AND TWO KIDS, JUST LIKE THIS ONE.

CAN YOU IMAGINE?

HOW CAN ANYONE DO SOMETHING LIKE THAT?

BUT I DIDN'T CALL YOU UP TO TELL YOU SAD STORIES.

LOOK WHAT I'VE GOT. READ THIS.

"TWO MEMBERS OF THE POLICE FORCE ACCUSED OF BLACKMAIL AND VIOLENT EXTORTION..."

"...ILLICIT TRAFFICKING INSIDE THE OPERATIONAL CENTER."

IT'S THEM.

THE TWO SONS OF BITCHES WHO FUCKED OUR LIVES.

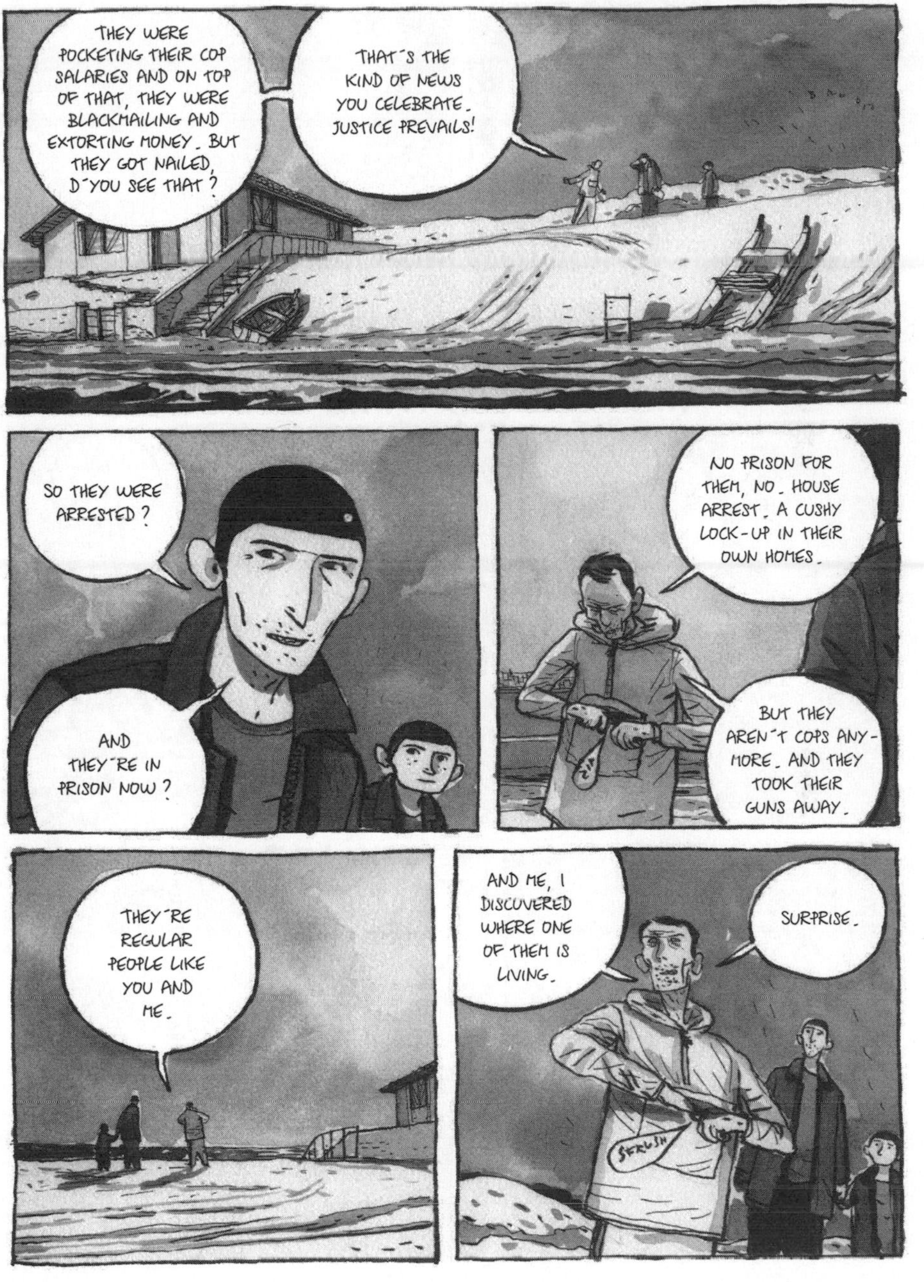
THEY WERE POCKETING THEIR COP SALARIES AND ON TOP OF THAT, THEY WERE BLACKMAILING AND EXTORTING MONEY. BUT THEY GOT NAILED, D'YOU SEE THAT?
THAT'S THE KIND OF NEWS YOU CELEBRATE. JUSTICE PREVAILS!
SO THEY WERE ARRESTED?
AND THEY'RE IN PRISON NOW?
NO PRISON FOR THEM, NO. HOUSE ARREST. A CUSHY LOCK-UP IN THEIR OWN HOMES.
BUT THEY AREN'T COPS ANY-MORE. AND THEY TOOK THEIR GUNS AWAY.
THEY'RE REGULAR PEOPLE LIKE YOU AND ME.
AND ME, I DISCOVERED WHERE ONE OF THEM IS LIVING.
SURPRISE.
SKRUSH

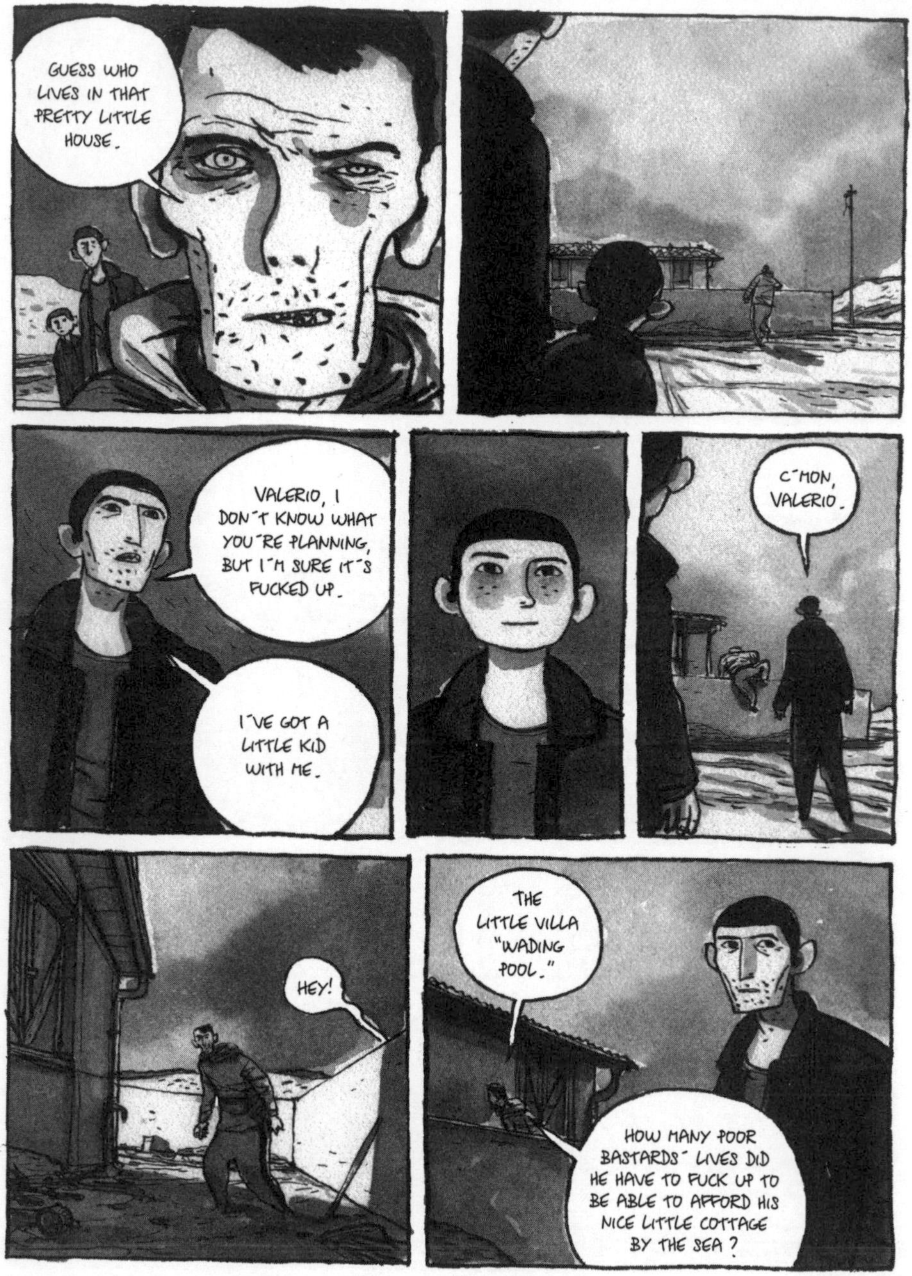
GUESS WHO LIVES IN THAT PRETTY LITTLE HOUSE.
VALERIO, I DON'T KNOW WHAT YOU'RE PLANNING, BUT I'M SURE IT'S FUCKED UP.
I'VE GOT A LITTLE KID WITH ME.
C'MON, VALERIO.
HEY!
THE LITTLE VILLA "WADING POOL."
HOW MANY POOR BASTARDS' LIVES DID HE HAVE TO FUCK UP TO BE ABLE TO AFFORD HIS NICE LITTLE COTTAGE BY THE SEA?

NGH
RATL RATL
FUCK!
thunk
thunk
ANDREA, GO TO THE CAR.
thunk
I'LL BE RIGHT THERE.
VALERIO, STOP IT!
THE HOUSE IS VACANT!

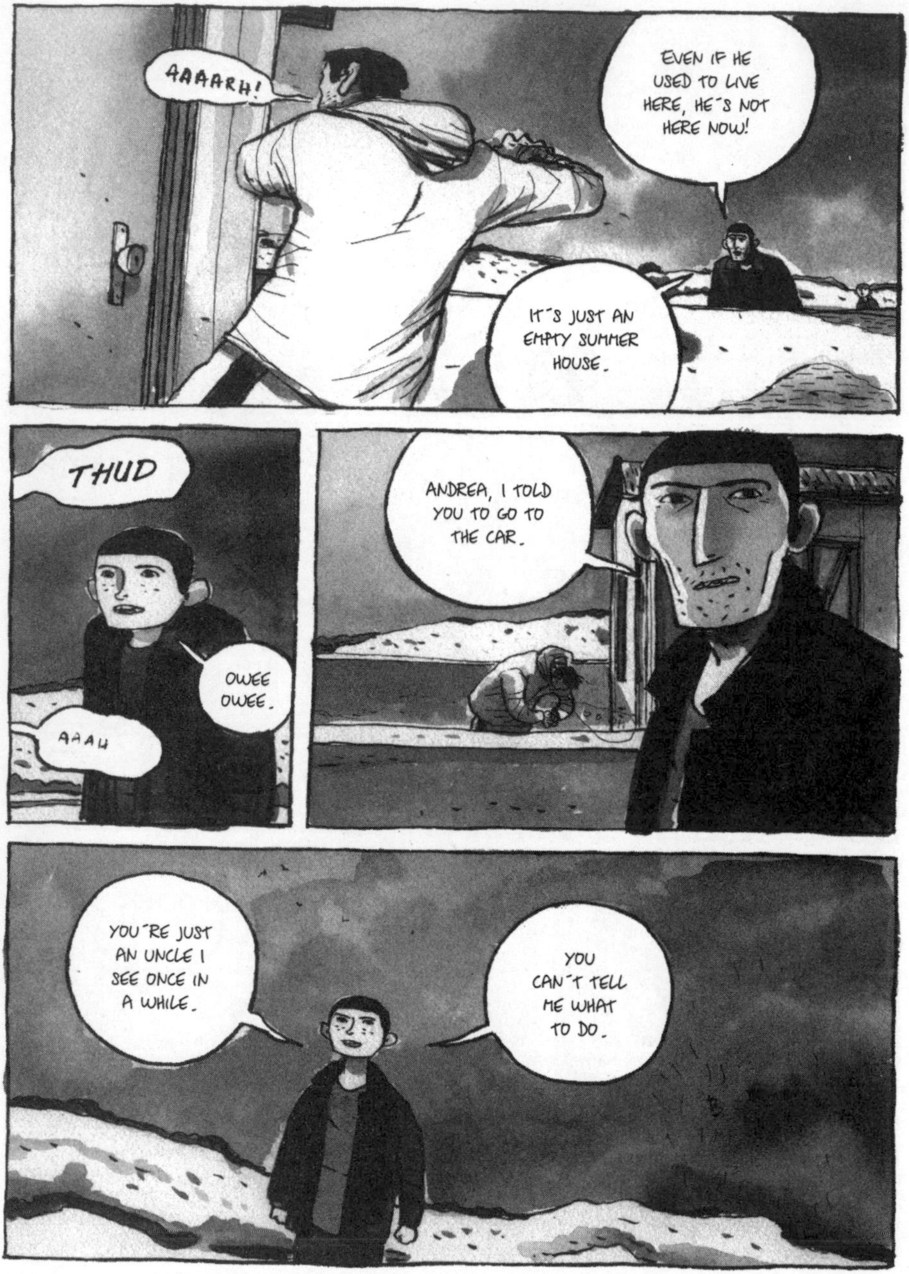
AAAARH!
EVEN IF HE USED TO LIVE HERE, HE'S NOT HERE NOW!
IT'S JUST AN EMPTY SUMMER HOUSE.
THUD
OWEE OWEE.
AAAH
ANDREA, I TOLD YOU TO GO TO THE CAR.
YOU'RE JUST AN UNCLE I SEE ONCE IN A WHILE.
YOU CAN'T TELL ME WHAT TO DO.

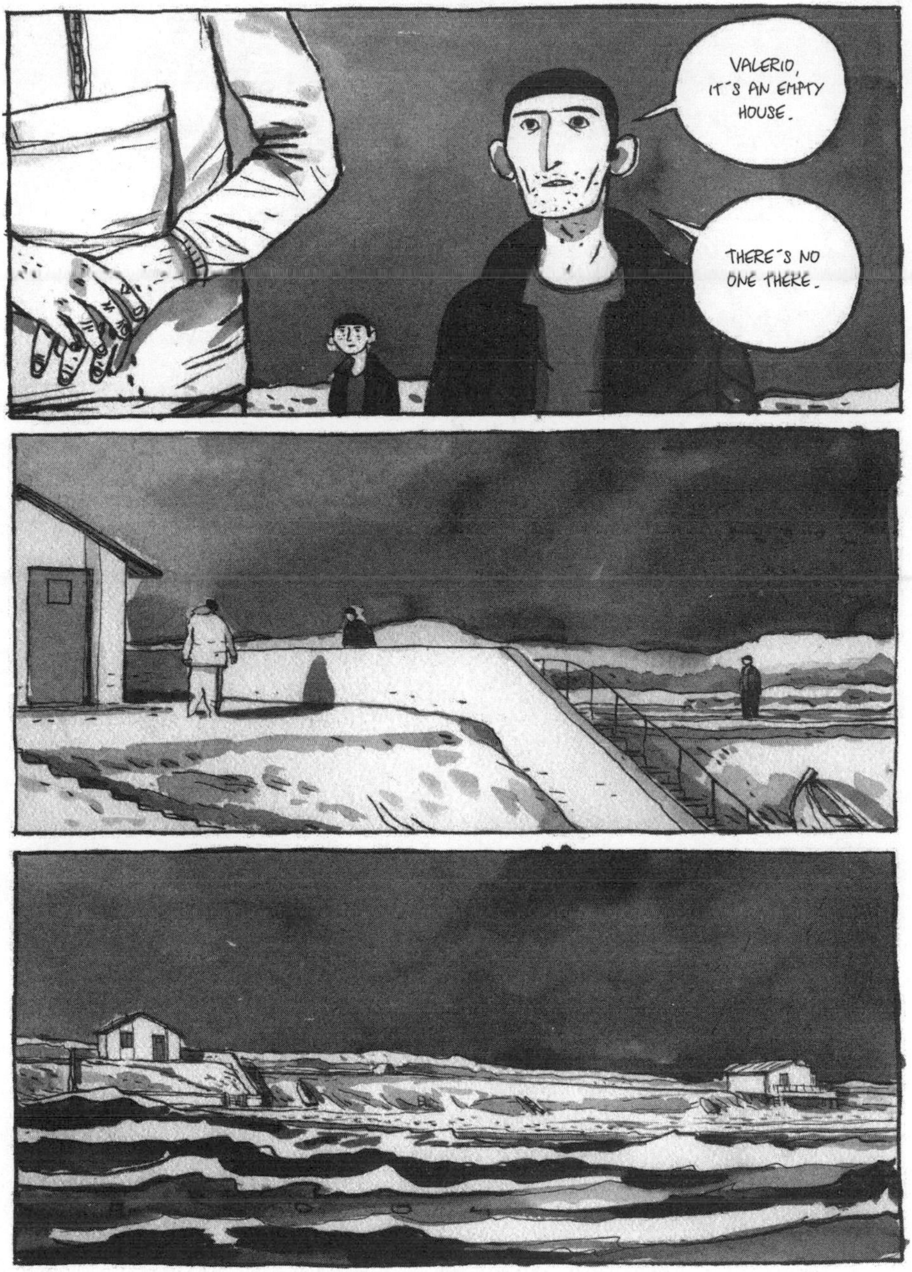
VALERIO, IT´S AN EMPTY HOUSE.
THERE´S NO ONE THERE.

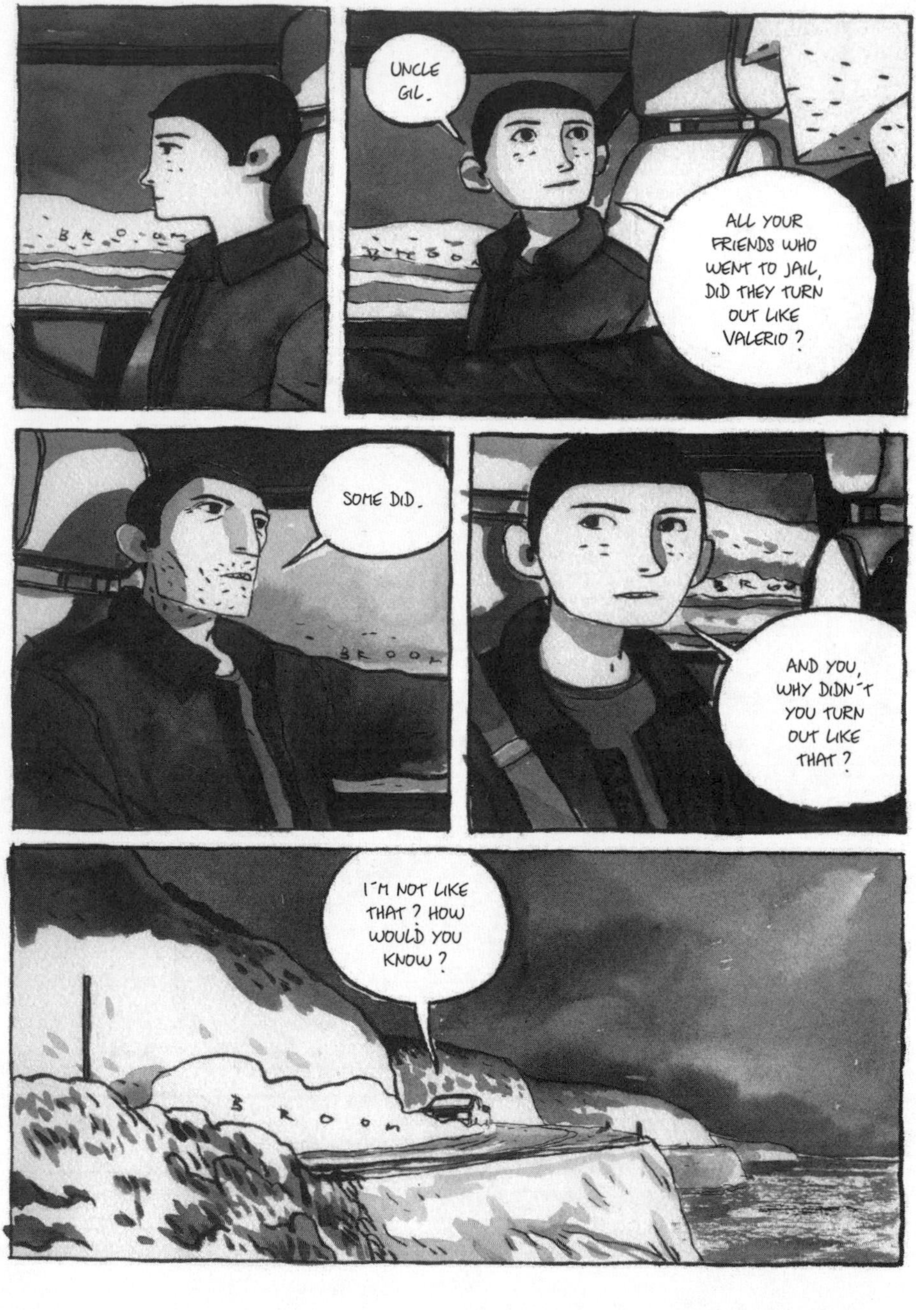
B R O O M
UNCLE GIL.
ALL YOUR FRIENDS WHO WENT TO JAIL, DID THEY TURN OUT LIKE VALERIO?
SOME DID.
B R O O M
AND YOU, WHY DIDN'T YOU TURN OUT LIKE THAT?
I'M NOT LIKE THAT? HOW WOULD YOU KNOW?
B R O O M

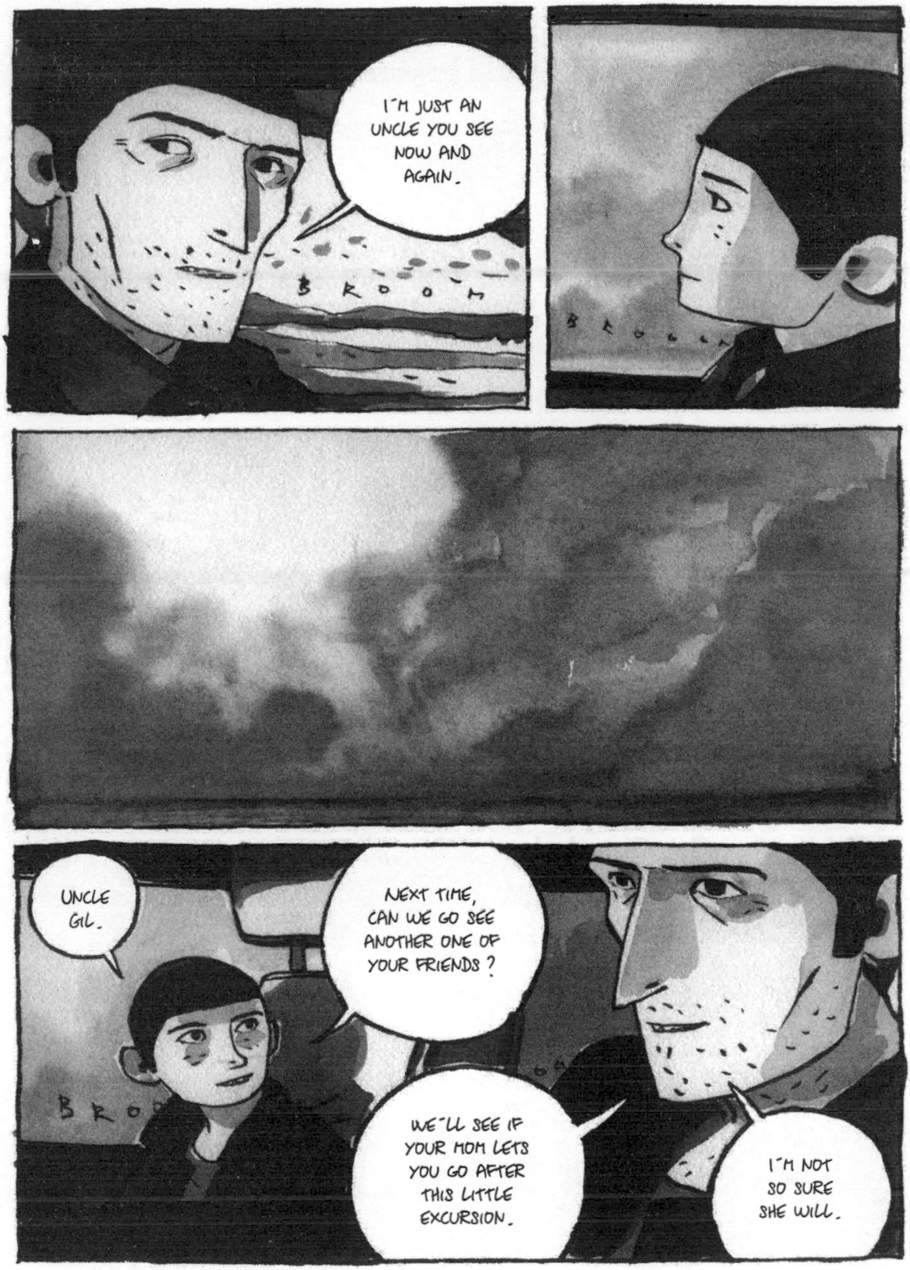
I'M JUST AN UNCLE YOU SEE NOW AND AGAIN.
BROOM
BROOM
UNCLE GIL.
NEXT TIME, CAN WE GO SEE ANOTHER ONE OF YOUR FRIENDS?
WE'LL SEE IF YOUR MOM LETS YOU GO AFTER THIS LITTLE EXCURSION.
I'M NOT SO SURE SHE WILL.

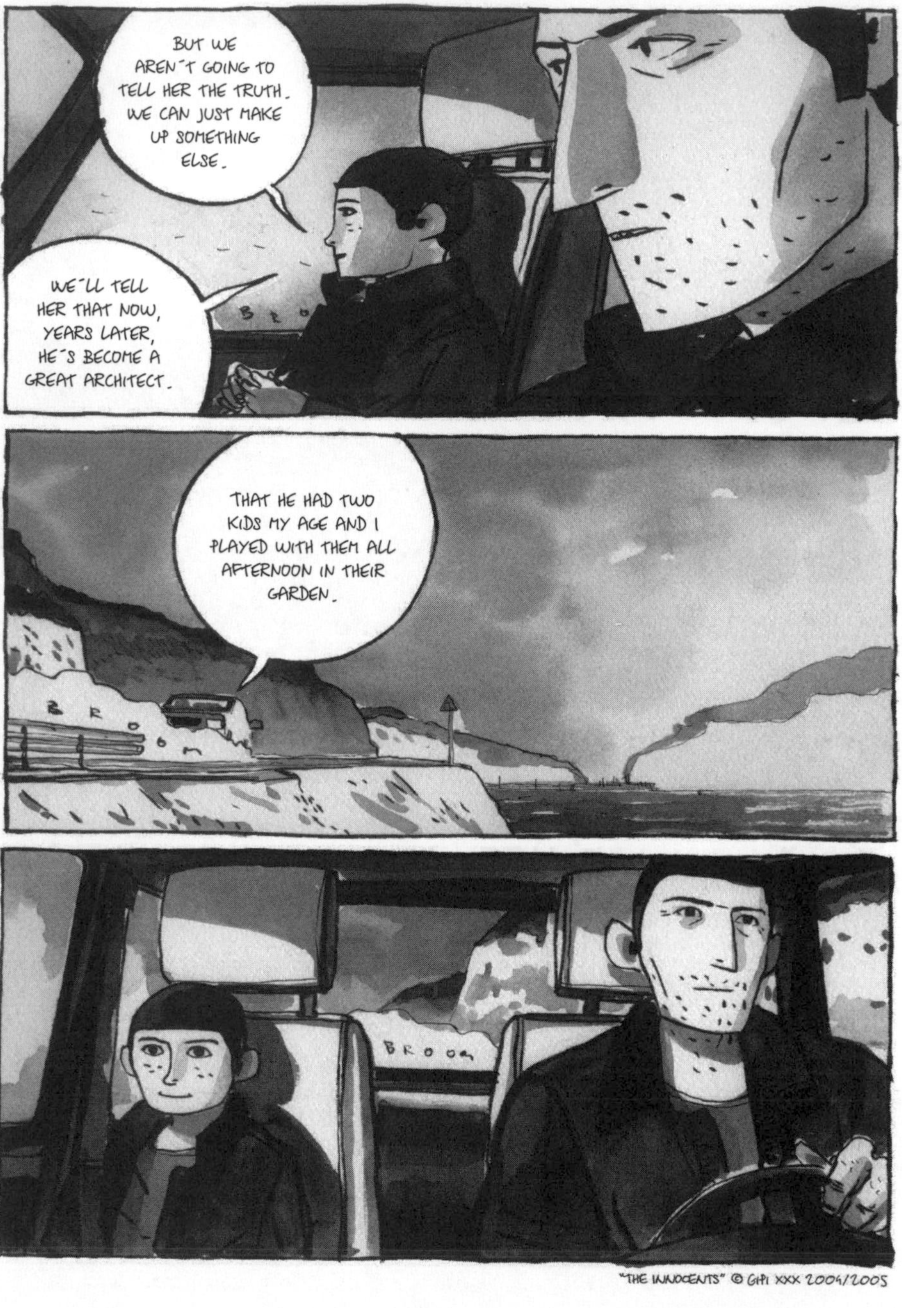
BUT WE AREN'T GOING TO TELL HER THE TRUTH. WE CAN JUST MAKE UP SOMETHING ELSE.
WE'LL TELL HER THAT NOW, YEARS LATER, HE'S BECOME A GREAT ARCHITECT.
THAT HE HAD TWO KIDS MY AGE AND I PLAYED WITH THEM ALL AFTERNOON IN THEIR GARDEN.
BROOM

The Iraqi Constitution

FROM *The Washington Post*

The following is the full text of the Iraqi Constitution, which was ratified by the Iraqi electorate in October 2005.

THE PREAMBLE

In the name of God, the most merciful, the most compassionate.

We have honored the sons of Adam.

We are the people of the land between two rivers, the homeland of the apostles and prophets, abode of the virtuous imams, pioneers of civilization, crafters of writing and cradle of numeration. Upon our land the first law made by man was passed, the most ancient just pact for homelands policy was inscribed, and upon our soil, companions of the Prophet and saints prayed, philosophers and scientists theorized and writers and poets excelled.

Acknowledging God's right over us, and in fulfillment of the call of our homeland and citizens, and in response to the call of our religious and national leaderships and the determination of our great (religious) authorities and of our leaders and reformers, and in the midst of an international support from our friends and those who love us, marched for the first time in our history toward the ballot boxes by the millions, men and women, young and old, on the thirtieth of January two thousand and five, invoking the pains of sectarian oppression, sufferings inflicted by the autocratic clique and inspired by the tragedies of Iraq's martyrs, Shiite and Sunni, Arabs and Kurds and Turkmen and from all the other components of the people and recollecting the darkness of the ravage of the holy cities and the South in the Sha'abaniyya uprising and burnt by the flames of grief of the mass graves, the marshes, Al-Dujail and others and articulating the sufferings of racial oppression in the massacres of Halabcha, Barzan, Anfal and the Fayli Kurds and inspired by the ordeals of the Turkmen in Basheer and as is the case in the remaining areas of Iraq where the people of the west suffered from the assassinations of their leaders, symbols and elderly and from the displacement of their skilled individuals and from the drying out of their cultural and intellectual wells, so we sought hand in hand and shoulder to shoulder to create our new Iraq, the Iraq of the future free from sectarianism, racism, locality complex, discrimination and exclusion.

Accusations of being infidels and terrorism did not stop us from marching forward to build a nation of law. Sectarianism and racism have not stopped us from marching together to strengthen our national unity, and to follow the path of peaceful transfer of power and adopt the course of the just distribution of resources and providing equal opportunity for all.

We the people of Iraq who have just risen from our stumble, and who are looking with confidence to the future through a republican, federal, democratic, pluralistic system, have resolved with the determination of our men, women, the elderly and youth, to respect the rules of law, to establish justice and equality, to cast aside the politics of aggression, and to tend to the concerns of women and their rights, and to the elderly and their concerns, and to children and their affairs, and to spread a culture of diversity and defusing terrorism.

We the people of Iraq of all components and shades have taken upon ourselves to decide freely and with our choice to unite our future and to take lessons from yesterday for tomorrow, to draft, through the values and ideals of the heavenly messages and the findings of science and man's civilization, this lasting constitution. The adherence to this constitution preserves for Iraq its free union, its people, its land and its sovereignty.

SECTION ONE: FUNDAMENTAL PRINCIPLES

Article 1: (The Republic of Iraq is a single, independent federal state with full sovereignty. Its system of government is republican, representative (parliamentary) and democratic. This Constitution is the guarantor of its unity.)

Article 2: First: Islam is the official religion of the State and it is a fundamental source of legislation:

A. No law that contradicts the established provisions of Islam may be established.

B. No law that contradicts the principles of democracy may be established.

C. No law that contradicts the rights and basic freedoms stipulated in this constitution may be established.

Second: This Constitution guarantees the Islamic identity of the majority of the Iraqi people and guarantees the full religious rights of all individuals to freedom of religious belief and practice such as Christians, Yazedis, and Mandi Sabeans.

Article 3: (Iraq is a country of many nationalities, religions and sects and is a founding and active member of the Arab League and is committed to its covenant. Iraq is a part of the Islamic world.)

Article 4: First: The Arabic language and Kurdish language are the two official languages of Iraq. The right of Iraqis to educate their children in their mother tongue, such as Turkmen, Syriac and Armenian, in government educational institutions in accordance with educational guidelines, or in any other language in private educational institutions, is guaranteed.

Second: The scope of the term official language and the means of applying the provisions of this article shall be defined by law which shall include:

A. Publication of the official gazette, in the two languages;

B. Speech, conversation and expression in official settings, such as the Council of Representatives, the Council of Ministers, courts, and official conferences, in either of the two languages;

C. Recognition and publication of the official documents and correspondences in the two languages;

D. Opening schools that teach the two languages, in accordance with the educational guidelines,

E. Use of both languages in any settings enjoined by the principle of equality such as bank notes, passports and stamps.

(Third: The federal institutions and agencies in the Kurdistan region shall use the Arabic and Kurdish languages.)

Fourth: The Turkmen language and Syriac language are two other official languages in the administrative units in which they represent density of population.

Fifth: Each region or governorate may adopt any other local language as an additional official language if the majority of its population so decide in a general referendum.

Article 5: The law is sovereign. The people are the source of authorities and its legitimacy, which the people shall exercise in a direct general secret ballot and through their constitutional institutions.

Article 6: Transfer of authority shall be made peacefully through democratic means as stipulated in this Constitution.

Article 7: First: No entity or program, under any name, may adopt racism, terrorism, the calling of others infidels, ethnic cleansing, or incite, facilitate, glorify, promote, or justify thereto, especially the Saddamist Ba'ath in Iraq and its symbols, regardless of the name that it adopts. This may not be part of the political pluralism in Iraq. This will be organized by law.

Second: The State shall undertake combating terrorism in all its forms, and shall work to protect its territories from being a base or pathway or field for terrorist activities.

Article 8: Iraq shall observe the principles of a good neighborliness, adhere to the principle of non-interference in the internal affairs of other states, endeavor to settle disputes by peaceful means, establish relations on the basis of mutual interests and reciprocity, and respect its international obligations.

Article 9: First:

A. The Iraqi Armed Forces and Security Services will be composed of the components of the Iraqi people with due consideration given to its balance and its similarity without discrimination or exclusion and shall be subject to the control of the civilian authority. The Iraqi Armed Forces shall defend Iraq and shall not be used as an instrument of oppression against the Iraqi people, shall not interfere in the political affairs and shall have no role in the transfer of authority.

B. The formation of military militia outside the framework of the armed forces is prohibited.

C. The Iraqi Armed Forces and its personnel, including military personnel working at the Ministry of Defense or any subordinate departments or organizations, may not stand for election to political office, campaign for candidates, or participate in other activities prohibited by the Ministry of Defense regulations. This ban encompasses the activities of the personnel mentioned above acting in their personal or official capacities. Nothing in this Article shall infringe upon the right of these personnel to cast their vote in the elections.

D. The Iraqi National Intelligence Service shall collect information, assess threats to national security, and advise the Iraqi government. This service shall be under civilian control and shall be subject to legislative oversight and shall operate in accordance with the law and pursuant to the recognized principles of human rights.

E. The Iraqi Government shall respect and implement Iraq's international obligations regarding the non-proliferation, non-development, non-production, and nonuse of nuclear, chemical, and biological weapons, and shall prohibit associated equipment, materiel, technologies, and delivery systems for use in the development, manufacture, production, and use of such weapons.

Second: National service will be stipulated by law.

Article 10: The holy shrines and religious places in Iraq are religious and cultural entities. The State is committed to confirming and safeguarding their sanctity, and guaranteeing the free practice of rituals in them.

Article 11: Baghdad is the capital of the Republic of Iraq.

Article 12: First: The flag, national anthem, and emblem of Iraq shall be fixed by law in a way that represents the components of the Iraqi people.

Second: A law shall regulate the decorations, official holidays, religious and national occasions and the Hijri and Gregorian calendar.

Article 13: First: This constitution is the sublime and supreme law in Iraq and shall be binding in all parts of Iraq without exception.

Second: No law shall be enacted that contradicts this constitution. Any text in any regional constitutions or any other legal text that contradicts it is deemed void.

SECTION TWO: RIGHTS AND LIBERTIES
CHAPTER ONE: RIGHTS
FIRST: Civil and Political Rights
Article 14: Iraqis are equal before the law without discrimination based on gender, race, ethnicity, origin, color, religion, creed, belief or opinion, or economic and social status.

Article 15: Every individual has the right to enjoy life, security and liberty. Deprivation or restriction of these rights is prohibited except in accordance with the law and based on a decision issued by a competent judicial authority.

Article 16: Equal opportunities are guaranteed for all Iraqis. The state guarantees the taking of the necessary measures to achieve such equal opportunities.

Article 17: First: Every individual shall have the right to personal privacy, so long it does not contradict the rights of others and public morals.

Second: The sanctity of the homes is inviolable and homes may not be entered, searched, or put in danger, except by a judicial decision, and in accordance with the law.

Article 18: (First: Iraqi nationality is the right of every Iraqi and shall be the basis of his citizenship.)

(Second: An Iraqi is any person born to an Iraqi father or mother. This will be regulated by law.)

Third:

A. An Iraqi citizen by birth may not have his nationality withdrawn for any reason. Any person who had his nationality withdrawn shall have the right to reclaim it, and this will be stipulated by law.

B. The Iraqi nationality shall be withdrawn from the naturalized in the cases stipulated by law.

Fourth: An Iraqi may have multiple nationalities. Everyone who assumes a senior, security sovereign position must abandon any other acquired nationality. This will be organized by law.

Fifth: Iraqi citizenship shall not be granted for the purposes of the policy of settling people that cause an imbalance in the population composition of Iraq.

Sixth: A law shall regulate the provisions of nationality. The competent courts shall consider the suits resulting from it.

Article 19: First: The judiciary is independent and no power is above the judiciary except the law.

Second: There is no crime or punishment except by a stipulation. The punishment shall only be for an act that the law considers a crime when perpetrated. A harsher sentence than the applicable sentence at the time of the offense may not be imposed.

Third: Litigation shall be a safeguarded and guaranteed right for all.

Fourth: The right to a defense shall be sacred and guaranteed in all phases of investigation and trial.

Fifth: The accused is innocent until proven guilty in a fair legal trial. The accused may not be tried on the same crime for a second time after acquittal unless new evidence is produced.

Sixth: Every person has the right to be treated with justice in judicial and administrative proceedings.

Seventh: The proceedings of a trial are public unless the court decides to make it secret.

Eighth: Punishment is personal.

Ninth: A law does not have a retroactive effect unless the law stipulates otherwise. This exclusion shall not include laws relating to taxes and fees.

Tenth: Criminal law does not have a retroactive effect, unless it is to the benefit of the accused.

Eleventh: The court shall delegate a lawyer at the expense of the state for an accused of a felony or misdemeanor who does not have a defense lawyer.

Twelfth:

A. (Unlawful) detention is prohibited.

B. Detention or arrest is prohibited in places not designed for it, pursuant to prison regulations covered by health and social care and subject to the scrutiny of the law.

Thirteenth: The preliminary investigative documents must be submitted to the competent judge in a period not to exceed twenty-four hours from the time of the arrest of the accused. It may be extended only once and for the same period.

Article 20: The citizens, men and women, have the right to participate in public affairs and to enjoy political rights including the right to vote, to elect and to nominate.

Article 21: First: No Iraqi shall be surrendered to foreign entities and authorities.

Second: A law shall regulate the right of political asylum to Iraq. No political refugee shall be surrendered to a foreign entity or returned forcibly to the country from which he fled.

Third: No political asylum shall be granted to a person accused of committing international or terrorist crimes or any person who inflicted damage on Iraq.

SECOND: Economic, Social and Cultural Liberties

Article 22: First: Work is a right for all Iraqis so as to guarantee them a decent living.

Second: The law regulates the relationship between employees and employers on economic basis and with regard to the foundations of social justice.

Third: The State guarantees the right of forming and joining professional associations and unions. This will be organized by law.

Article 23: First: Personal property is protected. The proprietor shall have the right to benefit from, exploit and utilize personal property within the limits of the law.

Second: No property may be taken away except for the purposes of public benefit in return for just compensation. This will be organized by law.

Third:

A. Every Iraqi has the right to own property throughout Iraq. No others may possess immovable assets, except as exempted by law.

B. Owning property for the purposes of population change shall be prohibited.

Article 24: The State guarantees freedom of movement of Iraqi manpower, goods and capitals between regions and governorates. This will be organized by law.

Article 25: The State guarantees the reform of the Iraqi economy in accordance with modern economic principles to ensure the full investment of its resources, diversification of its sources and the encouragement and the development of the private sector.

Article 26: The State guarantees the encouragement of investments in the various sectors. This will be organized by law.

Article 27: First: Public property is sacrosanct, and its protection is the duty of each citizen.

Second: The provisions related to the protection of State properties and its management and the conditions for its disposal and the limits under which none of these properties can be relinquished shall all be regulated by law.

Article 28: First: No taxes or fines may be imposed, amended, exempted or pardoned from, except in accordance with law.

Second: Low wage earners shall be exempted from taxes in a manner that ensures the upholding of the minimum wage required for survival. This will be organized by law.

Article 29: First:

A. The family is the foundation of society; the State preserves its entity and its religious, moral and patriotic values.

B. The State guarantees the protection of motherhood, childhood and old age and shall care for children and youth and provides them with the appropriate conditions to further their talents and abilities.

Second: Children have right over their parents in regard to upbringing, care and education. Parents shall have right over their children in regard to respect and care especially in times of need, disability and old age.

Third: Economic exploitation of children shall be completely prohibited. The State shall take the necessary measures to protect them.

Fourth: All forms of violence and abuse in the family, school and society shall be prohibited.

Article 30: First: The State guarantees to the individual and the family — especially children and women — social and health security and the basic requirements for leading a free and dignified life. The State also ensures the above a suitable income and appropriate housing.

Second: The State guarantees the social and health security to Iraqis in cases of old age, sickness, employment disability, homelessness, orphanage or unemployment, and shall work to protect them from ignorance, fear and poverty. The State shall provide them housing and special programs of care and rehabilitation. This will be organized by law.

Article 31: First: Every citizen has the right to health care. The State takes care of public health and provide the means of prevention and treatment by building different types of hospitals and medical institutions.

Second: Individuals and institutions may build hospitals or clinics or places for treatment with the supervision of the State and this shall be regulated by law.

Article 32: The State cares for the handicapped and those with special needs and ensure their rehabilitation in order to reintegrate them into society. This shall be regulated by law.

Article 33: First: Every individual has the right to live in a safe environment.

Second: The State undertakes the protection and preservation of the environment and biological diversity.

Article 34: First: Education is a fundamental factor in the progress of society and is a right guaranteed by the State. Primary education is mandatory and the State guarantees to eradicate illiteracy.

Second: Free education is a right for all Iraqis in all its stages.

Third: The State encourages scientific research for peaceful purposes that serve man and supports excellence, creativity, invention and the different aspects of ingenuity.

Fourth: Private and public education is guaranteed. This shall be regulated by law.

CHAPTER TWO: LIBERTIES

Article 35: First:

A. The liberty and dignity of man are safeguarded.

B. No person may be kept in custody or interrogated except in the context of a judicial decision.

C. All forms of psychological and physical torture and inhumane treatment shall be prohibited. Any confession coerced by force, threat, or torture shall not be relied on. The victim shall have the right to compensation in accordance with the law for material and moral damages incurred.

Second: The State guarantees the protection of the individual from intellectual, political and religious coercion.

Third: Compulsory service (unpaid labor), serfdom, slave trade (slavery), trafficking of women and children, and the sex trade is prohibited.

(Fourth: The State will promote cultural activities and institutions in a way that is appropriate with Iraq's civilizational history and culture. It will take care to depend on authentic Iraqi cultural trends.)

Article 36: The State guarantees in a way that does not violate public order and morality:

A. Freedom of expression, through all means.

B. Freedom of press, printing, advertisement, media and publication.

C. Freedom of assembly and peaceful demonstration. This shall be regulated by law.

(D. Every Iraqi has the right to engage in sports, and the State should encourage its activities and promotion and will provide its necessities.)

Article 37: First: The freedom of forming and of joining associations and political parties is guaranteed. This will be organized by law.

Second: It is prohibited to force any person to join any party, society or political entity or force him to continue his membership in it.

Article 38: The freedom of communication, and mail, telegraphic, electronic, and telephonic correspondence, and other correspondence shall be guaranteed and may not be monitored, wiretapped or disclosed except for legal and security necessity and by a judicial decision.

Article 39: Iraqis are free in their commitment to their personal status according to their religions, sects, beliefs, or choices. This shall be regulated by law.

Article 40: Each individual has freedom of thought, conscience and belief.

Article 41: First: The followers of all religions and sects are free in the:

A. Practice of religious rites, including the Husseini ceremonies (Shiite religious ceremonies)

B. Management of the endowments, its affairs and its religious institutions. The law shall regulate this.

Second: The State guarantees freedom of worship and the protection of the places of worship.

Article 42: First: Each Iraqi enjoys the right of free movement, travel, and residence inside and outside Iraq.

Second: No Iraqi may be exiled, displaced or deprived from returning to the homeland.

Article 43: First: The State shall seek to strengthen the role of civil society institutions, to support, develop and preserve its independence in a way that is consistent with peaceful means to achieve its legitimate goals. This will be organized by law.

Second: The State shall seek the advancement of the Iraqi clans and tribes and shall attend to their affairs in a manner that is consistent with religion and the law and upholds its noble human values in a way that contributes to the development of society. The State shall prohibit the tribal traditions that are in contradiction with human rights.

Article 44: There may not be a restriction or limit on the practice of any rights or liberties stipulated in this constitution, except by law or on the basis of it, and insofar as that limitation or restriction does not violate the essence of the right or freedom.

SECTION THREE: FEDERAL POWERS

Article 45: The federal powers shall consist of the legislative, the executive and the judicial powers. They exercise their specialization and tasks on the basis of the principle of separation of powers.

CHAPTER ONE: THE LEGISLATIVE POWER

Article 46: The federal legislative power shall consist of the Council of Representatives and the Federation Council.

First: The Council of Representatives

Article 47: First: The Council of Representatives shall consist of a number of members, at a ratio of one representative per 100,000 Iraqi persons representing the entire Iraqi people. They shall be elected through a direct secret general ballot. The representation of all components of the people in it shall be upheld.

Second: A candidate to the Council of Representatives must be a fully eligible Iraqi.

Third: A law shall regulate the requirements for the candidate, the voter and all that is connected with the elections.

Fourth: The elections law aims to achieve a percentage of women representation not less than one-quarter of the Council of Representatives members.

Fifth: The Council of Representatives shall promulgate a law dealing with the replacement of its members on resignation, dismissal or death.

Sixth: No member of the Council of Representatives shall be allowed to hold any other official position or work.

Article 48: Each member of the Council of Representatives must take the following constitutional oath before the Council prior to assuming his duties:

(I swear by God the Almighty to carry out my legal tasks and responsibilities devotedly and honestly and preserve the independence and sovereignty of Iraq, and safeguard the interests of its people, and watch over the safety of its land, skies, waters, resources and federal democratic system, and I shall endeavor to protect public and private liberties, the independence of the judiciary and adhere to the applications of the legislation neutrally and faithfully. God is my witness).

Article 49: The Council of Representatives shall set its bylaws to regulate its work.

Article 50: First: The Council of Representatives shall decide by a two-thirds majority, the membership authenticity of its members within thirty days from the date of filing an objection.

Second: The decision of the Council of Representatives may be appealed before the Federal Supreme Court within thirty days from the date of its issuance.

Article 51: First: Sessions of the Council of Representatives shall be public unless it deems them otherwise.

Second: Minutes of the sessions shall be published in means regarded appropriate by the Council.

Article 52: The President of the Republic shall call upon the Council of Representatives to convene by a presidential decree within fifteen days from the date of the ratification of the general elections results. Its eldest member shall chair the first session to elect the president of the Council and his two deputies. This period may not be extended by more than the aforementioned one.

Article 53: The Council of Representatives shall elect in its first session its president, then his first deputy and second deputy, by an absolute majority of the total number of the Council members by direct secret ballot.

Article 54: First: The electoral term of the Council of Representatives shall be limited to four calendar years, starting with its first session and ending with the conclusion of the fourth year.

Second: The new Council of Representatives shall be elected forty-five days before the conclusion of the previous electoral term.

Article 55: The Council of Representatives shall have one annual term with two legislative sessions lasting eight months. The bylaw shall define the method of convention. The session in which the general budget is being presented shall not end until its approval.

Article 56: First: The President of the Republic or the Prime Minister or the President of the Council of Representatives or fifty members of the Council of Representatives may call the Council to an extraordinary session. The session shall be restricted to the topics that necessitated the request.

Second: The President of the Republic, or the Prime Minister or the President of the Council or fifty members of the Council of Representatives, may ask for an extension of the legislative session of the Council of Representatives for no more than thirty days in order to complete the tasks that required the extension.

Article 57: First:

A. The Council of Representatives quorum shall be fulfilled by an absolute majority of its members.

B. Decisions in the sessions of the Council of Representatives shall be made by a simple majority after quorum is fulfilled, unless stipulated otherwise.

Second:

A. Bills shall be presented by the President of the Republic and the Prime Minister.

B. Proposed laws shall be presented by ten members of the Council of Representatives or by one of its specialized committees.

Article 58: The Council of Representatives specializes in the following:

First: Enacting federal laws.

Second: Monitoring the performance of the executive authority.

Third: Elect the President of the Republic.

Fourth: A law shall regulate the ratification of international treaties and agreements by a two-thirds majority of the members of the Council of Representatives.

Fifth: To approve the appointment of the following:

A. The President and members of the Federal Court of Cassation, Chief Public Prosecutor and the President of Judicial Oversight Commission based on a proposal from the Higher Juridical Council, by an absolute majority.

B. Ambassadors and those with special grades based on a proposal from the Cabinet.

C. The Iraqi Army Chief of Staff, his assistants and those of the rank of division commanders and above and the director of the intelligence service based on a proposal from the Cabinet.

Sixth:

A. Question the President of the Republic based on a justifiable petition by an absolute majority of the Council of Representatives members.

B. Relieve the President of the Republic by an absolute majority of the Council of Representatives members after being convicted by the Supreme Federal Court in one of the following cases:

1 Perjury of the constitutional oath.

2 Violating the Constitution.

3 High treason.

Seventh:

A. The Council of Representatives member may direct questions to the Prime Minister and the Ministers on any subject within their specialty and they may answer the members' questions. The Member who has asked the question solely has the right to comment on the answer.

B. At least twenty-five members of the Council of Representatives may table a general issue for discussion to obtain clarity on the policy and the performance of the Cabinet or one of the Ministries. It must be submitted to the President of the Council of Representatives, and the Prime Minister or the Ministers shall specify a date to come before the Council of Representatives to discuss it.

C. A Council of Representatives member with the agreement of twenty-five members may direct a question to the Prime Minister or the Ministers to call them to account on the issues within their authority. The discussion on the question shall begin at least seven days after submitting the question.

Eighth:

A. The Council of Representatives may withdraw confidence from one of the Ministers by an absolute majority and he is considered resigned from the date of the decision of confidence withdrawal. The issue of no confidence in the Minister may be tabled only on that Minister's wish or on a signed request of fifty members after an inquiry discussion directed at him. The Council of Representatives shall not issue its decision regarding the request except after at least seven days of its submission.

B.

1 The President of the Republic may submit a request to the Council of Representatives to withdraw confidence from the Prime Minister.

2 The Council of Representatives may withdraw confidence from the Prime Minister based on the request of one-fifth (1/5) of its members. This request may be submitted only after a question has been put to the Prime Minister and after at least seven days from submitting the request.

3 The Council of Representatives shall decide to withdraw confidence from the Prime Minister by an absolute majority of its members.

C. The Government is considered resigned in case of withdrawal of confidence from the Prime Minister.

D. In case of a vote of withdrawal of confidence in the Cabinet as a whole, the Prime Minister and the Ministers continue in their positions to run everyday business for a period not to exceed thirty days until a new cabinet is formed in accordance with the provisions of article 73 of this constitution.

E. The Council of Representatives may interrogate independent commission heads in accordance with the same procedures as for the ministers and may dismiss them by an absolute majority.

Ninth:

A. To consent to the declaration of war and the state of emergency by a two-thirds majority based on a joint request from the President of the Republic and the Prime Minister.

B. The period of the state emergency shall be limited to thirty days, extendable after approval each time.

C. The Prime Minister shall be authorized with the necessary powers that enable him to manage the affairs of the country within the period of the state of emergency and war. A law shall regulate these powers that do not contradict the constitution.

D. The Prime Minister shall present to the Council of Representatives the measures taken and the results within the period of declaration of war and within 15 days of the end of the state of emergency.

Article 59:

First: The Council of Ministers shall submit the draft general budget bill and the closing account to the Council of Representatives for approval.

Second: The Council of Representatives may conduct transfers between the sections and chapters of the general budget and reduce the total of its sums, and it may suggest to the Cabinet to increase the total expenses, when necessary.

Article 60:

First: A law shall regulate the rights and privileges of the speaker of the Council of Representatives, his two deputies and the members of the Council of Representatives.

Second:

A. Each member of the Council of Representatives shall enjoy immunity for statements made while the Council is in session, and the member may not be prosecuted before the courts for such.

B. A Council of Representatives member may not be placed under arrest during the legislative term of the Council of Representatives, unless the member is accused of a felony and the Council of Representatives members consent by an absolute majority to lift his immunity or if caught in flagrante delicto in the commission of a felony.

C. A Council of Representatives member may not be arrested after the legislative term of the Council of Representatives, unless the member is accused of a felony and with the consent of the speaker of the Council of Representatives to lift his immunity or if he is caught in flagrante delicto in the commission of a felony.

Article 61:

First: The Council of Representatives may dissolve itself with the consent of the absolute majority of its members, upon the request of one-third of its members or upon the request of the Prime Minister and the consent of the President of the Republic. The Council may not be dissolved during the period in which the Prime Minister is being questioned.

Second: Upon the dissolution of the Council of Representatives, the President of the Republic shall call for general elections in the country within a period not to exceed sixty days from the date of its dissolution. The Cabinet in this case is considered resigned and continues to run everyday business.

Second: The Federation Council

Article 62: A legislative council shall be established named the "Federation Council" to include representatives from the regions and the governorates that are not organized in a region. A law, enacted by a two-third majority of the members of the Council of Representatives, shall regulate the Federation Council formation, its membership conditions and its specializations and all that is connected with it.

CHAPTER TWO: THE EXECUTIVE POWER

Article 63: The Federal Executive Power shall consist of the President of the Republic and the Council of Ministers and shall exercise its powers in accordance with the constitution and the law.

First: The President of the Republic

Article 64: The President of the Republic is the Head of the State and a symbol of the unity of the country and represents the sovereignty of the country. He safeguards the commitment to the Constitution and the preservation of Iraq's independence, sovereignty, unity, the security of its territories in accordance with the provisions of the Constitution.

Article 65: A nominee to the Presidency must meet the following conditions:

A. Must be an Iraqi by birth, born to Iraqi parents.

B. Must be fully eligible and has completed forty years of age.

C. Must be of good reputation and political experience, and known for his integrity, righteousness, fairness and loyalty to the homeland.

D. Must not have been convicted of a crime involving moral turpitude.

Article 66: First: A law shall regulate the nomination to the post of the President of the Republic.

Second: A law shall regulate the nomination of one deputy or more for the President of the Republic.

Article 67: First: The Council of Representatives shall elect, from among the nominees, the President of the Republic by a two-thirds majority of its members.

Second: If any of the candidates does not receive the required majority vote then the two candidates who received the highest number of votes shall compete and the one who receives the highest number of votes in the second election shall be declared as President.

Article 68: The President shall take the Constitutional Oath before the Council of Representatives in the form stipulated in Article 48 of the Constitution.

Article 69: First: The President of the Republic's term in office shall be limited to four years and may be elected for a second time and no more.

Second:

A. The term of the President of the Republic shall finish at the end of the Council of Representatives' term.

B. The President of the Republic will continue to exercise his functions until the elections for the Council of Representatives is completed and until it meets. The new President shall then be elected within thirty days of its first meeting.

C. If the position of president of the republic is vacant, for whatever reason, a new president will be elected in order to fill the vacancy for the remaining period of that president's term.

Article 70: The President of the Republic shall assume the following powers:

A. To issue a special pardon on the recommendation of the Prime Minister, except for anything concerning private claim and for those who have been convicted of committing international crimes, terrorism, and financial and administrative corruption.

B. To ratify international treaties and agreements after the approval by the Council of Representatives. Such international treaties and agreements are considered ratified after fifteen days from the date of receipt.

C. To ratify and issue the laws enacted by the Council of Representatives. Such laws are considered ratified after fifteen days from the date of receipt.

D. To call the elected Council of Representatives to convene during a period not to exceed fifteen days from the date of approval of the election results and in the other cases stipulated in the Constitution.

E. To award medals and decorations on the recommendation of the Prime Minister in accordance with the law.

F. To accredit Ambassadors.

G. To issue Presidential decrees.

H. Ratify death sentences issued by the competent courts.

I. Perform the duty of the Higher Command of the armed forces for ceremonial and honorary purposes.

J. Exercise any other presidential powers stipulated in this Constitution.

Article 71: A law shall fix the salary and the allowances of the President of the Republic.

Article 72: First: The President of the Republic shall have the right to submit his resignation in writing to the Speaker of the Council of Representatives, and is considered effective after seven days from the date of its submission to the Council of Representatives.

Second: The "Vice" President shall assume the office of the President in case of his absence.

Third: The Vice President shall assume the duties of the President of the Republic or in the event of the post of the President becomes vacant for any reason whatsoever. The Council of Representatives must elect a new President within a period not to exceed thirty days from the date of the vacancy.

Fourth: In the case the post of the President of the Republic becomes vacant, the Speaker of the Council of Representatives shall replace the President of the Republic in case he does not have a Vice President, on the condition that a new President is elected during a period not to exceed thirty days from the date of the vacancy and in accordance with the provisions of this Constitution.

SECOND: Council of Ministers

Article 73: First: The President of the Republic shall name the nominee of the Council of Representatives bloc with the largest number to form the Cabinet within fifteen days from the date of the election of the president of the republic.

Second: The Prime Minister–designate shall undertake the naming of the members of his Cabinet within a period not to exceed thirty days from the date of his designation.

Third: In case the Prime Minister–designate fails to form the Cabinet during the period specified in clause "Second," the President of the Republic shall name a new nominee for the post of Prime Minister within fifteen days.

Fourth: The Prime Minister–designate shall present the names of his Cabinet members and the ministerial program to the Council of Representatives. He is deemed to have gained its confidence upon the approval, by an absolute majority of the Council of Representatives, of the individual Ministers and the ministerial program.

Fifth: The President of the Republic shall name another nominee to form the cabinet within fifteen days in case the Cabinet did not gain the confidence.

Article 74: First: The conditions for assuming the post of the Prime Minister shall be the same as those for the President of the Republic, provided that he has completed thirty-five years of age and has a college degree or its equivalent.

Second: The conditions for assuming the post of Minister shall be the same as those for members of the Council of Representatives provided that he holds a college degree or its equivalent.

Article 75: The Prime Minister is the direct executive authority responsible for the general policy of the State and the commander in chief of the armed forces. He directs the Council of Ministers, and presides over its meetings and has the right to dismiss the Ministers on the consent of the Council of Representatives.

Article 76: The Prime Minister and members of the Cabinet shall take the Constitutional Oath before the Council of Representatives in the form stipulated in Article 48 of the Constitution.

Article 77: The Cabinet shall exercise the following powers:

First: Plan and execute the general policy and the general plans of the State and oversee the work of the ministries and departments not associated with a ministry.

Second: To propose bills.

Third: To issue rules, instructions and decisions for the purpose of implementing the law.

Fourth: To prepare the draft of the general budget, the closing account, and the development plans.

Fifth: To recommend to the Council of Representatives to approve the appointment of under secretaries, ambassadors, State senior officials, Chief of Staff of the Armed Forces and his assistants, Division Commanders or higher, Director of the National Intelligence Service, and heads of security institutions.

Sixth: To negotiate and sign international agreements and treaties or designate any person to do so.

Article 78: First: The President of the Republic shall take up the office of the Prime Minister in the event the post becomes vacant for any reason whatsoever.

Second: The President must designate another nominee to form the cabinet within a period not to exceed fifteen days in accordance with the provisions of article 73 of this Constitution.

Article 79: A law shall regulate the salaries and allowances of the Prime Minister and Ministers, and anyone of their grade.

Article 80: The responsibility of the Prime Minister and the Ministers before the Council of Representatives is of a joint and personal nature.

Article 81: First: A law shall regulate the work of the security institutions and the National Intelligence Service and shall define its duties and authorities. It shall operate in accordance with the principles of human rights and be subject to the oversight of the Council of Representatives.

Second: The National Intelligence Service shall be attached to the Cabinet.

Article 82: The Council of Ministers shall establish internal bylaws to organize the work therein.

Article 83: A law shall regulate the formation of ministries, their tasks, their responsibilities and the authorities of the minister.

CHAPTER THREE: THE JUDICIAL AUTHORITY

Article 84: The Judicial authority is independent. The courts, in their various types and classes, shall assume this authority and issue decisions in accordance with the law.

Article 85: Judges are independent and there is no authority over them except that of the law. No authority shall have the right to interfere in the Judiciary and the affairs of Justice.

Article 86: The Federal Judicial Authority is comprised of the Higher Juridical Council, Supreme Federal Court, Federal Court of Cassation, Public Prosecution Department, Judiciary Oversight Commission and other federal courts that are regulated in accordance with the law.

FIRST: Higher Juridical Council

Article 87: The Higher Juridical Council shall oversee the affairs of the Judicial Committees. The law shall specify the method of its establishment, its authorities, and the rules of its operation.

Article 88: The Higher Juridical Council shall exercise the following authorities:

First: To manage the affairs of the Judiciary and supervise the Federal Judiciary.

Second: To nominate the Chief Justice and members of the Federal Court of Cassation, the Chief Public Prosecutor, the Chief Justice of the Judiciary Oversight Commission and present them to the Council of Representatives to approve their appointment.

Third: To propose the draft of the annual budget of the Federal Judiciary Authority and present it to the Council of Representatives for approval.

SECOND: Federal Supreme Court

Article 89: First: The Federal Supreme Court is an independent judicial body, financially and administratively.

Second: The Federal Supreme Court shall be made up of number of judges, and experts in Islamic jurisprudence and law experts whose number, the method of their selection and the work of the court shall be determined by a law enacted by a two-third majority of the members of the Council of Representatives.

Article 90: The Federal Supreme Court shall have jurisdiction over the following:

First: Oversight of the constitutionality of laws and regulations in effect.

Second: Interpretation of the provisions of the constitution.

Third: Settle matters that arise from the application of the federal laws, decisions, regulations, instructions, and procedures issued by the federal authority. The law shall guarantee the right of each of the Cabinet, the concerned individuals and others of direct contest with the Court.

Fourth: Settle disputes that arise between the federal government and the governments of the regions and governorates, municipalities, and local administrations.

Fifth: Settle disputes that arise between the governments of the regions and governments of the governorates.

Sixth: Settle accusations directed against the President, the Prime Minister and the Ministers. That shall be regulated by law.

Seventh: Ratify the final results of the general elections for membership in the Council of Representatives.

Eight:

A. Settle competency dispute between the Federal Judiciary and the judicial institutions of the regions and governorates that are not organized in a region.

B. Settle competency dispute between judicial institutions of the regions or governorates that are not organized in a region.

Article 91: Decisions of the Federal Supreme Court are final and binding for all authorities.

Third: General Provisions

Article 92: Special or exceptional courts may not be established.

Article 93: The law shall regulate the establishment of courts, their types, classes and jurisdiction and the method of appointing and the terms of service of judges, public prosecutors, their discipline and their retirement.

Article 94: Judges may not be removed except in cases specified by law; such law will determine the particular provisions related to them and shall regulate their disciplinary measures.

Article 95: A judge or public prosecutor may not:

First: Combine a position in the judiciary, and a position in the legislature and executive or any other employment.

Second: Joining any party or political organization or perform any political activity.

Article 96: A law shall regulate military judiciary and shall specify the jurisdiction of military courts, which will be limited to crimes of military nature that occur by members of the armed forces, security forces and within the limits stipulated by law.

Article 97: It is prohibited to stipulate in law the immunization from appeal of any administrative work or decision.

Article 98: It is permitted to regulate in a law the establishment of a State Council specialized in the functions of administrative judiciary, interpretation, drafting, and the State and various public institutions representation before the judicial bodies except those exempted by law.

CHAPTER FOUR: INDEPENDENT COMMISSIONS

Article 99: The High Commission for Human Rights, Independent Electoral High Commission and Commission on Public Integrity are independent commissions, which shall be subject to monitoring by the Council of Representatives. A law shall regulate their functions.

Article 100: First: The Central Bank of Iraq, Board of Supreme Audit, Communication and Media Commission, and the Endowment Commissions are financially and administratively independent institutions. A law shall regulate the work of each of these institutions.

Second: The Central Bank of Iraq is responsible before the Council of Representatives. The Board of Supreme Audit and the Communication and Media Commission shall be attached to the Council of Representatives.

Third: The Endowment Commissions shall be attached to the Council of Ministers.

Article 101: A commission named Foundation of Martyrs shall be established and attached to the Council of Ministers. Its functions and competencies shall be regulated by law.

Article 102: A public commission shall be established to guarantee the rights of the regions and governorates that are not organized in a region in fair participation in managing the various state federal institutions, missions, fellowships, delegations, and regional and international conferences. The Commission shall be comprised of representatives of the federal government, and representatives of the regions and governorates that are not organized in a region and shall be regulated by a law.

Article 103: A public commission shall be established by a law to audit and appropriate federal revenues. The commission shall be comprised of federal government experts and representatives and experts and representatives from the regions and governorates and shall assume the following responsibilities:

First: Ensure the fair distribution of grants, aid, and international loans pursuant to the entitlement of the regions and governorates that are not organized in a region.

Second: Ensure the ideal use and division of the federal financial resources.

Third: Guarantee transparency and justice in appropriating funds to the governments of the regions and governorates that are not organized in a region in accordance with the established percentages.

Article 104: A council named the Federal Public Service Council shall be established and shall regulate the affairs of the federal public service, including the appointment and promotion. A law shall regulate its formations and competencies.

Article 105: Other independent commissions may be established according to need and necessity by a law.

SECTION FOUR: POWERS OF THE FEDERAL GOVERNMENT

Article 106: The federal authorities shall preserve the unity, integrity, independence, sovereignty of Iraq, and its federal democratic system.

Article 107: The federal government shall have exclusive authorities in the following matters:

First: Formulating foreign policy and diplomatic representation; negotiating, signing, and ratifying international treaties and agreements; negotiating, signing and ratifying debt policies and formulating foreign sovereign economic and trade policy;

Second: Formulating and executing national security policy, including creating and managing armed forces to secure the protection, and to guarantee the security of Iraq's borders and to defend Iraq;

Third: Formulating fiscal and customs policy, issuing currency, regulating commercial policy across regional and governorate boundaries in Iraq; drawing up the national budget of the State; formulating monetary policy, and establishing and administering a central bank;

Fourth: Regulating standards, weights and measures;

Fifth: Regulating the issues of citizenship, naturalization, residency and the right to apply for political asylum.

Sixth: Regulating telecommunications and mail policy.

Seventh: To draw up the general and investment budget bill.

Eighth: Plan policies relating to water sources from outside Iraq, and guarantee the rate of water flow to Iraq and its fair distribution, in accordance with international laws and norms.

Ninth: General population statistics and census.

Article 108: Oil and gas are the ownership of all the people of Iraq in all the regions and governorates.

Article 109: First: The federal government with the producing governorates and regional governments shall undertake the management of oil and gas extracted from current fields provided that it distributes oil and gas revenues in a fair manner in proportion to the population distribution in all parts of the country with a set allotment for a set time for the damaged regions that were unjustly deprived by the former regime and the regions that were damaged later on, and in a way that assures balanced development in different areas of the country, and this will be regulated by law.

Second: The federal government with the producing regional and governorate governments shall together formulate the necessary strategic policies to develop the oil and gas wealth in a way that achieves the highest benefit to the Iraqi people using the most advanced techniques of the market principles and encourages investment.

(Antiquities and antiquity sites, traditional constructions, manuscripts and coins are considered part of the national wealth which are the responsibility of the federal authorities. They will be administered in cooperation with the regions and governorates, and this will be regulated by law.)

Article 110: The following competencies shall be shared between the federal authorities and regional authorities:

First: To administer customs in coordination with the governments of the regions and governorates that are not organized in a region. This will be organized by law.

Second: To regulate the main sources of electric energy and its distribution.

Third: To formulate the environmental policy to ensure the protection of the environment from pollution and to preserve its cleanness in cooperation with the regions and governorates that are not organized in a region.

Fourth: To formulate the development and general planning policies.

Fifth: To formulate the public health policy in cooperation with the regions and governorates that are not organized in a region.

Sixth: To formulate the public educational and instructional policy in consultation with the regions and governorates that are not organized in a region.

Seventh: To formulate and organize the main internal water sources policy in a way that guarantees fair distribution. This will be organized by law.

Article 111: All powers not stipulated in the exclusive authorities of the federal government shall be the powers of the regions and governorates that are not organized in a region. The priority goes to the regional law in case of conflict between other powers shared between the federal government and regional governments.

SECTION FIVE: POWERS OF THE REGIONS
CHAPTER ONE: REGIONS

Article 112: The federal system in the Republic of Iraq is made up of a decentralized capital, regions and governorates, and local administrations.

Article 113: First: This Constitution shall approbate the region of Kurdistan and its existing regional and federal authorities, at the time this constitution comes into force.

Second: This Constitution shall approbate new regions established in accordance with its provisions.

Article 114: The Council of Representatives shall enact, in a period not to exceed six months from the date of its first session, a law that defines the executive procedures to form regions, by a simple majority.

Article 115: One or more governorates shall have the right to organize into a region based on a request to be voted on in a referendum submitted in one of the following two methods:

A. A request by one-third of the council members of each governorate intending to form a region.

B. A request by one-tenth of the voters in each of the governorates intending to form a region.

Article 116: The region shall adopt a constitution that defines the structure of the regional government, its authorities and the mechanisms of exercising these authorities provided that it does not contradict with this Constitution.

Article 117: First: The regional authorities shall have the right to exercise executive, legislative, and judicial authority in accordance with this constitution, except for those powers stipulated in the exclusive powers of the federal government.

Second: In case of a contradiction between regional and national legislation in respect to a matter outside the exclusive powers of the federal government, the regional authority shall have the right to amend the application of the national legislation within that region.

Third: Regions and governorates shall be allocated an equitable share of the national revenues sufficient to discharge its responsibilities and duties, but having regard to its resources, needs and the percentage of its population.

Fourth: The regions and governorates shall establish offices in the embassies and diplomatic missions, in order to follow up cultural, social and developmental affairs.

Fifth: The Regional Government shall be responsible for all the administrative requirements of the region, particularly the establishment and organization of the internal security forces for the region such as police, security forces and guards of the region.

CHAPTER TWO: GOVERNORATES THAT ARE NOT INCORPORATED INTO A REGION

Article 118: First: The governorates shall be made up of a number of districts, sub-districts and villages.

Second: Governorates that are not incorporated in a region shall be granted broad administrative and financial authorities to enable it to manage its affairs in accordance with the principle of decentralized administration. This will be organized by law.

Third: The governor, who is elected by the Governorate Council, is the highest executive official in the governorate to practice his powers authorized by the council.

Fourth: A law shall regulate the election of the Governorate Council, the governor and their powers.

Fifth: The Governorate Council shall not be subject to the control or supervision of any ministry or any institution not linked to a ministry. The Governorate Council shall have an independent finance.

Article 119: Powers exercised by the federal government can be delegated to the governorates or vice versa, with the consent of both governments and shall be regulated by law.

CHAPTER THREE: THE CAPITAL

Article 120: First: Baghdad with its municipal borders is the capital of the Republic of Iraq and shall constitute, with its administrative borders, the governorate of Baghdad.

Second: A law shall regulate the status of the capital.

Third: The capital may not merge with a region.

CHAPTER FOUR: THE LOCAL ADMINISTRATIONS

Article 121: This Constitution shall guarantee the administrative, political, cultural and educational rights for the various nationalities, such as Turkmen, Caldeans, Assyrians and all other components. This will be organized by law.

SECTION SIX: FINAL AND TRANSITIONAL PROVISIONS

CHAPTER ONE: FINAL PROVISIONS

Article 122: First: The President of the Republic and the Council of the Ministers collectively or one-fifth ($\frac{1}{5}$) of the Council of Representatives members may propose to amend the Constitution.

Second: The fundamental principles mentioned in Section One and the rights and liberties mentioned in Section Two of the Constitution may not be amended except after two successive electoral terms, with the approval of two-thirds of the Council of Representatives members, and the approval of the people in a general referendum and the ratification of the President of the Republic within seven days.

Third: Other Articles not stipulated in clause "Second" of this Article may not be amended, except with the approval of two-thirds of the Council of Representatives members and with the approval of the people in a general referendum and the ratification of the President of the Republic within seven days.

Fourth: Articles of the constitution may not be amended if such amendment takes away from the powers of the regions that are not within the exclusive powers of the federal authorities except by the consent of the legislative authority of the concerned region and the approval of the majority of its citizens in a general referendum.

Fifth:

A. The amendment is considered ratified by the President of the Republic after the expiration of the period stipulated in clauses "Second" and "Third" of this Article in case he does not ratify it.

B. An amendment shall enter into force on the date of its publication in the Official Gazette.

Article 123: The President of the Republic, the Prime Minister, members of the Council of Ministers, the Speaker of the Council of Representatives, his two Deputies and members of the Council of Representatives, members of the Judicial Authority and people of the special grades may not use their influence to buy or rent any of the State properties, or to rent or sell any of their assets to the State, or to sue the State for it or to conclude a contract with the State under the pretense of being building contractors, suppliers or concessionaires.

Article 124: The laws and judicial judgments shall be issued in the name of the people.

Article 125: Laws shall be published in the Official Gazette and shall take effect on the date of its publication, unless stipulated otherwise.

Article 126: Existing laws shall remain in force, unless annulled or amended in accordance with the provisions of this constitution.

Article 127: Every referendum mentioned in this constitution is valid with the approval of a simple majority of the voters unless otherwise stipulated.

CHAPTER TWO: TRANSITIONAL PROVISIONS

Article 128: First: The State guarantees care for political prisoners and victims of the oppressive practices of the defunct dictatorial regime.

Second: The State guarantees compensation to the families of the martyrs and those injured due to terrorist acts.

Third: A law shall regulate matters mentioned in clauses "First" and "Second" of this Article.

Article 129: The Council of Representatives shall adopt in its first session the bylaws of the Transitional National Assembly until it adopts its own bylaws.

Article 130: The Iraq High Criminal Court shall continue its duties as an independent judicial body, in examining the crimes of the defunct dictatorial regime and its symbols. The Council of Representatives shall have the right to dissolve by law the Iraqi High Criminal Court after the completion of its work.

Article 131: First: The High Commission for De-Ba'athification shall continue its functions as an independent commission, and in coordination with the Judicial Authority and the Executive institutions within the framework of the laws regulating its functions. The Commission shall be attached to the Council of Representatives.

Second: The Council of Representatives shall have the right to dissolve this Commission after the completion of its function by absolute majority.

Third: The nominee to the Position of the President of the Republic, the Prime Minister and the members of the Ministers Council, the Speaker and the members of the Council of Representatives, the President and members of the Federation Council, the corresponding positions in the regions, members of the Judicial committees and other positions included in the De-Ba'athification pursuant to the law may not be subject to De-Ba'athification judgments.

Fourth: The conditions stated in clause "Third" of this article shall remain in force unless the commission provided for in clause "First" of this article is dissolved.

(Fifth: Membership in the defunct Ba'ath party alone is not considered a sufficient basis for transfer to the courts, and a member enjoys equality before the law and its protection, as long as he is not subject to the rulings of the De-Ba'athification Commission and its bylaws.)

(Sixth: The Council of Representatives will form a parliamentary committee from its members to oversee and review the executive activities of the Supreme De-Ba'athification Commission and state agencies to guarantee justice, objectivity and transparency, and to examine its accordance with the law. The committee's decisions will be subject to agreement by the Council of Representatives.)

Article 132: First: The Property Claims Commission shall continue its functions as an independent commission in coordination with the Judicial authority and the Executive institutions in accordance with the law. The Property Claims Commission shall be attached to the Council of Representatives.

Second: The Council of Representatives shall have the right to dissolve the Commission by a two-thirds majority vote of its members.

Article 133: Application of the provisions of the articles related to the Federation Council, wherever it may be cited in this Constitution, shall be postponed until the Council of Representatives issues a decision by a two-thirds majority vote in its second electoral term that is held after this Constitution comes into force.

Article 134: First: The expression "the Presidency Council" shall replace the expression "the President of the Republic" wherever it is mentioned in this Constitution. The provisions related to the President of the Republic shall be reactivated one successive term after this Constitution comes into force.

Second:

A. The Council of Representatives shall elect the President of the State and two

Vice Presidents who shall form a Council called "the Presidency Council," which shall be elected by one list and with a two-thirds majority.

B. The provisions to remove the President of the Republic present in this constitution shall apply to the President and members of the Presidency Council.

C. The Council of Representatives may remove a member of the Presidency Council with a three-fourths majority of its members for reasons of incompetence and dishonesty.

D. In the event of a vacant seat in the Presidency Council, the Council of Representatives shall elect a replacement by a two-thirds majority vote of its members.

Third: The members of the Presidency Council shall be subject to the same conditions as members of the Council of Representatives and must also:

A. Have completed forty years of age.

B. Enjoy good reputation, integrity and uprightness.

C. Have quit the defunct Party ten years prior to its fall, in case he was a member of the dissolved Ba'ath Party.

D. Have not participated in suppressing the 1991 uprising and the Anfal campaign. He must not have committed a crime against the Iraqi people.

Fourth: The Presidency Council shall issue its decisions unanimously and a member may delegate his place to any of the other members.

Fifth:

A. Legislation and decisions enacted by the Council of Representatives shall be forwarded to the Presidency Council to approve it unanimously and to issue it within ten days from the date of delivery to the Presidency Council, except the stipulations of Articles (114) and (115) that pertain to the formation of regions.

B. In the event the Presidency Council does not approve, legislation and decisions shall be sent back to the Council of Representatives to re-examine the disputed issues and to vote on by the majority of its members and then shall be sent for the second time to the Presidency Council for approval.

C. In the event the Presidency Council does not approve the legislation and decisions for the second time within ten days of receipt, the legislation and decisions are sent back to the Council of Representatives who have the right to adopt it by a three-fifths non-appealable majority vote and shall be considered ratified.

Sixth: The Presidency Council shall practice the powers of the President of the Republic stipulated in this Constitution.

Article 135: The Prime Minister shall have two deputies in the first electoral cycle.

Article 136: First: The Executive Authority shall undertake the necessary steps to complete the implementation of the requirements of all subparagraphs of Article 58 of the Transitional Administrative Law.

Second: The responsibility placed upon the executive branch of the Iraqi Transitional Government stipulated in Article 58 of the Transitional Administrative Law shall extend and continue to the executive authority elected in accordance with this constitution, provided that it completes (normalization and census and concludes with a referendum in Kirkuk and other disputed territories to determine the will of their citizens), in a period not to exceed (the thirty first of December two thousand and seven).

Article 137: Legislation enacted in the region of Kurdistan since 1992 shall remain in force, and decisions issued by the government of the region of Kurdistan — including court decisions and agreements — shall be considered valid unless it is amended or annulled pursuant to the laws of the region of Kurdistan by the competent entity in the region, provided that they do not contradict with the constitution.

(First: At the start of its functioning, the Council of Representatives shall form a committee from its members, which will be representative of the main components of Iraqi society and the duty of which will be to present within a period no longer than four months to the Council of Representatives a report that includes recommendations for the necessary amendments that can be made to the Constitution. The committee will be dissolved after a decision is made on its proposals.

Second: The amendments proposed by the committee will be put before the Council of Representatives in a single batch for approval. It will be considered approved by the agreement of an absolute majority of the number of council members.

Third: The articles amended by the Council of Representatives under the second clause of this article will be put before the people for a referendum within two months of the Council of Representatives' approval of them.

Fourth: The referendum on the amended articles will be considered successful with the agreement by an absolute majority of those who vote, unless it is rejected by two-thirds of those who vote in three governorates or more.

Fifth: This is an exception to Article 61 of this Constitution, which concerns amending the constitution. After the amendments discussed in this article are decided on, work will return to the terms of Article 61.

Article 138: The Transitional Administrative Law and its Annex shall be annulled on the seating of the new government, except for the stipulation of Article 53(A) and Article 58 of the Transitional Administrative Law.

Article 139: This Constitution shall come into force after the approval of the people thereon in a general referendum, its publication in the Official Gazette and the seating of the government that is formed pursuant to this constitution.

■

Me and You and
Everyone We Know

FROM the original shooting script

ME AND YOU AND EVERYONE WE KNOW *is the story of a newly divorced father, Richard, his two sons, Robby (six) and Peter (fourteen), and a lot of other people. Richard sells shoes in a department store and is prepared for amazing things to happen. One of these amazing things comes in the form of a persistent customer named Christine. Richard's sons are also looking for a connection, and are frequently unsupervised. The following five scenes are from the original shooting script.*

1

Int. Eden Roc, Swersey Apartment, the Sons' Bedroom, Night

Robby and Peter are playing on the computer. There are no Disney sheets — just old blankets on the beds. The decorations are all the things Robby and Peter have made and put on the walls. Duffel bags are in view. There is no room for anything more than the two beds and the desk that the computer is on. The boys are doing a one-on-one instant-message chat with a woman. NightWarrior is their chat name; their chat friend calls him/herself UNTITLED. Their responses are hastily thought up, madly typed.

UNTITLED: I'm wearing pants and a blouse.
ROBBY: Ask her if she likes baloney! What are you putting?

PETER: (*typing and then hitting Send*) I asked her what kind of bosom she had. It's probably a man.

Peter pronounces "bosom" wrong, to rhyme with "blossom."

ROBBY: Why is it a man?

PETER: 'Cuz everyone just makes stuff up on these things. It's probably a man pretending to be a woman. OK? So picture a fat guy with a little wiener.

ROBBY: What's a bosom?

PETER: It's a nice word for titties.

A pause.

ROBBY: Where's Mom?

PETER: What do you mean?

ROBBY: What do you think she's doing right now?

PETER: I don't know. Screwing her new boyfriend probably.

ROBBY: I think she's buying us presents.

PETER: Yeah, Robby, right now she's probably buying us each a car.

Noise sounds from instant message. They both read it quietly to themselves, Robby with more difficulty.

UNTITLED: I have a deliciously full "bosom."

PETER: It's a man —

ROBBY: I think it's a woman. I can tell it is.

Robby is now very serious, breathing heavily.

PETER: (*laughing, less serious*) Well, what should we write? "I have a big wiener"?

Pause.

ROBBY: "I want to poop back and forth."

PETER: What?! What does that mean?

ROBBY: (*very serious, quietly*) Like I'll poop into her butt hole and then she'll poop it back into my butt hole and then we'll just keep doing it back and forth. With the same poop.

PETER: (*louder, knowing this is a crazy, silly thing to write*) Oh my God,

I'm going to put that! "I . . . want . . . to . . . poop . . . back and forth!"
Oh God, she's gonna think we're a crazy perverted person!

Peter and Robby nervously wait for a response. Finally one appears.

UNTITLED: What does that mean exactly?

PETER: Ooh . . . she thinks we're crazy!

ROBBY: No, tell her like how I said it.

PETER: *(pleading but laughing still)* She'll never write back, Robby. We
have to sound like we're a man, you know, that's just lame. It's stupid.

ROBBY: But you said I could do half and you've done all of them before this.

PETER: OK, whatever. We're probably gonna get arrested. What do
you want me to put?

ROBBY: Like how I said it.

PETER: "I'll poop . . . in your . . . butt hole . . . and then you . . . will . . .
poop it . . . back into my . . . butt . . . and we will . . . keep doing it . . ."

ROBBY: Back . . .

PETER: "Back . . ."

ROBBY: . . . and forth

PETER: "And forth . . ."

ROBBY: With the same poop.

PETER: "With the same poop . . ."

ROBBY: Forever.

PETER: "Forever."

The instant-message noise sounds.

UNTITLED: You are crazy and you are making me very hot.

2

Ext. Department Store, Next Moment

*Richard has just exited the store; a moment later Christine walks quickly
out the doors, her eyes trained on Richard.*

CHRISTINE: (*catching up with him*) I'm not following you, my car's parked over there.

RICHARD: In Smart Park?

CHRISTINE: No, on Front Street.

RICHARD: Oh. I parked in Smart Park.

They walk in silence side by side.

CHRISTINE: So at the end of the next block we'll separate. At Tyrone Street.

RICHARD: Yep. The Iceland sign is halfway. (*filling an awkward silence*) It's the halfway point.

CHRISTINE: (*with nervous laughter*) Iceland is kind of like that point in a relationship, you know, where you suddenly realize it's not going to last forever? You know, you can see the end in sight . . . Tyrone Street?

Richard takes this in. There is a moment where we wonder if he'll be able to flow with it. He slows his walking pace way down and Christine laughs.

RICHARD: Yeah, but we're not even there yet. We're still at the good part. We're not even sick of each other yet.

CHRISTINE: I'm not sick of you at all and, whoa, it's been a good . . .

She looks behind her to gauge their progress.

CHRISTINE: . . . like six months.

RICHARD: What? Six months! Then the Iceland sign is like eight months. You think we'd only last a year and a half?

CHRISTINE: Well, I don't know . . . I don't want to be presumptuous. I don't know if you're married or what.

RICHARD: I'm not. Well, I'm separated. We separated last month. (*Beat.*) I was thinking that Tyrone was like twenty years away at least.

They are walking very slowly at this point. This is the first time we have seen Richard be this playful and happy. His energy is high.

CHRISTINE: Yeah? OK. Well, actually I was thinking Tyrone was like when we die of old age, and this is like our whole life together. This block.

RICHARD: That's perfect. Let's do it that way.
CHRISTINE: OK.

They walk, close together, slowly down to Tyrone Street. Richard looks as if he is suddenly in heaven and he doesn't know how he got there. They look all around themselves but are together. At Tyrone they stop. Richard is jolted out of their happy shared reality. He looks at her desperately.

CHRISTINE: Well . . . guess it can't be avoided, everyone dies.
RICHARD: I could walk you to your car.
CHRISTINE: Um, maybe we should just be glad that we lived this long, good life together. You know, it's so much more than most people ever get to have.
RICHARD: OK.
CHRISTINE: OK.
RICHARD: OK.
CHRISTINE: OK.
CHRISTINE: Well, don't be afraid.
RICHARD: OK.
CHRISTINE: Here we go.
RICHARD: Here we go.

They turn and walk in opposite directions. Christine is forcing herself to look straight ahead and keep walking, eyes wide open. She thinks she can feel his eyes on her back. Against her best instincts she turns to looks back, very quickly, and sees him walking away.

CUT TO:

Int. Richard's Car, A Moment Later

Richard is driving, passing the spot where he parted with Christine. He glances, sees hand, which is heavily bandaged, on the steering wheel. His face falls, he loses faith and becomes panicked. Suddenly he is jarred by a voice. It is Christine, calling from the sidewalk where she is walking.

CHRISTINE: Richard! Hi!
RICHARD: (*flustered*) Hi! I thought your car was over here.
CHRISTINE: It is, it's down there.

She points down the street. He looks down the street and doesn't respond.

CHRISTINE: You could give me a ride to it.
RICHARD: Doesn't that break the rules of the . . . thing?

Christine walks around the car, smiling, stands by the passenger window. He looks at her, almost terrified. Christine gets in.

CHRISTINE: This can be like the afterlife. You know, like we're angels or something?

Richard doesn't respond. He is immobile, suddenly humorless. She gradually comes to feel this. She nervously touches a sticker on the dashboard, something Robby had stuck there.

CHRISTINE: Cute.
RICHARD: What are you doing in my car? I don't know you. And you certainly don't know anything about me. I mean, what if I'm a . . . killer of children?

Christine is taken aback, but hangs in.

CHRISTINE: Yeah, well that would put a damper on things, wouldn't it?
RICHARD: *(makes a disgusted noise)* See, you're acting like I'm just this regular man, like a man in a book who the woman in the book meets.
CHRISTINE: I'm not doing that. Did I just invite myself into your car, is that what I just did? Well, I'm sorry.
RICHARD: *(angrily)* No, *I'm* sorry. *I'm* sorry.
CHRISTINE: You should be.
RICHARD: Good, terrific, can you get out of my car now?
CHRISTINE: OK.
RICHARD: OK.
CHRISTINE: OK.
RICHARD: OK.

These OKs are intense. They are hovering between anger and wanting to reverse what just happened. But neither gives in, and anger wins and

Christine gets out of the car, slamming the door. We see him drive away.
She stands there.

3

Int. Buckman School Library

Close-up on Robby's face, looking intently at the library computer. There
are no other students in this part of the library or on the other computers.
He types with one finger.

NIGHTWARRIOR: (typing) Hi.
UNTITLED: Hi friend.

Surprised and heartened by this, he repeats his first move and then waits
expectantly with his hands folded in his lap.

NIGHTWARRIOR: Hi.
UNTITLED: I've been thinking about the "back and forth."

This is shocking. He looks around the library to see if anyone has noticed.
He is suddenly in a big, real situation of his own creation, and he is alone.
He can't decide what to do, so he turns off the monitor. The computer sits
there blankly. He slowly picks up a pen and paper and makes the simple
drawing of two butts with a poop connecting them. He turns the monitor
back on. She's added a sentence.

UNTITLED: Do you remember what you said the last time? ("Back
and forth. Forever.")

He is all alone, except, as he slowly realizes, he has UNTITLED. *He leans*
into the screen and copies/pastes the [big] word "remember" from her sen-
tence.

NIGHTWARRIOR: I remember. The poop.
UNTITLED: Yes, the poop.

He can't think of what to write. She writes again.

UNTITLED: It makes me want to touch myself.

He is quite a bit out of his league, hugely excited, but almost distressed. He's unsure of what to do — very hampered by his typing skills and feeling more than he can contain/express.

UNTITLED: Is that very bad?
NIGHTWARRIOR: Maybee. (*He hesitates before the second e, then types it. The spell check indicates an error. In an attempt to cover up his spelling, he holds down the E key, stops, exhales, types a careful period.*) Maybeeeeeeeeeeeeeeeeeeeeeeeeeeeeeeeeeeee.
UNTITLED: Sounds like you're excited too.

His childlike short phrases come off as a "mysterious man of few words." This becomes slowly obvious, though initially it seems as though he will not be convincing. She writes:

UNTITLED: I am touching my "bosoms." What are you doing?
(*he writes, sounding it out*)
NIGHTWARRIOR: (*typing*) I am drowing. (*Spell check indicates his error. He then replaces the o.*) I am drawing.
UNTITLED: OK . . . drawing what. (*he tries a few ways before coming to this*)
NIGHTWARRIOR:))<>((
UNTITLED: Huh?
NIGHTWARRIOR: (*copying/pasting*) Back and forth.
UNTITLED: I get it. When can we meet?

4

Int. Department Store, Makeup Counter

Christine is holding a small, circular compact, using the mirror to reflect the light onto Richard. But just then the mirror falls out of the compact, onto the floor. It doesn't break; Christine picks it up, embarrassed. She looks at the MAKEUP-COUNTER WOMAN and at Richard, across the way.

She takes a deep breath and leaves the makeup counter, compact and mirror in hand.

We see him from her point of view. Christine arrives in front of Richard, who at the last minute pretends to be looking at a shoe. She holds out the compact and mirror.

CHRISTINE: Hi. Do you have any glue?
RICHARD: Oh . . . we have Shoo Goo.
CHRISTINE: Yeah, that might work.

He rummages through a drawer and brings out the Shoo Goo. He takes the mirror and compact from her and tries to apply the glue; it's too much for him to hold with the bandaged hand. Christine holds the mirror. He applies the glue. They both press it down. He looks at the instructions on the glue.

RICHARD: We have to hold this for one to two minutes.

They both hold the mirror and compact in silence for a moment. It is nervous between them. People are rushing past them on all sides.

CHRISTINE: So how's the separation going? Or was that temporary . . . or maybe even momentary?
RICHARD: No, we're really separated. But we have two kids.
CHRISTINE: OK. How old are they?
RICHARD: God, it's a real madhouse in here; it's 'cause of this sale we're having.
CHRISTINE: *(coldly defensive)* Well, go — if you need to go.

Richard stays, feeling like a fool for what he just said.

CHRISTINE: *(nodding at his bandaged hand)* How did you do that?
RICHARD: Ohh, well, do you want the long version or the short version?
CHRISTINE: The long one.
RICHARD: *(takes a deep breath, as if beginning an epic)* I was trying to save my life, and it didn't work.

They lock eyes. Suddenly they are in their own intense world, with much more passing between them than words. People swirl around them, but they are very still.

CHRISTINE: What's the short one?
RICHARD: I burned it.
CHRISTINE: And when do you get to take that off?
RICHARD: I don't know, I think when it . . . stops hurting.

They hold each other's gaze.

CHRISTINE: Let's give it another fifteen seconds.
RICHARD: Do you want to . . . sit down, together, sometime, with . . .
   like, with coffee, or something?
CHRISTINE: Yeah.

They stand together, holding the compact, people move around them.

CHRISTINE: Six, five, four, three, two, one.

*Richard lets go of the compact and she breaks away like a spacecraft from
the mother ship. There is an unsureness between them. Finally:*

CHRISTINE: (*awkwardly*) OK, well, if you ever feel too old to drive,
   just call that number.

*She presents him with an Eldercab business card. He looks down at the
card, and when he looks up, she's walking away.*

5

Int. Living Room

Richard is beginning to unwrap his bandaged hand.

RICHARD: I'm taking off the bandage now! If anyone wants to see.

*No one appears. Richard unbinds his hand slowly, almost timidly. The
hand is very white and raw-looking, moist. Robby quietly comes out of his
room and watches silently. Richard continues. Peter watches from the
kitchen. Richard looks at his hand. He waves it around in the air.*

RICHARD: It's so sensitive! It needs air. (*waves it around some more*) It
   needs to do some living.

He looks at Peter and Robby.

RICHARD: Let's take my hand for a walk!

Peter and Robby say nothing, stay rooted where they are.

RICHARD: Talk to me!

Peter and Robby look at Richard.

RICHARD: So this is it? This is the end of our relationship? That makes me sad, it really does.

After a moment Peter walks out and Robby follows, visibly upset. The boys walk out into the night.

CUT TO:

Ext. Eden Roc, Still Wide Shot, Next Moment, Night

RICHARD: Do you have questions you want to ask me? Do you want advice from your dad? Ask me for advice on anything. Anything at all, anything.

Neither boy responds.

RICHARD: OK, OK. Name a song, I'll whistle it, any song, any song that I know.

After a long silence Peter speaks, the first time in ages.

PETER: "Every Stone Shall Cry."
RICHARD: (*shocked that Peter spoke/doesn't know the song*) What?
PETER: It's a hymn.
RICHARD: A hymn? How do you know a hymn?
ROBBY: (*dying to talk*) We learned it at school!
RICHARD: Oh. Well all right, let's hear it.

Robby suddenly opens his mouth and starts singing it. Peter joins in after a moment. It is a very beautiful, sad song. Richard is completely struck by it. It is as if his boys have turned into angels; they are suddenly, finally externalizing everything he keeps inside himself.

ROBBY AND PETER:
A stable-lamp is lighted
Whose glow shall wake the sky;
The stars shall bend their voices,
And every stone shall cry.
And every stone shall cry
In praises of the child
By whose descent among us
The worlds are reconciled.

Int. Swersey Apartment, Night, Post-Hymn

Richard is lying on the fold-out bed, no bandage. He looks down at his now healed hand, which is resting on the sheets. It slides across the couch to the Eldercab card, which we now see is on the bed too, a couple feet away. His hand continues moving as he pushes the card off the edge of the couch, into the recesses of the sofabed.

MICHAEL LEWIS

■

Wading Toward Home

FROM *The New York Times Magazine*

1. Kings and Queens (and Squires) in Old, Old New Orleans

THERE'S A FINE LINE between stability and stagnation, and by the time I was born, New Orleans had already crossed it. The difference between growing up in New Orleans, starting in 1960, and growing up most other places in America was how easy it was to believe, in New Orleans, that nothing meaningful occurred outside it. No one of importance ever seemed to move in, just as no one of importance ever moved away. The absence of any sort of movement into or out of the upper and upper-middle classes was obviously bad for business, but it was great for what are now called family values. Until I went away to college, I had no idea how scattered and disjointed most American families were. By the time I was nine, I could ride my bike to the houses of both sets of grandparents. My mother's parents lived six blocks away; my father's parents, the far-flung ones, lived about a mile away. I didn't think it was at all odd that so much of my family was so near at hand: one friend of mine had all four of her grandparents next door, two on one side, two on the other. At the time, this struck me as normal.

Every Christmas, my mother's side of the family gathered for a party that confirmed for me that just about all white New Orleanians, even the horrible ones, were somehow blood relations. Before I could do long division, I knew the difference between a third cousin and a first cousin twice removed. Wherever I went, I was defined by family, living and dead.

My mother's family, the Monroes, were the *arrivistes:* they had been in New Orleans since only the 1850s. Nevertheless, my great-grandfather J. Blanc Monroe, descended from James Polk on one side and James Monroe on the other, became the spearhead of the New Orleans aristocracy. In *Rising Tide,* John Barry's history of the 1927 flood, Papa Blanc, as he was known, is cast as one of the villains who pressed the government to dynamite the levees below New Orleans and flood the outlying parishes in order to spare the city; he then stiffed the victims, on behalf of the city, when they came for reparations. My father's side, the Lewises, were the old New Orleanians. They came down from Virginia in 1803, when Thomas Jefferson sent my father's great-great-grandfather Joshua Lewis to be a judge for the territory of Orleans after the Louisiana Purchase. Eventually he joined the Louisiana Supreme Court, wrote the state's first legal opinion, gave the celebratory toast at the banquet given to honor Andrew Jackson in 1815 after the Battle of New Orleans, and, as the Protestant candidate, narrowly lost the governor's race to his Catholic opponent, Jacques Philippe Roi de Villere, whose descendant Sandy lived across the street from my parents until last year. Joshua's son John Lewis was elected mayor of New Orleans and was wounded at the Battle of Mansfield.

As a boy, I had no idea when the Lewises arrived in Louisiana, or that Thomas Jefferson himself had sent them. I just knew that everyone around me had been there forever, mostly in the same houses. I took it as the normal state of affairs, the done thing, that when the old carnival organizations went looking for royalty, they came to my Uptown neighborhood. There was, for instance, a Mardi Gras krewe for adolescents called Squires, which mimicked exactly the masked balls of the adults. When I was sixteen, I was dubbed its king: a group of five young men in suits, led by the departing king, turned up in our living room to tap my shoulders. After school for the next several weeks, I went straight from baseball practice to a school for royals in a cottage just off St. Charles Avenue, where a woman experienced in the ways of European royalty had taken up residence — presumably because we had the one growth market in the world for kings and queens. The tone of her sessions was serious, bordering on solemn. In that little cottage, I spent hours practicing to be king, a crown on my head, an ermine cape on my shoulders, and a glittering scepter in my left hand that I waved over imaginary subjects, unaware that there was anything the slightest bit unusual about any of it.

Perhaps because their position in it was so fixed, my parents were never all that interested in New Orleans society — my father once said to me, "My idea of hell is a cocktail party." On the other hand, they have always been deeply engaged in civic life; they are, I suppose, what's left of that useful but unfashionable attitude of noblesse oblige. Without making any sort of show of it at all, my mother has run just about every major charitable organization in the city: as camouflage in the public-housing projects, where she spends a lot of her time, she has always insisted on driving the world's oldest and least desirable automobiles. (And, yes, she has many black friends.) My father is a different sort, less keen on getting his hands dirty. For forty years, from the comfort of his private library, he has, every other Saturday, watched my mother push a lawn mower back and forth across the front lawn without so much as a passing thought that he might lend a hand. He was fond of citing the Lewis family motto:

> Do as little as possible
> And that unwillingly
> For it is better to incur a slight reprimand
> Than to perform an arduous task.

Like my mother, he seldom mentioned what he did away from home. Yet at one point in my childhood, he was president of so many civic and business enterprises that I didn't understand why they didn't just get it over with and make him president of the United States, too. He is still president of an unelected board of city elders, the Board of Liquidation, an artifact of Reconstruction that has, incredibly, the powers to issue bonds on behalf of New Orleans and to levy taxes to pay off those bonds.

But my parents have lived their entire adult lives fighting an unwinnable war. In their lifetimes, New Orleans has gone from the leading city of the South to a theme park for low-rollers and sinners. All the unpleasant facts about a city that can be measured — crime, poverty and illiteracy rates, the strange forms of governmental malfunction — have remained high. The public schools are a hopeless problem, and the public housing is a source of endless misery. A disturbing number of my parents' white neighbors have fled to white towns on the far side of Lake Pontchartrain. My parents would never put it this way, but they are fatalists; they have come to view change as unfortunate and inevitable. That's one difference between stability and stagnation. A stable society has the ability to reject or adapt to change. A stagnant one has change imposed on it, unpleasantly. The only question is from what direction it will come.

On the night of Sunday, August 28, it came from the south. That's when my mother reached me in California to let me know that she and my father, along with my sister (a former, reluctant Mardi Gras queen) and her husband and their children, were stuck in a traffic jam heading for central Alabama. "We had to evacuate for the hurricane," she said. HURR-i-cun. New Orleanians generate many peculiar accents, but nothing like a conventional southern one. Anyone in New Orleans with a southern accent is either faking it or from somewhere else. My mother often changes the standard pronunciation of words by stressing a first syllable. (Umbrella is UM-brella.)

"What HURR-i-cun?" I asked.

We had never left New Orleans to escape a hurricane. Betsy, in 1965, and Camille, in 1969, the meteorological stars of my youth, were wildly entertaining. Each in turn wiped out the weekend house built by Papa Blanc on the Mississippi Gulf Coast — Camille left behind nothing but the foundation slab — but that's what Mississippi was for: to get wiped out by hurricanes. A hurricane in Mississippi was not a natural disaster but an excuse for a real estate boom.

In this unchanging world, something else was about to change . . . but what? My father believes in knocking on wood, and also that bad things come in threes. Having endured this past summer both a nasty heart operation and the death of his closest friend, he was happy to see that the third bad thing was merely another hurricane. He, like I, assumed they would drive to their friend's place in central Alabama, wait a day or two, and then return to the same New Orleans they had fled. That was Sunday. The storm hit Monday morning, and the levees that protected the city from the lake broke. Then, of course, all hell broke loose. The mayor started saying that ten thousand people might be dead and that the living wouldn't be allowed to return for months. My parents left Alabama for a house in Highlands, North Carolina, that Papa Blanc bought in 1913. When the water is rising, it's nice to own a house in the highest incorporated town east of the Rocky Mountains — even if it is an old, chilly house without modern conveniences and a big sign inside that reads, "Yee Cannot Expect to Be Both Grand and Comfortable."

It's even nicer when you have immediate family accounted for. But on Sunday evening, my little brother, in hot pursuit of one of those Darwin Awards that are bestowed upon the unintentionally suicidal, looked at the traffic jam heading north out of New Orleans and decided instead to go south, toward Katrina, where the roads were clear and he could drive fast.

2. Rumors, Rumors Everywhere — and Haywood Hillyer

Three days after Katrina made landfall, I flew to Dallas and then, the next morning, squeezed between two FEMA workers on a flight into Baton Rouge. My father, even more risk-averse than usual, had phoned me and insisted that I shouldn't go home. When I wouldn't listen, he became testy with me for the first time in my adult life. "After what we've been through the past few months, you want to go and do this . . . ," he started, though when he realized he wasn't going to change my mind, he changed his tune. "In that case," he said, "grab me a couple of tropical-weight suits and a pair of decent shoes. And just a handful of bow ties."

On my way into the city, at a gas station, I ran into two young men leaving in a pickup truck. They had just been stopped by the police in New Orleans and related the following exchange:

> cops: Are you armed?
> young men: Heavily.
> cops: Good. Shoot to kill.

The first surprise was that a city supposedly blockaded wasn't actually all that hard to get into. The TV reports insisted that the National Guard had arrived — there were pictures of soldiers showing up, so how could it not be true? — but from the Friday morning of my arrival through the weekend after Katrina hit, there was no trace of the Guard, or any other authority, on high ground. New Orleans at that moment was experiencing the fantasy of the neutron bomb: people obliterated, buildings intact. No city was ever more silent. No barks, shouts, honks, or wails: there weren't even cockroaches scurrying between cracks in the sidewalks. At night, I soon learned, the sound of the place was different. At night, the air would be filled with helicopters reprising the soundtrack from *Apocalypse Now*. But on that bright blue summer Friday, the city could not have been more tranquil. It was as if New Orleans had a pause button, and the finger that reached in to press it also inadvertently uprooted giant magnolias and snapped telephone poles in two.

The next surprise was that a city supposedly inundated had so much dry land. When the levees broke, Lake Pontchartrain stole back the wetlands long ago reclaimed for housing. Between the new lake shore and the Mississippi River of my youth is dry land with the houses of about 185,000 people. The city government in exile has categorized the high-ground population as 55 percent black, 42 percent white, and 3 percent Hispanic. The flood did not discriminate by race or class. It took out a lot of poor people's homes, but it took out a lot of rich people's homes too. It did discriminate historically: it took out everything but the old city. If you asked an architecture critic or a preservationist to design a flood of this size in New Orleans, he would have given you something like this one.

This wasn't supposed to be. After the levees broke, Mayor Ray Nagin, who grew up in New Orleans, predicted that even Uptown would be under fifteen to twenty feet of water. But most of Uptown was dry. Chris O'Connor, vice president of the Ochsner Clinic, the one hospital still open, would tell me: "As the water rose, everyone was quoting different elevation levels. One doctor said Ochsner was 2.6 feet above sea level. Someone else said Ochsner was 12 feet above sea level. No one knew where the water would stop." But it stopped a far way from Ochsner. There's a long history to this sort of confusion: as a child I was told many times that the highest point in New Orleans was "Monkey Hill." Monkey Hill was a pile of dirt near the Audubon Zoo, Uptown, used chiefly as a bike ramp by ten-year-old boys. The rest of the city was "below sea level." That the whole city was below sea level, along with the fact that we buried people in tombs above ground because we couldn't dig into the soil without hitting water, was what every New Orleans child learned from seemingly knowledgeable grownups about the ground he walked on. If there was ever a serious flood, the only place that would be above water was Monkey Hill — which caused a lot of us to wonder what the grownups were thinking when they brought in earth-moving machinery and flattened it. Now we didn't even have Monkey Hill to stand on.

Apart from a few engineers, no one in New Orleans knew the most important fact about the ground he stood on: its elevation. It took some weaving to get a car to my family's house, but water wasn't the obstacle. There was no water here; the damage from the wind, on the other hand, was sensational, like nothing I had ever seen. Telephone poles lay like broken masts in the middle of the street. Wires and cables hung low over the streets like strings of popcorn on a Christmas tree. But the houses, the gorgeous old New Orleans houses, were pristine, untouched.

Beyond Uptown, here is what I knew, or thought I knew: Orleans Parish prison had been seized by the inmates, who also controlled the armory. Prisoners in their orange uniforms had been spotted outside, roaming around the tilapia ponds — there's a fish farm next to the prison — and whatever that meant, it sounded ominous: I mean, if they were getting into the tilapias, who knew what else they might do? Gangs of young black men were raging through the Garden District, moving toward my parents' house, shooting white people. Armed young black men, on Wednesday, had taken over Uptown Children's Hospital, just six blocks away, and shot patients and doctors. Others had stolen a forklift and carted out the entire contents of a Rite Aid and then removed the whole front of an Ace Hardware store farther uptown, on Oak Street. Most shocking of all, because of its incongruity, was the news that looters had broken into Perlis, the Uptown New Orleans clothing store, and picked the place clean of alligator belts, polo shirts with little crawfish on them, and tuxedos, most often rented by white kids for debutante parties and the Squires' Ball.

I also knew, or thought I knew, that right up to Thursday night, there had been just two houses in Uptown New Orleans with people inside them. In one, a couple of old coots had barricaded themselves behind plywood signs that said things like "Looters Will Be Shot" and "Enter and Die." The other, a fort-like house equipped with a massive power generator, was owned by Jim Huger — who happened to grow up in the house next door to my parents'. (When I heard that he had the only air conditioning in town and I called to ask if I could borrow a bed, he said, "I'm that little kid you used to beat on with a Wiffle Ball bat, and I gotta save your ass now?") In Jim Huger's house, until the night before, several other young men had holed up, collecting weapons and stories. Most of these stories entered the house by way of a reserve officer in the New Orleans Police Department, a friend of Jim's, who had gone out in full uniform each day and come back with news directly from other cops. From Tuesday until Thursday, the stories had grown increasingly terrifying. On Thursday, a police sergeant told him: "If I were you, I'd get the hell out of here. Tonight they gonna waste white guys, and they don't care which ones." This reserve cop had looked around and seen an amazing sight, full-time New Orleans police officers, en masse, fleeing New Orleans. "All these cops were going to Baton Rouge to sleep because they thought it wasn't safe to sleep in New Orleans," he told me. He had heard that by the time it was dark "there wouldn't be a single cop in the city."

On Thursday night, Fort Huger was abandoned. Forming a six-car, heavily armed convoy, the last of Uptown New Orleans, apart from the two old coots, set off into the darkness and agreed not to stop, or even slow down, until they were out of town. They also agreed that they would try to come back in the morning, when it was light.

With one exception: one of the men who had taken his meals inside Fort Huger declined to leave New Orleans. Haywood Hillyer was his name. He had been two years behind me in school. We weren't good friends, just pieces of furniture in each other's lives. He had grown up four blocks away from me and now lived two blocks down the street, in the smallest house in the neighborhood. Any panel of judges would have taken one look at Haywood's house and voted it Least Likely to Be Looted. Haywood nevertheless insisted on risking his life to protect it. Outwardly conformist — clean-shaven, bright smile, well-combed dark wavy hair, neatly pressed polo shirts, gentle and seemingly indecisive manner — Haywood was capable all the same of generating a great deal of original behavior. This he did in the usual New Orleans way, by thinking things through at least halfway for himself before leaping into action. This quality in Haywood, the instinct to improvise, is also in the city; it's why New Orleans is so hospitable to jazz musicians, chefs, and poker players.

The others couldn't decide whether to pity or admire Haywood, but in the end they gave him all their extra guns and ammo. By the time the convoy left the city Thursday night, Haywood had himself a .357 magnum, a .38 Special, a 9-millimeter Beretta, and a sleek, black military-grade semiautomatic rifle, along with a sack holding one thousand rounds of ammunition. Like most of the men in Uptown New Orleans, Haywood knew how to shoot a duck. But he had never fired any of these weapons or weapons remotely like them. He didn't even know what the sleek black rifle was; he just called it an "AK Whatever It Is." But that Thursday night, he took the three pistols and the AK Whatever It Was and boarded himself up inside his house.

Immediately he had a problem: a small generator that powered one tiny window air-conditioning unit. It cooled just one small room, his office. But the thing made such a racket that, as he put it, "they could have busted down the front door and be storming inside and I wouldn't have heard them. There could have been twenty natives outside screaming, 'I'm gonna burn your house down,' and I'd a never heard it." Fearing he might nod off and be taken in his sleep, he jammed a rack filled with insurance-industry magazines against the door. (Haywood sells life insurance.) In his little office, he sat all night — as far as he knew, the last white person left in New Orleans. He tried to sleep, he said, but "I kept dreaming all night long someone was coming through the door." He didn't leave his air-conditioned office until first light, when he crept out and squinted through his mail slot. In that moment, he was what Uptown New Orleans had become, even before the storm: a white man, alone, peering out through a slot in search of what might kill him. All he needed was the answer.

But that moment passed, and when the sun rose, he did, too, and went back to Fort Huger for food and clean water and a bath, in the form of a dip in the swimming pool. An hour later, in his underpants, and with a pistol in his hand, he discovered that he had accidentally locked the door to Fort Huger behind him, leaving all his keys and clothes and guns, save the one pistol, inside the fort. He couldn't think of what to do — he certainly didn't want to do anything so rash as break one of Jim Huger's cut-glass windows — so he plopped down on the porch in his soggy boxer shorts with the gun in his lap and waited, hoping that the good guys would reach him before the bad guys did.

3. The Ex-Israeli Commandos and Their Russian Flying Machines

That's when I arrived — on the heels of the young men who fled town the night before. Unaware of Haywood's plight, I pulled up across the street from my parents' house, into the only spot clear of debris, in front of old Ms. Dottie Perrier's place. For many years now, the easiest way to determine if she was home had been to pull your car right up in front: if she was in, she would throw open her upstairs shutter and ask, sweetly, that you park someplace else. Now, along with going the wrong way down one-way streets, running stop signs, and crossing Audubon Park on the grass, parking right in front of Ms. Perrier's house was one of the new pleasures of driving around a city without any people in it.

The moment I cut the engine, her shutters sprang open. Out the front door she flew, with her white hair nicely coiffed and her big blue eyes blinking behind the oversize spectacles perched on her nose without earpieces. She had the air of an owl who has mistaken day for night. After spending the past five days inside her house, she was intensely curious.

"Where is everybody?" she asked.

"There's been a hurricane," I said. "The city has been evacuated. Everybody's gone."

"Really! So they've all left, et cetera?"

Her surprise was as genuine as her tone was pleasant. Two days before, it turned out, one of the men inside Fort Huger passed by and noticed outgoing mail in her slot. One letter was her electric bill — four days after the entire city lost power. He knocked on her door, told her she really should get out of town, and then tried to explain to her that the postman wasn't coming, perhaps for months. Whereupon Ms. Perrier put her hands on her hips and said, "Well, no one informed me!"

Just then a car turned the corner, rolled up to a house on the next block, and stopped. Its appearance was as shocking as the arrival of a spaceship filled with aliens — apart from Ms. Perrier, I hadn't seen a soul, or a car, for miles. Four men with black pistols leapt out of it. Two of them looked as if they belonged in the neighborhood — polo shirts, sound orthodontia, a certain diffidence in their step. But the other two, with their bad teeth and battle gear, marched around as if they had only just captured the place. Leaving Ms. Perrier, I wandered down and met my first former Israeli commandos, along with their Uptown New Orleans employers, who had come to liberate their homes.

They had just landed Russian assault helicopters in Audubon Park. Not one, but two groups of Uptown New Orleanians had rented these old Soviet choppers, along with four-to-six-man Israeli commando units (platoons? squads?), and swooped down onto the soccer field beside the Audubon Zoo. Down, down, down they had come, then jumped out to, as they put it, "secure the perimeter." Guns aimed, eyes darting, no point of the compass uncovered. As a young man in this new militia later told me: "Hell, yes, I was scared. We didn't know what to expect. We thought Zulu Nation might be coming out of the woods." But the only resistance they met was a zookeeper, who came out with his hands up.

All of this happened just moments before. Right here, in my hometown. All four men were still a little hopped up. The commandos went inside to "clear the house." A nice little yellow house just one block from my childhood home. Not a human being — apart from Ms. Perrier and me — for a mile in each direction. And yet they raised their guns, opened the door, entered, and rattled around. A few minutes later they emerged, looking grim.

"You got some mold on the upstairs ceiling," one commando said gravely.

4. Fears, from High Ground to Troubled Waters

Pretty quickly, it became clear that there were more than a few people left in the city and that they fell into two broad categories: extremely well-armed white men prepared to do battle and a ragtag collection of irregulars, black and white, who had no idea that there was anyone to do battle with. A great many of the irregulars were old people, like Ms. Perrier, who had no family outside New Orleans and so could not imagine where else they would go. But there were also plenty of people who, like the portly, topless, middle-aged gay couple in short shorts walking their dogs down St. Charles Avenue every day, seemed not to sense the slightest danger.

The city on high ground organized itself around the few houses turned into forts. By Saturday morning, Fort Huger was again alive with half a dozen young men who spent their day checking on houses and rescuing the two groups of living creatures most in need of help: old people and pets. Two doors down from my sister's house on Audubon Park was Fort Ryan, under the command of Bill Ryan, who lost an eye to a mortar in Vietnam, was hit by a hand grenade, and was shot through the arm and then returned home with a well-earned chestful of ribbons and medals. Him you could understand. He had passed the nights sitting on his porch with his son at his side and a rifle on his lap. "The funny thing is," he told me, "is that before now my son never asked me what happened in Vietnam. Now he wants to know."

The biggest fort of all was Fort Ramelli, a mansion on St. Charles Avenue. At Fort Ryan, they joked, lovingly, about Fort Ramelli. "We used to say that if a nuclear bomb went off in New Orleans, the only thing left would be the cockroaches and Bobby Ramelli," said Nick Ryan, Bill's son. "Now we're not so sure about the cockroaches." Bobby Ramelli and his son spent the first five days of the flood in his flatboat, pulling, they guessed, about three hundred people from the water.

The police had said that gangs of young black men were looting and killing their way across the city, and the news had reached the men inside the forts. These men also had another informational disadvantage: working TV sets. Over and over again, they replayed the same few horrifying scenes from the Superdome, the convention center, and a shop in downtown New Orleans. If the images were to be reduced to a sentence in the minds of Uptown New Orleans, that sentence would be: *Crazy black people with automatic weapons are out hunting white people, and there's no bag limit!* "The perspective you are getting from me," one of Fort Huger's foot soldiers said as he walked around the living room with an M-16, "is the perspective of the guy who is getting disinformation and reacting accordingly." He spoke, for those few days, for much of the city, including the mayor and the police chief.

No emotion is as absurd as fear when it is proved to be unjustified. I was aware of this; I was also aware that it is better to be absurdly alive than absurdly dead. I broke into the family duck-hunting closet, loaded a shotgun with birdshot, and headed out into the city. Running around with a 12-gauge filled with birdshot was, in the eyes of the local militia, little better than running around with a slingshot — or one of those guns that, when you shoot them, spit out a tiny flag. Over the next few days, I checked hundreds of houses and found that none had been broken into. The story about the children's hospital turned out to be just that, a story. The glass door to the Rite Aid on St. Charles near Broadway — where my paternal grandfather collapsed and died in 1979 — was shattered, but the only section disturbed was the shelf stocking the Wild Turkey. The Ace Hardware store on Oak Street was supposed to have had its front wall pulled off by a forklift, but it appeared to be, like most stores and all houses, perfectly intact. Of all the stores in town, none looked so well preserved as the bookshops. No one loots literature.

Oddly, the only rumor that contained even a grain of truth was the looting of Perlis. The window of the Uptown clothing store was shattered. But the alligator belts hung from their carousel, and the shirts with miniature crawfish emblazoned on their breasts lay stacked as neatly as they had been before Katrina churned up the gulf. On the floor was a ripped brown paper sack with two pairs of jeans inside: the thief lacked both ambition and conviction.

The old houses were also safe. There wasn't a house in the Garden District, or Uptown, that could not have been easily entered; there wasn't a house in either area that didn't have food and water to keep a family of five alive for a week; and there was hardly a house in either place that had been violated in any way. And the grocery stores! I spent some time inside a Whole Foods choosing from the selection of Power Bars. The door was open, the shelves groaned with untouched bottles of water and food. Downtown, twenty-five thousand people spent the previous four days without food and water when a few miles away — and it's a lovely stroll — entire grocery stores, doors ajar, were untouched. From the moment the crisis downtown began, there had been a clear path, requiring maybe an hour's walk, to food, water, and shelter. And no one, not a single person, it seemed, took it.

Here, in the most familial city in America, the people turned out to know even less of one another than they did of the ground on which they stood. Downtown, into which the people too poor to get themselves out of town had been shamefully herded by local authorities, I found the mirror image of the hysteria uptown. Inside the Superdome and the convention center, rumors started that the police chief, the mayor, and the national media passed along: of two hundred people murdered, of countless rapes, of hundreds of armed black gang members on the loose. (Weeks later, the *Times-Picayune* wrote that just two people were found killed and there had been no reports of rape. The murder rate in the city the week after Katrina hit was unchanged.) There, two poor people told me that the flood wasn't caused by nature but by man: the government was trying to kill poor people. (Another reason it may never have occurred to the poor to make their way into the homes and grocery stores of the rich is that they assumed the whole point of this event was for the rich to get a clean shot at the poor.) In their view, the whole thing, beginning with the levee break and ending with the cramming of thousands of innocent people into what they were sure were death chambers with murderers and rapists, was a setup.

My great-grandfather J. Blanc Monroe is dead and gone, but he didn't take with him the climate of suspicion between rich and poor that he apparently helped foster. On St. Claude Avenue, just below the

French Quarter, there was a scene of indigents, old people, and gay men employed in the arts fleeing what they took to be bombs being dropped on them by army helicopters. What were being dropped were, in fact, ready-to-eat meals and water in plastic jugs. But falling from the sky, these missiles looked unfriendly, and when the jugs hit concrete, they exploded and threw up shrapnel. The people in the area had heard from the police that George W. Bush intended to visit the city that day, and they could not imagine he meant them any good — but this attack, as they took it, came as a shock. "Run! Run!" screamed a man among the hordes trying to outrun the chopper. "It's the president!"

5. Securing Things, Including Dottie Perrier

Four days after I arrived, I walked down St. Charles Avenue and watched the most eclectic convoy of official vehicles ever assembled. It included (I couldn't write fast enough to list them all) the New York City Police Department, the Alameda County Fire Department, the Aspen Fire Department, the SPCA from somewhere in Kentucky, emergency-rescue trucks from Illinois and Arizona, the Austin Fire Department, the U.S. Coast Guard, the Consulate of Iceland, and several pickup trucks marked, mysteriously, "FPS: Federal Protection Services." The next day, the police chief said that New Orleans was "probably the safest city in America right now," and the mayor, removed to Dallas, announced that the city would be forcibly evacuated. The old social logic of New Orleans was now turned on its head: the only people welcome inside were those who had never before been there.

Overnight, the city went from being a place that you couldn't get out of to a place you had to be a conniver to stay in. In the few people who still needed to be saved there was a striking lack of urgency. When Lieutenant Governor Mitch Landrieu, rescuing people in a boat, spotted three young men on a roof and tried to ferry them out, they told him to leave them be and said, "We want to be helicoptered out." After my host, Jim Huger, took a pirogue to help an old man surrounded by floodwaters, he passed an old woman sitting on her porch and offered to rescue her too. "Are you the official Coast Guard?" she asked. He said he wasn't. "I'm waiting for the *official* Coast Guard," she said, and sat back down.

I had a half-dozen equally perplexing encounters. For instance, on one occasion I ran into a lady of a certain age, wearing a broad straw hat, pedaling a decrepit bicycle down the middle of St. Charles Avenue. She rode not in a straight line but a series of interlinked S's; it was as close as bike riding gets to wandering. I pulled up beside her in my car, rolled down the window, and saw, in her lap, a dog more odd than she. "It has two purebred pedigrees," she said. "One is Chihuahua and the other is poodle."

"Are you all right?" I asked.

"I'm fine!" she said. "It's a beautiful day."

"Do you want to evacuate?" I asked, because I couldn't think of what else to say.

"I have eighty dollars," she said, still smiling. "I'd like to go to New York, but you tell me how far you can go in New York with eighty dollars."

In the back of my car, I now had about sixty gallons of water, picked up from beside Uptown houses, with the intention of redistributing them to the needy. "Do you need anything?" I asked her. "Water? Food?"

"No," she said, still pedaling. "I have a lot of water and even more food."

As I pulled away toward the water, she shouted, "But I could use some ice!"

Until now it had been possible to get around without credentials. But with the National Guard banging on doors, telling people they had to leave the city, out came the most outlandish fake IDs I had laid eyes on since high school. One fellow got around on a Marriott Hotel security badge, another dummied up a laminated picture of himself that said he was a doctor. On Louisiana Avenue, one of the world's leading dealers of African sculpture, Charlie Davis, answered his door to National Guardsmen. He told them he was employed by newspapers as a photographer, but when he turned to get his (fake) press pass, he told me, "the guns went up." When asked how much force he would use to remove people from their homes, Police Chief

Eddie Compass said that he couldn't be precise because "if you are somebody who is 350 pounds, it will obviously take more force to move you than if you are 150 pounds." (Compass has since resigned.) Even the people who had come back home in Russian assault helicopters made a hasty exit, invariably leaving behind them, flying from a porch, the American flag. It was a symbol not of liberty but of personal defiance, a tribute to underdog-dom. It was aimed at the enemy and said, *Take that!* The Confederate flag had become unnecessary.

I drove over to give Ms. Perrier the news. Ms. Perrier weighs far less than 150 pounds. It would take almost no force, and little time, for the soldiers to cart her away. Wouldn't it be better if I drove her quietly out to the one hospital still open, the Ochsner Clinic, where she could be cared for?

"I'd rather go to Touro," she said. Touro is another New Orleans hospital, not as distinguished as Ochsner, but closer to her house.

"Touro's closed," I said. "Ochsner's the only hospital open in the city."

"Really! Why?"

We agreed that she would be packed and ready to go in the morning — and she was. She came out wearing a bright dress and a brave smile, carrying an ancient silver suitcase.

"When's the hurricane coming?" she asked.

"It already hit," I said, then realized it must seem callous to her to relate this shocking news in such a dull tone.

"You're kidding!" she said. "Well, I'm glad the worst is over."

It went like this all the way to the Ochsner ER. I left her at check-in, with an understanding that she would be evaluated and, I assumed, admitted. She sat down at the bank-teller-like window and produced her wallet with various ID cards. The lady in the window assured me that Ms. Perrier would be taken care of.

6. Afloat and Adrift

From there I set out into the water with a purpose. My brother had been found unjustifiably alive in Lafayette, Louisiana, studying satellite photographs on the Internet to determine just how many miles he would need to swim to get to his house. He alone of my immediate family had set up home beyond Uptown, but even so, he had bought an old house. For some time now, he has had this thing about his little shotgun cottage — it isn't just an ordinary affection; it's true love — and so the past few days he had been contemplating total loss. *It's all gone!*

I reached the floodwater a mile or so from the river. A mile farther, the street signs vanished below the surface, and the upper branches of old oak trees rose from the water like the fingers of drowning men. But the water didn't simply get deeper the closer you got to the lake. There were local highs and lows, so that it was actually very hard to get around in anything but a pirogue or an airboat without scraping the bottom. I picked up Charlie Davis, the African sculpture dealer masquerading as a photojournalist, and we drove down the Esplanade Ridge through a foot or so of water until we were as close as we assumed we could get to my brother's place. I had no idea that there was such a thing as the Esplanade Ridge — a strip of high ground that runs from the (high) river to the (low) lake — but in retrospect I should have. It is the one strip of land apart from old Crescent City that is decorated with lovely old homes. (It's where Degas lived during his year in New Orleans.) People built here originally because it was dry.

Before plunging off the side of the ridge, we shimmied into duck-hunting waders, surgical masks, and rubber gloves. The water was black and viscous and smelled only of petroleum, but the doctors at the Ochsner Clinic had said they were finding chemical burns on people who had been in it. Waist-deep, we gently ascended to the back of my brother's house — which was high and dry. The leaves in his yard crunched underfoot like fresh cornflakes. He had made his home on what amounted to a peninsula off one side of the Esplanade Ridge, saved by his preference for old New Orleans architecture.

On the way out, we were able to loop around to the car without getting wet. That's when we first heard the gunshots.

Pop!

Pop!

Pop!

They were coming from a house just across the street, maybe thirty yards away.

"That's a twenty-two," Charlie said. The last time Charlie was amid gunfire was when he went to Liberia to buy African sculpture and wound up hiding in an elevator shaft during a coup. He knows his gunshots.

Several things happened all at once. A hissing sound *(Psst! Psst!)* that, it occurred to me only later, and a bit hopefully, must have been bullets whizzing past us. (After the fact, more danger is always better than less.) Overhead, two sheriffs' helicopters swooped down. Coming toward us by land was the 82nd Airborne in their jaunty red berets. We ran.

The trouble was, there was nowhere to go. We reached the end of the Esplanade Ridge and found that the only way out was back the way we came. Retracing our path, we passed the house of the man with the gun, now surrounded by the 82nd Airborne. "He's not actually shooting at anybody," the soldier in charge said wearily. "He was just trying to get someone to bring him some water."

Three hours after I dropped her off, I returned to visit Ms. Perrier, who, I assumed, would be propped up in the geriatric ward, sipping warm milk, maybe watching a game show. The lady behind the desk looked down at a sheet. "She's been discharged," she said.

"How? She doesn't even have a car."

"She'd have been bused out," she said.

It was that word, "bused," that chilled the spine. The buses were controlled by the authorities. New Orleans now had a new word for what happens to people unlucky enough to fall into the hands of the authorities purporting to save them: domed. As in "I just got domed," or "If the police knock on your door, don't answer, 'cause you might get domed." To be domed is to be herded into a domed sports building — the Superdome, the Astrodome, the Maravich basketball arena at Louisiana State University — for your own safety. Ms. Perrier hadn't really wanted to leave her house in the first place. She had entrusted herself to me. Now she had been domed.

7. Two Very New Orleanian Reasons for Staying in New Orleans

New Orleanians often are slow to get to the point: in my youth it was not unusual for someone to call my mother, keep her on the phone for twenty minutes, hang up, then call back because she never got around to what the call was about in the first place. The point is never really the point. Conversation in New Orleans is not a tool but a pastime. New Orleans stories are given perhaps too much room to breathe; they go on and on so entertainingly that only later do you realize that there were things in them that made no sense.

At some moment, I realized that Haywood Hillyer's story made no sense. Why, really, had he stayed? The first time I asked him, he replied: "These other guys had children, so they felt it wasn't worth the risk. I didn't have children." This may have been true as far as it went, but it didn't really answer the question: childlessness is not a reason to risk your life. Just three months earlier, he married a lovely young woman who was reason enough to live. He wasn't by nature defiant, or belligerent. He was just different, in some hard-to-see but meaningful way.

The fourth time (in four days) that I put the same question to him — Yeah, but why did you stay? — Haywood stood and, with the air of a man ready to make his final statement, said: "OK, I'll tell you why I stayed. *But this is totally off the record.*"

"Fine, it's off the record."

"*Totally* off the record."

"OK, totally off the record."

"There were these feral kittens under my house," he began, and off he went, explaining how these little kittens had come to depend on him, how three of them now live with him but two still refuse to let him near them, even though he feeds them. There's a long story that he swore was interesting about how these cats got under his house in the first place, but the point was this: *If he left, there would be no one in New Orleans to feed the cats.*

Haywood Hillyer stayed and, for all anyone knew then, risked being skinned alive or worse to feed cats. And the cats didn't even like him.

Two days later, as he was pulling out of town, I explained to Haywood that he just had to let me put his story on the record. "It'll make me look like a wuss," he said. I convinced him that in view of the fact that his bravery exceeded that of the entire police department and possibly the armed forces of the United States, the last thing he would look like is a wuss.

"All right," he finally said, "but then you got to get the story exactly straight. There was one other reason I stayed. It wasn't as important as the cats. But it wouldn't be a true story unless you mentioned the other reason."

"What's the other reason?"

"The traffic."

"What?"

"It took my wife twelve *hours* to drive from New Orleans to Jackson on Sunday," he said. "She left Sunday at one P.M. and arrived in Jackson at one A.M."

"So?"

"That's usually a two-and-a-half-hour drive."

"Right. So what?"

"You don't understand: I *hate* traffic."

8. A City of Storytelling — and a Little Hope

There's a reason that New Orleanians often turn out to be as distinctive as their homes. The city doesn't so much celebrate individualism as assume it. It has a social reflex unlike any other I've encountered: people's first reaction to other people is to be amused by them — unless of course they've been told by the police that they are about to be killed by them.

If the behavior of the people was peculiar once the flooding started, it was peculiar in the way New Orleanians are peculiar. At the outset people were shockingly slow-footed. But then New Orleanians are always shockingly slow-footed. Even the most urgent news, the levee break, took twenty hours to officially reach the people in harm's way, long after the water itself did. But news isn't what New Orleanians tell; stories are. And the long days after the waters leveled off were a perfect storytelling environment — no reliable information, a great many wild rumors, the most outlandish fictions suddenly plausible — and the people used it to do what they do best. But so far as I can tell — and I covered much of the city, along with every inch of the high ground — very few of the many terrible things that people are reported to have done to one another ever happened. With the brutal exception of the violent young men forcibly detained in the Super-dome and the convention center with twenty-five thousand or so po-tential victims, civilians actually treated one another extremely well. (There's a different story to tell about government officials.) So far as I can tell, no one supposedly defending his property actually fired a shot at anyone else — though there have been a couple of stories, unconfirmed, of warning shots being fired. Yet even as the water flowed back out of the city, my father called to say that a friend in exile had just informed him that "they had to shoot about five hundred looters." The only looter admitted to Ochsner, the city's one function-ing hospital, was a white guy who was beaten, not shot — though badly enough that a surgeon had to remove his spleen.

Driving out of New Orleans to search for Ms. Perrier, I had a deli-cious sensation I associate with home, of feeling something that I ought not to feel and of being allowed to feel it. I had come to New Or-leans because I felt obliged: I had skipped too many funerals already and didn't think I should miss the last big one. But the flood did not drown the past; it forced it to the surface, like one of those tightly sealed plastic coffins that, when the water comes in over the grave-yard, shoot through the dirt and into broad daylight. (Yes, it turns out that we buried some of our dead in the ground too, and that the ground was perfectly capable of receiving them.) The levees were breached, but something else cracked, too, inside the people behind them. The old façade: the pretense that New Orleans was either the Big Easy or it was nothing; that no great change was ever possible. A lot of New Orleanians, from the mayor on down, obviously did not feel so easy. They harbored a deep distrust of their own city and their fellow citizens — which is why they were so quick to believe the most hysterical rumors about one another. The waters came to expose those fears and to mock them. The ghosts have been flushed out of their hiding places; now there's a chance to chase them away, or at least holler at them a bit.

The late great novelist Walker Percy, a lifelong New Orleanian, was attracted to the psychological state of the ex-suicide. The ex-suicide is the man who has tried to kill himself and failed. Before his suicide attempt, he had nothing to live for. Now, expecting to be dead and discovering himself alive, something inside him awakens: so long as he's alive, he might as well give living a shot. The whole of New Orleans is in this psychological state. The waters did their worst but still left the old city intact. They did to the public schools and the public-housing projects what the government should have done long ago. They called forth tens of billions of dollars in aid, and the attention of energetic people, to a city long starved of capital and energy. For the first time in my life, outsiders are pouring into the city to do something other than drink. For the first time in my life, the city is alive with possibilities. For the first time in my life, it doesn't matter one bit who is born to be a king. Whatever else New Orleans is right now, it isn't stagnant. As I left, I thought about what an oddly characteristic thing it would be if it was a flood that saved New Orleans.

There was to be no finding Ms. Perrier in the flesh, only the spot where her trail went cold. After a frantic search, a woman at Ochsner found that Dorothy Perrier of State Street had been bused with other refugees to the Maravich arena in Baton Rouge. From there, no one could say what had become of her. "This isn't going to take five minutes," a woman working in Missing Persons at the basketball arena said. "We have no records for most of the people who came through here." But it took exactly five minutes for her to return with the news that there were no records for Ms. Perrier. Anywhere. "Even if she did go through here, we wouldn't necessarily have a record," she said. Most likely, she added, she was bused to a shelter in Alexandria or Lake Charles. To me that sounded like wishful thinking: there wasn't room in the state for but a relative handful of the one million New Orleanians who evacuated in the past week. But on my way out, she handed me a piece of paper with phone numbers for the Red Cross. "You might try them," she said. "Sometimes they can find lost people."

I don't know why it never occurred to me to call the Red Cross. I suppose I always thought of them as something to give money to, not ask help from. But from my gate at the airport, I phoned the Red Cross, and in what seemed like an instant, a man told me, "Here she is — in Battle Creek."

"Battle Creek, Louisiana?" I asked hopefully.

"Battle Creek, Michigan," he said. He gave me another number, and in a minute or so Ms. Perrier herself was on the other end of the line. She couldn't have been more pleasant, even as she remained bewildered by what had just happened to her. It all took place so fast, she said, that she didn't even remember how she got from her house on State Street all the way to Michigan. (And thank God for that.) "Everyone up here is so nice, et cetera," she said. "But I really just want to go home."

■

Are Iraqis Optimistic?

In late 2005, the Pentagon contracted the Lincoln Group, a Washington-based defense contractor, to aid the U.S. military in a covert effort to plant articles in a number of Iraqi newspapers. These stories, written by American soldiers but presented as unbiased accounts from independent Iraqi journalists and citizens, denounced the insurgency and gave a positive spin to the U.S. occupation of Iraq. This piece, targeted at the national Iraqi newspaper As-Safeer, *was never published.*

I WAS SURPRISED when last month I saw a poll of our people that showed that most Iraqis are optimistic about the future of our country. Many Iraqis complain about security, corruption, and lack of electricity, so I wondered how this could be true. I decided to look deeper into this statement.

First I had to find out what exactly a poll is. A poll is an instrument used to scientifically measure public opinion, just like a ruler is an instrument used to scientifically measure distance. Under Saddam, public opinion wasn't something anyone in power wanted to know about, so no polls were conducted, save the ten-year census. Even that was more of a propaganda tool than a scientific instrument.

Polling works because people of various backgrounds, education, religious affiliation, and ethnic groups are asked about their opinion. For instance, people with a university education are chosen in proportion to their population in Iraq, as are urban residents and rural residents. Their answers are tallied up and the results are representative of the Iraqi population. If used properly, a poll measures people's opinions.

In September, an Iraqi polling firm asked 3,000 Iraqis to participate in a poll, and 2,728 people agreed to participate, in 17 of Iraq's
governorates. The poll showed that most Iraqis believe that life in
Iraq will be better in six months. Fully fifty percent of Iraqis think
the situation in our country will be better in six months. Sixty-three
percent of Iraqis think the situation in our country will be better after
one year.

Why do they think things are getting better? Twenty-six percent
find hope in the fact that we now have a nationally elected government. Twenty-two percent say that democracy and liberty give them
optimism for the future. The constitution makes eleven percent of
Iraqis think that the future is getting better for our country.

Concern about security and stability is the number one reason
Iraqis are not optimistic about the future. Forty-four percent of those
who participated in the poll named this concern as their number one
concern about the future of Iraq.

This is not surprising. We are constantly reminded of our insecu-
rity in our country. The foreign terrorists bomb another target every
day — sometimes several times a day. My heart breaks every time I
hear about another innocent child killed by terrorists whose personal
vision of jihad makes them think that blowing up Iraqi children will
provide riches from Allah to them.

But half of our countrymen look past our lack of security and find
reason to be optimistic, and there are reasons to be optimistic. Our
national wealth is once again our own, instead of that of a terrible dic-
tator. Hundreds of thousands of satellite TVs are in Iraqi homes —
once a crime that would get one thrown in prison. Traffic in Baghdad
is bad, but it is because more people now have the money to own a
nice car, and everybody has the freedom to visit their families and
friends without fear of government retribution. Most important, we
can now practice our religion as we choose, whether we are Sunni,
Shia, or Christian.

Iraq certainly has problems. But the biggest problem — the lack of
security — is something that we can solve ourselves. The foreign terrorists are friend to nobody in Iraq, and cannot operate here if we as
Iraqis do not let them. Brave Iraqis in Al Anbar are standing up to the
terrorist thugs and refusing to give them shelter. Some pay the ulti-

mate price for being loyal to Iraq, although many find that the foreign religious extremists are cowards who only have the bravery to kill unsuspecting women and children with a bomb disguised as a car. If you stand up to them, they will back down.

And Sunni religious and political leaders are encouraging the Iraqi insurgency to lay down their arms with honor, rejoin their families, and make their voice heard peacefully, through participating in elections.

Everybody has something to be optimistic about in our country. We must stand united as Iraqis and solve our problems and create a beautiful future for our children.

■

Room No. 12

FROM *Zoetrope: All-Story*

THE HOTEL MANAGER RECALLS, like a photo he can never forget, how one day a woman came to take a room for just twenty-four hours. The time was exactly 10 A.M. The sight of such a stunning member of the opposite sex approaching him, utterly unaccompanied, made him stare at her, intrigued. Equally unforgettable: she seemed a woman of formidable influence — obvious in the firmness of her build, the fineness of her features, and the sharpness of her gaze. She stopped at the front desk, standing bolt upright in her red gown and white hat. She had no personal identity card, and was neither employed nor married. Most likely she was divorced or a widow. Her name was Bahiga al-Dahabi, and came from Mansoura in the Delta. The man recorded all the necessary information, then pointed her toward a bellhop. The bellhop walked ahead of her, carrying her bag — one heavier than he was used to — leading her to room no. 12 in the little hotel.

The bellhop returned after half an hour, an amazed look on his face. When the manager asked him what had happened, he replied, "She's a very eccentric woman."

"What do you mean?" the manager wondered.

The bellhop said that she'd asked him to strip the coverlet, blanket, and sheets from the bed and to put them in the corner of the room until nightfall. As for the bed itself, she requested that he move it outside the room altogether, with the excuse that she could not sleep so long as there was a space beneath her large enough to conceal a man. He told her that her fear was groundless, that there had never been any kind of incident in the hotel since its founding. But she insisted, so he bowed to her will.

"You should have come back to me immediately," said the manager.

The bellhop apologized, saying that while her request was peculiar, it did not exceed any of the duties the hotel was bound to fulfill. Then he resumed his story: she had ordered him to open wide the doors of her wardrobe and to leave them open. The bellhop could tell from her voice that she was afraid a stranger could hide inside the wardrobe if it were closed. So he carried out her command, smiling as he did so, he said.

"The amazing part is that she seemed so strong and brave," remarked the manager.

He thought for a bit longer, then asked, "Did she cough up a tip?"

"A whole half-pound," bragged the bellhop.

"She's certainly not typical, but there's no harm in that," the manager replied.

"I was passing by her locked-up room on my way to the laundry when I heard a voice speaking very excitedly inside," said the bellhop.

"But isn't she by herself?"

"Still, she was talking angrily, and her voice kept getting louder as she did."

"A lot of people do that," the manager said. "Just because you talk to yourself doesn't mean that you're crazy."

The bellhop shook his head without saying anything, so the manager asked him, "Were you able to make out anything she was saying?"

"No — except one expression: 'It's not important.'"

The manager signaled firmly that he wanted to end their discussion. Then, as he was writing in the register, he added to the bellhop, "Be ever more vigilant — that's our obligation, in any case."

Thunder sounded, and the manager looked at the sky through the window and found it thickly overcast with clouds. The weather had been very cold, with occasional showers of rain. At precisely 1 P.M., the woman telephoned from room no. 12.

"May I order lunch?" she inquired.

"We have no food in the hotel, but there's a restaurant on the street," the manager told her. "What would you like, ma'am?"

"Mixed vegetables with chicken," she answered, "plus rice with minced meat and onions, a kilogram of varied sorts of kebab, a set of Oriental salads, a loaf of bread grilled with lamb, soft pastries, and two oranges."

The manager ordered all that she requested. Yet he was astounded by how much food she wanted, especially the meat. That alone would have been enough for six persons!

"She's crazy not just with fear, but with gluttony, too," he said to himself. "Most likely she'll leave the hotel during the afternoon, and I'll be able to get a look inside her room."

The food arrived, and an hour later the man from the restaurant returned to collect the tray and china. The manager couldn't resist looking at the plates — and found them all licked clean, except for the remains of some bones and congealed sauce. He decided to put the whole business out of his mind, but nonetheless found that the woman — the strange way she looked and acted — kept pursuing him, pressing in on his thoughts. He couldn't say that she was beautiful, yet she had a kind of force and attraction. There was something frightening about her, along with things that aroused curiosity and even submission. And though he'd seen her for the very first time only that day, she'd left an impression of familiarity that comes with faces that have embedded themselves in one's memory from days of old.

He saw a man and woman coming toward him. "Is Madam Bahiga al-Dahabi staying here?" the man queried.

The hotel manager answered in the affirmative, then telephoned to ask if the lady would let the visitors go up to her room. Obviously these people were from the upper crust, at least in terms of material wealth. The wind wailed powerfully, making the chandeliers dance in the hotel's small lobby. Then quickly another eight persons arrived — four men and four women — and repeated the same question.

"Is Mrs. Bahiga al-Dahabi staying here?"

Again the manager telephoned to obtain the guest's permission. That being granted, the group, with a lofty air — they were from the same elevated crowd as the couple that preceded them — mounted the stairs to room no. 12. There were now ten visitors in all — either relatives from one family, or friends, or friends and relatives combined. Whatever the case might be, there was no doubt that Madam Bahiga was no ordinary dame.

Why did she choose our hotel? he wondered.

Bustle spread through the establishment's bar as the staff carried tumblers of tea above, and it occurred to the manager that he had seen some of the faces in the second group before. But then he said to himself that the best thing would be to purge his brain of any thoughts of Bahiga al-Dahabi. Tomorrow she would be just another one of hundreds of lost memories that cluttered the little hotel.

Then he found before him a woman of about fifty, possessing the ultimate in poise and comportment. "Is Madam Bahiga al-Dahabi in residence?"

When he said yes, she told him, "Tell her, if you please, that the lady doctor is here."

He contacted the Madam, who said the physician could come up. Then he yielded to an insistent urge by asking, before she left him, "What is your specialization, Doctor?"

"Obstetrics," the woman replied.

He noticed that she had introduced herself with her professional title, but without her name. *Is she visiting the woman in that capacity? Is Bahiga al-Dahabi suffering from a feminine condition? Is she pregnant?* Yet he was not able to give full rein to his thoughts before a short, fat man with a scowling face marched in, introducing himself as Yusuf Qabil, contractor. He posed the much-repeated question, "Is Madam Bahiga al-Dahabi here?"

After the hotel manager had sought and obtained permission for the contractor to go up to her room, he bid the man goodbye with a perplexed and sarcastic smile. Meanwhile, one of the bellhops returned from an errand outside, shivering from the cold under his thick, rustic galabia. Darkness, he said, was gathering in the four corners of the sky, and soon the day would be turned into night. The manager glanced again out the window, but he was really thinking about the woman in room no. 12 — the mysterious femme fatale with her top-drawer coterie. He began to feel that a current of unrest and unease had spread through the hotel since her arrival. It permeated his own inner being, arousing within him adolescent dreams of the languorous splendor of rich, worldly occupations.

He was jolted from his reverie by a voice asking, "Is Madam Bahiga al-Dahabi here?"

He beheld a big man wrapped in a jubba and caftan, a tarbouche tilted back on his head, his hand gripping a gray umbrella. "Tell her that Blind Sayyid the Corpse Washer has come."

His chest heaving with revulsion, the manager gritted his teeth and cursed the man and the woman both — but he did his duty by calling her. For the first time, he met a contrary response.

"Please wait in the lobby, sir," he told the undertaker.

What did he *come to do here? Why doesn't he wait outside?* The manager had worked in the hotel for fifty years, yet had never seen anything like what was happening that day. He was afraid that the rain would start coming down in torrents, keeping them all locked inside the hotel for no one knew how long — and with this messenger of death!

New visitors arrived. They came separately, but in succession: the owner of a furniture store, a grocer, a sugarcane-juice vendor, the proprietor of a shop for cosmetics and perfumes, a high official in the revenue department, the editor of a well-known newspaper, a fish wholesaler, a procurer of furnished flats, an agent for an Arab millionaire. The manager thought the lady would move her meeting down to the lobby, but instead she kept granting permission for them to come up, one after the other. The bellhops brought them more and more tea and chairs, while the manager wondered how they could all find places to sit. *Did they all know each other before? And what, exactly, has brought them together now?* He summoned the head bellhop and asked him what he knew about these things.

"I don't know what's going on inside," he answered. "Hands reach out to take the chairs and the tea, then the door closes again immediately."

The manager shrugged his shoulders. So long as no one complained, he told himself, he was not to blame for anything.

Blind Sayyid the Corpse Washer came up to him. "I'd like to remind the lady that I am here waiting," he said.

"She promised to call you at the appropriate time," the manager told him with a feeling of futility.

The man wouldn't move, so the manager called the lady again, handing the mortician the telephone at her request.

"Madam, it's already past the afternoon prayer, and the days in winter are very short," the man chided.

He bent into the receiver, listening for a moment, then put it back and returned to the lobby, clearly disturbed. The manager damned him from his deepest heart. *The woman is responsible for inviting this ghoul to the hotel,* he thought as he glanced at the lobby's door with aversion and disgust. Meanwhile, some of the lady's guests came down on their way outside, and the manager's apprehensions about the goings-on in room no. 12 seemed to lessen.

"Some of the visitors will go sooner and some later; they'll all be gone by nightfall," he said to himself defensively.

He began to worry that his position of responsibility would force him into a confrontation with them — and they were from a powerful class. His dismay redoubled with the wind that whistled violently outdoors and the sense of distress that cloaked the roads. Yet despite these forbidding conditions, he saw a group of men and women wearing raincoats gathered at the hotel door, and his heart sank in his chest. He surprised them by asking, "Madam Bahiga al-Dahabi?"

One of them, laughing, replied, "Tell her, if you please, that the delegates from the Association for Heritage Revival have arrived."

So he telephoned the woman, and as she gave her consent for them to come up, he pleaded with her: "There are ten of them, Madam, and the lobby downstairs is at your disposal for any number of visitors."

"There's plenty of space in the room," she retorted.

As the delegates ascended, the manager shook his head in total confusion. *Sooner or later there's going to be a clash,* he thought. The fury of heaven was about to descend outside, provoked by the assorted oddballs in room no. 12. The manager chanced to turn to the lobby, and caught sight of Blind Sayyid the Corpse Washer creeping toward him. He rapped the table with his knuckles in agitation, then put the man directly in touch with the woman by telephone before he could open his mouth. The manager listened to him complain to her, then heard him accede. The undertaker hung up the receiver by himself, but then grumbled as the manager began to walk away, "Waiting around with nothing to do is very boring."

The manager became enraged, and would have scolded him if the lady hadn't telephoned at that moment, asking to be connected to the restaurant. Her conversation with them continued for some minutes. *Will she and her guests remain in the room until dinner,* the manager pondered, *and where will they dine?* How he wished he could examine her room as it was right then. It had to be a scene beyond all imagining — an insane spectacle indeed.

While the torrent continued outside without any hint of slowing, a group of university professors and men of religion came, so immersed in deep discussion that the manager simply let them go upstairs. The situation was becoming more and more nightmarish as a mysterious man went up without first passing by the desk. The manager called out to the intruder, who did not respond. One of the bellhops followed him, but stopped when the man ducked into room no. 12. The manager now felt he was alone, that he had lost fundamental control of the hotel. He considered summoning the head bellhop, but then a man appeared, the mere sight of whom brought him relief. They shook hands and the manager told him, "You've come at the right time, Honorable Informer, sir."

"Show me the register," the informer said calmly.

"Strange things are happening here," the manager blurted.

As the informer perused the names in the ledger, jotting down notes as he read, the manager said, "I suppose you've come because of room number twelve." He added, "Mad depravity is running riot in there."

"Anything found in nature must be natural," the informer said dismissively. Then, taking his leave, he said, "If anyone wants me on the phone, I'll be in room number twelve."

The manager became even more confused, yet at the same time he was comforted to think that the government's eyes and ears knew what was happening in the hotel. He remembered that he was going to summon the head bellhop, and just as he pressed the ringer to call him, he observed Blind Sayyid once again slinking up to him. Losing his grip on his nerves, he shouted, "She told you to wait until she invited you up!"

The man grinned at the rebuke in habitual servility, then pleaded, "But I've been waiting so long . . ."

"Wait without any back talk — and remember, you're in a hotel, not a boneyard!" the manager fumed.

The man retreated in feigned patience as the manager called the head bellhop. "How are things going in room number twelve?" he queried.

"I don't know, but there's a lot of racket in there."

"How can they all squeeze into that place? They must be sitting on top of each other!" the manager marveled.

"I don't know any more than you do," the head bellhop answered. "In any case, the officer is inside with them."

The manager went to look once more out the window and saw the night weighing heavily in the void. The lights had gone on throughout the hotel, casting a wan radiance over the atmosphere, thick with damp from the howling, raging wind outside. A battalion of waiters came from the restaurant, bearing trays crammed with all kinds of food, and the manager's astonishment grew. *The room has only one dining table, so where will the woman's guests put all those plates? How can they consume their meals?* One of the bellhops told him that the room's door no longer opened, and that the food now went in only through the little peep window. What's more, the uproar from the room was afflicting the entire hotel: the whole spectacle was simply incredible.

After a half-hour, the bellhop came back from room no. 12 to confirm that the lot of them were drunk.

"But I haven't seen a single bottle go up there!" exclaimed the manager.

"Maybe they hid them in their pockets," the bellhop surmised. "They're singing, shouting, and clapping. A case of drunken rowdiness, to be sure, and sinfulness too, for there are as many women as men in that room."

"And the informer?"

"I heard his voice singing 'The World Is a Smoke and a Drink,'" said the bellhop.

Thunder boomed outside as the manager said to himself, "I could well be dreaming, and I could just as well have gone mad." At that instant, a group of common people approached; their faces and clothes proclaimed their low social status. They asked the inevitable question: "Is Mrs. Bahiga al-Dahabi staying here?"

The manager smiled despairingly and contacted the woman. She asked him to keep them waiting in the lobby and to serve them drinks as well. The lobby was now overflowing, upsetting the undertaker. The manager again smiled hopelessly, muttering, "This hotel is no longer a hotel, and I'm no longer the manager, and today is not a day, and lunacy is laughing at us in the shape of meat and wine!"

The rain began to gush down again in sheets, and the sky to thunder. The asphalt at the hotel's entrance gleamed with the light of the electric lamps as feet scurried in from outside. The bellhops all cried, "There is no god but God!" while the passersby took refuge in the foyer. The battering blows of the rain rattled the windowpanes without ceasing. The manager left his post and went to the entrance, turning his face up to the blackened sky. Then he looked down at the water sluicing stones over the sloping ground. First the rain beat down, then it flared up with wrath, before detonating in a surging deluge over the hapless earth.

"There hasn't been rain like this for at least a generation," he declared.

Digging back in his past, he remembered a similar flood from his childhood. He recalled how it stopped all means of transport, filling up the alleys and completely drowning rooms — and those in them — beneath porous roofs. He then went back to his desk, intent upon his work with the hotel records and expenditures, but he also issued orders to tighten surveillance of the rooms and of the roof. He called the head bellhop and asked him, "What news of room number twelve?"

"The singing and laughing shows no sign of stopping," the man said, twisting his lips. "They're crazy in there!"

Blind Sayyid the Corpse Washer loomed at the lobby's door.

"Get back to your place!" shrieked the manager.

The undertaker held up his hand in entreaty, and the manager yelled at him once more, "Not another word!"

The thunder clapped like bombs and the rain pounded the pavement with intensity. The manager mused that the old hotel wasn't built with reinforced concrete — and the night warned of yet more travails.

Another bellhop told him, "There are complaints in number twelve about the leaky roof and the water pouring in."

"You mean they've stopped laughing and singing?" the manager demanded, exasperated. "Then let them all leave the room now!"

"But they can't!" protested the bellhop.

The manager dismissed him and once again called the head bellhop, asking him about what his assistant had said.

"The rooms are all leaking, so I've mobilized the men to plug the holes in the roof with sandbags."

"And room number twelve?"

"They're all jammed in there too tightly. Their stomachs have inflated so much they can't open the door. They can't even move!"

Cosmic ire was smiting the night outside, while inside a frenzied air filled the hotel as the bellhops scurried about with sandbags to halt the invading rain.

Then a most peculiar thing happened: the people who'd been waiting in the lobby rushed to aid in the effort. The manager watched all this with delight, made greater by the fact that Blind Sayyid the Corpse Washer did not take part.

After a while the head bellhop reported on the work's progress. "They're putting all they've got into it," he said with pride. "But as for our friends in room number twelve, their condition is very bad, and getting worse and worse all the time."

What the man said struck the manager like a shock, and amid the violent, pent-up tension of the entire day, he snapped. His anger taking hold of his flesh, his blood, and his nerves at once, he finally surrendered his last shred of sanity.

"Listen," he said. "Remember exactly what I'm about to tell you." The bellhop stared at his face in terror as the manager shouted with stark resolve, "Ignore room number twelve and everyone in it!"

"Sir, the men are screaming and the women are crying!"

Bellowing like a beast, the manager railed, "Concentrate on the roof over the guest rooms, but as for room number twelve, *leave it alone — and everyone inside it!*"

The bellhop tarried for merely a second, and the manager foamed with an even more animal-like fervor: "Carry out my instructions to the letter without dragging your feet!"

The manager moved to face the window and watched the storm crashing in the heart of the darkness, waxing more and more perilous with each passing moment. Yet he felt his great burden lighten, as his confidence returned with his clarity of mind.

Translated by Raymond Stock

RICK MOODY

■

Pirate Station

FROM *Gargoyle*

FOR THE FIRST TWENTY-FOUR HOURS, the pirate station broadcasts
the sound of someone coughing nervously. An august beginning. It's
not the dead air of the rural FM dial. It's someone coughing nervously. Much nervousness at the pirate station, and thus much nervous coughing. The next Tuesday a jazz band is convened, so that live
jazz might be broadcast on the pirate station. None of the players has
ever had a lesson on his instrument. These include soprano sax,
vibes, electric guitar, bass, drums, mellotron. Three idioms of jazz are
agreed upon: cool jazz, smooth jazz, Afro-Cuban jazz. At the count of
three, the ensemble begins. The pirate station broadcasts the music
of this ensemble for six days, without ceasing. There's no agreed-
upon coda for the piece, the pirate station simply pulls the plug.

That fall, after weeks of casting about, a symphony is written by filling in notes on a staff at random. A local orchestra attempts to pick
out the piece without rehearsal. However, the symphony is considered too sentimental for broadcast. A bird-call program is surprisingly popular, however, with the great horned howl coming in for
most requests, these issuing from the sheriff's office. Perhaps it's the
lonely night patrolman of the graveyard shift. The sounds of south-
western cacti are broadcast for several weeks until, by general assent,
it is agreed that cacti make no sounds.

The pirate station branches out. It broadcasts, over twelve nights, a
comparative study of whistles, including pennywhistles, the starter's
whistle that your high school track coach favored when in an ornery
mood, and that guy up the street who can whistle like nobody's business. Briefly, the pirate station backpedals reluctantly and agrees

to play musical recordings of the conventional sort, but only if the selections alternate in the following way: salsa, mariachi, tejana, reggae, Tuvan throat singing, thumb-piano concertos, music released in 1964, and songs sung by tone-deaf people. And yet these categories are considered too easy to fill, and after a week or so the pirate station loses interest.

The pirate station broadcasts news programs, but never at the top of the hour, and only when bootlegged from other stations. The substance of the news in these programs is altered slightly in order to mislead: the weather is said to be sunny, no matter the weather; the stock market is said to be going down without respite; the high school football team is said to be losing; newcomers are said to be bringing prosperity to the town; and the war is always said to be going smoothly, with little loss of civilian life. The pirate station broadcasts a single chord, a major third, key of A, for four consecutive days. Here's the secret to this particular broadcast: a toy organ has the relevant keys held down with duct tape.

Upon the return of pirate station employees from the holidays, a period of reflection sets in. The microphone is turned on and all the pirate station disc jockeys gather around and speak of their uncertainty about the pirate station. What could be done differently with the medium? What can the pirate station do that no one has done before? Is complete liberty not terrifying in some fundamental way? Can we burn in effigy a classic-rock deejay and a shock jock and broadcast these burnings live? A recording of this staff meeting is then played backward, sped up slightly, on the pirate station, with the harmonious conclusion first and the confusion at the end.

The pirate station sends people out into the street, humming, with contact mikes, the only requirement being that they hum songs with the word "joy" in the title, though not that song by Three Dog Night. Inducing strangers and townspeople on the street to hum along is considered particularly exciting. At the conclusion of the program, the unpleasant man at the dollar store is persuaded to hum "Frosty the Snowman," though it is spring. A contest is announced on the pirate station to find the person who has the best radio voice. This person is then tickled mercilessly on air and driven blindfolded to a distant metropolis. The sounds of people making love are broadcast for

the entire month of May, rising to a crescendo of simultaneous or-
gasms on May the fourteenth and then dwindling away to some
heavy breathing and delicate sighs by the first of June, just in time for
summer.

The doors of the pirate station are thrown open and anyone is invited in. The building that houses the pirate station is demolished,
and the station moves out into the rubble. Soon the pirate station begins moving, night after night, never staying in one place for more
than a few hours. Interns carry the transmitter in its small red tool-
box. The pirate station becomes a condition of all possible sounds, so
that everything is a song, and there is no commercial interruption
and no fundraising drives. The people who began the pirate station
grow old, marry, have children, make out wills, and leave the pirate
station behind. The children of the pirate station owners take up
incendiary devices in lieu of better-paying professions. They move
to different cities where they claim to be uninterested in radio, which
they consider less avant-garde than crayons on construction paper,
but then they order transmitter kits from foreign countries nonetheless.

The sounds of freight trains begin to sound suspiciously like
broadcasts on the pirate station, and the sounds of police sirens begin
to sound suspiciously like broadcasts on the pirate station, the sounds
of cheerleaders goading on the local football team are definitely prere-
corded and borrowed from the pirate station, and any music produced in the year 1964 seems to suggest that the pirate station is back
on line and up to its old tricks. The Federal Communications Commission becomes obsessed with the possibility that the pirate station
is continuing to broadcast but at wattages so meager and in places so
far flung that no one at all can tune the programming. Still, this is un-
acceptable.

The pirate station refuses to cooperate with finding the enemy. The
pirate station refuses to inform on its neighbors. The pirate station no
longer takes photographs the way it did when young. The pirate station once thought gardening was satisfying, but no longer. The pirate
station makes its own bricks, using mud from the backyard. The pirate station forgets the name of distant relations and people it met
only recently. The pirate station goes off its medication. The pirate

station quarrels frequently and is testy about things that never used to bother it. The pirate station eats infrequently. The pirate station loses interest in worldly things. The pirate station never calls. The pirate station imagines it can hear the music of the spheres and begins to totter down a long narrow corridor the color of purple, in which many dead friends beckon to it, but just when it is about to sleep its eternal sleep, the pirate station reconsiders, and remarks, haltingly, that it has work yet to do.

HARUKI MURAKAMI

■

The Kidney-Shaped Stone That Moves Every Day

FROM *The New Yorker*

JUNPEI WAS SIXTEEN YEARS OLD when his father made a surprising pronouncement. True, they were father and son; the same blood flowed through their veins. But they were not so close that they often opened their hearts to each other and it was extremely rare for Junpei's father to offer him views of life that might (perhaps) be called philosophical. So that day's exchange would remain vivid in his memory long after he had forgotten what prompted it.

"Among the women a man meets in his life, there are only three who have real meaning for him. No more, no less," his father said — or, rather, declared. He spoke coolly but with utter certainty, as he might have in noting that the earth takes a year to revolve around the sun. Junpei listened in silence, partly because his father's speech was so unexpected; he could think of nothing to say on the spur of the moment.

"You will probably become involved with many women in the future," his father continued, "but you will be wasting your time if a woman is the wrong one for you. I want you to remember that."

Later, several questions formed in Junpei's young mind: Has my father already met his three women? Is my mother one of them? And if so, what happened with the other two? But he was not able to ask his father these questions. As noted earlier, the two were not on such close terms that they could speak heart to heart.

*

When Junpei was eighteen, he left home and went to college in To-kyo, where over time he became involved with several women, one of whom had "real meaning" for him. Before he could express his feel-ings, however (by nature, it took him longer than most people to express his feelings), she married his best friend, and soon after that became a mother. For the time being, therefore, she had to be elimi-nated from the list of possibilities that life had to offer Junpei. He had to harden his heart and sweep her from his mind, as a result of which the number of women remaining who would have real meaning in his life — if he accepted his father's theory — was reduced to two.

Whenever Junpei met a new woman, he would ask himself, Is this a woman who has real meaning for me? And the question would cre-ate a dilemma. For even as he continued to hope (as who does not?) that he would meet someone who had real meaning for him, he was afraid of playing his few remaining cards too early. Having failed to connect with the very first important Other he encountered, Junpei had lost confidence in his ability — the crucial ability — to give out-ward expression to love at the appropriate time and in the appropriate manner. *I may be the type who manages to grab all the pointless things in life but lets the really important things slip away.* Whenever this thought crossed his mind, which was often, his heart would descend to a place devoid of light and warmth.

Whenever, after he had been with a new woman for some months, he began to notice something about her character or behavior, how-ever trivial, that displeased him or touched a nerve, somewhere in a recess of his heart he would feel a twinge of relief. As a result, it be-came a pattern for him to carry on tepid, indecisive relationships with one woman after another. Each of these relationships dissolved on its own. The breakups never involved any discord or shouting matches, because he never became involved with women who seemed as if they might be difficult to get rid of. Before he knew it, he had devel-oped a kind of nose for convenient partners.

Junpei was unsure whether this ability stemmed from his own in-nate character or whether it had been formed by his environment. If the latter, it might well have been the fruit of his father's curse. Around the time that he graduated from college, he had a violent ar-gument with his father and cut off all contact with him, but still the "three-women theory," its basis never fully explained, clung tenaciously to him. At one point, he even half jokingly considered becoming gay: maybe then he'd be able to free himself from this ridiculous countdown. For better or for worse, however, women were the only objects of Junpei's sexual interest.

The next woman Junpei met was older than he was. She was thirty-six. Junpei was thirty-one. An acquaintance of his was opening a little French restaurant on a street leading out of central Tokyo, and Junpei was invited to the party. He wore a Perry Ellis shirt of deep blue silk with a matching summer sports jacket. He had planned to meet a close friend at the party but the friend canceled at the last minute, which left Junpei with no one to talk to. He nursed a large glass of Bordeaux alone at the bar. Just as he was ready to leave and beginning to scan the crowd for the owner in order to say goodbye, a tall woman approached him holding a purple cocktail. Junpei's first thought on seeing her was: Here is a woman with excellent posture.

"Somebody over there told me that you're a writer. Is that true?" she asked, resting an elbow on the bar.

"I suppose so, in a way," Junpei answered.

"A writer 'in a way'?"

Junpei nodded.

"How many books have you published?"

"Two volumes of short stories and one book I translated. None of them sold much."

She gave him a quick head-to-toe inspection and smiled with apparent satisfaction.

"Well, anyhow, you're the first real writer I've met."

"I might be a little disappointing," Junpei said. "A pianist could play you a tune. A painter could draw something for you. A magician could perform a trick. There's not much a writer can do on the spot."

"Oh, I don't know. Maybe I can just enjoy your artistic aura or something."

"Artistic aura?" Junpei said.

"That special radiance — something you don't find in ordinary people."

"I look at my face in the mirror every morning when I'm shaving, but I've never noticed anything like that."

She smiled and asked, "What kind of stories do you write?"

"People ask me that a lot, but my stories don't really fit into any particular genre."

She ran a finger around the lip of her cocktail glass. "I suppose that means you write *literary* fiction?"

"I suppose it does. You say that the way you might say 'chain letters.'"

She smiled again. "Could I have heard your name?"

"Do you read literary magazines?"

She gave her head a small, sharp shake.

"Then you probably haven't. I'm not that well known."

Without asking his permission, she sat on the barstool next to his, sipped what was left of her cocktail, and told him her name: Kirie.

Junpei guessed that she was an inch or more taller than he was. She had a deep tan, her hair was short, and her head was a beautiful shape. She wore a pale green linen jacket, with the sleeves rolled up to her elbows, and a knee-length flared skirt. Under the jacket, she had on a simple cotton blouse with a small turquoise brooch at the collar. The swell of her breasts was neither large nor small. She dressed with style, and while there was nothing affected about it, her entire outfit seemed to express a strong and independent personality. Her lips were full, and they marked the ends of her sentences by spreading or pursing. This gave her a strangely lively quality. Three parallel creases formed across her broad forehead whenever she stopped to think about something; when she finished thinking, they disappeared.

Junpei was aware that he was attracted to her. Something indefinable but persistent was exciting him, pumping adrenaline to his heart. Suddenly aware that his throat was dry, he ordered a Perrier from a passing waiter, and as always he began to ask himself, Is she someone with real meaning for me? Is she one of the remaining two? Will she be my second strike? Should I let her go, or take a swing?

"Did you always want to be a writer?" Kirie asked.

"Hmm. Let's just say I could never think of anything else I wanted to be."

"So your dream came true."

"I wonder. I wanted to be a *great* writer." Junpei spread his hands about a foot apart. "There's a pretty big distance between the two, I think."

"Everybody has to start somewhere. You have your future ahead of you. You can't attain perfection right away." Then she asked, "How old are you?"

Being older than he was didn't seem to bother her in the least. It didn't bother Junpei either. He preferred mature women to young girls. In most cases, it was easier to break up with an older woman.

"What kind of work do you do?" he asked.

Her lips formed a perfectly straight line, and her expression became earnest for the first time.

"What kind of work do you *think* I do?"

Junpei jogged his glass, swirling the red wine inside it exactly once. "Can I have a hint?"

"No hints. Is it so hard to tell? Observation and judgment are your business."

"Not really," he said. "What a writer is supposed to do is observe and observe and observe again, and put off making judgments till the last possible moment."

"Of course," she said. "All right, then, observe and observe and observe again, and then use your imagination. That wouldn't clash with your professional ethics, would it?"

Junpei raised his eyes and studied Kirie's face with new concentration, hoping to find a secret sign there. She looked straight into his eyes, and he looked straight into hers.

After a short pause, he said, "All right, this is what I imagine, based on nothing much: You're a professional of some sort. Not just anyone can do your job. It requires some kind of special expertise."

"Bull's-eye! But try to narrow it down a little."

"Something to do with music?"

"No."

"Fashion design?"

"No."

"Tennis?"

"No," she said.

Junpei shook his head. "Well, you've got a tan, you're solidly built, your arms have a good bit of muscle. Maybe you do a lot of outdoor sports. I don't think you're an outdoor laborer. You don't have that vibe."

Kirie rested her arms on the counter and turned them over, inspecting them. "You seem to be getting there."

"But I still can't give you the right answer."

"It's important to keep a few little secrets," Kirie said. "I don't want to deprive you of your professional pleasure — observing and imagining . . . I will give you one hint, though. It's the same for me as for you."

"The same how?"

"I mean, my profession is exactly what I always wanted to do, ever since I was a little girl. Like you. Getting to where I am, though, was not an easy journey."

"Good," Junpei said. "That's important. Your work should be an act of love, not a marriage of convenience."

"An act of love," Kirie said. The words seemed to make an impression on her. "That's a wonderful metaphor."

"Meanwhile, do you think I might have heard your name somewhere?" Junpei asked.

"Probably not," she answered, shaking her head. "I'm not that well known."

"Oh, well, everybody has to start somewhere."

"Exactly," Kirie said with a smile. Then she turned serious. "My situation is different from yours in one way. I'm expected to attain perfection right from the start. No mistakes allowed. Perfection or nothing. No in-between. No second chances."

"I suppose that's another hint."

"Probably."

A waiter circulating with a tray of champagne approached them. She took two glasses from him and handed one to Junpei.

"Cheers," she said.

"To our respective areas of expertise," Junpei said.

They clinked glasses.

"By the way," she said, "are you married?"

Junpei shook his head.

"Neither am I," Kirie said.

She spent that night in Junpei's room. They drank wine — a gift from the restaurant — had sex, and went to sleep. When Junpei woke at ten o'clock the next morning, she was gone, leaving only an indentation, like a memory, in the pillow next to his and a note: "I have to go to work. Get in touch with me if you like." She included her cellphone number.

He called her, and they had dinner at a restaurant the following Saturday. They drank a little wine, had sex in Junpei's room, and went to sleep. Again the next morning she was gone. It was Sunday, but her note said again, "Got to go to work."

Junpei still had no idea what kind of work Kirie did, but it certainly started early in the morning. And — on occasion, at least — she worked on Sundays.

The two were never at a loss for things to talk about. She had a sharp mind and was knowledgeable on a broad range of topics. She enjoyed reading, but generally favored books other than fiction — biography, history, psychology, and popular science — and she retained an amazing amount of information. One time, Junpei was astounded at her detailed knowledge of the history of prefabricated housing.

"Prefabricated housing? Your work must have something to do with construction or architecture."

"No," she said. "I just tend to be attracted to highly practical topics. That's all."

She did, however, read the two story collections that Junpei had published, and found them "wonderful." "They were far more enjoyable than I expected," she told him. "To tell you the truth, I was worried. What would I do if I read your work and didn't like it? What could I say? But there was nothing to worry about. I enjoyed them thoroughly."

"I'm glad to hear that," Junpei said, relieved. He had had the same worry when, at her request, he gave her the books.

"I'm not just saying this to make you feel good," Kirie said, "but you've got something special — that special element it takes to become an outstanding writer. Your stories are lively, and the style is beautiful, but mainly it's that your writing is so balanced. For me, that is always the most important thing — in music, in fiction, in painting. Whenever I encounter a work or a performance that lacks balance, it makes me sick. It's like motion sickness. That's probably why I don't go to concerts and hardly read any fiction."

"Because you don't want to encounter unbalanced things?"

"Exactly."

"Sounds a little far out to me."

"I'm a Libra. I just can't stand it when things are out of balance. No, it's not so much that I can't stand it as . . ."

She closed her mouth in search of the right words, but she wasn't able to find them, releasing instead a few tentative sighs. "Oh, well, never mind," she went on. "I just wanted to say that I believe someday you are going to write novels. And, when you do that, you will become a more important writer. It may take a while, but that's what I feel."

"No, I'm a born short story writer," Junpei said dryly. "I'm not suited to writing novels."

He offered nothing more on the subject, just lay quietly and listened to the hum of the air conditioner. In fact, he had tried several times to write a novel, but had always bogged down partway through. He simply could not maintain the concentration it took to write a story over a long period of time. He would start out convinced that he was going to write something incredible. The story would flow out almost by itself. But the farther he went with it, the more its energy and brilliance would fade — gradually at first, but undeniably, until, like an engine coming to a halt, it petered out entirely.

The two of them were in bed. It was autumn. They were naked after a long, warm session of lovemaking. Kirie's shoulder pressed against Junpei, whose arms were around her. Two glasses of white wine stood on the night table.

"Junpei?"

"Uh-huh."

"You're in love with another woman, aren't you? Somebody you can't forget?"

"It's true," Junpei admitted. "You can tell?"

"Of course," she said. "Women are very sensitive to such things. You can't see her?"

"There are problems."

"And no possibility those 'problems' could be solved?"

"None," Junpei said with a quick shake of the head.

Kirie drank a little wine. "I don't have anybody like that," she said almost under her breath. "I like you a lot, Junpei. You really move me. When we're together like this, I feel tremendously happy and calm. But that doesn't mean that I want to have a serious relationship with you. How does that make you feel? Relieved?"

Junpei ran his fingers through her hair. Instead of answering her question, he asked one of his own. "Why is that?"

"Why don't I want to be with you?"

"Uh-huh."

"Does it bother you?"

"A little."

"I can't have a serious everyday relationship with anybody. Not just you, anybody," she said. "I want to concentrate completely on what I'm doing now. If I were living with somebody — if I had a deep emotional involvement with somebody — I might not be able to do that."

Junpei thought for a minute. "You mean you don't want to be distracted?"

"That's right."

"If you were distracted, you could lose your balance, and that might prove to be an obstacle to your career."

"Exactly." She nodded.

"But you still won't tell me what that is."

"Guess."

"You're a burglar."

"No," Kirie answered with amusement. "What a sexy guess! But a burglar doesn't go to work early in the morning."

"You're a hit man."

"Hit *person*," she corrected him. "But no. Why are you coming up with these awful ideas?"

"So what you do is perfectly legal?"

"Perfectly."

"Undercover agent?"

"No. OK, let's stop for today. I'd rather talk about your work. Tell me about what you're writing. You are writing something now?"

"Yes, a short story."

"What kind of story?"

"I haven't finished it yet."

"So tell me what has happened so far."

Junpei fell silent. He had a policy of not talking to anyone about his works in progress. If he put his story into words and those words left his mouth, he feared, something important would evaporate like morning dew. Delicate shades of meaning would be flattened into a shallow surface. Secrets would no longer be secrets. But here in bed, running his fingers through Kirie's short hair, Junpei felt that it might be all right to tell her. After all, he was taking a break from the story because he didn't know how to finish it. He hadn't been able to move forward for some days now.

"It's in the third person, and the protagonist is a woman," he began. "She's in her early thirties, a skilled internist who practices at a big hospital. She's single, but she's having an affair with a surgeon at the same hospital. He's in his late forties and has a wife and kids."

Kirie took a moment to imagine the heroine. "Is she attractive?"

"I think so. Quite attractive," Junpei said. "But not as attractive as you."

Kirie kissed Junpei on the neck. "That's the right answer," she said.

"So, anyway, she takes a vacation and goes off on a trip by herself. It's autumn. She's staying at a little hot-spring resort in the mountains and she goes for a walk along a stream. She's a bird watcher, and she especially enjoys seeing kingfishers. She steps down into the dry streambed and notices an odd stone. It's black with a tinge of red, it's smooth, and it has a familiar shape. She realizes right away that it's shaped like a kidney. I mean, she's a doctor, after all. Everything about it is just like a real kidney — the size, the thickness."

"So she picks it up and takes it home."

"Right," Junpei said. "She takes it to her office at the hospital and uses it as a paperweight. It's just the right size and weight."

"And it's the perfect shape for a hospital."

"Exactly," Junpei said. "But a few days later she notices something strange."

Kirie waited silently for him to continue with his story. Junpei paused as if deliberately teasing his listener, but in fact this was not deliberate at all. He had not yet written the rest of the story. This was the point at which he had stopped. Standing at this unmarked intersection, he surveyed his surroundings and worked his brain. Then he thought of how the story should go.

"Every morning, she finds the stone in a different place. She's a very methodical person, so she always leaves it in exactly the same spot on her desk when she goes home at night, but in the morning she finds it on the seat of her swivel chair, or next to the vase, or on the floor. Her first thought is that her memory is playing tricks on her. The door to her office is locked, and no one else can get in. Of course, the night watchman has a key, but he has been working at the hospital for years and he would never take it upon himself to enter anyone's office. Besides, what would be the point of his barging into her office every night just to change the position of a stone she's using as a paperweight? Nothing else in the office has changed, nothing is missing, and nothing has been tampered with. The position of the rock is the only thing that changes. She's totally stumped. What do *you* think is going on? Why do you think the stone moves during the night?"

"The kidney-shaped stone has its own reasons for doing what it does," Kirie said with simple assurance.

"What kind of reasons can a kidney-shaped stone have?"

"It wants to shake her up. Little by little. Over a long period of time."

"All right, then, why does it want to shake her up?"

"I don't know," she said. Then, with a giggle, she added, "Maybe it just wants to *rock* her world."

"That's the worst pun I've ever heard," Junpei groaned.

"Well, *you're* the writer. Aren't you the one who decides?"

Junpei scowled. He felt a slight throbbing behind his temples from having concentrated so hard. Maybe he had drunk too much wine. "The ideas aren't coming together," he said. "My plots don't move unless I'm actually sitting at my desk and moving my hands, making sentences. Talking about it like this, though, I'm beginning to feel as if the rest of the story is going to work itself out."

"I'll wait," Kirie said. She reached over for her glass and took a sip of wine. "But the story is really getting interesting. I want to know what happens with the kidney-shaped stone."

She turned toward him and pressed her shapely breasts against his side. Then, quietly, as if sharing a secret, she said, "You know, Junpei, everything in the world has its reasons for doing what it does." Junpei was falling asleep and could not answer. In the night air, her sentences lost their shape as grammatical constructions and blended with the faint aroma of the wine before reaching the hidden recesses of his consciousness. "For example, the wind has its reasons. You just don't notice it as you go about your life. Then, at some point, you are made to notice. The wind envelops you with a certain purpose in mind and shakes you up. It knows everything that's inside you. And it's not just the wind. Everything, even a stone, knows you. And all you can do is go with those things. As you take them in, you survive and deepen."

For the next five days, Junpei hardly left the house; he stayed at his desk, writing the rest of the story of the kidney-shaped stone. As Kirie had predicted, the stone continues quietly to shake the doctor — little by little, but decisively. She is engaged in a hurried coupling with her lover in an anonymous hotel room one evening when she stealthily reaches around to his back and feels for the shape of a kidney. Something tells her that her kidney-shaped stone is lurking in there. The kidney is a secret informer that she herself has buried in her lover's body. Beneath her fingers it squirms like an insect, sending her messages. She converses with the kidney, exchanging intelligence. She can feel its sliminess against the palm of her hand.

The doctor grows gradually used to the existence of the kidney-shaped stone that shifts position every night. She comes to accept it as natural. She is no longer surprised when she finds that it has moved. When she arrives at the hospital each morning, she looks for the stone, picks it up, and returns it to her desk. This has simply become part of her routine. As long as she remains in the room, the stone does not move. It stays quietly in one place, like a cat napping in the sun. It awakes and begins to move only after she has left the room and locked the door.

Whenever she has a spare moment at her desk, she reaches out and caresses the stone's smooth dark surface. After a while, it becomes increasingly difficult for her to take her eyes off the stone; it is as if she has been hypnotized. She gradually loses interest in anything else. She can no longer read books. She stops going to the gym. Talking to her colleagues bores her. She becomes indifferent to her own grooming. She loses her appetite. Even the embrace of her lover becomes a source of annoyance. When there is no one else around, she speaks to the stone in a lowered voice — the way lonely people converse with a dog or a cat — and she listens to the wordless words the stone speaks to her. The dark kidney-shaped stone now controls the greater part of her life.

Surely the stone is not an object that has come to her from without: Junpei becomes aware of this as his story progresses. The main point is something inside herself. Something inside herself is activating the kidney-shaped stone and urging her to take some kind of action. It keeps sending her signals for that purpose — signals in the form of the stone's nightly movements.

While he writes, Junpei thinks about Kirie. He senses that she (or something inside her) is propelling the story; it was never his intention to write something so divorced from reality. What Junpei had imagined vaguely beforehand was a more tranquil, psychological story line. In that story line, rocks did not take it upon themselves to move around.

Junpei imagined that the doctor would cut her ties to the married surgeon. She might even come to hate him. This was probably what she had been seeking all along, unconsciously.

Once the rest of the story had become visible to him, writing it out was relatively easy. Listening to the songs of Mahler at low volume, Junpei sat at his computer and wrote the conclusion at what was, for him, top speed.

The doctor makes her decision to part with her lover. "I can't see you anymore," she tells him. "Can't we at least talk this over?" he asks. "No," she tells him firmly, "that is impossible." On her next free day, she boards a Tokyo Harbor ferry, and from the deck she throws the kidney-shaped stone into the sea. The stone sinks to the bottom of the ocean, plunging toward the core of the earth. She resolves to start her life over. Having cast away the stone, she feels a new sense of lightness.

The next day, however, when she arrives at the hospital, the stone is on her desk, waiting for her. It sits exactly where it is supposed to be, as dark and kidney-shaped as ever.

As soon as he finished writing the story, Junpei called Kirie. She would probably want to read the finished work, which she, in a sense, had inspired him to write. His call, however, did not go through. "Your call cannot be completed as dialed," a recorded voice said. "Please check the number and try again." Junpei tried it again — and again. But the result was always the same. She was probably having some kind of technical problem with her phone, he thought.

Junpei stuck close to home, waiting for word from Kirie, but nothing came. A month went by. One month became two, and two became three. The season changed to winter, and a new year began. His story came out in the February issue of a literary magazine. A newspaper ad for the magazine listed Junpei's name and the title, "The Kidney-Shaped Stone That Moves Every Day." Kirie might see the ad, buy the magazine, read the story, and call him to share her impressions — or so he hoped. But all that reached him were new layers of silence.

The pain that Junpei felt when Kirie vanished from his life was far more intense than he could have imagined. In the course of a day he would think any number of times, If only she were here! He missed her smile, he missed the words shaped by her lips, he missed the touch of her skin as they held each other. He gained no comfort from his favorite music or from the arrival of new books by authors that he liked. Everything felt distant, divorced from him. Kirie may have been woman number two, Junpei thought.

Junpei's next encounter with Kirie occurred one day in early spring — though you couldn't really call it an encounter.

He was in a taxi stuck in traffic. The driver was listening to an FM broadcast. Kirie's voice emerged from the radio. At first, Junpei didn't realize that he was hearing Kirie. He simply thought the voice was similar to hers. But the more he listened, the more it sounded like her, her manner of speaking — the same smooth intonation, the same relaxed style, the special way she had of pausing between thoughts.

Junpei asked the driver to turn up the volume.

"Sure thing," the driver said.

Kirie was being interviewed by a female announcer. "So you've liked high places since you were a little girl?" the announcer asked.

"Yes," Kirie — or a woman with exactly the same voice — said. "As long as I can remember, I've liked being up high. The higher I am, the more peaceful I feel. I was always nagging my parents to take me to tall buildings. I was a strange little creature," she said with a laugh.

"Which is how you got started in your present line of work, I suppose."

"First I worked as an analyst at a securities firm. But I knew right away that it wasn't right for me. I left the company after three years, and the first thing I did was get a job washing windows in tall buildings. What I really wanted to be was a steeplejack, but that's such a macho world — they don't let women in very easily."

"From securities analyst to window washer — that's quite a change!"

"To tell the truth, washing windows was much less stressful for me. If something's going to fall, it's just me, not stock prices." Again the laugh.

"Now, by 'window washer' you mean one of those people who get lowered down the side of a building on a platform?"

"Right. Of course, they give you a lifeline, but some spots you can't reach without taking the lifeline off. That didn't bother me at all. No matter how high we went, I was never scared — which made me a very valuable worker."

"I suppose you like to go mountain climbing?"

"I have almost no interest in mountains. I've tried climbing a few times, but it does nothing for me. The only things that interest me are man-made structures that rise straight up from the ground. Don't ask me why."

"So now you run a window-washing company that specializes in high-rise buildings in the Tokyo metropolitan area."

"Correct," she said. "I saved up and started my own little company about six years ago. Of course, I go out with my crews, but basically I'm an owner now. I don't have to take orders from anybody, and I can make up my own rules."

"Meaning you can take the lifeline off whenever you like?"

"In a word." Another laugh.

"You really do like high places, don't you?"

"I do. I feel it's my calling to be up high. I can't imagine doing any other kind of work. Your work should be an act of love, not a marriage of convenience."

"It's time for a song now," the announcer said. "James Taylor, with 'Up on the Roof.' We'll talk more about tightrope walking after this."

While the song played, Junpei leaned over the front seat and asked the driver, "What does this woman do?"

"She puts up ropes between high-rise buildings and walks across them," the driver explained. "With a long pole in her hands for balance. She's some kind of performer. I guess she gets her kicks that way. I get scared just riding in a glass elevator."

"That's her *profession?*" Junpei asked. He noticed that his voice was dry and the weight had gone out of it. It sounded like someone else's voice.

"Yeah. I guess she gets a bunch of sponsors together and puts on a performance. She just did one at some famous cathedral in Germany. She says she wants to do it on higher buildings but can't get permission. 'Cause if you go that high a safety net won't help. Of course, she can't make a living that way, so — well, you heard her say she's got this window-cleaning company. Weird chick."

"The most wonderful thing about it is that when you're up there you change as a human being," Kirie told the interviewer. "You have to change or you can't survive. When I come out to a high place, it's just me and the wind. Nothing else. The wind envelops me, shakes me up. It understands who I am. At the same time, I understand the wind. We accept each other and we decide to go on living together. That's the moment I love more than anything. No, I'm not afraid. Once I set foot in that high place and enter completely into that state of concentration, all fear vanishes."

She spoke with cool assurance. Junpei could not tell whether the interviewer understood what she was saying. When the interview ended, Junpei stopped the cab and got out, walking the rest of the way to his destination. Now and then he would look up at a tall building and at the clouds flowing past. No one could come between her and the wind, he realized, and he felt a violent rush of jealousy. But jealousy of what? The wind? Who could possibly be jealous of the wind?

Junpei waited several more months for Kirie to contact him. He wanted to see her and talk to her about lots of things, including the kidney-shaped stone. But the call never came, and his calls to her could never be completed as dialed. When summer came, he gave up. She obviously had no intention of seeing him again. And so the relationship ended calmly, without discord or shouting matches — exactly the way he had ended relationships with so many other women. At some point, the calls would stop coming, and everything would come to an end quietly, naturally.

Should I add her to the countdown? Was she one of my three women with real meaning? Junpei agonized over the question for some time without reaching a conclusion. I'll wait another six months, he thought. Then I'll decide.

During those six months, he wrote with great concentration and produced a large number of short stories. As he sat at his desk polishing a story, he would think, Kirie is probably in some high place with the wind right now. Here I am, all alone at my desk writing stories, while she's all alone up there, without a lifeline. Once she enters that state of concentration, all fear vanishes: it's just her and the wind. Junpei would often recall her words and realize that he had come to feel something special for Kirie, something that he had never felt for another woman. It was a deep emotion, with clear outlines and real weight. He was still unsure what to call this emotion. It was, at least, a feeling that could not be exchanged for anything else. Even if he never saw Kirie again, this feeling would stay with him forever. Somewhere in his body — perhaps in the marrow of his bones — he would continue to feel her absence.

As the year came to an end, Junpei made up his mind. He would count her as number two. She was one of the women who had real meaning for him. Strike two. Only one left.

But he was no longer afraid. Numbers aren't the important thing, he told himself. The countdown has no meaning. Now he knew: what matters is deciding in your heart to accept another person completely. When you do that, it is always the first time and the last.

One morning, the doctor notices that the dark kidney-shaped stone has disappeared from her desk. And she knows: it won't be coming back.

Translated by Jay Rubin

JEFF PARKER

■

False Cognate

FROM *Hobart*

WHEN I FIRST ARRIVED HERE, I had a simple request of our liaison, a handsome, tall woman with steel-blue eyes and a pancake face. I wasn't yet confident in my Russian and needed a haircut. I asked her in English, "Do you know, Tanya, where I can get a barber? I heard they go for about thirty rubles here."

She looked at me with a rather sharp glance and said, "Thirty rubles is one dollar."

"About what my last one was worth," I said, mussing up my hair.

"That's not for me to judge," she said. "The best thing to do is wait at the bus stops. They'll come up to you."

"Come up to me?" I said.

"Eventually," she said.

"That's how people go about it?"

"I think so," she said, then clip-clopped away.

I spent the better part of a week hanging out at the bus stops trying to look like I wanted a haircut. The only people who ever approached me were thin-lipped prostitutes.

Tanya avoided me after that. The whole cohort avoided me. At first I thought they were just an unsociable bunch, but sometimes, walking home at night, I'd see them all at the beer garden near my flat, laughing and having a good time. I'd pull up a chair and they'd suddenly evacuate. Later on, I convinced this Spanish guy who considered himself a Defender of Women to tell me why everyone hated me, and he said word got around that I had shown up the first day and asked the program liaison where I could find a whore. He added that I was what was wrong with Americans and didn't I have a sister and — poking me in the chest with his finger — how would I feel if his Spanish ass came over to America expressly to fuck her?

I couldn't figure out what he was talking about, but he looked like he was going to hit me. I left.

I gave it some thought, and the only explanation was that she'd mistaken the English word "barber" for the Russian word *baba* — a funny thing, because I had a history with the word *baba*. I had written a prizewinning essay for my upper-level Russian composition class in which I'd identified a flaw in a notorious Babel translation. Babel had a situation in which a simple young peasant girl, referred to as a *baba*, strolls into a bar drawing all the men's attention. The word has three meanings: plumpish old woman, simple young peasant girl, and, in slang, whore. The translator had rendered it as an old haggard babushka, which didn't make any sense. Why would the men find their attention inexplicably drawn to her, except for her hideousness, which wasn't the point at all? I found the original, identified the problem, and composed the essay, winning the prize.

Since "barber" is not a common English word, and our liaison's English was about as good as my Russian, she could only hear a Russian approximate. False cognate. This was the only explanation. They work the other way too. When Russians, in the course of normal conversation, describe a lecture as "exciting and inspirational," the Russian word for which is *pathetichiske*, I hear only "pathetic." At the kiosks late at night, young men ask for *preservativi*, and I'm imagining cured pears when it's the Russian word for condoms.

For a couple of days, I tried to set the record straight. I spoke to Tanya about it. "Why do you think I was mussing my hair while I asked you? What do *babas* have to do with hair?" She clearly didn't believe me. I spoke to others in the cohort as well. "Like from my essay?" I said. "The one that won the prize? Imagine the irony!"

No one believed me.

So I was there with a group and by myself at the same time.

It turned out to be the best thing going for me. While the others dance a vodka-flavored merengue at a club called Havana Nights, I wash my socks in a bathroom designed so that you have to straddle the toilet to take a shower.

While the others are in classes, I check out the obscure museums and see Rasputin's actual penis and Peter the Great's collection of deformed babies, which float in jars like smooth balls of fresh mozzarella. I live the real Russian life: isolated, wet feet, maligned.

And on weekends they check out the city of fountains or the tsar's summer palace or sun themselves, bare- and flabby-assed, on the rocky beach at the Peter and Paul Fortress. I take the bus to the provinces.

The Novgorod bus is late, so I sit in the beer garden in the courtyard of my building and read the newspaper. Lena is sitting there with a friend, dark-skinned, maybe Tajik or Azerbaijani. Lena hates me too. She hates me because I pee behind her office, a wooden shed with a keg inside it. My bladder is worthless, and five minutes after a beer I have to go. All the Russian guys go back there, and so I do too.

Lena doesn't like this, but the only option is to take the eight flights of stairs to my apartment and stand in the shower to pee.

Lena, who doesn't think much of my Russian, says to her friend, "Take this goat, Choika. He doesn't speak a word of Russian, and he pees behind this box every day."

I buy a bottle of beer and some dried squid from her.

"You're very beautiful," I say in my admittedly heavily accented Russian.

"Three words in Russian. Oh, look at that — seven, twelve." She spits over her shoulder.

Lena *is* very beautiful, but her friend is even more so. I watch them over the top edge of the newspaper, and when they look, I drop my eyes to some paragraph: *Sergei V. Yastrzhembsky, Putin's senior adviser on Chechnya, suggests that Islamic extremists co-opt the black widows against their will to become suicide bombers. "Chechens are turning these young girls into zombies using psychotropic drugs," Mr. Yastrzhembsky said. "I have heard that they rape them and record the rapes on video. After that, such Chechen girls have no chance at all of resuming a normal life in Chechnya. They have only one option: to blow themselves up with a bomb full of nails and ball bearings."*

Choika stands up. She is wearing a half-shirt and there's a square Band-Aid displayed prominently on her hip. It looks like a nicotine patch, but the guide at the Erotica Museum who showed me Rasputin's penis said that they're the new fashion in birth control.

Choika and Lena hug each other and cry. Then Choika scurries across the street to where the bus has pulled into the station. I chug the rest of my beer and run after her.

The driver stands outside the bus, smoking and collecting tickets. "Nice shoes," he says to me. He's in New Balance sneakers identical to mine. It's obvious mine are authentic and his are fake, the imitations you buy in the market. Already the threads along the tongue are pulled and loose. The sole rubber is separating. *USA* is embroidered on both our heels. "How much?" he says.

"They're my only shoes."

"It's OK. Not a problem."

Ahead of me in line, two babushkas lecture Choika on the length of her skirt. She tells them it's the fashion. They say something about she won't be welcome in Novgorod like that. She says in her opinion she'll be very welcome.

I watch her shoes, white strappy things with heels like ice picks, and wonder why it is I think the word "babushka" rather than "old lady." It comes easier than other words. I wonder when I'll think *devushka* instead of "girl." I want to think *devushka* instead of "girl."

I grab the last seat, across from Choika and the two babushkas, next to two passed-out soldiers. I smile at Choika. She clutches her bag and looks out the window.

The driver stands on the steps at the front of the bus and shouts, "Attention, attention. I am very sorry to report that the bathroom on this bus is out of order today. In light of this unfortunate development we will be stopping once or twice whenever the possibility for a bathroom opportunity presents itself."

The soldier to my left comes to. He reaches across the aisle and puts his hand on Choika's stockinged knee. "O Caucasian beauty," he says.

The babushkas bang their canes against the seats.

"Relax, my friends," the soldier says. He removes his hand from her knee and puts it on mine. Choika never looks away from the window.

"Do you know the game Submarine?" he asks me.

"I've heard," I say. The game is very popular among students. I had heard of those in my cohort playing it. But no one was inviting me.

From what I gather, a kind of game-master they call Captain locks a group of friends in a flat with several bottles of vodka and some pickles. They cannot bring watches, and all clocks are unplugged. The telephone and television are removed by the Captain, and no cell phones are permitted. He locks them in the flat and goes about his life, taking the key. The players block the light from all the windows and drink, sleep, drink, sleep, eat pickles, drink, sleep, etc. They are not allowed to peek out the window or stop drinking while they are awake. Two days later the Captain returns and lets them out.

He smiles at me. "We have been operating Submarine for ten days."

"It's a long time," I say.

"Our Captain — he forgot about us."

With his hand still on my knee, the soldier falls asleep again.

"You are giving away so much," the babushka whispers to Choika.

"Much or not much," Choika says.

Dear Motherfucking Travel Diary, all this business before the bus takes off.

I play out this fantasy: Choika is one of the "black widows" from the article.

And it makes a lot of sense. Her eyes never flinch, even when the bus slams into potholes; her gaze is steady out the window. Her bag is not quite big enough for luggage yet larger than an ordinary purse, the perfect size to conceal a wad of nails and ball bearings. She is just old enough to have had a young husband die recently in the Chechen war.

How would she know Lena, then? That was the hole. Unless Lena's family, hard up for money like most Russian families, had become Chechen sympathizers purely out of financial necessity, taking in black widows, housing them, feeding them, taking care of them while plotting out the best, most populated, most unexpected routes. That was how they had managed to buy that box with the keg in it, where they sold dried squid and *preservativi*. I look around the bus. It's packed.

I kind of get off on this idea. I can already imagine the cutline on the national news back home: "Black widow suicide bomber blows up bus outside St. Petersburg, Russia. One American is among the dead."

My one life reduced to that one line. I lean across the seat to Choika and say, "Your way is fraught with peril; your plight, an admirable one."

She does not turn her head.

"Devil," the babushka says, crunching on sunflower seeds. "Now you've got foreigners drooling."

I disturb the soldier's hand from my knee and he jumps to his feet, wobbling slowly into the aisle and teetering to the back of the bus.

The driver, looking up at us from his rear-view mirror the size of an ironing board, yells at him. "Hey, jerk," he says, "the bathroom is out of order."

"I'll piss on the floor then," the soldier says.

The driver swings the bus onto the shoulder, knocking the soldier down. The brakes are still hissing and the driver is up, halfway down the aisle. The other soldier grabs his arm as he goes by.

"Reconsider any manly man," the other soldier says.

"No," the driver says, "nothing like that." The soldier in the aisle crawls to his feet and lights a cigarette. "Friends," the driver says, "let me talk to you then, outside. Everybody, let's take a bathroom break."

"Where are we supposed to go?" a woman shouts from the back. "Under some death cap?"

"Find a nice tree," the driver says.

Choika stands up. I think, Detonation.

"I believe someone asked you kindly, sir," she says. "Where exactly are women supposed to go?"

"I believe someone answered, miss. There's some congenial trees in the area," the driver says. "They're cleaner than most bathrooms. You have five minutes or we leave without you."

"And what about ticks?" one of the babushkas says.

"Make sure you get their heads," the driver says.

The babushkas break out some toilet paper and sell squares for four rubles each. Choika buys two. The passengers disperse into the forest. I hold it and eavesdrop. The soldiers and driver stand around a rock, talking. There is a lot of nodding, but I can't hear them. The soldiers deliberate with each other and say something back to the driver. Then they all shake hands and pee together on the rock.

I go toward the tree I remember Choika going toward. Another woman I don't recognize steps out and yells at me for sneaking up on her. I use her tree after she's gone, and when I'm done, Choika and the soldiers are back on the bus and the driver is beeping.

I take the small portion of the seat the soldiers leave me. The soldier who'd kept his hand on my knee holds out his hand, this time to shake. "Andre Andreevich," he says. "Let me guess: Fritz?"

"American," I say.

"Even better," he says, scooting over to give me more room. "Share some beer with us." He takes a warm bottle from his duffel bag and hands it to me. "The danger in playing Submarine is in the doors. Russian doors are the problem, but, well, let's say you don't have to worry about them when you have a responsible Captain. Our Captain was also interested in drinking. And one of the rules of Submarine — strictly enforced by players — is that you cannot look out the window and you cannot know the time, and as a consequence you never know how long you've been playing."

"You don't get light through the crevices?" I ask.

"You get, which is why you tape the curtains to the wall with electrical tape."

The other soldier knocks on the window to get Choika's attention. She is like a statue, a perfect flesh statue with a birth control patch on her hip. The other soldier hunkers down in his seat to try to see up her skirt.

"You should be in Submarine for two days, but sometimes time goes slow and sometimes fast. We think it was the sixth day when we realized perhaps time was going too slow."

"It seems impossible to me to mistake six days for two," I say.

"Luckily we had good amounts of vodka and pickled garlic."

He replaces my beer and takes the empty. He puts the empties on the floor and says, "Watch this." He points at his watch. The babushkas set their newspaper hats full of sunflower seeds on their seat and pick up the empties. They drop them in plastic sacks and go back to eating their seeds. "Five seconds," he says, "a new record."

"You're throwing away money," one of the babushkas says. "You could use a manicure, but you are not accurate."

"You cannot hear through Russian doors," Andre says. "We were shouting. We thought we would die there. We were pounding on the door, but this is like a mouse running on a pipe. We were on the top floor, Vadim screaming for help out the windows. Everyone thought we were just drunk."

"We were fucking drunk," Vadim, the other soldier, says.

"When the Captain finally arrived, he tried to tell us that it had only been two days. I told him, 'Prepare to suffer,' and he admitted that he had forgotten us, and he confessed — you will never believe this — he had been off playing Submarine himself. He was a player in two other games of Submarine before he remembered about us. Since he didn't shower, he didn't find the key in his pocket. He also lost our cell phones."

I tell Andre my story about barber and *baba,* which he laughs at once I explain that in English a barber is someone who cuts hair. He elbows Vadim and tells him my story. He and Vadim crack up.

"Let me tell you," Andre says, "*all* women are whores."

"Watch your mouth," one of the babushkas says.

"I've written an essay about this phenomenon," I say to Andre. "It was awarded a very prestigious collegiate prize in the U.S."

Choika sits like a statue. Her bag in her lap, her legs crossed official-like. She hardly jostles. I am more and more disappointed that she has not blown us all up. I contemplate peeing into an empty beer bottle. Instead I set the bottle on the floor and one of the babushkas snatches it up.

The cops pull over our bus, and the driver calls another bathroom break to deal with them. I am happy for the bathroom break, the first one on the ground, whizzing behind the wheel, and I'm climbing back aboard before everyone else is even off. The cops and the driver are talking near the front of the bus, and I see the driver hand them some money.

Choika steps off the bus and walks around the cops and the driver. I hurry back to my seat to watch her. She goes across the street and chooses a thin birch. She plants her feet in front of the tree, then squats, staring at her knees. I wonder if I'm becoming weird.

She stands again, tugging down the hem of her skirt. She doesn't even look when she steps onto the highway. She stands there in the middle of the asphalt. She lifts up one heel, wiping off the mud with toilet paper. Then she does the same to the other heel.

When she slides back into the seat, one of the babushkas holds out the paper hat of sunflower seeds to her and says, "Here, girl, you need to eat."

"There's no place to wash hands," Choika says.

The police come aboard, forcing their way to the back of the bus. They crowbar the locked bathroom door open and a tower of shoe-boxes collapses on them. The driver breaks for it, but Andre and Vadim trounce him in the aisle.

"You bitches," the driver says. "They were in on it," he says to the police as they bend him over the seatback and handcuff him. "They wanted free pairs. Size forty-three and forty-five. Check them."

"A cunt to your mouth," someone in back yells. "You unscrupulous shit-ass," says another.

Choika stands awkwardly, like she has to sneeze, and whips some kind of ball with wires out of her bag. She pushes something on it and hunches. She hunches again, like she's pushing in the top of a de-flated volleyball with her thumbs.

"What is this?" one of the babushkas says.

I close my eyes.

When I open them, the aisle is a knot of perfectly unharmed scream-ing bodies.

"Move," Andre says to me, and I push out into the aisle.

The soldiers lunge across the seat, tackling Choika. A policeman pitches the bomb out the window. It lands in the street and rolls into the ditch.

As I'm swept off the bus, I'm thinking: Was she going to do that? Did she have that bomb before I thought it? "Did I do that?" I say out loud and in English, and no one can hear me.

*

Once off the bus, the soldiers yell furiously for us to get as far away from the bomb as possible. We are off the bus, dispersing into the woods. I move more hesitantly than the rest.

When the police stuff Choika into the back of the cop car, I can see her knees are bleeding, but she's not crying or shaking. She sits in the back seat staring out the window, just like she'd stared out the bus window the whole ride, like nothing mattered.

The police and the soldiers crouch over the bomb. Andre tinkers with it, and Vadim and the police back up.

"I never saw a Muslim dressed like that," one of the babushkas says.

"She was masquerading as one of our girls," the other says. "Sluts," she says, and dumps a little purse full of coins on the ground.

"What are you doing?" one babushka says.

"She gave me eight rubles for the toilet paper."

A little boy runs up and starts collecting the money. His mother yells at him to put it down and come back to her. When he does, she hugs his head and says, "I wish we'd be there," or something like that — I don't understand the exact phrasing.

I approach the solider and the police. Andre is still fiddling with the bomb.

"I know her name," I say.

The police turn around. Their faces twitch. They're really shaken up. "Who are you?" one of them asks.

"Foreigner," Vadim says.

"I know her name," I say. Then, "I heard her say it."

"It's crap," Andre says, "total crap." He leaves the bomb in the ditch. "What's her name?" Andre says.

"Choika," I say.

"Choika," one of the policemen says. He says it again, louder, looking her way, and she turns her head. I suddenly feel ashamed, like I gave her up.

"What is that?" Andre says. "Choika."

"Chukchi?" Vadim says.

"Never heard of it," Andre says.

"Friends," the driver says. He's still in the handcuffs. "Feel free to retake your seat, friend," the driver says to me.

I'm the first one back on the bus, and one of Choika's gorgeous shoes is on the floor near my seat. There's a scrap of toilet paper stuck to the bottom of the heel.

The driver talks to the police and the soldiers as the other passengers reboard, absolutely silent. Even the chatty babushkas. They sit cramped together in the exact same spots they'd sat in before, leaving a wide space where Choika had been. A policeman unlocks the driver's handcuffs and the driver comes aboard. He goes back to the bathroom and selects two boxes, restacking those that had fallen and shutting the bathroom door, which refuses to latch at first but eventually clicks. He hands the two boxes to the policemen. Then the soldiers and the driver reboard.

I point to the shoe on the ground.

"Don't touch it," Andre says. "Forget about it." He kicks it under the seat.

The driver stands at the front of the bus. "Any more crazy terrorists here?" he says. No one says anything. "I sure hope not. Next stop is Novgorod. Unfortunately, I'm sorry to say that the bathroom on the bus is still out of order."

The engine fires and everyone breathes deeply. Andre hands me a beer. From the first sip, I feel the pressure build in my bladder. I am still waiting for something to blow.

DAVID RAKOFF

■

Love It or Leave It

FROM *Don't Get Too Comfortable*

GEORGE W. BUSH made me want to be an American. It was a need I had not known before. A desire that came over me in a rush one day, not unlike that of the pencil-necked honors student suddenly overwhelmed with the inexplicable urge to make a daily gift of his lunch money to the schoolyard tough. I have lived in the United States, first as a student and then as a resident alien, under numerous other administrations, including what I once thought of as the nadir of all time: the Cajun-scented, plague-ravaged Reagan eighties in New York; horrible, black years of red fish and blue drinks. A time when greed was magically transformed from vice to virtue. And after that, the even greedier nineties, when money flowed like water and everybody's boat rose with the tide (except, of course, for those forgotten souls who had been provided not with boats but with stones, and no one told them; oh well, *tra-la*), and all through that time, aside from having to make sure not to get myself arrested at demonstrations, I was sufficiently satisfied with a civic life of paying taxes and taking part in the occasional protest.

But George changed all that. Even though I am not a Muslim and I come from a country that enjoys cordial relations with the United States, I no longer felt safe being here as just a lawful permanent resident. Under the cudgel-like USA Patriot Act, a shoot-first-ask-questions-later bit of legislation, there are residents who have been here since childhood, other folks who have sired American-born children, who have found themselves deported — often to countries of which they have almost no firsthand knowledge — for the most minor, not remotely terrorist-related infractions. Those people are never coming back, at least not during this administration. I don't want to be put out of my home, and like it or not this is my home. I have been here longer than I haven't. After twenty-two years, it seemed a little bit coy to still be playing the Canadian card. I felt like the butt of that old joke about the proper lady who, when asked if she would have sex with a strange man for a million dollars, allows that yes, she would do it. But when asked if she would do the same thing for a can of Schlitz and a plastic sleeve of beer nuts, reels back with an affronted "What do you think I am?" To which the response is "Madam, we have already established what you are. Now we're just quibbling about the price." Becoming a citizen merely names a state of affairs already in place for a long time.

Even so, once I reach my decision, I don't make my intentions widely known. I tell almost no one, especially no one in Canada. You can know this only if you grew up in a country directly adjacent to a globally dominating, culturally obliterating economic behemoth, but becoming an American feels like some kind of defeat. Another one bites the dust.

The naturalization application can be downloaded from the government's Web site. It is ten pages long but can be filled out over the course of an industrious day or two. It takes me four months and one week. I got delayed twice, although not by the usual pitfalls of questions requiring a lot of documentation from over a long period. I have no problem, for example, with Part 7, Section C, in which I have to account for every trip I have taken outside the United States of more than twenty-four hours' duration over the last ten years, including every weekend jaunt to Canada to see the family. I have kept every datebook I have ever owned. I pore over a decade's worth of pages and list all of my travels, from the most recent backward. I create a table with columns, listing exact dates of departure and return, plus my destination. It is a document of such surpassing beauty, it is virtually scented. Not since I threaded puffy orange yarn through the punched holes of my fourth-grade book reports have I so shamelessly tried to placate authority with meaningless externals.

No, my first hang-up occurs at Part 10, Section G, question 33: *Are you a male who lived in the United States at any time between your 18th and 26th birthdays in any status except as a lawful nonimmigrant?* I make my living with words, and yet I cannot for the life of me begin to parse this question, with its embedded double negatives and hypotheticals. How are any nonnative speakers managing to become citizens? I wonder. Part of my clouded judgment is due to fear. I don't want to piss them off, and I am worried that a wrong answer will immediately feed my name into a database for a wiretap, a tax audit, or an automatic years-long "misplacement" of my application; some casual, gratuitous harassment that a thuggish administration might decide to visit upon someone they identified as a troublemaker. I spend an entire afternoon trying to map the grammar and come away with nothing but a headache and no idea.

This is in early March. I put the form away in my drawer and forget about it, my dreams of inalienable rights felled by just one question. I put all thoughts of citizenship out of my head, until one evening in July, four months later, when, as I'm dropping off to sleep, the clauses fall into place and the lock turns and I realize the answer is a simple "no." With inordinate self-satisfaction, I soldier on. Have I ever been a habitual drunkard? I have not. A prostitute, a procurer, or a bigamist? Nuh-uh. Did I in any way aid, abet, support, work for, or claim membership in the Nazi government of Germany between March 23, 1933, and May 8, 1945? *Nein!* Do I understand and support the Constitution? You betcha. If the law required it, would I be willing to bear arms on behalf of the United States?

Again I stop. The same headache as before marches its little foot soldiers across my cranium. I put the application back into the drawer and return to bed, not picking it up again until seven days later, when I surprise myself by checking "yes."

I figure it's grass soup. Grass soup is exactly what it sounds like. It's a recipe for food of last resort that my father apparently has squirreled away somewhere. I have never actually seen this recipe, but it was referred to fairly often when I was a child. Should everything else turn to shit, we could always derive sustenance from nutritious grass soup! At heart, it's an anxious, romantic fantasy that disaster and total financial ruin lurk just around the corner, but when they do come, they will have all the stark beauty and domestic fine feeling of a Dickens novel. Young Tiny Tim's palsied hand lifting a spoon to his rosebud mouth. "What delicious grass soup. I must be getting better after all," he will say, putting on a good show of it just as he expires, the tin utensil clattering to the rough wood table.

A grass-soup situation is a self-dramatizing one based on such a poorly imagined and improbable premise as to render it beneath consideration. Michael Jackson's saying with no apparent irony, for example, that were he to wake up one day to find all the children in the world gone, he would throw himself out the window. Mr. Jackson's statement doesn't really take into consideration that a planet devoid of tots would likely be just one link in a chain of geopolitical events so cataclysmic that to assume the presence of an intact building with an intact window out of which to throw himself is plain idiotic. As for grass soup itself, from what I've seen on the news, by the time you're reduced to using the lawn for food, any grass that isn't already gone — either parched to death or napalmed into oblivion — is probably best eaten on the run.

All by way of saying that if there ever came a time when the government of my new homeland was actually calling up the forty-something asking-and-telling homosexuals with hypoactive thyroids to take up arms, something very calamitous indeed will have to have happened. The streets would likely be running with blood, and such moral gray areas as might have existed at other times will seem so beside the point that I will join the fight, or so terrifying and appallingly beyond the pale that I'd already be either dead or underground.

For most of my life, I would have automatically said that I would opt for conscientious objector status, and in general, I still would. But the spirit of the question is would I *ever*, and there are instances when I might. If immediate intervention would have circumvented the genocide in Rwanda or stopped the Janjaweed in Darfur, would I choose pacifism? Of course not. Scott Simon, the reporter for National Public Radio and a committed lifelong Quaker, has written that it took looking into mass graves in the former Yugoslavia to convince him that force is sometimes the only option to deter our species' murderous impulses.

While we're on the subject of the horrors of war, and humanity's most poisonous and least charitable attributes, let us not forget to mention Barbara Bush. (That would be the former First Lady and presidential mother, as opposed to W's liquor-swilling, Girl Gone Wild, human ashtray of a daughter. I'm sorry, that's not fair: I've no idea if she smokes.) When the administration censored images of the flag-draped coffins of the young men and women being killed in Iraq — purportedly to respect "the privacy of the families" and not to minimize and cover up the true nature and consequences of the war — the family matriarch expressed her support for what was ultimately her son's decision by saying on *Good Morning America* on March 18, 2003, "Why should we hear about body bags and deaths? I mean, it's not relevant. So why should I waste my beautiful mind on something like that?"

Mrs. Bush is not getting any younger. When she eventually ceases to walk among us, we will undoubtedly see photographs of *her* flag-draped coffin. Whatever obituaries that run will admiringly mention those wizened, dynastic loins of hers and praise her staunch refusal to color her hair or glamorize her image. But will they remember this particular statement of hers, this "Let them eat cake" for the twenty-first century? Unlikely, since it received far too little play and definitely insufficient outrage when she said it. So let us promise herewith to never forget her callous disregard for other parents' children when her own son was sending them to make the ultimate sacrifice, while asking of the rest of us little more than to promise to go shopping. Commit the quote to memory, and say it whenever her name comes up. Remind others how she lacked even the bare minimum of human integrity, the most basic requirement of decency that says if you support a war, you should be willing, if not to join those nineteen-year-olds yourself, then at least, *at the very least,* to acknowledge that said war was actually going on. Stupid fucking cow.

So that's why I answered "yes." But, like I said, it is grass soup. (I hope.)

There has been much talk about a post–September 11 backlog of applications and how I should expect to wait far longer than the usual year. But ten months after filing, I am notified that I have been provisionally approved, pending an interview. I am to report to the Bureau of Citizenship and Immigration Services at Federal Plaza. It is a scorcher of a May day when I go downtown. Even now there are equivalents of first class and steerage. Those of us with scheduled appointments are immediately ushered inside and through the metal detectors, while the line of people who have just shown up snakes around the block. I check in at the window and am asked if, before starting the official process of my glorious, butterfly-like transformation into David Rakoff, American, I'd like to change my name. The hairy-knuckled, pinkie-ringed lawyer for a Vietnamese fellow behind me nudges his client and says, "Hear that? You wanna change your name? To George Bush? Saddam Hussein? Anything you want. Haw haw," he laughs, clapping his client on the back. The young man shoots me an apologetic look to suggest that, yes, even with the obvious cultural and language barriers, he knows that he has unwittingly hired a shithead.

There are about fifty of us waiting for our interviews. Many people are in their best clothes. I wonder if I've adversely affected my chances by having opted for comfort in Levi's and sneakers, but so long as the Russian woman in her early forties is across from me, I have nothing to worry about. She wears painted-on acid-wash jeans, white stilettos, and a tight blouse of sheer leopard-print fabric. The sleeves are designed as a series of irregular tatters clinging to her arms, as if she's just come from tearing the hide off the back of an actual leopard. A really slutty leopard.

My name is called, and Agent Morales brings me back to her office. From her window I can see the Brooklyn Bridge, hazy under a humid sky the color of a soiled shirt collar. Agent Morales's desk is crowded with small plaster figures of cherubic children holding fishing poles, polka-dot-hankie hobo bundles, small wicker picnic baskets, etc. The walls, however, are almost completely bare. Perhaps it's bureau policy, but all of those typical examples of office humor — that in other work environments might get their own piece of paper, perhaps with Garfield or Dilbert saying them — have been printed on the same $8\frac{1}{2}$ × 11 sheet and listed like bulleted items in a PowerPoint presentation. There are old standbys like "You don't have to be crazy to work here, but it sure helps," along with some gags that are new to me: "Chocolate, coffee, men: some things are just better rich" and "I'm out of estrogen and I have a gun!" The latter frankly seems to push the envelope of acceptable discourse in a government office.

She has me raise my right hand while swearing to tell the truth. That's it — no Bible, no Koran, no sacred text of any sort to solidify my oath. Perhaps the increased blood flow from my upheld arm down to my heart is enough to safeguard against perjury. She questions me about any potential criminal past. (A boy could get ideas, or at least a distorted view of his own allure, seeing as how regularly I am asked if I have ever turned tricks.) Agent Morales then administers my citizenship test. Along with my application, I downloaded the list of one hundred possible questions, any handful of which she might choose to ask. Some of them are incredibly basic, like When is Independence Day?, while others delve more deeply into the three branches of government, or ask you to name some of the better-known constitutional amendments.

Here are the four questions I am asked: What do the stripes on the flag represent? What were the original states called? What is the judiciary? And who takes over if the president dies?

"Dick Cheney, God help us," I answer with a shudder. Agent Morales gives me a small half-smile. She then has me write down on a piece of paper, "I watch the news every day." It's the literacy test, the final hurdle of the interview. She looks at it and, picking up my application, she compares them, her eyes going back and forth between the two documents.

"Wait a second. Who wrote your application?" she asks, confused.

"I did, but I was really, really careful."

"Oh my God," she says, almost with relief. " 'Cause the writing is so different. We couldn't believe it, your application was so tidy. It looked so good, and *this* was so good . . . ," she says, unfolding my painstaking table of trips outside the country. She reads through it once more, as if reminiscing over a pleasant memory. Pathetically, in that moment, being approved for citizenship is secondary to the thrill that her kind words about my penmanship give me. I am out of there within five minutes, a provisional American. I have now only to wait for my swearing-in. I exit the same door onto lower Broadway that I did almost exactly ten years earlier when I got my green card, and the same bleakness overtakes me. It is a feeling more unrooted than mere statelessness. It's as though all my moorings have been cut. Any connection that I might have had to anything or anyone has been, for the moment, severed. It's a cold realization that I am now, as indeed I always have been, an official unit of one.

Coincidentally, the Canadian-born newscaster Peter Jennings also became a citizen around the same time, after almost forty years in the United States. According to the papers, his swearing-in took place in a swanky Manhattan courthouse. I, on the other hand, am forced to catch the 6:55 A.M. train to Hempstead, Long Island. My friend Sarah, a self-described civics nerd, very sweetly agrees to come with me. She is a good deal more excited than I am. This all feels like monumentally bad timing, or possibly the wrong move altogether. Just a couple of days earlier, the front page of the paper had two news stories. The first was about how Canada was on the brink of legalizing gay marriage, and the second told of an appeals court in the District of Columbia circuit that ruled that the detainees at Guantánamo Bay are legally outside the reach of the protections of the Constitution.

The INS center, a one-story sprawl devoid of character, fits into its very unprepossessing surroundings on a highway of strip malls with empty storefronts. Still, the air is electric with a sense of occasion as we line up at the door. No one has come alone, and people are dressed to the nines. We are separated from our friends and family and pass through the final sheep dip before becoming Americans. I have to answer once again whether, in the intervening four weeks between my interview and now, I have become a dipsomaniac, a whore, or traveled backward in time to willingly participate in Kristallnacht. They take back my green card, which after ten years is barely holding up. It was always government property. There is a strange lightness I feel having turned in the small laminated object that has been on my person for an entire decade. Something has been lanced. For the brief walk from this anteroom to the main auditorium, I am a completely undocumented human. The only picture ID I have is my gym membership, and it has my name spelled wrong.

There is absolutely nothing on the walls of the huge, fluorescent-lit, drop-ceilinged room into which we are corralled. It's the new federalist architecture. Even travel agencies give out free posters of the Grand Canyon or the Chicago Loop at night. Alternately, how hard could it be to get a bunch of schoolchildren in to paint a lousy mural of some politically neutral rainbows and trees? Our guests are already seated way in the back; I cannot find Sarah in the sea of faces. I am grateful for the newspaper I have brought with me, since it takes well over an hour for everyone to register and find their seats. Across the aisle from me, one of my fellow soon-to-be new citizens has a paperback. He is reading *American Psycho*. Give me your tired, your poor, your huddled masses yearning to read about a murderous yuppie dispatching live rodents into women's vaginas. Welcome, friend.

I catnap a little and one of the guards turns on a boom box perched on a chair for the musical prelude. A typical pompy instrumental of "The Star-Spangled Banner," followed by a very atypical "America the Beautiful," rendered in a minor key with full string orchestration, straight out of a forties film noir. Three women and one man then get up on the dais. The man checks that everyone has turned in all their documents. It's a minor federal offense to keep them. "Your old passports from the countries you came from are souvenirs and can never be used again." The people in the back are instructed to applaud loudly, people with cameras are told to take lots of pictures. There is pretty well only joy in this room, save for some extreme Canadian ambivalence.

They lead us in the Pledge of Allegiance. I leave off "under God" as I say it. Oh, maverick! I feel about as renegade as the mohawked young "anarchist" I once watched walking up Third Avenue on a Saturday evening. For some reason the streets were choked with limousines that night. My young friend spat contemptuously at each one that sat unoccupied and parked, while letting the peopled vehicles go saliva-free.

To lead us in singing the national anthem for our first time as Americans, we have a choir. Not a real choir, but a group of employees who come up to the front. We sing and I cry, although I'm not sure why. I'm clearly overcome by something. It's a combination of guilt over having shown insufficient appreciation for my origins, of feeling very much alone in the world, and — I am not proud to say — of constructing life-and-death grass-soup scenarios for the immigrants standing around me. Strangely, no one else that I can see sheds a tear. Perhaps it is because they are not big drama queens.

One of the women on the dais addresses us. "There are many reasons each of you has come to be here today. Some of you have relatives or spouses. Either way, you all know that this is the land where you can succeed and prosper. You've come to live the American dream and to enjoy the country's great freedom and rights. But with rights come great responsibilities."

Shouldering that great responsibility is primarily what I came here for today. Question 87 of the citizenship test is "What is the most important right granted to U.S. citizens?" The answer, *formulated by the government itself*, is "the right to vote." As we file out of the room, I ask someone who works there where the voter registration forms are. I am met with a shrug. "A church group used to hand them out, but they ran out of money, I think."

I don't go to the post office to then have to buy my stamps from a bunch of Girl Scouts outside, and if the Girl Scouts are sick that day, then I'm shit out of luck. A church group? Why isn't there a form clipped to my naturalization certificate? It is difficult not to see something insidious in this oversight while I stand in this sea of humanity, the majority of whom are visible minorities.

Sarah presents me with a hardbound copy of the U.S. Constitution and we head back to the station. We have half an hour to kill before our train. If I thought the lack of America-related decor in the main room of the citizenship facility was lousy public relations, it is as nothing compared with this port of entry, the town of Hempstead itself. Sarah and I attempt a walk around. My first glimpse as a citizen of this golden land is not the Lady of the Harbor shining her beacon through the Atlantic mist but cracked pavement, cheap liquor stores with thick Plexiglas partitions in front of the cashiers, shuttered businesses, and used-car lots. The only spot of brightness on the blighted landscape is the window of the adult book and video store, with its two mannequins, one wearing a shiny Stars-and-Stripes bra-and-G-string set, and the other in a rainbow thong. Just like the dreamy former New Jersey governor Jim McGreevey, I could comfortably dance in either of these native costumes of my twin identities.

My first Independence Day as an American comes scarcely two weeks later. I mark it by heading down to the nation's capital to celebrate with my old friend Madhulika, who is newly American herself. Washington, D.C., is a sultry place in July. We stay indoors, hanging out and preparing a proper July Fourth meal of barbecued beer-can chicken and corn on the cob. In the evening, once the heat has broken, we head off with her husband, Jim, and their two daughters to see the fireworks. In the past, we might have lain out on the vast lawns of the Mall, but they have been fenced and cordoned off for security, so we park ourselves in a group of several hundred, sitting down on the pavement and grassy median in front of the DAR building.

The fireworks are big and bombastic and seem much louder and more aggressive than those in New York. Then again, in New York I'm usually on a rooftop miles away from the action. We are right under the explosions here. A little girl behind me, strapped into her stroller, twists in fear and panic as the percussive reports of the rockets thud through her rib cage. "No no no," she moans softly throughout the entire thirty-minute show.

She has my sympathies 100 percent. I have made a terrible miscalculation, at least regarding my decision to go down to D.C. I adore my friends, and the floodlit Greek Revival buildings of Capitol Hill are undeniably beautiful and a suitable representation of the majesty of this great nation of which I am now a part, but I'm not being glib when I say that one of the most compelling reasons for my having become a citizen was to entrench and make permanent my relationship with New York, the great love of my life. Being down here feels a bit like I chose to go on my honeymoon with my in-laws while my beloved waits for me back at the apartment. There is a supercomputer somewhere in the Nevada desert whose sole function is to count the number of times that I have said the following, because it is unquantifiable by human minds at this point, but this time it's really true: I should have stayed home.

There are already forty people waiting on line by seven o'clock on Election Day morning. My local polling place is in the basement of a new NYU dormitory on the corner of Fourteenth Street and Third Avenue. An ugly box of a building, it was erected on the site of the old dirty bookstore where, coincidentally, one could also enter booths to manipulate levers of a different sort.

It has been an awfully long time between drinks for me. I haven't voted since I was eighteen, when I cast a ballot in Canada during my first summer back from college. It's not that I take voting lightly. Quite the opposite. Living in the United States, where the coverage of Canadian politics is pretty well nonexistent, I never felt well enough informed to have an opinion. But even if I had made it my business to stay abreast of things — going to the library to read the foreign papers in those pre-Internet years — after a certain point I no longer felt entitled to have a say in Canada's affairs, having essentially abandoned the place. I suspect this is going to happen for the next little while every time I have to do something unmistakably American, like cast a ballot in a nonparliamentary election or go through customs on my U.S. passport, but standing here on line, I am stricken with such guilt and buyer's remorse, overcome with a feeling of such nostalgia for where I came from, with its socialized medicine and gun control, that it is all I can do not to break ranks and start walking uptown and not stop until I reach the 49th parallel. There is also an equal part of me that is completely thrilled to finally be part of the electoral process. I am not alone in my exuberance this morning. Many people around me also seem filled with a buoyant and tentative excitement that George Bush might very well lose *this* election as well. Complete strangers are talking to one another, almost giddy at the prospect. Others emerge from having voted and raise both their hands with crossed fingers, shaking them at us like maracas. "Good luck!" they wish us as they head off to work. It's almost like a party in this crowded dormitory basement that smells like a foot.

I love everything about the booth: the stiff, pleated curtain; the foursquare, early-industrial heaviness of the brass switches; the no-nonsense 1950s primary-school font of the labels; the lever that gives out a satisfying *tchnk* when I pull it back. It all feels solid and tried and tested. In the very best way, un-Floridian.

For the rest of the day I bound the floor of the apartment like a caged tiger, unable to settle. I make and receive dozens of phone calls. My in-box is full of well over a hundred e-mails from friends, all on precisely the same theme: early numbers and preliminary exit polls, predictions from the pundits, all pointing to a Kerry victory. We are contacting one another the way my immediate family obsessively did in the final days of my sister's first pregnancy, leading up to the birth of my oldest nephew. We are trying to bear witness for one another in these last few moments of the never-to-be-returned-to time of Before. It's overblown and starry-eyed, we know. Even if Kerry wins, he's going to inherit some pretty insurmountable messes both here and abroad, but it is a function of what a shitty four years it has been that we still feel we are on the cusp of something potentially miraculous and life-changing.

The city that evening feels like New Year's Eve, without the menace. My neighborhood is full of people walking by with bottles of booze, on their way to watch the returns with friends; restaurants and bars have their doors open and their TVs on. Even I have no fewer than four parties to go to. I plan to skip lightly from venue to venue, until I end up somewhere, standing in a crowd of like-minded (albeit younger and more attractive) Democrats just as the final polls close and the new president is announced. It will be one big booty call for justice.

That was before everything turned brown. Before the ever-reddening map rooted me to one spot. Before I parked myself at my friends' apartment, overstaying my welcome and slowly getting drunk. I eventually give up before Ohio is lost, and stagger home sometime after midnight. I turn off the alarm before I go to sleep. I don't want to hear the news in the morning.

Daybreak rouses me anyway. I lie awake, unable to move. If I put my foot on the floor, it will make it true: four more years. I stay where I am, frozen, my bladder full. I'll have to get up soon, but for a few more minutes I try not to waste my beautiful mind. Eventually I turn on the radio and cold reality comes flooding in. I know of a journalist who, when Reagan was reelected, called everyone she knew — friends, acquaintances, everyone — and sweepingly screamed "President Shithead! President Shithead!" into the phone. I understand the impulse, but I try to be philosophical as I start my day. He can't be president forever. Besides, I can wait him out. It's not like I'm going anywhere.

JOE SACCO

■

Trauma on Loan

FROM *The Guardian*

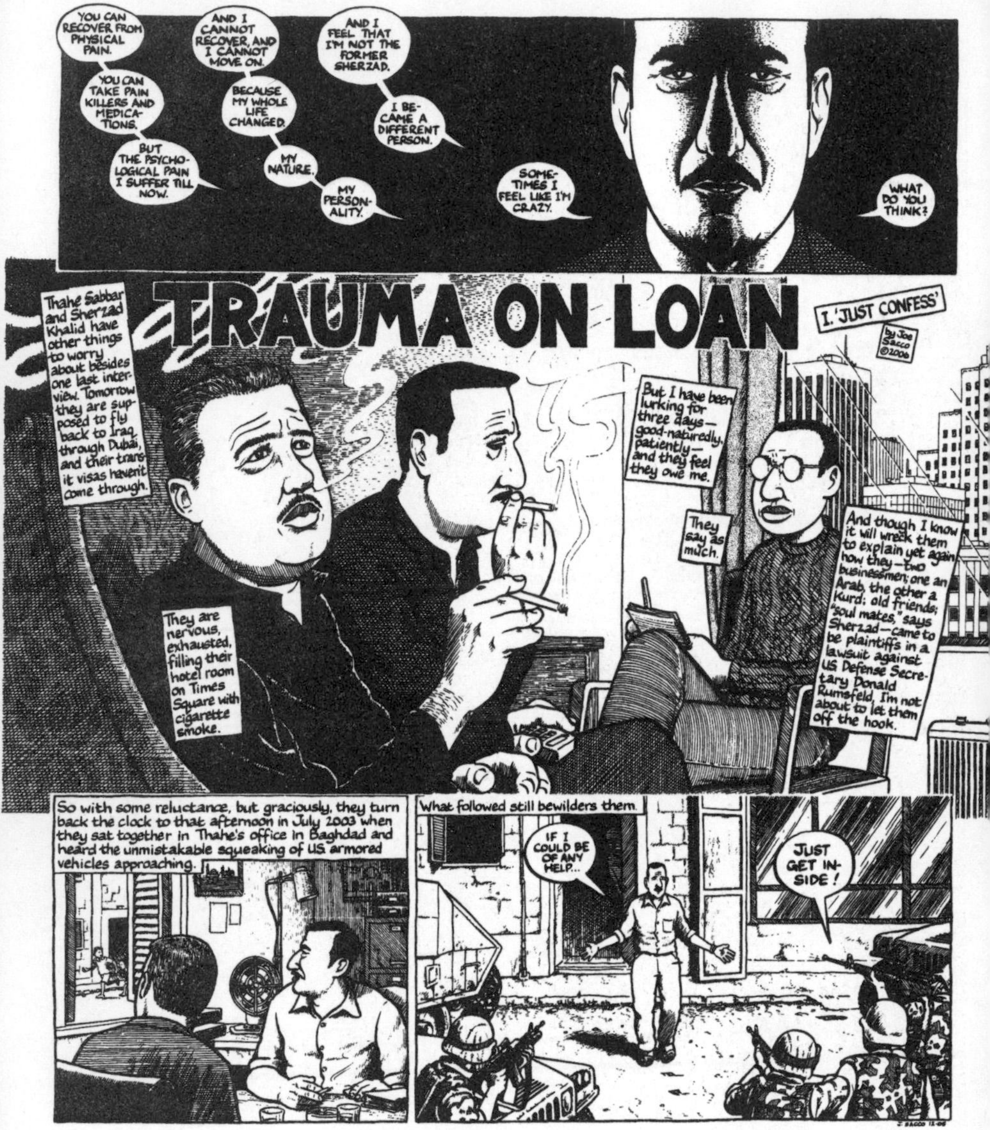

YOU CAN RECOVER FROM PHYSICAL PAIN.
YOU CAN TAKE PAIN KILLERS AND MEDICATIONS.
BUT THE PSYCHOLOGICAL PAIN I SUFFER TILL NOW.
AND I CANNOT RECOVER, AND I CANNOT MOVE ON.
BECAUSE MY WHOLE LIFE CHANGED.
MY NATURE.
MY PERSONALITY.
AND I FEEL THAT I'M NOT THE FORMER SHERZAD.
I BECAME A DIFFERENT PERSON.
SOMETIMES I FEEL LIKE I'M CRAZY.
WHAT DO YOU THINK?
TRAUMA ON LOAN
I. 'JUST CONFESS'
by Joe Sacco ©2006
Thahe Sabbar and Sherzad Khalid have other things to worry about besides one last interview. Tomorrow they are supposed to fly back to Iraq through Dubai, and their transit visas haven't come through.
They are nervous, exhausted, filling their hotel room on Times Square with cigarette smoke.
But I have been lurking for three days— good-naturedly, patiently— and they feel they owe me.
They say as much.
And though I know it will wreck them to explain yet again how they—two businessmen; one an Arab, the other a Kurd; old friends; "soul mates," says Sherzad—came to be plaintiffs in a lawsuit against U.S. Defense Secretary Donald Rumsfeld, I'm not about to let them off the hook.
So with some reluctance, but graciously, they turn back the clock to that afternoon in July 2003 when they sat together in Thahe's office in Baghdad and heard the unmistakable squeaking of U.S. armored vehicles approaching.
What followed still bewilders them.
IF I COULD BE OF ANY HELP...
JUST GET INSIDE!

According to the two men, American troops then entered the building "from all sides," including from the roof.

Sherzad: "They were yelling... and aiming their guns. And they started beating everybody."

Along with others in the building, they were cuffed, hooded, and driven away. It was nighttime when the vehicle stopped. "They kicked us off," according to Thahe.

"We fell on the ground... Our hands were still tied behind our backs, and we were still hooded."

Thahe's left shoulder was dislocated in the fall.

When their hoods were removed, they say they found themselves in one of Saddam Hussein's presidential palaces—standing in front of a cage of lions. The lions, evidently, once had been the personal property of Uday, one of Saddam's notorious sons.

One by one, the detainees were taken to the cage and, according to Sherzad, told to confess.

WHAT DO YOU WANT US TO CONFESS?

YOU DON'T KNOW WHY YOU'RE HERE? JUST CONFESS!

Thahe: "They opened the door... We went in, maybe a meter"...

"But when the lions came running toward us, they pulled us outside"...

"I lost consciousness. I was unconscious most of the time now. And the way they woke me up was by beating me..."

The men then were taken to a wall behind the cage.

THE OFFICER HAS DECIDED TO EXECUTE YOU BY SHOOTING. SO YOU BETTER CONFESS.

Sherzad: "And we didn't confess because we didn't know what they wanted us to say."

YOU KNOW WHEN YOU WATCH MOVIES AND YOU HEAR THE WORD "FIRE!"

IT WAS THE SAME.

THEY SAID, "FIRE!" AND THEY FIRED.

"I fell down to the ground. And then I heard the soldiers' laughter. So I started looking at my body, trying to find a trace of blood. I realized it was just a mock execution..."

According to Thahe and Sherzad, by then a number of detainees had pissed on themselves.

They spent the night shackled to a tennis court fence, and the next day they were taken to the prison at Baghdad's international airport, where they were made to run a gauntlet of baton-wielding soldiers before reaching their cells.

II. 'THE LION THING'

In America, another sort of gauntlet awaited them:

Cameramen!

Photographers!

Reporters!

By the time I met them in Washington, D.C., their lawyers, who include members of the American Civil Liberties Union and Human Rights First, fretted that all the interviews had pushed their clients to the edge.

ATTORNEY HINA SHAMSI, HUMAN RIGHTS FIRST

SOMETIMES WE DON'T KNOW WHEN THEY'VE HAD ENOUGH, AND SOMETIMES THEY DON'T KNOW THEMSELVES UNTIL AFTERWARDS.

Thahe and Sherzad's visit to the States is meant to draw attention to their legal complaint, which alleges "torture or other cruel, inhuman or degrading punishment" while they were in U.S. military custody.

They "are representative of so many hundreds or thousands of others...whose shockingly brutal mistreatment" is ultimately Mr. Rumsfeld's responsibility, according to Emily Whitfield, the ACLU's media relations director.

In effect, Thahe and Sherzad are standing in for all the hooded and beaten. For this case, they are sacrificial detainees."

* THEY ARE JOINED BY SIX OTHER PLAINTIFFS: FOUR AFGHANS AND TWO IRAQIS

J. SACCO 11-05

So when their lawyers expressed misgivings about Thahe and Sherzad reopening their wounds for one last journalist—me!—when they hinted *my* interview might be cancelled, I wanted to snap back—

"Come on!"

"You brought them here to reopen their wounds."

"No point worrying about their feelings *now*."

Besides, the media blitz has had an impact. Even the chief defendant has taken notice.

THE LION THING WAS MENTIONED AT THE RUMSFELD BRIEFING.

Yes, it's "the lion thing" that is raising eyebrows. Much else of what Thahe and Sherzad allege —the shackling in extreme temperatures, the electric shocks, the desecration of the Koran—might seem ho-hum to an American public that has long digested the enormities of Abu Ghraib.

And at his press conference, Mr. Rumsfeld called Thahe and Sherzad's lion story "farfetched" and referred to Al Qaeda documents that—

—TRAIN PEOPLE, TERRORISTS, TO LIE ABOUT THEIR TREATMENT.

Thahe and Sherzad might take exception to Mr. Rumsfeld's implication that they have studied Al Qaeda manuals or that they are "terrorists."

Neither of them was ever charged with anything by the Americans.

III. "WHAT IS YOUR FAVORITE SPORT?"

WHEN I WAS FIRST TAKEN FOR INTERROGATION, I WAS HAPPY.

I THOUGHT, NOW I CAN EXPLAIN MYSELF.

"But the first question was—

WHERE IS SADDAM?*"

"I laughed, and he hit me."

After perfunctory questions about weapons of mass destruction, Al Qaeda, etc., the interrogator asked—

WHAT IS YOUR FAVORITE BREAKFAST?

WHAT IS YOUR FAVORITE SPORT?

WHAT TIME DO YOU GO TO SLEEP?

WHY WAS HE ASKING YOU THOSE LAST THINGS!

I DON'T KNOW.

But then, does Sherzad know why he was subjected to "simulat[ed] anal rape" with a water bottle? Does Thahe know why "one or more soldiers in the presence of male and female soldiers inserted their fingers" into his anus?

*SADDAM HUSSEIN WAS STILL IN HIDING WHEN THIS INTERROGATION TOOK PLACE

J. SACCO 12-05

I've quoted Thahe's and Sherzad's sexual assault allegations from the lawsuit. Their attorneys ask me not to bring up the subject with the men. When CNN broke that ground rule and badgered Thahe about his ordeal, he was retraumatized, I'm told.

IV. 'I HAVE NO DESIRE TO TELL A SAD STORY'

In the morning, an interview with 'Time' magazine; in the afternoon, a meeting with earnest Senate staffers who promise to relay Thahe and Sherzad's story to their bosses.

And now one of the attorneys suggests a quick get-together with her colleagues in an office nearby.

IT'S UP TO YOU.

But Thahe is only being diplomatic. He boards the van rented for the day's activities and waits for his handlers to follow.

WE WANT TO GO SEE THE WHITE HOUSE.

The lawyers are sensitive to the moods of their clients. The rest of the day will be given over to sightseeing.

For an hour or two, Thahe and Sherzad smile in front of America's monuments to liberty.

But the cell phones are ringing again.

A senator has agreed to meet with Thahe and Sherzad personally.

When?!

Now!

Thahe is almost despondent.

He has to remind himself why he's here.

WE DIDN'T COME AS TOURISTS.

Sherzad, on the other hand, won't have it.

AFTER SEEING THIS BEAUTIFUL VIEW, I HAVE NO DESIRE TO TELL A SAD STORY.

The attorneys turn down the senator. And they tell Thahe and Sherzad they will get to see the White House in the morning.

V. THE AIRPORT

AT THE AIRPORT, THERE WERE 75 TO 150 DETAINEES IN EACH TENT.

"There was a place for people to sit, but not to sleep. The ground was earth. We were given one blanket. My pillow was my shoes.

"I had a beard. I had long hair just like a beast.

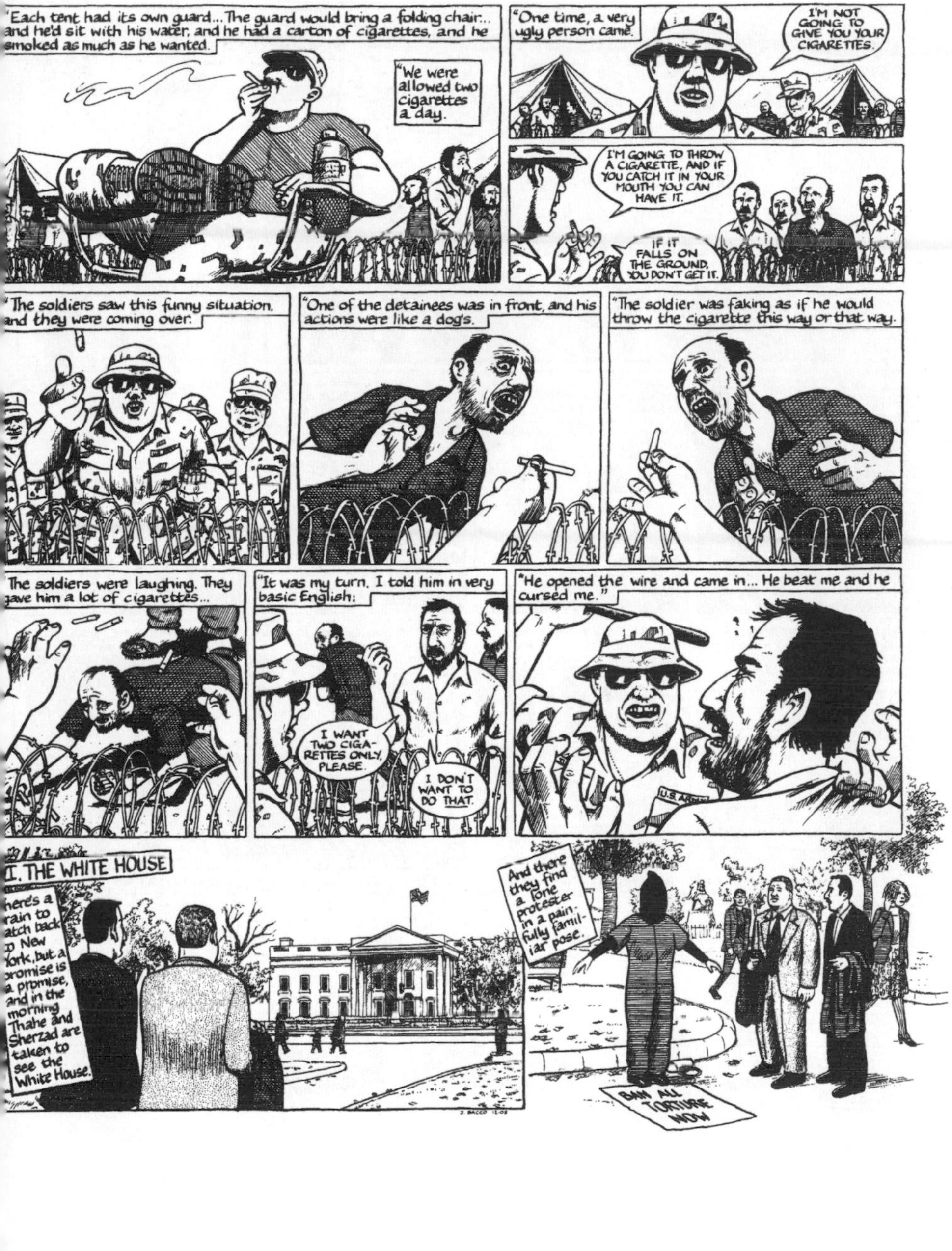
"Each tent had its own guard... The guard would bring a folding chair... and he'd sit with his water, and he had a carton of cigarettes, and he smoked as much as he wanted.
"We were allowed two cigarettes a day.
"One time, a very ugly person came.
I'M NOT GOING TO GIVE YOU YOUR CIGARETTES.
I'M GOING TO THROW A CIGARETTE, AND IF YOU CATCH IT IN YOUR MOUTH YOU CAN HAVE IT.
IF IT FALLS ON THE GROUND, YOU DON'T GET IT.
"The soldiers saw this funny situation, and they were coming over.
"One of the detainees was in front, and his actions were like a dog's.
"The soldier was faking as if he would throw the cigarette this way or that way.
The soldiers were laughing. They gave him a lot of cigarettes...
"It was my turn. I told him in very basic English:
I WANT TWO CIGARETTES ONLY, PLEASE.
I DON'T WANT TO DO THAT.
"He opened the wire and came in... He beat me and he cursed me."
U.S. ARMY
I. THE WHITE HOUSE
There's a train to catch back to New York, but a promise is a promise, and in the morning Thahe and Sherzad are taken to see the White House.
And there they find a lone protester in a painfully familiar pose.
BAN ALL TORTURE NOW

It is Jennifer Harbury.

She was in the news several years ago.

Her husband, a Guatemalan resistance leader, had been interrogated and tortured to death by Guatemalan forces working with the Central Intelligence Agency.

Like Thahe and Sherzad she filed a lawsuit.

Hers also reached for the top.

She named high-level U.S. officials who, she says, withheld information that could have helped her save her husband's life.

Her case went all the way to the Supreme Court— and lost.

Ms. Harbury resumes her pose.

Thahe and Sherzad leave to catch their train.

VII. CAMP BUCCA

YOU KNOW, TOWARD THE LAST PERIOD, MY MORALE WAS BECOMING VERY LOW. AND I REALLY BROKE DOWN.

"There was this guy in the detention center who knew English so I asked him to write a petition on my behalf.

"I just asked, 'What is going to happen to me?... I have not been charged.' So I asked for their mercy. I really pleaded and begged.

"And I gave it to the guards.

"After a few hours they came and asked for me so I was really happy. I thought there was some sort of response...

"They took me to the 'silent tent.'... In this tent you are prohibited from speaking or sleeping.

"Anytime you closed your eyes and were about to sleeping—

"— they would come yelling at you, cursing and insulting—

"— and two of them would carry you—

"— and throw you outside the tent.

"And then, after that beating, insulting, cursing, they would bring you in the same way."

I ask Sherzad how many times he was thrown in this way.

I DON'T REALLY KNOW BECAUSE, FOR ME, UP TILL NOW, IT'S JUST LIKE A DREAM.

IT WASN'T REALITY.

VIII. RELEASE

Honestly, I've been gentle.

I haven't pushed.

I've jumped over whole allegations, entire beatings and humiliations.

I've curbed my enthusiasm for detail.

Yet even without the hints from the attorney monitoring our conversation, it's clear to me that Thahe has had enough.

CONTINUE WITH ME BECAUSE I'M STRONGER THAN HE IS.

So I go on with Sherzad for a few minutes more, but I know it's time to leave.

Because after a while, in certain situations, a journalist in a room begins to smell; even he notices.

Still—I have one more question. Just one more and I'm going.

How were you released?

YOU KNOW, THE RELEASE IS RANDOM JUST LIKE THE ARREST.

"Once you're released, you don't believe it. You look behind you because you're so scared that they're going to jump you and arrest you again."

"And I did not believe that I was released until I arrived at my house and saw my children."

"And I closed the door."

"And I asked my brother to bring me a lock so I could lock the door from the inside."

"And they were laughing at me."

I pack my pen and notebook and tape recorder.

I get up to go.

I tell Thahe and Sherzad that I was honored to meet them.

I thank them.

I wish them a good journey back to Iraq.

And, once again, they are released.

J. SACCO 12-06

GEORGE SAUNDERS

■

The New Mecca

FROM *GQ*

Put That Stately Pleasure Palace There Between Those Other Two

IF YOU ARE like I was three weeks ago, before I went to Dubai, you may not know exactly where Dubai is. Near Venezuela? No, sorry, that is incorrect. Somewhere north of Pakistan, an idyllic mountain kingdom ruled by gentle goatherds? Well, no.

Dubai, actually, is in the United Arab Emirates, on the Arabian Peninsula, 100 miles across the Gulf from Iran, about 600 miles from Basra, 1,100 from Kabul.

You might also not know, as I did not know, what Dubai is all about or why someone would want to send you there. You might wonder: Is it dangerous? Will I be beheaded? Will I need a translator? Will my translator be beheaded? Just before we're beheaded, will my translator try to get out of it by blaming everything on me?

No, no, not to worry. Dubai, turns out, is quite possibly the safest great city in the world. It is also the newest great city in the world. In the 1950s, before oil was discovered there, Dubai was just a cluster of mud huts and Bedouin tents along Dubai Creek: the entire city has basically been built in the last fifty years. And actually, the cool parts — the parts that have won Dubai its reputation as "the Vegas of the Middle East" or "the Venice of the Middle East" or "the Disney World of the Middle East, if Disney World were the size of San Francisco and out in a desert" — have been built in the last ten years. And the supercool parts — the parts that, when someone tells you about them, your attention drifts because these morons have to be lying (no one dreams this big or has that much available capital) — those parts are all going to be built in the next five years.

By 2010, if all goes according to plan, Dubai will have: the world's tallest skyscraper (2,300 feet), largest mall, biggest theme park, longest indoor ski run, most luxurious underwater hotel (accessible by submarine train); a huge (2,000-acre, 60,000-resident) development called International City, divided into nation-neighborhoods (England, China, France, Greece, etc.) within which all homes will be required to reflect the national architectural style; not to mention four artificially constructed island mega-archipelagoes (three shaped like giant palm trees, the fourth like a map of the world), built using a specially designed boat that dredges up tons of ocean-bottom sand each day and sprays it into place.

Before I saw Dubai for myself, I assumed this was bluster: brag about ten upcoming projects, finally build one — smaller than you'd bragged — hope everyone forgets about the other nine.

But no.

I've been to Dubai, and I believe. If America was looking for a pluralistic, tax-free, laissez-faire, diverse, inclusive, tolerant, no-holds-barred, daringly capitalist country to serve as a shining City on the Hill for the entire Middle East, we should have left Iraq alone and sponsored a National Peaceful Tourist Excursion to Dubai and spent our ninety quadrillion Iraq War dollars there. Maybe.

In Which I Fall in Love with a Fake Town

From the air, Dubai looked something like Dallas circa 1985: a vast expanse of one- or two-story white boxes, punctuated by clusters of freakish skyscrapers. (An Indian kid shouted, "Dad, looks like a microchip!") Driving in from the airport, you're struck by the usual first-night-in-new-country exotica ("There's a *Harley-Davidson* dealership — right in the *Middle East!*"), and the skyscraper clusters were, OK, odd-looking (like four or five architects had staged a weird-off, with unlimited funds) — but all in all, it was, you know, a city. And I wondered what all the fuss was about.

Then I got to my hotel.

The Madinat Jumeirah is, near as I can figure, a superresort consisting of three, or possibly six, luxury subhotels and two, or maybe three, clusters of luxury villas, spread out over about forty acres, or for all I know it was twelve subhotels and nine luxury-villa clusters — I really couldn't tell, so seamless and extravagant and confusing was all the luxury. The Madinat is themed to resemble an ancient Arabian village. But to say the Madinat is themed doesn't begin to express the intensity and opulence and unreal extent of the theming. The site is crisscrossed by 2.3 miles of fake creeks, trolled night and day by dozens of fake Arabian water taxis (*abras*), piloted by what I can only describe as fake Arabs because, though dressed like old-timey Arabs, they are actually young, smiling, sweet-hearted guys from Nepal or Kenya or the Philippines, who speak terrific English as they pilot the soundless electrical *abras* through this lush, created Arabia, looking for someone to take back to the lobby, or to the largest outdoor pool in the Middle East, or over to Trader Vic's, which is also themed and looks something like a mysterious ancient casbah inexplicably filled with beautiful contemporary people.

And so, though my first response to elaborate Theming is often irony (Who *did* this? And *why*? Look at that *modern exit sign* over that *eighteenth-century bedstead*. Haw!), what I found during my stay at the Madinat is that irony is actually my first response to tepid, lame Theming. In the belly of radical Theming, my first response was to want to stay forever, bring my family over, set up shop in my hut-evoking villa, and never go home again.

Because the truth is, it's beautiful. The air is perfumed, you hear fountains, the tinkling of bells, distant chanted prayers, and when the (real) Arabian moon comes up, yellow and attenuated, over a (fake) Arabian wind tower, you feel you are a resident of some ancient city — or rather, some ancient city if you had dreamed the ancient city, and the ancient city had been purged of all disease, death, and corruption, and you were a Founder/Elder of that city, much beloved by your Citizens, the Staff.

Wandering around one night, a little lost, I came to the realization that verisimilitude and pleasure are not causally related. How is this "fake"? This is real flowing water, the date and palm trees are real, the smell of incense and rosewater is real. The staggering effect of the immense scale of one particular crosswalk — which joins two hotels together and is, if you can imagine this, a four-story ornate crosswalk that looks like it should have ten thousand cheering Imperial Troops clustered under it and an enigmatic young Princess waving from one of its arabesquey windows — that effect is *real*. You feel it in your gut and your legs. It makes you feel happy and heroic and a little breathless, in love anew with the world and its possibilities. You have somehow entered the landscape of a dream, the Platonic realization of the idea of Ancient Village — but there are real smells here, and when, a little dazzled, you mutter to yourself ("This is like a freaking dream, I love it, I, wow . . ."), you don't wake up, but instead a smiling Filipino kid comes up and asks if you'd like a drink.

On the flight over, I watched an interview with an employee of Jumeirah International, the company that manages the Madinat. Even though he saw it going up himself, he said, he feels it is an ancient place every time he enters, and finds it hard to believe that, three years ago, it was all just sand.

A Word about the Help

UAE nationals comprise about 20 percent of the city's population. Until three years ago, only nationals were allowed to own property in Dubai, and they still own essentially all of it. Visually identifiable by their dress — the men wear the traditional white dishdashas; the women, long black gowns and abayas — these nationals occupy the top rung of a rigid social hierarchy: imagine Hollywood, if everyone who'd been wildly successful in the movie business had to wear a distinctive costume.

A rung down from the Emiratis are some 200,000 expats (mostly Brits but also other Europeans, Russians, Lebanese, Indians), who comprise a kind of managerial class: the marketing people, the hotel managers, the human-resource gurus, the accountants, the lawyers, etc. But a majority of Dubai's expat population — roughly two thirds of it — comes from poorer countries around the world, mainly South Asia or Africa. They built Dubai, they run it with their labor, but can't afford to own homes or raise their families here. They take their dirhams home and cash them in for local currency, in this way increasing their wealth by as much as tenfold. They live here for two years, five years, fifteen years, and take home-leaves as often as every three months or as infrequently as never.

And even within this class there are stratifications. The hotel workers I met at the Madinat, for example, having been handpicked by Jumeirah scouts from the finest hotels in their native countries, are a class, or two, or three, above the scores of South Asian laborers who do the heavy construction work, who live in labor camps on the outskirts of town (where they sleep ten to a room), and whose social life, according to one British expat I met, consists of "a thrilling evening once a month of sitting in a circle popping their bulbs out so some bloody Russian chickie can race around hand-jobbing them all in a mob."

You see these construction guys all over town: somewhat darker-complexioned, wearing blue jumpsuits, averting their eyes when you try to say hello, squatting outside a work site at three in the morning because Dubai construction crews work twenty-four hours a day, seven days a week.

There is much to be done.

The Wild Wadi Epiphany

A short, complimentary golf-cart ride down the beach from the Madinat is Wild Wadi, a sprawling, themed water park whose theme is: a wadi is flooding! Once an hour, the sound of thunder/cracking trees/rushing waves blares through the facility-wide PA system, and a waterfall begins dropping a thousand gallons of water a minute into an empty pond, which then violently overflows down the pedestrian walkways, past the gift shop.

Waiting in line, I'm part of a sort of United Nations of partial nudity: me, a couple of sunburned German women, three angry-looking Arab teens, kind of like the Marx Brothers if the Marx Brothers were Arabs in bathing suits with cigarettes behind their ears, who, I notice, are muttering to one another while glowering. Then I see what they're muttering/glowering about: several (like, fifteen) members of the United States Navy, on shore leave. You can tell they're Navy because they're huge and tattooed and innocently happy and keep bellowing things like "Dude, fuck that, I am all *about* dancing!" while punching each other lovingly in the tattoos and shooting what I recognize as Rural Smiles of Shyness and Apprehension at all the people staring at them because they're so freaking loud.

Then the Navy Guys notice the Glowering Muttering Arabs, and it gets weirdly tense there in line. Luckily, it's my turn to awkwardly blop into a tube, and off I go.

This ride involves a series of tremendous water jets that blast you, on your tube, to the top of Wild Wadi, where, your recently purchased swim trunks having been driven up your rear by the jets, you pause, looking out over the entire city — the miles of stone-white villas, the Burj Al Arab (sail-shaped, iconic, the world's only seven-star hotel) out in the green-blue bay — just before you fly down so fast that you momentarily fear the next morning's headline will read "Middle-aged American Dies in Freak Waterslide Mishap; Bathing Suit Found Far Up Ass."

Afterward, I reconvene with my former line mates in a sort of faux river bend. Becalmed, traffic-jammed, we bob around in our tubes, trying to keep off one another with impotent little hand flips, bare feet accidentally touching ("Ha, wope, sorry, heh . . ."), legs splayed, belly-up in the blinding 112-degree Arabian sun, self-conscious and expectant, as in: "Are we, like, stuck here? Will we go soon? I hope I'm not the one who drifts under that dang *waterfall* over there!"

No one is glowering or muttering now. We're sated, enjoying that little dopey buzz of quasi accomplishment you feel after a surprisingly intense theme-park ride. One of the Arab kids, the one with the Chico hair, passes a drenched cigarette to me, to pass to his friend, and then a lighter, and suddenly everybody's smiling — me, the Arab Marxes, the sunburned German girls, the U.S. Navy.

A disclaimer: it may be that, when you're forty-six and pearl white and wearing a new bathing suit at a theme park on your first full day in Arabia, you're especially prone to Big Naive Philosophical Realizations.

Be that as it may, in my tube at Wild Wadi, I have a mini-epiphany: given enough time, I realize, statistically, despite what it may look like at any given moment, we *will* all be brothers. All differences will be bred out. There will be no pure Arab, no pure Jew, no pure American American. The old dividers — nation, race, religion — will be overpowered by crossbreeding and by our mass media, our world Culture o' Enjoyment.

Look what just happened here: hatred and tension were defused by Sudden Fun.

Still bobbing around (three days before the resort bombings in Cairo, two weeks after the London bombings), I think-mumble a little prayer for the great homogenizing effect of pop culture: Same us out, Lord MTV! Even if, in the process, we are left a little dumber, please proceed. Let us, brothers and sisters, leave the intolerant, the ideologues, the religious Islamist Bolsheviks, our own solvers-of-problems-with-troops behind, fully clothed, on the banks of Wild Wadi. We, the New People, desire Fun and the Good Things of Life, and through Fun we will be saved.

Then the logjam breaks and we surge forward, down a mini-waterfall.

Without exception, regardless of nationality, each of us makes the same sound as we disappear: a thrilled little self-forgetting *whoop*.

We Buy, Therefore We Am

After two full days of blissfully farting around inside the Madinat, I reluctantly venture forth out of the resort bubble, downtown, into the actual city, to the Deira souk. This is the real Middle East, the dark *Indiana Jones*–ish Middle East I'd preimagined: an exotic, cramped, hot, chaotic, labyrinthine, canopied street bazaar, crowded with room-size, even closet-size stalls, selling everything there is in the world to buy, and more than a few things you can't imagine anyone ever wanting to buy, or even accept for free.

Here is the stall of Plastic Flowers That Light Up; the stall of Tall Thin Blond Dolls in Miniskirts with Improbably Huge Eyes; the stall of Toy Semiautomatic Weapons; the stall of Every Spice Known to Man (SAFFRON BUKHOR, BAHRAT, MEDICAL HERBS, NATURAL VIAGRA); the stall of Coffee-Grinding Machines in Parts on the Floor; the stall of Hindi Prayer Cards; the stall of Spangled Kashmiri Slippers; of Air Rifles; Halloween Masks; Oversize Bright-Colored Toy Ships and Trucks; a stall whose walls and ceiling are completely covered with hundreds of cooking pots. There is a Pashtun-dominated section, a hidden Hindi temple, a section that suddenly goes Chinese, entire streets where nothing is sold but bolts of cloth. There's a mind-blowing gold section — two or three hundred gold shops on one street, with mysterious doors leading to four-story mini-malls holding still more gold shops, each overflowing with the yellow high-end gold that, in storybooks and Disney movies, comes pouring out of pirate chests.

As I walk through, a kind of amazed mantra starts running through my head: *There is no end to the making and selling of things there is no end to the making and selling of things there is no end . . .*

Man, it occurs to me, is a joyful, buying-and-selling piece of work. I have been wrong, dead wrong, when I've decried consumerism. Consumerism is what we are. It is, in a sense, a holy impulse. A human being is someone who joyfully goes in pursuit of things, brings them home, then immediately starts planning how to get more.

A human being is someone who wishes to improve his lot.

Speaking of Improving One's Lot: The Great Dubai Quandary

Dubai raises the questions raised by any apparent utopia: What's the downside? At whose expense has this nirvana been built? On whose backs are these pearly gates being raised?

Dubai is, in essence, capitalism on steroids: a small, insanely wealthy group of capital-controlling haves supported by a huge group of overworked and underpaid have-nots, with, in Dubai's case, the gap between haves and have-nots so wide as to indicate different species.

But any attempt to reduce this to some sort of sci-fi Masters and 'Droids scenario gets complicated. Relative to their brethren back home (working for next to nothing or not working at all), Dubai's South Asian workers have it great; likewise, relative to their brethren working in nearby Saudi Arabia. An American I met, who has spent the past fifteen years working in the Saudi oil industry, told me about seeing new South Indian workers getting off the plane in Riyadh, in their pathetic new clothes, clutching cardboard suitcases. On arrival, as in a scene out of *The Grapes of Wrath*, they are informed (for the first time) that they will have to pay for their flight over, their lodging, their food (which must be bought from the company), and, in advance, their flight home. In this way, they essentially work the first two years for free.

Dubai is not, in structure, much different: the workers surrender their passports to their employer; there are no labor unions, no organizing, no protests. And yet in Dubai, the workers tell you again and again how happy they are to be here. Even the poorest, most overworked laborer considers himself lucky — he is making more, much more, than he would be back home. In Saudi, the windfall profits from skyrocketing oil prices have shot directly upstairs, to the five thousand or so members of the royal family, and from there to investments (new jets, real estate in London). In Dubai, the leaders have plowed the profits back into the national dream of the New Dubai — reliant not on oil revenue (the Dubai oil will be gone by 2010) but on global tourism. Whatever complaints you hear about the Emirati ruling class — they buy $250,000 falcons, squash all dissent, tolerate the financial presence of questionable organizations (Al Qaeda, various national Mafias) — they seem to be universally respected, even loved, because, unlike the Saudi rulers, they are perceived to put the interests of the people first.

On the other hand, relative to Western standards, Dubai is so anti-labor as to seem medieval. In the local paper, I read about the following case: A group of foreign workers in Dubai quit their jobs in protest over millions of dirhams in unpaid wages. Since by law they weren't allowed to work for another company, these men couldn't afford plane tickets back home and were thus stuck in a kind of Kafka loop. After two years, the government finally stepped in and helped send the men home. This story indicates both the potential brutality of the system — so skewed toward the employer — and its flexibility relative to the Saudi system, its general right-heartedness, I think you could say, or at least its awareness of, and concern with, Western opinion: the situation was allowed to be reported and, once reported, was corrected.

Complicated.

Because you see these low-level foreign workers working two or three jobs, twelve, fourteen, sixteen hours a day, longing for home (a waiter shows me exactly how he likes to hold his two-year-old, or did like to hold her, last time he was home, eight months ago), and you think: Couldn't you haves cut loose with just a little more?

But ask the workers, in your intrusive Western way, about their Possible Feelings of Oppression, and they model a level of stoic, noble determination that makes the Ayn Rand in you think, Good, good for you, sir, best of luck in your professional endeavors!

Only later, back in your room, having waded in through a lobby full of high rollers — beautifully dressed European/Lebanese/Russian expats, conferring Emiratis, all smoking, chatting, the expats occasionally making a scene, berating a waitress — thinking of some cabdriver in the thirteenth hour of his fourteen-hour shift, worrying about his distant grandchild; thinking of some lonely young Kathmandu husband, sleeping fitfully in his sweltering rented room — do you get a sudden urge to move to Dubai and start a chapter of the Wobblies.

On the other hand:

A Kenyan security guard who works fourteen-hour days at Wild Wadi, euphoric about his new earning power, says to me: "I expect, in your writing, you will try to find the dark side of Dubai? Some positive, some negative? Isn't that the Western way? But I must say: I have found Dubai to be nearly perfect."

Complicated.

The University of the Back of the Cab

A partial list of wise things cabdrivers said to me in Dubai:

1. "If you good Muslim, you go straight, no talking talking, bomb blast! No. You go to mosque, to talk. You go straight!"
2. "This, all you see? So new! All new within! Within one year! Within within within! That building there? New within three year! All built within! Before, no! Only sand."
3. "You won't see any Dubai Arab man driving cab. Big boss only."
4. Re the Taliban: "If you put a man into a room with no way out, he

will fight his way out. But if you leave him one way out, he will take it."

5. "The Cyclone Club? Please to not go there. It is a disco known for too many fuck-girls."

One night my driver is an elderly Iranian, a fan of George W. Bush who hates the Iranian government. He tells me the story of his spiritual life. When young, he says, he was a donkey: a donkey of Islam. Then a professor said to him: You are so religious, so sure of yourself, and yet you know absolutely nothing. And this professor gave him books to read from his personal library. "I read one, then more, more," he says, nearly moving himself to tears with the memory. After two years, the driver had a revelation: all religious knowledge comes from the hand of man. God does not talk to us directly. One can trust only one's own mind, one's own intelligence. He has five kids, four grandkids, still works fourteen-hour days at sixty-five years old. But he stays in Dubai, because in Iran there are two classes: the religious and the not. And the religious get all the privileges, all the money, all the best jobs. And if you, part of the not-religious, say something against them, he says, they put you against a wall and . . .

He turns to me, shoots himself in the head with his finger.

As I get out, he says, "We are not different, all men are . . ." and struggles to remember the word.

"Brothers?" I say.

"No," he says.

"Unified?" I say.

"No," he says.

"Part of the same, uh . . . transcendent . . ."

"No," he says. He can't remember the word. He is old, very old, he says, sorry, sorry.

We say goodbye, promising to pray for our respective governments, and for each other.

Cleaning amid the Mayhem

Dubai is a city of people who come from elsewhere and are going back there soon. To start a good conversation — with a fellow tourist, with the help, with just about anybody — simply ask, "Where are you from?" Everyone wants to tell you. If white, they are usually from England, South Africa, Ukraine. If not, they are from Sri Lanka, the Philippines, Kenya, Nepal, India.

One hotel seems to hire only Nepalese. One bar has only Ukrainians. You discover a pocket of Sri Lankan golf-cart drivers, all anxious to talk about the tsunami.

One day, inexplicably, everyone you meet, wherever you go, is from the Philippines.

"Where are you from?" you say all day, and all day people brightly answer, "Philippines!"

That night, at a club called Boudoir, I meet L, an employee of Ford in Dubai, a manic, funny, Stanley Tucci–looking guy from Detroit, who welcomes me into his party, gets me free champagne, mourns the circa-1990 state of inner-city Detroit: feral dogs roaming the streets, trees growing out of the upper stories of skyscrapers where "you know, formerly, commerce was being done, the real 1960s automobile fucking world-class commerce, man!" The night kind of explodes. This, I think, this is the repressive Arabian Peninsula? Apparently, anything is permitted, as long as it stays within the space in which it is permitted. Here is a Palestinian who lives in L.A. and whose T-shirt says LAPD — WHERE EVERYBODY IS KING. A couple of blond Russian girls dance on a rail, among balloons. On the dance floor, two other blonds dance alone. A guy comes up behind one and starts passionately grinding her. This goes on awhile. Then he stops, introduces himself, she shakes his hand, he goes back to grinding her. His friend comes up, starts grinding her friend. I don't get it. Prostitutes? Some new youthful social code? Am I possibly too old to be in here? The dance floor is packed, the whole place *becomes* the dance floor, the rails are now packed with dancers, a Lebanese kid petulantly shouts that if this was *fucking Beirut,* the girls would be *stripped off* by now, then gives me a snotty look and stomps off, as if it's my fault the girls are still dressed. I drop my wallet, look down, and see the tiniest little woman imaginable, with whisk broom, struggling against the surge of the crowd like some kind of cursed Cleaning Fairy, trying to find a small swath of floor to sweep while being bashed by this teeming mass of gyrating International Hipsters. She's tiny —

I mean *tiny*, like three feet tall, her head barely reaching all the gyrating waists — with thick glasses and bowl-cut hair.

Dear little person! It seems impossible she's trying to sweep the dance floor at a time like this. She seems uncommonly, heroically dedicated, like some kind of OCD janitor on the *Titanic*.

"Where are you from?" I shout.

"Philippines!" she shouts, and goes back to her sweeping.

My Arrival in Heaven

The Burj Al Arab is the only seven-star hotel in the world, even though the ratings system only goes up to five. The most expensive Burj suite goes for $12,000 a night. The atrium is 590 feet from floor to ceiling, the largest in the world. As you enter, the staff rushes over with cold towels, rosewater for the hands, dates, incense. The smell, the scale, the level of loving, fascinated attention you are receiving, makes you realize you have never really been in the lap of true luxury before. All the luxury you have previously had — in New York, L.A. — was stale, Burj-imitative crap! Your entire concept of *being inside a building* is being altered in real time. The lobby of the Burj is neither inside nor out. The roof is so far away as to seem like sky. The underbellies of the floors above you grade through countless shades of color from deep blue to, finally, up so high you can barely see it, pale green. Your Guest Services liaison, a humble, pretty Ukrainian, tells you that every gold-colored surface you see during your stay is actual twenty-four-karat gold. Even those four-story columns? Even so, she says. Even the thick fourth-story arcs the size of buses that span the columns? All gold, sir, is correct.

I am so thrilled to be checking in! What a life! Where a kid from Chicago gets to fly halfway around the world and stay at the world's only seven-star hotel, and *GQ* pays for it!

But there was a difficulty.

Help, Help, Heaven Is Making Me Nervous

Because, for complicated reasons, *GQ* couldn't pay from afar, and because my wife and I share a common hobby of maxing out all credit

cards in sight, I had rather naively embarked on a trip halfway around
the world without an operative credit card: the contemporary version
of setting sail with no water in the casks. So I found myself in the odd
position of having to pay the off-season rate of $1,500 a night, in cash.
And because, turns out, to my chagrin, my ATM has a daily withdrawal limit (Surprise, dumbass!), I found myself there in my two-
floor suite (every Burj room is a two-story suite), wearing the new
clothes I had bought back in Syracuse for the express purpose of "arriving at the Burj," trying to explain, like some yokel hustler at a Motel
6 in Topeka, that I'd be happy to pay half in cash now, half on checkout, if that would be, ah, acceptable, would that be, you know, cool?

My God, if you could have bottled the tension there in my suite at
the Burj! The absolute electricity of disappointment shooting back
and forth between the lovely Ukrainian and my kindly Personal Butler, the pity, really . . .

Sorry, uh, sorry for the, you know, trouble . . . I say. No, sir, the
lovely Ukrainian says. We are sorry to make any difficulties for you.

Ha, I thought, God bless you, now *this* is service, this is freaking
Seven-Star Service!

But over the next few hours, my bliss diminished. I was approached by the Lebanese Floor Butler, by several Mysterious Callers
from Guest Services, all of whom politely but edgily informed me that
it would be much appreciated if the balance of the payment could be
made by me pronto. I kept explaining my situation (that darn bank!),
they kept accepting my explanation, and then someone else would
call or come by, once again encouraging me to pay the remaining
cash, if I didn't mind terribly, right away, as was proper.

So although the Burj is a wonder — a Themed evocation of a reality
that has never existed, unless in somebody's hashish dream — a kind
of externalized fantasy of Affluence, if that fantasy were being had in
real time by a very rich Hedonistic Giant with unlimited access to
some kind of Exaggeration Drug, a Giant fond of bright, mismatched
colors, rounded, huge, inexplicable structures, dancing fountains,
and two-story wall-lining aquariums — I couldn't enjoy any of it. Not
the electronic curtains that reveal infinite ocean; not the free-high-
speed-Internet-accessing big-screen TV; not the Burj-shaped box of
complimentary gourmet dates; not the shower with its six different

Rube Goldbergian nozzles arranged so that one can wash certain body parts without having to demean oneself by bending or squatting; not the complimentary $300 bottle of wine; not the sweeping Liberace stairs or the remote-control front-door opener; not the distant view of The Palm, Jumeirah, and/or the tiny inconsequential boats far below, full of little people who couldn't afford to stay in the Burj even in their wildest dreams, the schmucks (although by the time of my third Admonitory Phone Call, I was feeling envious of them and their little, completely paid-for boats, out there wearing shorts, shorts with possibly some cash in the pockets) — couldn't enjoy any of it, because I was too cowed to leave my room. I resisted the urge to crawl under the bed. I experienced a sudden fear that a group of Disapproving Guest Services People would appear at my remote-controlled door and physically escort me down to the lobby ATM (an ATM about which I expect I'll be having anxiety nightmares the rest of my life), which would once again prominently display the words PROVIDER DECLINES TRANSACTION. It's true what the Buddhists say: mind can convert heaven into hell. This was happening to me. A headline in one of the nine complimentary newspapers read, actually read: "American Jailed for Nonpayment of Hotel Bill."

Perhaps someone had put acid in the complimentary Evian.

Mon Petit Pathetic Rebellion

On one of my many unsuccessful missions to the ATM, I met an Indian couple from the United Kingdom who had saved up their money for this Dubai trip and were staying downtown, near the souk. They had paid $50 to come in and have a look around the Burj (although whom they paid wasn't clear — the Burj says it discontinued its policy of charging for this privilege), and were regretting having paid this money while simultaneously trying to justify it. Although we must remember, said the husband to the wife, this is, after all, a once-in-a-lifetime experience! Yes, yes, of course, she said, I don't regret it for a minute! But there is a look, a certain look about the eyes, that means: Oh God, I am gut-sick with worry about money. And these intelligent, articulate people had that look. (As, I suspect, did I.) There wasn't, she said sadly, that much to see, really, was there? And one felt rather watched, didn't one, by the help? Was there a limit on how long they could stay? They had already toured the lobby twice, been out to the ocean-overlooking pool, and were sort of lingering, trying to get their fifty bucks' worth.

At this point, I was, I admit it, like anyone at someone else's financial mercy, a little angry at the Burj, which suddenly seemed like a rosewater-smelling museum run for, and by, wealthy oppressors of the people, shills for the new global economy, membership in which requires the presence of A Wad, and your ability to get to it/prove it exists.

Would you like to see my suite? I asked the couple.

Will there be a problem with the, ah . . .

Butler? I said. Personal Butler?

With the Personal Butler? he said.

Well, I am a guest, after all, I said. And you are, after all, my old friends from college in the States. Right? Could we say that?

We said that. I sneaked them up to my room, past the Personal Butler, and gave them my complimentary box of dates and the $300 bottle of wine. Fight the power! Then we all stood around feeling that odd sense of shame/solidarity that people of limited means feel when their limitedness has somehow been underscored.

Later that night, a little drunk in a scurvy bar in another hotel (described by L, my friend from Detroit, as the place where "Arabs with a thing for brown sugar" go to procure "the most exquisite African girls on the planet," but which was actually full of African girls who, like all girls whose job it is to fuck anyone who asks them, night after night, were weary and joyless and seemed on the brink of tears), I scrawled in my notebook: *Paucity (ATM) = Rage.*

Then I imagined a whole world of people toiling in the shadow of approaching ruin, exhausting their strength and grace, while above them a whole other world of people puttered around, enjoying the good things of life, staying at the Burj just because they could.

And I left my ATM woes out of it and just wrote: *Paucity = Rage.*

Luckily, It Didn't Come to Jail

Turns out, the ATM definition of "daily" is: after midnight in the United States. In the morning, as I marched the 2,500 dirhams I owed proudly upstairs, the cloud lifted. A citizen of the affluent world again, I went openly to have coffee in the miraculous lobby, where my waiter and I talked of many things — of previous guests (Bill Clinton, 50 Cent — a "loud-laughing man, having many energetic friends") and a current guest, supermodel Naomi Campbell.

Then I left the Burj, no hard feelings, and went somewhere even better, and more expensive. *Heaven for real, plus in this case it was paid for in advance.*

The Al Maha resort is located inside a stunningly beautiful/bleak, rugged desert nature preserve an hour outside Dubai. My Personal Butler was possibly the nicest man I've ever met, who proudly admitted it was he who designed the linens, as well as the special Kleenex dispensers. He had been at Al Maha since the beginning. He loved it here. This place was his life's work.

Each villa had its own private pool.

After check-in, we're given a Jeep tour of the desert by a friendly and intensely knowledgeable South African guide, of that distinct subspecies of large, handsome guys who love nature. I learn things. The oryx at Al Maha have adapted to the sprinkler system in the following way: at dusk, rather than going down to the spring, they sit at the base of the trees, waiting for the system to engage. I see a bush called spine of Christ; it was from one of these, some believe, that Christ's crown of thorns was made. I see camel bones, three types of gazelle. We pass a concrete hut the size of a one-car garage, in a spot so isolated and desolate you expect some Beckett characters to be sitting there. Who lives inside? A guy hired by the camel farmer, our guide says. He stays there day and night for months at a time. Who is he? Probably a Pakistani; often, these camel-feeding outposts are manned by former child camel-jockeys, sold by their families to sheikhs when the kids were four or five years old.

For lunch, we have a killer buffet, with a chef's special of veal medallions.

I go back to my villa for a swim. Birds come down to drink from my private pool. As you lower yourself into the pool, water laps forward and out, into a holding rim, then down into the Lawrencian desert. You see a plane of blue water, then a plane of tan desert. Yellow bees

— completely yellow, as if spray-painted — flit around on the surface of the water.

At dusk we ride camels out to the desert. A truck meets us with champagne and strawberries. We sit on a dune, sipping champagne, watching the sunset. Dorkily, I am the only single. Luckily, I am befriended by B and K, a beautiful, affluent Dubai-Indian couple right out of Hemingway. She is pretty and loopy: Angelina Jolie meets Lucille Ball. He is elegant, reserved, kind-eyed, always admiring her from a little ways off, then rushing over to get her something she needs. They are here for their one-and-a-half-year anniversary. Theirs was a big, traditional Indian wedding, held in a tent in the desert, attended by four hundred guests, who were transported in buses. In a traditional Indian wedding, the groom is supposed to enter on a white horse. White horses being in short supply in Dubai, her grandfather, a scion of old Dubai, called in a favor from a sheikh, who flew in, from India, a beautiful white stallion. Her father then surprised the newlyweds with a thirty-minute fireworks show.

Fireworks, wow, I say, thinking of my wedding and our big surprise, which was, someone had strung a crapload of Bud cans to the bumper of our rented Taurus.

She is her father's most precious possession, he says.

Does her father like you? I say.

He has no choice, he says.

Back at my room, out of my private pool comes the crazed Arabian moon, which has never, in my experience, looked more like a Ball of Rock in Space.

My cup runneth over. All irony vanishes. I am so happy to be alive. I am convinced of the essential goodness of the universe. I wish everyone I've ever loved could be here with me in my private pool.

I wish *everyone* could be here with me in my private pool: the blue-suited South Indians back in town, the camel farmer in his little stone box, the scared, sad Moldavian girls clutching their ostensibly sexy little purses at hotel bars — I wish they could all, before they die, have one night at Al Maha.

But they can't.

Because that's not the way the world works.

"Dubai Is What It Is Because All the Countries Around It Are So Fucked Up"

In the middle of a harsh, repressive, backward, religiously excessive, physically terrifying region sits Dubai. Among its Gulf neighbors: Iraq and Iran, war-torn and fanatic-ruled, respectively. Surrounding it, Saudi Arabia, where stealing will get your hand cut off, a repressive terrorist breeding ground where women's faces can't be seen in public, a country, my oil-industry friend says, on the brink of serious trouble.

The most worrisome thing in Saudi, he says, is the rural lower class. The urban middle class is doing all right, relatively affluent and satisfied. But look at a map of Saudi, he says: all that apparently empty space is not really empty. People live there who are not middle class and not happy. I say the Middle East seems something like Russia circa 1900 — it's about trying to stave off revolution in a place where great wealth has been withheld from the masses by a greedy ruling class.

That's one way of saying it, he says.

Then he tells me how you get a date if you are a teenage girl in Saudi Arabia:

Go to the mall wearing your required abaya. When a group of young guys walks by, if you see one you like, quickly find a secluded corner of the mall, take out your cell phone, lift your veil, snap a picture of your face. Write your cell number on a piece of paper. When the boys walk by, drop the scrap at the feet of the one you like. When he calls, send him your photo. If he likes the photo, he will call again. Arrange a secret meeting.

The world must be peopled.

The Truth Is, I Can't Decide What's True, Honestly

One night, at dinner with some People Who Know, I blurt out a question that's been bothering me: Why doesn't Al Qaeda bomb Dubai, since Dubai represents/tolerates decadent Western materialism, etc., and they could do it so easily? The Man Who Knows says, I'll tell you why: Dubai is like Switzerland during World War II — a place needed by everyone. The Swiss held Nazi money, Italian Fascist money. And in Dubai, according to this Person, Al Qaeda has millions of dollars in independent, Dubai-based banks, which don't always adhere to the international banking regulations that would require a bank to document the source of the income. A Woman Who Knows says she's seen it: a guy walks into a bank with a shitload of money, and they just take it, credit it, end of story. In this way, the People Who Know say, Dubai serves various illicit organizations from around the world: the Italian Mafia, the Spanish Mafia, etc., etc. Is this known about and blessed from the top down? Yes, it is. Al Qaeda needs Dubai, and Dubai tolerates Al Qaeda, making the periodic token arrest to keep the United States happy.

Later, the People Who Know are contradicted, in an elevator, by another Man Who Knows, a suave Luxembourger who sells financial-services products to Dubai banks. Dubai has greatly improved its banking procedures since 9/11. Why would a terrorist group want to bank here? he asks. Think about it logically: Would they not be better served in a country sympathetic to them? Iran, Syria, Lebanon?

Good point, I say, thanking God in my heart that I am not a real investigative journalist.

In Which Snow Is Made by a Kenyan

Arabian Ice City is part of a larger, months-long festival called Dubai Summer Surprises, which takes place at a dozen venues around town and includes Funny Magic Mirrors, Snow Magician Show, Magic Academy Workshop, Magic Bubble Show, Balloon Man Show, and Ice Cave Workshop, not to mention Ice Fun Character Show.

But Arabian Ice City is the jewel.

Because at Arabian Ice City, Arab kids see snow for the first time.

Arabian Ice City consists, physically, of wall-length murals of stylized Swiss landscapes; two cardboard igloos labeled GENTS' MOSQUE and LADIES' MOSQUE, respectively (actual mosques, with shoes piled up inside the mock-ice doorways, through which people keep disappearing to pray); a huge ice cliff, which on closer inspection is a huge

Styrofoam cliff, being sculpted frantically to look more like ice by twenty Filipinos with steak knives; and a tremendous central cardboard castle, inside of which, it is rumored, will be the snow.

This is a local event, attended almost exclusively by Emiratis, sponsored by the local utility company; an opportunity, a representative tells me, to teach children about water and power conservation via educational activities and "some encouraging gifts." Has he been to America? He makes a kind of scoffing sound, as in, Right, pal, I'm going to America.

"America does not like Arabs," he says. "They think we are . . . I will not even say the word."

"Terrorists," I say.

He shuts his eyes in offended agreement.

Then he has to go. There is continued concern about the safety of the Arabian Ice City. Yesterday, at the opening, they expected one hundred people in the first hour, and instead got three thousand. Soon the ice was melting, and the children, who knew nothing of the hazards of snow, were slipping, getting hurt, and they'd had to shut the whole thing down, to much disappointment.

Waiting in the rapidly growing line, I detect a sense of mounting communal worry, fierce concern. This is, after all, for the children. Men rush in and out of the Ice Palace, bearing pillows, shovels, clipboards. Several Characters arrive and are ushered inside: a red crescent with legs; what looks like a drop of toothpaste, or, more honestly, sperm, with horizontal blue stripes; the crankiest-looking goose imaginable, with a face like a velociraptor and a strangely solicitous Sri Lankan handler, who keeps affectionately swatting the goose-raptor's tail and whispering things to it and steering it away from the crowd so they can have a private talk. The handler seems, actually, a little in love with the goose. As the goose approaches, a doorman announces robustly, "Give a way for the goose!" The goose and goose tender rush past, the tender swatting in lusty wonderment at the goose's thick tail, as if amazed that he is so privileged to be allowed to freely swat at such a thick, realistic tail.

The door opens, and in we go.

Inside is a rectangle about the size of a tennis court, green-bordered, like one of the ice rinks Sears used to sell. Inside is basically a shitload of crushed ice and one Kenyan with a shovel, madly crushing. And it does look like snow, kind of, or at least ice; it looks, actually, like a Syracuse parking lot after a freezing night.

Then the Arab kids pour in: sweet, proud, scared, tentative, trying to be brave. Each is offered a coat from a big pile of identical coats, black with a red racing stripe. Some stand outside the snow rink, watching. Some walk stiff-legged across it, beaming. For others the approach is: bend down, touch with one finger. One affects nonchalance: snow is nothing to him. But then he quickly stoops, palms the snow, yanks his hand back, grins to himself. Another boy makes a clunky snowball, hands it politely to the crescent-with-legs, who politely takes it, holds it awhile, discreetly drops it. The goose paces angrily around the room, as if trying to escape the handler, who is still swatting flirtatiously at its tail while constantly whispering asides up at its beak.

And the kids keep coming. On their faces: looks of bliss, the kind of look a person gets when he realizes he is in the midst of doing something rare, that might never be repeated, and is therefore of great value. They are seeing something from a world far away, where they will probably never go.

Women in abayas video. Families pose shyly, rearranging themselves to get more snow in the frame. Mothers and fathers stand beaming at their kids, who are beaming at the snow.

This is sweet, I scribble in my notebook.

And it is. My eyes well up with tears.

In the same way that reading the Bible, listening to radio preachers, would not clue the neophyte into the very active kindness of a true Christian home, reading the Koran, hearing about "moderate Islam," tells us nothing about the astonishing core warmth and familial sense of these Arab families.

I think: If everybody in America could see this, our foreign policy would change.

For my part, in the future, when I hear "Arab" or "Arab street" or those who "harbor, shelter, and sponsor" the terrorists, I am going to think of the Arabian Ice City, and that goose, moving among the cold-humbled kids, and the hundreds of videotapes now scattered around Arab homes in Dubai, showing beloved children reaching down to touch snow.

What Is Jed Clampett Doing in Gitmo?

After Arabian Ice City, while I have a Coke and try to get my crying situation sorted out, it occurs to me that the American sense of sophistication/irony — our cleverness, our glibness, our rapid-fire delivery, our rejection of gentility, our denial of tradition, our blunt realism — which can be a form of greatness when it manifests in a Gershwin, an Ellington, a Jackson Pollock — also causes us to (wrongly) assume a corresponding level of sophistication/irony/worldliness in the people of other nations.

Example one: I once spent some time with the mujahideen in Peshawar, Pakistan — the men who were at that time fighting the Russians and formed the core of the Taliban — big, scowling, bearded men who'd just walked across the Khyber Pass for a few weeks of rest. And the biggest, fiercest one of all asked me, in complete sincerity, to please convey a message to President Reagan from him, and he was kind of flabbergasted that I didn't know the president and couldn't just call him up for a chat, man to man.

Example two: On the flight over to Dubai, the flight attendant announced that if we'd like to make a contribution to the Emirates Airline Foundation children's fund, we should do so in the envelope provided. The sickly Arab man next to me, whose teeth were rotten and who had, with some embarrassment, confessed to a "leg problem," responded by gently stuffing the envelope full of the sugar cookies he was about to eat. Then he patted the envelope, smiled to himself, folded his hands in his lap, and went to sleep.

What one might be tempted to call simplicity could more accurately be called a limited sphere of experience. We round up a "suspected Taliban member" in Afghanistan and, assuming that Taliban means the same thing to him as it does to us (a mob of intransigent, nonconvertible terrorists), whisk this sinister Taliban member — who grew up in, and has never once left, what is essentially the Appalachia of Afghanistan; who possibly joined the Taliban in response to the lawlessness of the post-Russian warlord state, in the name of bringing some order and morality to his life or in a misguided sense of religious fervor — off to Guantánamo, where he's treated as if he personally planned 9/11. Then this provincial, probably not guilty, certainly rube-like guy, whose view of the world is more limited than we can even imagine, is denied counsel and a possible release date, and subjected to all of the hardships and deprivations our modern military-prison system can muster. How must this look to him? How must *we* look to him?

My experience has been that the poor, simple people of the world admire us, are enamored of our boldness, are hopeful that the insanely positive values we espouse can be actualized in the world. They are, in other words, rooting for us. Which means that when we disappoint them — when we come in too big, kill innocents, when our powers of discernment are diminished by our frenzied, self-protective, fearful post-9/11 energy — we have the potential to disappoint them bitterly and drive them away.

Look, Dream, but Stay Out There

My fourth and final hotel, the Emirates Towers, is grand and imperial, surrounded by gardens, palm trees, and an elaborate fountain/moat assembly that would look right at home on an outlying *Star Wars* planet.

One Thai prostitute I spoke with in a bar said she'd stayed at the Emirates Towers four or five times but didn't like it much. Why not? I wondered. Too business-oriented? Kind of formal, a bit stuffy? "Because every time, they come up in the night and t'row me out," she said.

Returning to the hotel at dusk, I find dozens of the low-level South Indian workers, on their weekly half-day off, making their way toward the Towers, like peasants to the gates of the castle, dressed in their finest clothes (cowboy-type shirts buttoned to the throat), holding clunky, circa-1980s cameras.

What are they doing here? I ask. What's going on?

We are on holiday, one says.

What are their jobs? When can they go home? What will they do tonight? Go out and meet girls? Do they have girlfriends back home, wives?

Maybe someday, one guy says, smiling a smile of anticipatory domestic ecstasy, and what he means is: Sir, if you please, how can I marry when I have nothing? This is why I'm here, so someday I can have a family.

Are you going in there? I ask, meaning the hotel.

An awkward silence follows. In there? Them?

No, sir, one says. We are just wishing to take photos of ourselves in this beautiful place.

They go off. I watch them merrily photographing themselves in front of the futuristic fountain, in the groves of lush trees, photos they'll send home to Hyderabad, Bangalore. Entering the hotel is out of the question. They know the rules.

I decide to go in but can't locate the pedestrian entrance. The idea, I come to understand, after fifteen minutes of high-attentiveness searching, is to discourage foot traffic. Anybody who belongs in there will drive in and valet park.

Finally I locate the entrance: an unmarked, concealed, marble staircase with wide, stately steps fifty feet across. Going up, I pass a lone Indian guy hand-squeegeeing the thirty-three (I count them) steps.

How long will this take you? I ask. All afternoon?

I think so, he says sweetly.

Part of me wants to offer to help. But that would be, of course, ridiculous, melodramatic. He washes these stairs every day. It's not my job to hand-wash stairs. It's his job to hand-wash stairs. My job is to observe him hand-washing the stairs, then go inside the air-conditioned lobby and order a cold beer and take notes about his stair-washing so I can go home and write about it, making more for writing about it than he'll make in many, many years of doing it.

And of course, somewhere in India is a guy who'd kill to do some stair-washing in Dubai. He hasn't worked in three years; any chance of marriage is rapidly fading. Does this stair washer have any inclination to return to India, surrender his job to this other guy, give up his hard-won lifestyle to help this fellow human being? Who knows? If he's like me, he probably does. But in the end, his answer, like mine, is: That would be ridiculous, melodramatic. It's not my job to give up my job, which I worked so hard these many years to get.

Am I not me? Is he not him?

He keeps washing. I jog up the stairs to the hotel. Two smiling Nepalese throw open the huge doors, greeting me warmly, and I go inside.

Goodbye, Dubai, I'll Love You Forever

Emirates Airline features unlimited free movies, music, and video games, as well as downward-looking and forward-looking live closed-circuit TV. I toggle back and forth between the downward-looking camera (there are the Zagros Mountains, along the Iraq-Iran border) and *Meet the Fockers*. The mountains are green, rugged. The little dog is flushed down the toilet and comes out blue.

It's a big world, and I really like it. In all things, we are the victims of the Misconception from Afar. There is the idea of a city, and the city itself, too great to be held in the mind. And it is in this gap between the conceptual and the real that aggression begins. No place works any differently than any other place, really, beyond mere details. The universal human laws — need, love for the beloved, fear, hunger, periodic exaltation, the kindness that rises naturally in the absence of hunger/fear/pain — are constant, predictable, reliable, universal, and are merely ornamented with the details of local culture. What a powerful thing to know: that one's own desires are mappable onto strangers, that what one finds in oneself will most certainly be found in the Other.

Just before I doze off, I counsel myself grandiosely: Fuck concepts. Don't be afraid to be confused. Try to remain permanently confused. Anything is possible. Stay open, forever, so open it hurts, and then open up some more, until the day you die, world without end, amen.

SAM SHAW

■

Peg

FROM *Open City*

Reception

FIRST THAW, and things were going to be all right. George sat on the cinderblock prow of his chimney with a compass and a level and a short length of twine. Here was the sun, streaming on wet conifers. And beneath the teeming sounds of early spring — tinny FM rock, the cannonade of pickup basketball, a lone honest hammer beating time — beneath it all there was the steady cheerful murmuring of snowmelt in gutters and drains.

The view had put him in an expansive mood. From this vantage, Prospect seemed a gentle and orderly place, all right angles and perfect arcs. Cars rolled slowly down the streets. Somewhere a rifle cracked, and George felt a fleeting kinship with the town's forefathers, small rational men who had almost certainly commanded the respect of their wives.

George restored the satellite to its proper azimuth and elevation. The work was slow, but agreeable too, and as he tightened the last bolt he had the sense that he had also brought his life into a kind of alignment. It was March, and the colors of the world shone bright and true.

He found Rita in the threshold to the den, regarding the TV screen with her arms folded. The picture was crystalline, brilliant even.

"How about that," he said in the tone of a surgeon who has just completed a radical new procedure.

"Don't start," she said. "It was the cord, not the dish. Practically detached. I fixed it myself an hour ago."

He stood with his compass in his hand.

"What are you smiling for? Anne Pomerantz phoned in a panic. She thought you were going to jump."

George sprawled across the sofa. On the television, a couple of tigers screwed in a vast green dale. Before long, the sights and sounds of this Technicolor world had displaced the paler appurtenances of the house — the rattan chairs arranged just so, the animal hum of the furnace. George closed his eyes. It was a perfect day on the veldt. But Rita kept intruding, talking dimly to herself, pacing, shutting kitchen drawers. Undoubtedly, she was filling out contest forms. It was Rita's talent in life to win prizes through the mail. Their closets were full of crockery, birdseed, baby clothes. The hallways, too. Blenders and radios, water picks, snorkels, leather-bound books. All manner of athletic and gardening equipment. What were George's talents? There was billiards. In high school, he'd played snare drum in the marching band.

A while later, the mailman arrived with today's bounty of junk mail and glinting sweepstakes appliances. Then it was dark, then dawn, then dark again.

Sleeves

George and Rita had been married only three years — they were newlyweds practically — but already an anxious silence had fallen on the house, and they greeted each other with the same weary enmity that had passed for tenderness between George's parents after five arid decades. It was troubling. George had been a recluse all his life, an exile of sorts, and he'd looked to Rita for relief. But his solitude was all the more complete for her presence. She was constantly shutting off lights or worrying the thermostat gauge. It unnerved him the way she never fully came to rest, the way she skimmed from room to room, in darkness, like a shark.

At first, Rita had seemed to George the most fragile and lovely creature in the state. She'd had a skittish greyhound named Silver, who followed her on errands. One afternoon, they were ambushed by another dog: it overtook them, a wiry, murderous thing, and when Rita came to Silver's aid, he bit her wrist, which promptly snapped. It was the ruined arm that won George's heart. He loved to carry things for her, to open doors and cut her steaks at Vern's. He loved to brush her red bangs from her eyes. After the wrist had healed, he would sometimes drape his coat over her shoulders on chilly night walks. It brought him a great deal of pleasure to look at the limp sleeves hanging at her sides.

Now her every gesture spoke of disappointment: around the house she wore the loose sweats and haggard eyes of a patient on a death ward; neglected jars of powder and containers of eye shadow and lipstick lined the bathroom counter like a monument to her vanished beauty.

Failures

It was raining, and as he fumbled for the house key in the low light from the kitchen window, George slipped and split the seat of his pants.

"God bless," he sputtered.

He balanced his cigarette on the iron rail and probed the tear with both hands.

Probably Rita could sew it up, but the thought of asking vexed him. Not that she'd refuse. Rita relished the few household chores she performed, as if through suffering her life might acquire an aspect of the heroic; she'd become a kind of domestic martyr, a saint of Cascade Pure-Rinse Flakes and Lemon Cheer.

He knocked his cigarette into the hedge, opened the door, and draped his coat on his wife's listless hydrangea.

Among the bills and gaily colored circulars fanned across the floor was a postcard from his brother:

> Beware the Ides, etc., etc.!
> Fondly, Chuck

George turned it over in his hands. In the picture three coffee-colored ladies washed a sports car. One of them was drinking from a hose. George held the card to his face. It had a sweet, gluey odor.

After his divorce, Chuck had fled to Pompano Beach, where he lived in a condo with a whirlpool tub and a marble bar. It was a bachelor's paradise: sixty-five in winter, and his job as trainer at the airport Marriott's gym guaranteed him a steady diet of svelte, undemanding sex partners, many of them actual flight attendants. George had always hated his brother, who was unequivocally his better — older, stronger, quicker, and more handsome. Even in the final throes of his marriage, Chuck maintained a brute, vigorous health. He and Susan fought like wolves; more than once the police appeared at their door, called by sleepless neighbors. There were shattered glasses and plates, a ten-gallon tank full of startled fish upended on the bedroom floor. Occasionally he had shown up at George's late at night with a wide, humorless grin and a six-pack of Pabst, once with a frozen steak-tip sandwich held to his purpled eye. George would give him a blanket and Chuck would lie on the couch in the dark, the TV roaring.

With George and Rita it was steady and silent, a sort of intravenous drip. There was no violence, no betrayal, no tearful recrimination. In this too it seemed that he had failed.

Penny's

George worked the night shift at Penny's Video. Some of his most loyal customers were young women, about whom he indulged lavish filmic daydreams. Typically his fantasies involved acts of sacrifice or heroism: there were blazing fires, bar fights, donations of blood that left him pale and depleted. Occasionally he'd spy one of his lady patrons in town talking with another man, and he would want briefly to die.

Tonight, two girls from the high school had spent nearly an hour in the store, and he had scrutinized them head to toe while they roved the interminable shelves of movies. They were all of seventeen, he guessed. The more conventionally attractive of the two wore a man's hockey jersey, altered to expose a few inches of tender stomach. The other was more to his liking: squat and round, with powdered eyes that lent her a haunted, raccoonish aspect. Or Asian, somehow, and geisha-like. She was precisely Chuck's type.

George's temples throbbed. This was the weight of yearning, green love expressed as barometric pressure in his head. He felt that he knew this one, really and truly knew her, better than her friends and family even, perhaps better than she knew herself. Light flared in her reddish hair with a special brilliance that suggested she was different from the others, touched. Her future was elsewhere, far from Prospect; no bagging waxy fruit or filing memos in a window-less box — though probably she would make a fine secretary, the sort of quiet, dutiful employee who is consistently passed over for promotion. George felt a wave of hatred for her gray-flanneled tyrant of a supervisor, who wouldn't know raw talent if it was sharing his thirty-dollar entrée in a restaurant in Tokyo — or thirty yen, he guessed — and he pictured her dressed in a sheer kimono, and chok-ing on a square of unchewed eel, clawing the air, and in his mind he shoved aside the useless gaping manager and swept to Raccoon Girl's aid, applying first a Heimlich, then slow CPR, below the tables now on the soft, carpeted restaurant floor, tasting dusky soy sauce on her lips.

"My card?" she asked, and George found that he'd stowed it in the pocket of his shirt.

After they'd left, he retrieved her record on the office computer and penned her home number on his wrist.

Telephone

Seated now in his kitchen and looking into a glass of milk, George tried to picture Raccoon Girl's face. Black eyes and full, disappointed lips. Through the tear in his pants the chair was cold, though not dis-agreeably so. What a pleasant shock it would be to hold her round face, to breathe life into her parted mouth.

George considered the number written on his arm. He picked up the Nortel Execu-Talk — one in a long and distinguished line of sweepstakes phones — and pondered the electric void of the dial tone. Then he restored the handset to its cradle. Down the hall, the bedroom door was ajar. The thought of sinking into bed with Rita stung his eyes. He stood up and poured his milk into the sink, where it pooled over carelessly stacked dishes and cups. He put on his coat, opened the door, and stepped into the night.

Vern's

At the corner, George turned south toward town. All in all, Prospect wasn't much on the eyes. The houses were more or less identical: pre-fabricated single-story numbers, painted white or yellow or some-times powder blue. Desiccated hedges flanked the yards, and every forty feet or so a street lamp threw circles of sallow light on the black-top. Where was he going? The options were few and too familiar. There were three bars in town, only one that would be open. Vern's: a falling-down house at the foot of the highway, a structure that had for-merly served as a Methodist church.

During the months of their courtship, Rita had been sick with mis-trust, sure that half of Prospect wanted George, and though he knew that she was wrong, the notion had pleased him. Whenever he shot pool at Vern's, whenever he broke a date or failed to call, she requited him with reddened tearful eyes. Since the wedding, though, she was a new woman, coolly disinterested. It was as if George were one more object gained in a contest — as if all pleasure lay in acquisition, none in ownership.

A Friend

In the hope of reviving Rita's passion, George had contrived a phony mistress. Late at night he would whisper loving phrases to the dial tone on the pink Princess phone in the den. He would sleep in a chair at Penny's, return home at dawn with rumpled clothes and dampened tousled hair. On an airless summer evening, he had given her a name. Rita sat in the bed, clipping proofs of purchase from spent packages of cereal and long-grain rice. George paced the yard, talking on the black Precision cordless.

"No, no," he said to the shrill note in his ear. "I'm the lucky one. A woman like you is a once-in-a-lifetime special gift."

In his enthusiasm, he almost believed there was someone on the line.

Periodically, he veered past the bedroom window. On each such oc-casion, he furtively angled his head, hoping to catch Rita watching him. After a while he gave up and joined her in the bedroom.

"Don't worry," he said. "She's a friend, and nothing but."

Rita paused, scissor raised at a martial slant. "Who?" she asked.

"Peg," he said. Where had it come from? George had never known a Peg.

"Peg," George said again, testing the sound of it. "From Vern's. I'm sure I've mentioned her. My billiards partner, Peg."

She resumed cutting.

"I'm thinking of inviting Peg to dinner. She's recently divorced."

"So invite her," said Rita.

"I'm thinking that I will," said George.

120v AC

Had the game progressed too far? That fall, George had cried "Peg" in the heat of sex. The next week, he'd found Rita in the darkened bedroom, making love with a small plastic cylinder.

"What are you looking at?" she'd panted, and the thing had seemed to mock him with its nasal insect hum.

Waltz

In truth, Rita seemed only vaguely aware of his comings and goings, and if his talk of Peg concerned her, she betrayed no sign. Despite all his maneuvers, she seemed implicitly to trust him. And perhaps she was right: that winter, at Vern's, he'd met a true Peg — or was it Paige? — and in his beery condition he'd felt it was fate, that she'd been sent to free him from his cell. They danced a slow waltz, and she let him rest his hands on the firm plane of her back, and at closing time, in the rain-glossed parking lot, she kissed him roughly on the mouth. But George withdrew. Because in spite of everything, he wasn't a man who broke a vow. In spite of everything, he was true to Rita, true as north.

Lack

"Peg," he said to the empty street. "Peg."

For the first time, he heard the name for what it was. Empty. Mournful. A word expressing everything he lacked.

He was halfway to Vern's when he heard the sound — a rupture in the night stillness, a howling of metal and glass. He held his breath for a minute. An uneasy quiet fell. He jogged to the corner and turned down the street.

The car stood a hundred yards away, a little white sedan. The hood had split around a tree. Steam rose from the engine, and the ruined windshield grinned. George approached it, tasting queer metallic smoke in the air. The car was bleeding. He dipped his toe in the fluid — oil or fuel, he didn't know — and traced a line on the ground.

Through the fogged glass of the side window, he discerned a figure bent across the steering wheel, inert. It took him a moment to understand what he was looking at. Like some exotic zoo animal: legs, a torso with crooked arms, and finally a neck that flared into nothing. George's eyes rested awhile on the incomplete body. At last he stood upright and surveyed the area. There were no houses in sight, no one to call for help. And frankly, he thought, the time for help had passed.

"Oh, man," George said to the thing in the car. "I wish I could do something. I wish there was something I could do."

He crossed to the front of the car and laid his hand on the wrinkled hood. It burned his palm. Reflexively, he touched his fingers to his mouth. And at that moment he saw it. At first he thought it was a possum nestled in the tall grass, and then he knew better. It was several feet away, lost in shadow: dark hair and a glimpse of skin.

George crouched beside the head and reached to touch its ragged neck, tentative and deliberate, like someone attempting a difficult shot in billiards. An older man, sixty at least, with a sharp nose, thin lips, and wide pearly eyes. Something in the face brought his brother to mind. The stare had an eerie limpid quality: it was as if the head had something to impart to him.

In school, George had read accounts of guillotined kings and queens who blinked and hissed in death.

"Hello?" he said, just to be safe.

The blood matting the hair and coating the cheeks and teeth was altogether too red, the color of grenadine. George cleaned the face with the cuff of his shirt. In spite of what must have been a terrible flight, its features were poised. This put him in mind of a circus act he'd witnessed as a boy: child trapezists drawing slow arcs in the summer air.

George cradled the head as one might hold a child. With his free hand, he lit a fresh cigarette. Then he opened and shut the jaw as if to make it speak. The teeth made a quiet clicking noise. Shamed by this act, George pressed the face to his chest.

Overhead, the cruciform lights of an aircraft winked.

He zipped his jacket over the head, turned his back on the ruined car, and walked briskly home.

Homecoming

George closed the door gently so as not to rouse his wife. He stood there in the darkness of the hallway, listening to the wash of heated air through vents. Having judged Rita asleep, he laid some newspapers on the kitchen table and set the head on top.

He walked around the room, running his hands over counters, opening and shutting cabinets and drawers. Inside the freezer he found two plastic ice trays, some TV dinners, a few packages of ground beef, a stick of butter, and a tub of yogurt missing its lid. He stacked these objects on a chair. Then he placed the head at the back of the freezer and walled it behind the frozen foods.

Next there was the business of cleaning. He wiped the counter and the floor, depositing the slick newspapers along with his pants, his jacket, and his shirt in a paper bag beneath the sink. The water from the tap was pleasant on his hands, and he gave them a vigorous washing, and his arms, and even his armpits, and then he wet his hair. Afterward, he crept to the bedroom. For a long minute he stood overlooking the prostrate shape of Rita, who was fast asleep. He could hear the steady tidal noise of her breath, but her chest was still. In sleep, she remained his wife.

Flight

They had taken the house in autumn, just weeks before the wedding. It was empty of furniture then, and the walls shone startling white. Silver had yet to be killed, and the high *tick tick* of his pacing filled the air, a sound as of fingers typing an interminable memo. On the first night they'd found a sparrow, stone dead on the kitchen floor; Silver offered it to Rita, who offered it to George. How had it come to be there? Through the chimney? George imagined its last days in the house: the dizzy indoor flight, its hundred frenzied dives against the glass panels of the sliding kitchen door. He would have fed it to the dog, but Rita demanded a proper burial in the yard, in a Dixie Cup coffin. Afterward, they lay together on the bedroom floor, she facing outward. He touched her cheek and found that it was wet, and he held her as tightly as he could. He had felt then that she was the kindest and most loving person he would ever know, moved to tears by the death of a bird.

Nocturne

George climbed into bed. Gingerly, he tucked a hand under the bottom of Rita's cotton shirt. Her stomach was an oven. He slipped a finger into the hollow of her navel and closed his eyes and lapsed into sleep.

Provisions

The next morning, George feigned sleep while Rita dressed for work. Before she left the bedroom, she paused in the doorway.

"I know perfectly well you're awake," she said.

He waited with his eyes shut until he heard the front door close.

While he ate breakfast, George stared fixedly at the freezer. What would've happened if she'd taken something out to thaw? He opened the freezer door, dug through the barricade of frozen foods, and retrieved the head. The skin had lost its color; the brows were thick with frost. George set the head down on its side in the center of the table and finished eating.

The head notwithstanding, it was a weekday like any other. He showered and brushed his teeth, made up the bed, cleaned the dishes, and watched *Knight Rider* and *Baretta* at lunchtime. Throughout the day, the head sat on the table, sizing him up.

At four o'clock he dressed for work, then leaned against the counter and contemplated the head.

"How about a drive?" he asked it.

George rummaged through the front hall closet until he found a red-and-white Igloo cooler, which he filled with ice. To his great satisfaction, the head fit perfectly. Atop its chilly bed, it looked like something from the seafood counter at the Freshmart. George swiveled the top of the cooler, and it locked in place with an authoritative click.

He was very glad not to encounter any neighbors on his way to the car. At the corner of Treasure Hill Road, he slowed to a crawl. Police tape lashed in the wind. There were cruisers and a couple of deputies trailing shrewd-looking dogs through the high grass. George sped toward town, his right hand tapping syncopations on the cooler.

Listen

At the video store, he felt a nagging urge to take out the head and put it on the counter. It didn't seem right to keep the head locked up all night. He compromised by opening the lid a crack, exposing a sliver of red ice.

Later, a bored-looking redhead appeared, and George felt his heart turn over like the engine of a car. She laid her tape on the counter and asked, "Where's the picnic at?"

George followed her eyes to the cooler.

"It's a heart," he said. "For transplant. Still beating if you listen."

She turned her head and closed her eyes. Outside, a car horn cried. George had been watching a trick-shot billiards tape; there was the sound of balls colliding, then damp applause. She gave him a high, forced laugh and shook her head and left.

At closing time, George took the head and propped it against a stack of tapes.

"This is where I work," he said. "It's called Penny's Video. The boss is named Cal. I don't know who Penny is."

The head watched him as he dusted the shelves and extinguished the lights.

Foil

In the car, George posed the question that had troubled him throughout the day: "How does it feel?"

"You'd be surprised," the head answered. The voice was high and hoarse. It made a sound like wrinkling tinfoil. "It feels like nothing. Nothing at all."

"That's good," George said. He tuned in a ballad on the radio and lit a cigarette.

"What about taking me out of the box?" the head asked. "It's cold as a polar bear's tit."

George lifted the head out of the cooler and set it on the seat beside him.

"Actually, it's all right," the head said after a time. "I'm grateful not to be wherever it is they've taken my body, for example."

"Probably the hospital," George offered, exhaling smoke that billowed against the windshield. "Or for all I know, they've buried it."

"A savage custom if I've ever heard one," said the head. "It's easy enough on the living. I don't guess they can stand the idea of death."

The sound of a steel guitar washed over them. At a red light, George offered his cigarette to the head, and for a few moments they both considered the problem of inhaling without lungs.

"Now there's something I'm going to miss," it said.

George parked a little ways from the house. He sat awhile, looking through the filmy windshield and biting his lip. As if sensing his ambivalence, the head made a faint clucking sound. The cigarette in George's hand had burned down nearly to the filter, and a long column of ash buckled and dropped onto his lap.

"I'm going to have to put you back in the box," he said to the head.

Louis

Mercifully, Rita had made herself scarce. George took a browned banana from the fruit basket on the counter and peeled and ate it.

"How about you wangle us a date," said the thing in the cooler. It was an interesting proposition.

"I don't know," he said. "Really?"

The number on his wrist was only faintly legible. He dialed, feeling a strange, warm calm. There was ringing — once, twice. Then all at once her breath was in his ear.

"What happened to ten o'clock?" she asked.

George faltered. It was not a question he'd anticipated.

"Louis?" she asked, and George set the phone on its cradle. He collected the cooler and walked to the bathroom. He shut the door behind him and laid the head on its side in the sink.

"We ought to give you a proper cleaning," George said to the head. And truly, it looked unwell, the features wilted, the skin raw and white. George turned on the faucet, so that a weak stream of water doused the hair and trickled onto the face.

"Too hot," said the head. George adjusted the temperature.

A Wedding

"If you'll permit," said the head, "let me tell you a story. When I was young like you, I had a lady, and what she wanted more than anything was to marry. She was sweet, like to rot your teeth. But I tell you that there's nothing that'll take the life out of a man as surely as a band on his finger."

George nodded, because he knew this to be the truth.

"Finally I gave in to her, and we drove to Las Vegas and had ourselves a safari wedding with a black priest and a choir of lady singers in tiger suits. When we got back to our hotel room, I took out an empty suitcase and put it out on the bed for her to see. I told her, 'Every time you fuck this thing up, every time you do me wrong, I'm going to take a piece of clothing, a shirt or pants or whatever, and I'm going to put it into the suitcase, and once the suitcase is full, I'm gone.' We weren't married a year before I'd packed my bag, and I stuck it in the back of my car and I left."

"You know," George said to the head, "in another time and place, I might have been a very good professional billiards player."

"Billiards," said the head, "is the sport of kings."

Improvements

George looked closely at the nicked cheeks. They were covered with stubble. When he squinted, he could almost see tiny hairs snaking out of the follicles. He spread shaving cream on his hands and lathered the face. In slow, careful strokes, he shaved it clean. He dried it

with one of Rita's hand towels and set it in front of the mirror to contemplate its reflection.

"I've looked worse," it said.

George rifled through Rita's makeup drawer and took out a compact of rouge. "Let's see what we can do about giving you some color,"
he said. He applied the makeup in generous streaks, massaged it into
the loose jowls until the head had a pleasant ruddy complexion.

George was poised with a tube of lipstick in one hand and a hairbrush in the other when the door swung open. Rita stood in the hallway, pale and bedraggled.

Rita

"Who's in there?" she demanded. Her eyes were fire. "I know it's not a
woman, in our house. In my bathroom."

And then she saw the head. She stopped in the threshold, a shaky
hand covering her mouth. George went cold.

"It's not how it looks," he stammered, gesturing at the head with
the hairbrush. He saw himself through Rita's eyes, and he felt
ashamed. "I thought I'd clean him up. I couldn't leave him, could I?
There are dogs and whatnot."

Rita made a low watery sound. She took a clumsy backward step
and pointed an unsteady finger at George.

"You get out of here right now," she cried. "You go to your Peg. You
get out of this house."

She retreated toward the bedroom, past chess sets and Walkmans
and free weights and cordless phones, and George watched her
shrink away and disappear behind the door, which shut without a
sound.

Fauna

George sat down on the tiled floor of the bathroom. He leaned his
head against the toilet.

"What am I supposed to do now?" he asked.

The head made a fine suggestion. "Let's drop in on your brother

Chuck," it said. "And listen, pick out a golf club from the closet in the hall."

"What for?" George asked.

"If this thing's going to work out," it said, "you'll have to learn to trust me."

George held the edge of the counter and staggered to his feet. He collected the head and lurched through the kitchen to the closet and out the front door. The air smelled fresh, like Christmas. It was a fine night for driving, mist suspended over vacant yards, curtains drawn on the few lit windows of the town. Through the windshield, the mailboxes suggested human forms, and George had the impression of his neighbors gathered at the ends of their driveways to see him off. Some time later, the car passed a bull elk idling in a stand of pines, still and noble and grave. The whole world seemed to pause to take in its breath. A premonition of light etched the mountains in fine relief, and the highway uncoiled, a kind of gentle offering. George was speechless, and on the seat beside him, so was the head.

JULIA SWEENEY

■

Letting Go of God?

FROM *This American Life*

NOT TOO LONG AGO, two Mormon missionaries came to my door. I live just off a main thoroughfare in Los Angeles, and my block is a natural beginning for people peddling things door to door. Sometimes I get little old ladies from the Seventh-day Adventist church showing me pictures of heaven, and sometimes I get teenagers who promise me they won't join a gang and start robbing people if only I'd buy some magazine subscriptions. Normally I just ignore the doorbell. But on this day, I answered.

And there stood two Mormon boys, each about nineteen, in white, starched, short-sleeved shirts. They had little nametags that identified them as official representatives of the Church of Jesus Christ of Latter-day Saints. And they said they had a message for me. From God.

I said, "A message from God, for me?" And they said, "Yes."

I was raised in the Pacific Northwest around a lot of Mormons, and I've worked with them and even dated them, but I never really knew the doctrine or what they said to people on a mission. And I guess I was curious. So I said, "Please come in." And they seemed really happy because I don't think that happens to them all that often. I sat them down in the living room and got them glasses of water and after our niceties, I said, "OK, I'm ready for my message from God."

But instead they had a question. Which threw me a little. I thought it would be more like a pitch at a movie studio: they would tell me their story and then, if I was interested, I would have my people call their people. But apparently this was going to be interactive. They asked, "Do you believe that God loves you with all his heart?"

I thought, "Well, of course I believe in God. But I don't like the word 'heart' because that anthropomorphizes God, and I don't like the word 'his' because that sexualizes God." But I didn't want to argue semantics with these boys, so after a long, uncomfortable pause I just said, "Yes. Yes. I do. I feel very loved."

They looked at each other and smiled, like that was the right answer. And then they said, "Do you believe that we're all brothers and sisters on this planet?" And I immediately said, "Yes, I do. Yes, I do." And I felt relieved that it was a question I could answer so quickly. And then they said, "Well, then we have a story to tell you."

And they told me this story of a guy named Lehi, who lived in Jerusalem in 600 B.C. Apparently, in 600 B.C. everyone in Jerusalem was completely bad and evil, every single one of them: man, woman, child, infant, fetus. And God came to Lehi and said, "Put your family on a boat and I will lead you out of here." And so he did. And God led them to . . . America.

I said, "America? From Jerusalem to America by boat in 600 B.C.?" And they said, "Yes." And I said, "Oh." And then they told me how Lehi and his descendants reproduced and reproduced and eventually, over the course of six hundred years, there were two races: the Nephites and the Lamanites. And the Nephites were totally good, each and every one of them, and the Lamanites were totally bad, each and every one of them, bad to the bone.

Then, after Jesus died on the cross for our sins, on his way up to heaven he stopped by America and visited the Nephites. And Jesus said that if the Nephites all remained totally good, each and every one of them, they would win the war against the Lamanites. But apparently someone blew it, and the Lamanites killed all the Nephites.

Except for one guy named Mormon, who managed to survive by hiding in the woods. And he made sure this whole story was written down in reformed Egyptian hieroglyphics and engraved on gold plates, which he then buried near Palmyra, New York.

Well, I was so into this story, I was on the edge of my seat. And I said, "What happened to the Lamanites?" And they said, "They became our Native Americans here in the U.S."

I said, "So you believe that the Native Americans are descended from people who were totally evil?" And they said, "Yes."

Then they told me how a man named Joseph Smith found the buried gold plates in his backyard. And he also found a magic stone that he put into his hat and buried his face in, and this allowed him to translate the plates (which he'd hid in the stump of a tree, being gold and all) from reformed Egyptian into English.

So I was just looking at these boys with wide eyes. And I was wishing I could give them some advice about their pitch. I wanted to say, "Don't start with this story. Even the Scientologists know to give you a personality test before they tell you all about Xenu, the evil intergalactic overlord."

Then they said, "Do you believe that God speaks to us through his righteous prophets?" And I said, "No, I don't," because I was sort of upset about the Lamanites story and this crazy golden-plate story. But the truth was, I hadn't thought this through. So I backpedaled a little and said, "Well, what do you mean by righteous? And what do you mean by prophets? Like . . . can the prophets be women?" And they said, "Uh, no. You see, God gave women a gift that is so fantastic, that is so wonderful, that the only gift he had left over to give men was the gift of prophecy."

I wondered, what is the wonderful gift he gave women? Maybe their greater ability to cooperate, their longer life span, their tendency to be less violent than men . . . ?

But no. They said, "It's their ability to bear children."

I said, "Oh, come on. I mean, even if a woman had a child every year from the time she was fifteen to the time she was forty-five, assuming she didn't die from exhaustion, she would still have time when she was older to hear the word of God." And they said, "Ah, no."

At this point they didn't look so fresh-faced and cute anymore.

But they had more to say. They told me that if you're a Mormon, and you're in good standing with the church, you go to heaven and get to be with your family for all eternity.

I said, "Oh, dear. That's not such a good incentive for me. I mean, I was sort of looking forward to death as a reprieve from some members of my family." And they said, "Well, when you go to heaven you get your body completely restored to you in its best state. Like, if you lost a leg, you have it back, and if you're blind, you can see."

And I said, "Now, I don't have a uterus, because I had cancer a few years ago, so does this mean that I would get my old uterus back if I went to heaven?" And they said, "Yes!" And I said, "I don't want it back! I'm happy without it! What if you had a nose job, and you liked it? Would God force you to get your old nose back?"

Well, then they gave me a Book of Mormon and told me to read this chapter and that chapter and that they would come back someday and check in on me, and I think I said something like "Please don't hurry." Or maybe it was just "Please don't." And they were gone.

All right. So, I initially felt really superior to these boys, and smug in my more conventional faith, but then I had to be honest with myself. If someone came to my door with Catholic theology, and I was hearing it for the first time, and they said, "We believe that God impregnated a very young girl without the use of intercourse, and the fact that she was a virgin is maniacally important to us, and she eventually had a baby and he was the son of God," I would think that was equally ridiculous. I'm just used to that story.

So I couldn't let myself feel condescending toward these boys. But the question they asked me when they first arrived — "Do you believe that God loves you with all his heart?" — stuck in my head. Because I wasn't exactly sure what I felt about that question. Now, if they had asked me, "Do you feel that God loves you with all his heart?" that would have been easy. I would have honestly said, "Yes, I feel it all the time. I feel God's love when I'm hurt and confused and I feel consoled and cared for. I take shelter in God's love when I don't understand why tragedy hits. I feel God's love when I look with gratitude at all the beauty I see."

But since they asked me the question with the word "believe" in it, somehow it was all different. Because I wasn't sure if I believed what I so clearly felt.

OK, my religious history, in a nutshell. I was raised Catholic, and for me, all in all, it was a great experience. We can't stop reading about all the people who've had horrific and abusive experiences as a child in the Catholic Church, but I always felt lucky to be a Catholic. It was easy for me to believe. I even had religious experiences — I mean, I know this is more of a Protestant thing than a Catholic thing, but a few times, maybe five or six times, I felt the power of the Holy Spirit come over me and shake me to the core. I felt a powerful force of love and transcendence when I knew that God had a plan for me.

So now you can sort of see, when, a few days later, the two Mormon boys arrived at my doorstep and said that God had a message for me, why I was stopped in my tracks and actually let them in. And in spite of their nutty story, they inspired me. I realized that I had been getting a bit lazy about my faith. I was inspired by the Mormon boys' dedication, and in them I glimpsed the girl inside me who had once wanted to be a nun, the person who was willing to go the distance in matters of faith.

So I decided I had to rededicate myself to my church. I went to Mass at a few different Catholic churches, and finally settled on one about ten miles from my house, near the ocean. It was liberal, it was big, and it had a dedicated and enthusiastic congregation. Their Masses were wonderful, so emotional and so full of feeling. I would have to choke back tears just to say the Nicene Creed every time I went. "We believe in one God, the Father Almighty, creator of heaven and earth. And of all that is seen and unseen." I love reciting that, the voices in church all together in unison. But I wanted to say it with conviction, not as a child who has absorbed these things over the years, but with a grownup's understanding, in my heart and soul, the way God says we should.

I noticed in the announcements that the church offered a Bible study class on Thursday nights and I decided to sign up for it. You know, the Catholics don't emphasize the Bible all that much. They sort of say, "Leave that book to the professionals. Don't you worry your little self with that complicated book." But of what little I did know, I knew there were parts I loved. Often when I felt scared or confused, I repeated Psalm 23: "Though I walk through the valley of the shadow of death, I shall not fear, because you are with me." And I felt so much better.

Now, I was happy to see that the Old Testament starts out with two conflicting stories about the origin of the universe: one where Adam and Eve are created at the same moment, and then a second creation story where Adam is created first and then Eve is created out of his rib after he gets lonely. And I thought, "Wow, for all those people who believe in the inerrancy of the Bible, or that every word of the Bible is true, they can't even have read the first two chapters of the Bible." I had always had the Bible served up to me piecemeal and in sections and it was edited, severely edited. It was quite different reading it as an adult. As an adult you could begin to see the whole puzzle. As an adult, it was disturbing.

We started with Noah and the Ark. And it was kind of funny: when I was studying this as a child, I don't remember Sister Mary Kevin highlighting the fact that Noah becomes an alcoholic after the flood. And spends time lying around passed out and naked, to the point where his sons have to back up into a room with a blanket to cover him up. And I didn't think about the fact that God purposefully killed everyone because he was angry — drowned them all because he thought they were all bad. And you have to assume that included a lot of kids and unborn fetuses. Which I guess was OK with God. But then I was relieved to read that God tells Noah afterward, "Y'know the whole flood thing? It might have been a big mistake." And he promises he'll never do it again. That was another surprise: God has regrets.

Then we got to stories like Sodom and Gomorrah. All I remembered was that they were sinful cities, like Las Vegas and Reno, and God got mad and wiped them out. And Lot's wife looked back when she was told not to and got turned into a pillar of salt. But the nuns of my grade school didn't tell us about what happens right before they flee. Right before they leave, two angels, masquerading as men, come for a visit and stay overnight at Lot's house. And a mob forms outside and they yell, "Send out those two angel-like men to us so we can have sex with them!" And Lot says, "No!" Which I think is a basic rule of hospitality: don't give up your guests to be raped by an angry mob.

But what does he say next? He says, "Instead of the men, please take my daughters and rape and do what you will with them. They're virgins!"

OK, so Lot is evil, right? How is it that the story we know is about his wife turning into salt? Maybe this was her only way out. Maybe being a big pillar of salt is preferable to being married to Lot.

So after Lot and his traumatized daughters flee Sodom and Gomorrah, they go up to a cave in the mountains. During the night, Lot's two daughters get Lot drunk and rape *him*. Do they do this in revenge for what their father did to them? No. The Bible says it's because there aren't any other men around. Even though the Bible also says they aren't that far from a city named Zoar. So I guess no men were around for maybe a few miles . . .

OK, so I knew the Bible had nutty stories, but I thought they'd be wedged in among an ocean of inspiration and history. But instead the stories got darker and more convoluted. God tests people's loyalty in the grizzliest ways. Like when he asks Abraham to murder his son, Isaac. As a kid, I remembered we were taught to admire it. I caught my breath reading it. We were taught to *admire* it. What kind of sadistic test of loyalty is that, to ask someone to kill his or her child? Isn't the proper answer "No, I will not kill my child, or any child, even if it means eternal punishment in hell"?

At the next class Father Tom reminded us that "Isaac represented what mattered to Abraham most. And that's what God asks us to give up for him."

I said, "But protecting and loving and caring for the welfare of your child is a deep, ethical, loving instinct. So what if what matters to you most is your own loving behavior? Should we be willing to give up our ethics for God?"

Father Tom said, "No, it's what matters to you most that isn't your ethics, because your ethics is your love and faith in God." That confused me, but I decided to let it go. Then I found that Abraham wasn't the only person willing to murder his own child for God. They're all over the place in the Bible.

For example, in the book of Judges, a guy named Jephthah tells God that if he can help him win a certain battle, he, Jephthah, will kill the first person to greet him when he returns home. And who is the first person Jephthah sees? His only child, his beloved daughter, who comes out of the house playing with tambourines and singing: "Hi, Daddy . . . What?"

And does God say "No, don't kill your daughter as a burnt offering to me"? Or even "Jephthah, who did you expect to be the first person out of the door to greet you when you came home?" No, it appears that the most important point of the story is that before Jephthah kills her, he allows his beautiful daughter to go off to the woods for two months to mourn her virginity (I kept thinking, "Run! Run!") But when she comes back he kills her — by lighting her on fire.

Even things that I thought were set in stone, like literally set in stone, like the Ten Commandments, were not. The Ten Commandments we're most familiar with are rules that God simply told Moses on Mount Sinai, without referring to them as commandments and without setting them in stone. It's only later in Exodus, when Moses goes back up to Mount Sinai, that God gives him a set of two tablets of stone with rules chiseled on them. When Moses comes down from the mountain, he sees people worshiping the golden calf, and he throws a tantrum and smashes the tablets before he reads them. So then Moses goes back up to Mount Sinai and God gives him *another* set of tablets, and this is the first time they're referred to as "the Commandments." And they are chiseled into stone, so you'd sort of think that God is firm on the subject of commandments by now.

But the rules are significantly different from the other rules. Like how all male children have to appear before God three times a year (however that's supposed to be accomplished), and how you can't boil a young goat in its mother's milk to cook it, and how every domestic animal's firstborn male has to be sacrificed. (This commandment goes on to say that if you don't want to sacrifice your donkey's firstborn male, you can substitute a lamb if you want to.) Some people argue that without the Ten Commandments, morality would be relative and wishy-washy. But in the Bible morality is relative and wishy-washy. In fact, it sure seems like our modern morality is much more loving and humane than the Bible's morality.

After Mass one Sunday, Father Tom saw me outside the church. He said, "Julia, you always look so very sad in Bible study class." And I said, "Well, God is so offensive in the Old Testament. I mean, really, like . . . bipolar."

Father Tom said, "Well, y'know, the Old Testament. Just remember, Julia, that the people who wrote it lived in a Bronze Age civilization. The stories are legends, tales of trickery and deception that were told around the campfire by shepherds who made God impressive by their ancient standards."

I said, "Oh. Wow. Looking at the Old Testament that way, it makes a lot of sense. In fact, looking at it that way is quite interesting. But Homer was also an ancient Bronze Age writer writing about gods. I mean, how much are we supposed to believe is actually true?"

And Father Tom said, "Well, look, there's no evidence that Abraham is anything other than legend, or Isaac or Moses, or even the whole Exodus story." I said, "The Exodus story is myth?" And Father Tom said, "Mythish." And I said, "How can something be mythish?" And he said, "Well, the Exodus story is myth in the sense that it never actually happened. But it's not a myth in the fact that the story was believed by a group of people who shaped their identity in the world based on thinking it was true. But Julia, you can't approach the Bible with modern, historical eyes. You have to read it with the eyes of faith. This is the story God wants us to know."

As I drove home, I thought, "OK, calm down. This is the Old Testament. Old. Old is right in the title. A New, Newer Testament is coming up. And that's why God sent his son, Jesus. Because we clearly hadn't gotten the message right, right? Jesus was all about tearing down those archaic ways of worship and reminding people that what mattered most was what we were like on the inside. I was so excited to meet Jesus again, as if it were the first time.

But, oh dear. When I did read the New Testament again, I realized that Jesus is much angrier than I had expected him to be. I mean, I knew Jesus got angry with the moneychangers in the Temple, but I didn't know he was *so* angry *so* much of the time. And very impatient.

For example, Jesus says he teaches in parables because people don't understand anything else. But the parables are often foggy and meaningless. And Jesus is snippy when the disciples don't get them. He says, "If you don't understand this parable, then how can you understand any parable?" And "Are you incapable of understanding?" I kept thinking, "Don't teach in parables, then. It's not working! Even your staff doesn't get them! Just say what you mean."

Many parables weren't just foggy, but offensive. In Luke, Jesus helps us understand God's relationship with humans by telling us a story about how God treats people like people treat their slaves. They beat some more than others. OK, I know this was a different time and everything, and I tried to keep this in mind since the Bible refers to slavery all over the place. And not only does the Bible not say slavery is wrong, it goes so far as to give advice about how to treat slaves and how slaves should behave obediently to their masters. You'd sort of think the son of God would say slavery is wrong.

It's hard to stay on Jesus' side when he says really aggressive, hateful things. In Luke, he says, "Anyone who does not recognize me, bring them here and slaughter them before me." Or in John, chapter 15, where Jesus says that anyone who doesn't believe in him is like a withered branch that will be cast into the fire and burned! In Matthew he says, "I come not to bring peace, but a sword." And in Luke he continues, "And if you don't have a sword, sell your clothes and buy one."

Then Jesus starts acting downright crazy. In Matthew, chapter 21, when a fig tree doesn't have a fig for him to eat, he condemns the fig tree to death. That's right, Jesus condemns a *fig tree* to death. Not a parable — just Jesus pissed off that the fig tree didn't have a fig for him to eat when he wanted one! Not exactly the Prince of Peace who taught us to turn the other cheek.

And then there's family. I have to say, one of the most deeply upsetting things about Jesus is his sense of family values. Which is amazing when you think how so many groups say they base their family values on the Bible.

He seems to have no close ties to his parents. He puts Mary off cruelly, over and over again. At the wedding feast he says to her, "Woman, what have I to do with you?" And one time while he was speaking to a crowd, his mother waited patiently off to the side to talk to him, and he said to the apostles, "Send her away, you are my family now."

Matthew, Mark, and Luke all tell this same story, but Mark actually tells us why Mary was there to see Jesus. He says Mary came to see Jesus to restrain him, because the people were saying, "He has gone out of his mind." I was thinking, "Yes. Let's go get Jesus and get him some help!"

Anyway, Jesus discourages any contact his converts have with their families. He himself does not marry or have children, and he explicitly tells his followers not to have families as well, and if they do, they should just abandon them.

Mostly Jesus says this because he believed the end of the world was imminent. He said that people who were alive when he was around would not die naturally, but see the End Time. He tells us this in Matthew, Mark, and Luke.

So, OK, Jesus said not to have a family because he mistakenly believed that the end of all time was upon us, but then Jesus also says not to care for the family that you do have already. In Luke, chapter 14, Jesus says, "Whoever comes to me and does not hate father and mother, wife and children, brothers and sisters, cannot be my disciple." I mean, isn't that what cults do? Get you to reject your family in order to indoctrinate you?

So those are the New Testament family values for you — the supposed big improvement on the Old Testament family values, which seemed to be mostly about incest and mass slaughter and protecting your specific genetic line at all costs.

After the Gospels, the Bible has lots of letters written by early Christians, the most important of which are by Saint Paul. You know, in general the Bible's view of women is dreadful, and I know that was a different time than now and everything. But Saint Paul? He really gets right to the point.

He writes, "Man is the image and glory of God, but woman is the glory of man. A woman should learn in quietness and full submission. I do not permit a woman to teach or have authority over a man; she must be silent. If there is anything a woman desires to know, let her ask her husband at home. For Adam was formed first, and then Eve. And it was not the man who was deceived; it was the woman who was deceived and became the sinner." I was so disillusioned by the time I finished the epistles, I didn't think it could get any worse, but it did. We were just about to read the last and most oddball book of the Bible, Revelation.

Revelation was apparently written by Saint John, the same person who wrote a Gospel and some of the epistles. The biblical historian Ken Smith says that "if his epistles can be seen as John on pot, then Revelation is John on acid." It describes the End of Days, with maybe a little too much gruesome enthusiasm.

Revelation tells us that in heaven there "is a throne, and the One who sat there had the appearance of a jasper . . . Around the throne were four living creatures, and they were covered with eyes, front and back. Day and night they never stop saying 'Holy, holy, holy is the

Lord God Almighty, who was and is and is to come.'" In heaven, Jesus resembles a dead lamb with seven horns and seven eyes. When the gates of hell are opened, locusts pour out with human faces, wearing tiny crowns, and they sting people with their tails.

Revelation tells us that only 144,000 people will be saved and go to heaven, and none of them will have, quote, "defiled themselves with women." Which I guess excludes most heterosexual men from heaven, and depending on how you interpret the word "defiled," I would say it excludes all women, too.

The Bible. The Bible. The Good News! The Good Book! What a great book! What great news!

As we finished Revelation, the whole Bible study group sat there dumbfounded, our Bibles on our laps. Father Tom said, "Revelation's a poem about the end of the world." I said, "Father Tom, I'm having a really hard time with this book." He told me to "pray for faith."

I left the church thinking, "Is this one big practical joke? Where is my God? The Jesus I thought I knew? The one I love and the one who loves me?"

I drove home, and when I stopped for a red light at Wilshire and Crenshaw, I saw all these people walking to church, holding their Bibles. I wanted to roll down the window and yell, "Have you read that book? I mean *really*, have you read it?"

I felt I was in a horror film and realized that the clue to the insanity was not a secret document, it was a book that everyone was holding, that was in every hotel room, the biggest bestseller of all time, the key to the underpinnings of the faith.

And yet if you cared enough to glance inside, you'd find you had opened a door to an asylum, where crazy people were dancing around yelling, "Yippity yippity yah! It's all a fake! And we hid it in plain sight!" And I had quickly shut that door, and how was I going to pretend I hadn't opened that door?

My mother said, "I just ignore what I don't like. Why would you go and do something like read the Bible cover to cover if you weren't just looking for reasons to be upset? Julie, you make your life so much harder than it has to be!"

So I tried to concentrate on what I liked about the church. The stained glass windows were pretty, as was the religious art. The songs. Not the words of the songs exactly, but the melodies were nice. Especially at Christmas. It was all so . . . pretty in the church around the holidays.

After Mass that Easter, Father Tom saw me outside the church and he said, "Happy Easter, Julia." And I said, "Happy Easter, Father." And he said, "You know, I can see you frowning from the pulpit." And I said, "I'm sorry. But Father, help me! What can I do? It all just seems so . . . impossible to believe." He pulled me toward the coffee-and-donuts table. He said, "I've spoken with some of the other priests about your . . . predicament." I loved how he said "predicament," like I was sixteen and knocked up.

I said, "Yeah, what do they suggest?" He said, "We all struggle with doubt. But we all come back. Remember Proverbs 3:5: 'Trust in the Lord with all your heart, and lean not on your own understanding.'"

"So, God gave us the gifts of reasoning and intelligence and curiosity," I said, "but we aren't supposed to use them?"

Father Tom sighed, like he was so tired of me and my struggle. And I felt so angry that he used that particular proverb. Like he was shutting the door.

Then Father Tom suddenly blessed me. It was kind of awkward — he started waving his hands over me and chanting a phrase in Latin. Not that this is so out of the ordinary or wrong; it just felt like he was trying to perform an exorcism.

As I drove home, I thought, "I tried so hard! I tried to learn more about my church and it just made everything else a lot worse. I can't go back there again. This is not the right church for me. Maybe I don't even need a church at all." And I could almost feel God sitting next to me in the passenger seat, saying, "I could barely stand it at church myself. Let's get the hell out of here!" And so we did.

When I got home it felt remarkably quiet. Just me and . . . God. Not saying much, just pondering. Not a big conversationalist, God.

The real truth was, I was starting to get nervous about our relationship. I felt like we were a married couple in trouble, trying to find some common ground. I started to wonder just who I was married to. How defined did it really need to be for me? Because the truth was, God worked for me. Did it work because it's true, or is it true because it worked? William James said it amounted to the same thing. I began to wonder if God wasn't just my imaginary friend. As they say, the invisible and the nonexistent often look very much alike.

At the time, I was dating a guy who was a big believer in intelligent design. Intelligent design is an idea that the world is so complex, especially the conscious, thinking, feeling human being, who is so complicated, that it just couldn't have happened by chance. Someone or something even smarter had to have a hand in creating us. And that someone or something is God. I mean, the watch requires a watchmaker.

One morning my intelligent-designer boyfriend and I woke up and he glanced at the books on the table next to my side of the bed, which were becoming increasingly more biological rather than religious. Then we gazed into each other's eyes, deeper than ever before. And he said, "It's the human eye, you know — that's the proof that there must have been a designer. You can't have half an eye. Half an eye is no good at all. You either have an eye so you can see or you don't. How could you possibly *evolve* an eye?"

"Yes," I said, "that's probably true. An eye, an eye is very complex. After all, it's the window to the soul."

So I began to read about eyes. I learned a lot more than I ever dreamed about eyes. It turns out that from an evolutionary perspective, the human eye is perfectly explainable. What began as a patch of skin more sensitive to light than other skin offers some advantage: those who have it, live. Those who don't, do not.

So half an eye *is* pretty valuable, about half as valuable.

Now if an intelligent designer, or God, designed our eyes, well, he would not get such a good grade. Because he put the blood vessels and the nerves that carry the visual information to the brain on top of our retinas. Imagine, that's like putting the wiring of a video camera on top of the lens. And where the blood vessels and nerves go through the retina, there is a blind spot that we have to compensate for, basically by hallucinating. That's bad. Bad, bad, bad. Not the best design for an eye. And it doesn't even have to be that way!

Octopuses and squids have eyes that evolved separately from ours and they don't have those annoying features. The wonderful biologist

Massimo Pigliucci wrote, "The only possible conclusions to this evidence are that God didn't design the eye, or He's pretty sloppy and not worthy of our unconditional admiration, or God likes squids a lot better than humans."

Intelligent design gets everything backward. It's like saying that our hands are miraculous because they fit so perfectly into our gloves: "Look at that! Four fingers *and* a thumb! That can't have been an accident!"

One day as I was Cometing out my bathtub, I thought: "What if it's true? What if humans are here because of pure random chance? What if there is no guiding hand, no external regulation, no one watching?" It is clearly possible that this may be true. In fact, this is what our scientific evidence is pointing toward. But if it is true, what would that mean?

I had spent so much time thinking about what God meant that I hadn't really spent any time thinking about what not-God meant.

A few days later, as I was walking from my office in my backyard to my house, I realized there was this teeny-weenie voice whispering in my head. I'm not sure how long it had been there, but it suddenly got one decibel louder. It whispered, "There is no God."

And I tried to ignore it. But it got a teeny bit louder. "There is no God. There is no God. Oh my God, there is no God."

I sat down in my backyard, under my barren apricot tree. (I didn't know trees were like people: they stop reproducing after they get old. Maybe that barren fig tree that Jesus condemned to death was just menopausal.) Anyway, I sat down and thought: "OK. I admit it. I do not believe there is enough evidence to continue to believe in God. The world behaves exactly as you would expect it would if there were no supreme being, no supreme consciousness, and no supernatural. And my best judgment tells me that it's much more likely that we invented God than that God invented us."

I shuddered. I felt I was slipping off the raft.

And then I thought: "But I can't. I don't know if I *can* not believe in God. I need God. I mean, we have a history."

But then I thought: "Wait a minute. If you look over my life, every step of maturing for me, every single one, had the same common denominator. It was accepting what was true over what I wished were true. This was the case about men, about my career, about my parents."

So how can I come up against this biggest question, the ultimate question, "Do I *really* believe in a personal God," and then turn away from the evidence? How can I believe just because I want to? How will I have any respect for myself if I do that?

I thought of Pascal's wager. Pascal argued that it's better to bet there is a God, because if you're wrong, there's nothing to lose, but if there is, you win an eternity in heaven. But I can't *force* myself to believe, just in case it turns out to be true.

The God I've been praying to knows what I think; he doesn't just make sure I show up for church. How could I possibly pretend to believe? I might convince other people, but surely not God. Plus, if I lead my life according to my own deeply held moral principles, what difference would it make if I believe in God or not? Why would God care if I "believed" in him?

Then I thought, "But I don't know *how* to not believe in God. I don't know how you do it. How do you get up, how do you get through the day?" I felt unbalanced. I thought, "OK, calm down. Let's try on the not-believing-in-God glasses for a moment. Put on the no-God glasses and take a quick look around and then immediately throw them off. And I put them on and I looked around.

I'm embarrassed to report that I initially felt dizzy. I actually had the thought, "Well, how does the earth stay up in the sky? You mean we're just hurtling through space? That's so vulnerable!" I wanted to run out and catch the earth as it fell out of space into my hands.

And then I remembered, "Oh, yeah, gravity and angular momentum are gonna keep us revolving around the sun for probably a long, long time."

Then I thought, "What's going to stop me from running out and murdering people?" And I had to walk myself through it: Why are we ethical? Well, because we have to be. We're social animals. We have to get along with each other. We evolved a moral sense, like an aversion to random murder, in order for communities to exist. Because communities help us survive better. And then we made laws against things like wanton murder, to codify our ethics. So I guess that's why I don't run out and murder people!

And then I felt like I'd cheated on God somehow, and I went into the house and prayed and asked God to help me have faith. But already it felt silly and vacant, and I felt like I was talking to myself. I thought, "I'll just not believe in God for one hour a day and see how it goes." So, the next day, I tried it again.

Then I thought: "Wait a minute. Wait a minute. What about those people who are unjustifiably jailed somewhere horrible, and they're in solitary confinement and all they do is pray? This means that they're praying to nobody. Is that possible?" And then I thought, "We gotta do something to get those people outta jail!" Because no one else is looking out for them but us; no God is hearing their pleas. And I guess that goes for really poor people too, or oppressed people. I had this vague notion that they had God to comfort them. And then an even vaguer notion, that God had orchestrated their lot for some unknowable grand design.

I wandered around in a daze, thinking, "No one is minding the store!" And I wondered how traffic worked, like how we weren't in chaos all the time. I had to rethink what I thought about everything. It's like I had to go change the wallpaper of my mind.

And slowly I began to see the world completely differently. And I wished I could say goodbye to God, and I wanted to say, "God, it's because I take you so seriously that I can't believe in you. If it's any consolation, it's really a sign of respect."

Eventually I was able to say goodbye to God. And I imagined him as this old man, this old guy — like a more broken-down version of the God on the ceiling of the Sistine Chapel. And if you looked closely, you could see the Jesus on the poster hanging in my high school bedroom, but older, much older, with long gray and white hair and lots of lines in his face. An old hippie who still smoked. And at one time he seemed so cool and loving and protective and all-powerful, but now he seemed a little stinky.

He was sitting on his suitcases by the front door of my house. And

I said to him, "I'm sorry, God; it's not you. It's me. It's just, I don't think you exist. I mean, God, look at it this way: it's really because I take you so seriously that I can't believe in you. If it's any consolation, it's sort of a sign of respect. So, you know, sit here as long as you want to, stay for a while if you need to, there's no big hurry."

And slowly, over the course of several weeks, he disappeared.

Looking back on it, I think I walked around in a daze for a few months. My mind became such a private place. I had shared my mind with God my whole life, and now, now I realized that my thoughts were completely my own. No one was monitoring them, no one was compassionately listening to them. My thoughts were my own private affair, something no one but me knew about.

I had so much thinking to do! One day I was sipping my coffee, walking along Larchmont Boulevard, a busy shopping area near my house. I was lost in thought: "So, I don't think anything happens to us after we die. Consciousness fades and stops like every other organ. So people just die."

Then: "Wait a minute. Hitler, Hitler just . . . died? No one sat him down and said, 'You fucked up, buddy! And now you're going to spend an eternity in HELL!' So Hitler just died," I thought. "We better make sure that doesn't happen again."

And my brother Mike. He just died. I always had the idea that his death, while premature, was his divine destiny somehow. That his spirit didn't really die, it lived on. Not just in the memory of those who knew him, but in a real, tangible sense. And I realized that I now thought he died. He *really* died. And he was gone, forever.

Then I thought about all the little happenstances that resulted in me being alive, me in particular, at this moment. All the random moves: not just my parents meeting, but even the millions of sperm against the hundreds of possible eggs. I thought about this randomness multiplying: my parents, their parents, Marie meeting Tom in Yakima, Henrietta meeting Will on the cruise to Cuba, and then their parents, their parents, their parents. All the ways it could have gone one way, but it went the way it went. And all the possible people who could just as easily be here in my place.

Richard Dawkins wrote, "Certainly those unborn ghosts include poets greater than Keats, scientists greater than Newton . . . In the teeth of these stupefying odds it is you and I, in our ordinariness, that are here."

I went to Spokane to visit my parents. My dad walked to church every morning, to Lourdes Cathedral for the 6:30 Mass, and then he took the bus back home. On the days I was in town, I went with him. It was fun to go to Mass with my dad. He had a special way of walking downtown that took him past certain store windows, and he could see if they changed things.

On the bus ride home, we would muse over the wording of certain prayers or recitations in the Mass. My dad loved it when the priest said, "Satan, who prowls through the world for the ruin of souls." We both agreed that it was the word "prowls" that made the phrase so great.

Later that day, I casually mentioned to my parents that I had stopped believing in God. They just looked at me blankly. Sometimes I feel sorry for my parents for having had me for a kid. Sometimes I am thankful that my parents had a lot of kids. My mom said, "This doesn't mean that you aren't going to go to Mass anymore, does it?"

I said, "No, I'll still go with you!" I suddenly felt so guilty about this religion, my parents' religion, the religion that they had given to us kids, and that I was now handing back to them.

A month later, I went to a conference in Washington, D.C., put on by the Center for Inquiry, a nonprofit group that promotes science and critical thinking. A lot of people spoke at the conference. I got to give a speech too, which included my views on God. The Associated Press covered it. And the wire story was picked up by my hometown paper, the *Spokesman Review.* Spokane, where I had recently hosted a Catholic Charities luncheon, where I had spoken repeatedly at my Catholic high school, where my parents took such pride in their Catholicism and their children: in retrospect, I believe my parents felt that my Catholicism was what connected me to my hometown, to my class, and to them, in spite of my having moved away.

So one day, weeks and weeks after this speech, and without my being aware that this article would appear, my parents went out and got their morning paper. And there I was, on the back of the front section, a huge half-page picture of me, and in bold letters, in huge type, it said, "Sweeney Loses Her Religion."

And the first two sentences of the article were: Julia Sweeney has come out of the closet. Period. As an atheist. Period.

It was the local angle, and they led with it. The article went on to speak about the conference in general and barely mentioned me again.

My first call from my mother was more of a scream: "Atheist? ATHEIST?!?!" My dad called and said, "You have betrayed your family, your school, your city." It was like I had sold secrets to the Russians. They both said they weren't going to talk to me anymore. My dad said, "I don't think you should come to my funeral." After I hung up, I thought, "Just try and stop me."

I think that my parents had been mildly disappointed when I'd said I didn't believe in God anymore, but being an atheist was another thing altogether. Frankly, I hadn't described myself as an atheist, although I suppose I am. I don't live my life under the assumption that there's a God, so I guess that makes me an atheist. A-theist. Non-theist. But I like the word "naturalist" more. "Atheist" defines me on religious terms. I believe in a wholly natural world; that makes religious people, in my mind, a-naturalists.

A few weeks went by, and there was no contact with my parents. This was a big deal: I usually spoke to my parents on the phone several times a week. Then one day, out of the blue, my mother called on her cell phone and she said, "I just got out of the foot doctor and he told me blah, blah, blah . . ." And then there was a pause. She had forgotten she wasn't speaking to me anymore.

That began a series of sporadic phone calls that I would get from my mother, sometimes in the early hours of the morning. Once, at about 5:30 A.M., I got a call from my mother, and she whispered, "Why can't you just say you're still searching?" And I said, "Ah, well, I *am* searching, if what you mean by searching is a continual yearning to understand. But when it comes to God, at some point, don't you have to decide one way or the other? The way you think when you believe there is a God is very different from the way you think when you don't."

She said, "Well then, why do you have to tell people? Everyone knows that there are those who don't believe in God, but they keep it quietly to themselves! Last night your father said he even wishes you'd announced you were gay. Because at least that's socially acceptable!"

I felt awful. To my parents it really was like I was rejecting them personally, or like saying I wasn't Irish anymore. Or worse, like I wasn't American anymore.

Once, I picked up the phone and my mother said, "Where do you get your peace?" And I repressed the urge to be sarcastic.

I said, "Well, I guess in some ways I do have less peace. I don't think everything works out for the best. Or there is some grand plan. The sad things in life *do* seem even sadder. But I guess I've learned how to live with it."

My mother said, "Julie, I just want you to be happy. Aren't you just so depressed all the time now?" And I said, "No. Every day I feel lucky to simply be here. The smallest things seem amazing. I see a bridge and now I think, 'Wow, we figured out how to make a bridge.' I mean, if this is all there is, everything becomes more meaningful, not less — right?"

Eventually my dad called me and said, "Listen, it's all right. I disagree with you, but I am proud of you for saying what you really think. Even though I think Satan might be prowling the world for the ruin of your soul." And I said, "Maybe he's just strolling." And my dad said, "Lurking." And I said, "Sauntering." And he said, "Meandering . . . with a sinister intent."

KURT VONNEGUT

■

Here Is a Lesson in Creative Writing

FROM *A Man Without a Country*

FIRST RULE: Do not use semicolons. They are transvestite hermaphrodites representing absolutely nothing. All they do is show you've been to college.

And I realize some of you may be having trouble deciding whether I am kidding or not. So from now on I will tell you when I'm kidding.

For instance, join the National Guard or the Marines and teach democracy. I'm kidding.

We are about to be attacked by Al Qaeda. Wave flags if you have them. That always seems to scare them away. I'm kidding.

If you want to really hurt your parents, and you don't have the nerve to be gay, the least you can do is go into the arts. I'm not kidding. The arts are not a way to make a living. They are a very human way of making life more bearable. Practicing an art, no matter how well or badly, is a way to make your soul grow, for heaven's sake. Sing in the shower. Dance to the radio. Tell stories. Write a poem to a friend, even a lousy poem. Do it as well as you possibly can. You will get an enormous reward. You will have created something.

I want to share with you something I've learned. I'll draw it on the blackboard behind me so you can follow more easily [*draws a vertical line on the blackboard*]. This is the G-I axis: good fortune — ill fortune. Death and terrible poverty, sickness down here — great prosperity, wonderful health up there. Your average state of affairs here in the middle [*points to bottom, top, and middle of line, respectively*].

This is the B-E axis. B for beginning, E for entropy. OK. Not every story has that very simple, very pretty shape that even a computer can understand [*draws horizontal line extending from middle of G-I axis*].

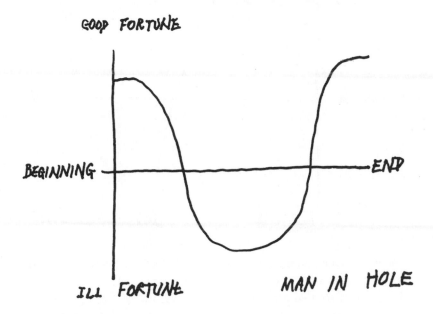

Now let me give you a marketing tip. The people who can afford to buy books and magazines and go to the movies don't like to hear about people who are poor or sick, so start your story up here [*indicates top of the G-I axis*]. You will see this story over and over again. People love it and it is not copyrighted. The story is "Man in Hole," but the story needn't be about a man or a hole. It's: Somebody gets into trouble, gets out of it again [*draws line A*]. It is not accidental that the line ends up higher than where it began. This is encouraging to readers.

Another is called "Boy Meets Girl," but this needn't be about a boy meeting a girl [*begins drawing line B*]. It's: Somebody, an ordinary person, on a day like any other day, comes across something perfectly wonderful: "Oh boy, this is my lucky day!" . . . [*drawing line downward*] "Shit!" . . . [*drawing line back up again*] And gets back up again.

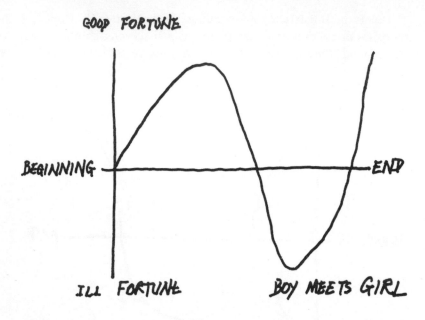

Now, I don't mean to intimidate you, but after being a chemist as an undergraduate at Cornell, after the war I went to the University of Chicago and studied anthropology, and eventually I took a master's degree in that field. Saul Bellow was in that same department, and neither one of us ever made a field trip. Although we certainly imagined some. I started going to the library in search of reports about ethnographers, preachers, and explorers — those imperialists — to find out what sorts of stories they'd collected from primitive people. It was a big mistake for me to take a degree in anthropology anyway, because I can't stand primitive people — they're so stupid. But anyway, I read these stories, one after another, collected from primitive people all over the world, and they were dead level, like the B-E axis here. So all right. Primitive people deserve to lose with their lousy stories. They really are backward. Look at the wonderful rise and fall of our stories.

One of the most popular stories ever told starts down here [*begins line C below B-E axis*]. Who is this person who's despondent? She's a girl of about fifteen or sixteen whose mother has died, so why wouldn't she be low? And her father got married almost immediately to a terrible battle-ax with two mean daughters. You've heard it?

There's to be a party at the palace. She has to help her two stepsis-
ters and her dreadful stepmother get ready to go, but she herself has
to stay home. Is she even sadder now? No, she's already a broken-
hearted little girl. The death of her mother is enough. Things can't get
any worse than that. So OK, they all leave for the party. Her fairy god-
mother shows up [*draws incremental rise*], gives her pantyhose, mas-
cara, and a means of transportation to get to the party.

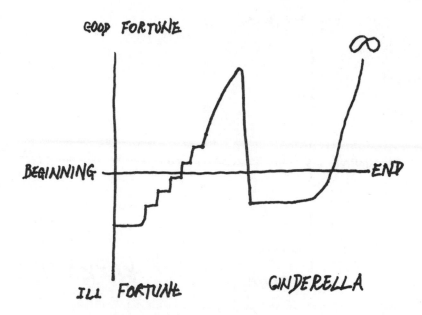

And when she shows up she's the belle of the ball [*draws line upward*]. She is so heavily made up that her relatives don't even recognize her. Then the clock strikes twelve, as promised, and it's all taken
away again [*draws line downward*]. It doesn't take long for a clock to
strike twelve times, so she drops down. Does she drop down to the
same level? Hell, no. No matter what happens after that, she'll remember when the prince was in love with her and she was the belle of
the ball. So she poops along, at her considerably improved level, no
matter what, and the shoe fits, and she becomes off-scale happy
[*draws line upward and then infinity symbol*].

Now there's a Franz Kafka story [*begins line D toward bottom of G-I axis*]. A young man is rather unattractive and not very personable. He has disagreeable relatives and has had a lot of jobs with no chance of promotion. He doesn't get paid enough to take his girl dancing or to go to the beer hall to have a beer with a friend. One morning he wakes up, it's time to go to work again, and he has turned into a cockroach [*draws line downward and then infinity symbol*]. It's a pessimistic story.

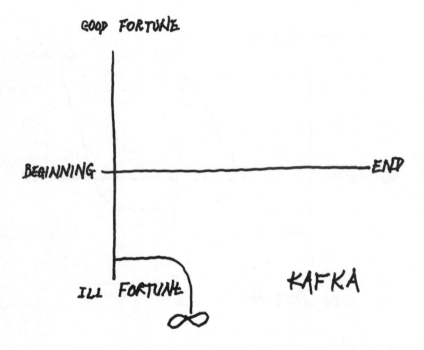

The question is, does this system I've devised help us in the evaluation of literature? Perhaps a real masterpiece cannot be crucified on a cross of this design. How about *Hamlet*? It's a pretty good piece of work, I'd say. Is anybody going to argue that it isn't? I don't have to draw a new line, because Hamlet's situation is the same as Cinderella's, except that the sexes are reversed.

His father has just died. He's despondent. And right away his mother went and married his uncle, who's a bastard. So Hamlet is going along on the same level as Cinderella when his friend Horatio comes up to him and says, "Hamlet, listen, there's this thing up in the parapet, I think maybe you'd better talk to it. It's your dad." So Hamlet goes up and talks to this, you know, fairly substantial apparition there. And this thing says, "I'm your father, I was murdered, you gotta avenge me, it was your uncle did it, here's how."

Well, was this good news or bad news? To this day we don't know if that ghost was really Hamlet's father. If you have messed around with Ouija boards, you know there are malicious spirits floating around, liable to tell you anything, and you shouldn't believe them. Madame Blavatsky, who knew more about the spirit world than anybody else, said you are a fool to take any apparition seriously, because they are often malicious and they are frequently the souls of people who were murdered, were suicides, or were terribly cheated in life in one way or another, and they are out for revenge.

So we don't know whether this thing was really Hamlet's father or if it was good news or bad news. And neither does Hamlet. But he says OK, I got a way to check this out. I'll hire actors to act out the way the ghost said my father was murdered by my uncle, and I'll put on this show and see what my uncle makes of it. So he puts on this show. And it's not like *Perry Mason*. His uncle doesn't go crazy and say, "I-I- You got me, you got me, I did it, I did it." It flops. Neither good news nor bad news. After this flop, Hamlet ends up talking with his mother when the drapes move, so he thinks his uncle is back there and he says, "All right, I am so sick of being so damn indecisive," and he sticks his rapier through the drapery. Well, who falls out? This wind-bag, Polonius. This Rush Limbaugh. And Shakespeare regards him as a fool and quite disposable.

You know, dumb parents think that the advice that Polonius gave to his kids when they were going away was what parents should always tell their kids, and it's the dumbest possible advice, and Shakespeare even thought it was hilarious.

"Neither a borrower nor a lender be." But what else is life but endless lending and borrowing, give and take?

"This above all, to thine own self be true." Be an egomaniac!

Neither good news nor bad news. Hamlet didn't get arrested. He's prince. He can kill anybody he wants. So he goes along, and finally he gets in a duel, and he's killed. Well, did he go to heaven or did he go to hell? Quite a difference. Cinderella or Kafka's cockroach? I don't think Shakespeare believed in a heaven or hell any more than I do. And so we don't know whether it's good news or bad news.

I have just demonstrated to you that Shakespeare was as poor a storyteller as any Arapaho.

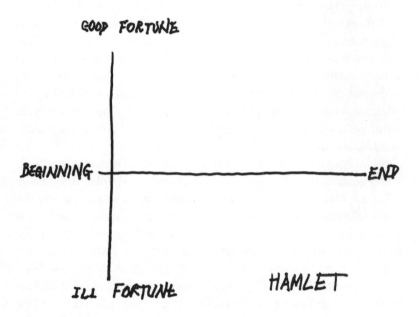

But there's a reason we recognize *Hamlet* as a masterpiece: it's that Shakespeare told us the truth, and people so rarely tell us the truth in this rise and fall here [*indicates blackboard*]. The truth is, we know so little about life, we don't really know what the good news is and what the bad news is.

And if I die — God forbid — I would like to go to heaven to ask somebody in charge up there, "Hey, what was the good news and what was the bad news?"

DAVID FOSTER WALLACE

∎

Kenyon Commencement Speech

GREETINGS, THANKS, and congratulations to Kenyon's graduating class of 2005.

There are these two young fish swimming along, and they happen to meet an older fish swimming the other way, who nods at them and says, "Morning, boys, how's the water?" And the two young fish swim on for a bit, and then eventually one of them looks over at the other and goes, "What the hell is water?"

This is a standard requirement of U.S. commencement speeches: the deployment of didactic little parable-ish stories. The story thing turns out to be one of the better, less bullshitty conventions of the genre . . . but if you're worried that I plan to present myself here as the wise old fish, please don't be. I am not the wise old fish. The immediate point of the fish story is merely that the most obvious, ubiquitous, important realities are often the ones that are hardest to see and talk about. Stated as an English sentence, of course, this is just a banal platitude — but the fact is that in the day-to-day trenches of adult existence, banal platitudes can have a life-or-death importance. Or so I wish to suggest to you on this dry and lovely morning.

Of course, the main requirement of speeches like this is that I'm supposed to talk about your liberal arts education's meaning, to try to explain why the degree you're about to receive has actual human value instead of just a material payoff. So let's talk about the single most pervasive cliché in the commencement-speech genre, which is that a liberal arts education is not so much about filling you up with knowledge as it is about, quote, "teaching you how to think." If you're like me as a college student, you've never liked hearing this, and you tend to feel a little insulted by the claim that you've needed anybody to teach you how to think, since the fact that you even got admitted to a college this good seems like proof that you already know how to think. But I'm going to posit to you that the liberal arts cliché turns out not to be insulting at all, because the really significant education in thinking that we're supposed to get in a place like this isn't really about the capacity to think, but rather about the choice of what to think about. If your complete freedom of choice regarding what to think about seems too obvious to waste time talking about, I'd ask you to think about fish and water and to bracket, for just a few minutes, your skepticism about the value of the totally obvious.

Here's another didactic little story. There are these two guys sitting together in a bar in the remote Alaskan wilderness. One of the guys is religious, the other's an atheist, and they're arguing about the existence of God with that special intensity that comes after about the fourth beer. And the atheist says, "Look, it's not like I don't have actual reasons for not believing in God. It's not like I haven't ever experimented with the whole God-and-prayer thing. Just last month, I got caught off away from camp in that terrible blizzard, and I couldn't see a thing, and I was totally lost, and it was fifty below, and so I did, I tried it: I fell to my knees in the snow and cried out, 'God, if there is a God, I'm lost in this blizzard and I'm gonna die if you don't help me!'" And now, in the bar, the religious guy looks at the atheist all puzzled: "Well, but you must believe now," he says. "After all, here you are, alive." The atheist rolls his eyes like the religious guy is a total simp: "No, man, all that happened was that a couple of Eskimos just happened to come wandering by, and they showed me the way back to the camp."

It's easy to run this story through a kind of standard liberal arts analysis: the exact same experience can mean two completely different things to two different people, given those two different people's templates and two different ways of constructing meaning from experience. Because we prize tolerance and diversity of belief, nowhere in our liberal arts analysis do we want to claim that one guy's interpretation is true and the other guy's is false or bad. Which is fine, except we also never end up talking about just where these individual templates and beliefs come from, meaning where they come from *inside* the two guys. As if a person's most basic orientation toward the world and the meaning of his experience were somehow automatically hard-wired, like height or shoe size, or absorbed from the culture like language. As if how we construct meaning were not actually a matter of personal, intentional choice, of conscious decision.

Plus there's the matter of arrogance. The nonreligious guy is so totally, obnoxiously confident in his dismissal of the possibility that the Eskimos had anything to do with his prayer for help. True, there are plenty of religious people who seem arrogantly certain of their own interpretations too. They're probably even more repulsive than atheists, at least to most of us here, but the fact is that religious dogmatists' problem is exactly the same as the story's atheist's — arrogance, blind certainty, a closed-mindedness that's like an imprisonment so complete that the prisoner doesn't even know he's locked up. The point here is that I think this is one part of what the liberal arts mantra of "teaching me how to think" is really supposed to mean: to be just a little less arrogant, to have some "critical awareness" about myself and my certainties . . . because a huge percentage of the stuff that I tend to be automatically certain of is, it turns out, totally wrong and deluded. I have learned this the hard way, as I predict you graduates will too.

Here's one example of the utter wrongness of something I tend to be automatically sure of. Everything in my own immediate experience supports my deep belief that I am the absolute center of the universe, the realest, most vivid and important person in existence. We rarely talk about this sort of natural, basic self-centeredness, because it's so socially repulsive, but it's pretty much the same for all of us, deep down. It is our default setting, hard-wired into our boards at birth. Think about it: there is no experience you've had that you were not at the absolute center of. The world as you experience it is there in front of you, or behind you, to the left or right of you, on your TV, or your monitor, or whatever. Other people's thoughts and feelings have to be communicated to you somehow, but your own are so immediate, urgent, *real*. You get the idea. But please don't worry that I'm getting ready to preach to you about compassion or other-directedness or all the other so-called virtues. This is not a matter of virtue — it is a matter of my choosing to do the work of somehow altering or getting free of my natural, hard-wired default setting, which is to be deeply and literally self-centered, and to see and interpret everything through this lens of self. People who *can* adjust their natural default setting this way are often described as being, quote, "well-adjusted," which I suggest to you is not an accidental term.

Given the academic setting here, an obvious question is how much of this work of adjusting our default setting involves actual knowledge or intellect. The answer, not surprisingly, is that it depends what kind of knowledge we're talking about. Probably the most dangerous thing about an academic education, at least in my own case, is that it enables my tendency to overintellectualize stuff, to get lost in abstract thinking instead of simply paying attention to what's going on in front of me. Instead of paying attention to what's going on *inside* me. As I'm sure you guys know by now, it is extremely difficult to stay alert and attentive instead of getting hypnotized by the constant monologue inside your head. What you don't yet know are the stakes of this struggle.

In the twenty years since my own graduation, I have come gradually to understand these stakes, and to see that the liberal arts cliché about "teaching you how to think" was actually shorthand for a very deep and important truth. "Learning how to think" really means learning how to exercise some control over *how* and *what* you think. It means being conscious of and aware enough to *choose* what you pay attention to and to *choose* how you construct meaning from experience. Because if you cannot or will not exercise this kind of choice in adult life, you will be totally hosed. Think of the old cliché about "the mind being an excellent servant but a terrible master." This, like many clichés, so lame and banal on the surface, actually expresses a great and terrible truth. It is not the least bit coincidental that adults who commit suicide with firearms nearly always shoot themselves in . . . the *head*. And the truth is that most of these suicides are actually dead long before they pull the trigger. And I submit that this is really what the real, no-shit value of your liberal arts education is supposed to be about: how to keep from going through your comfortable, prosperous, respectable adult life dead, unconscious, a slave to your head

and to your natural default setting of being uniquely, completely, im-
perially alone, day in and day out.

That may sound like hyperbole or abstract nonsense. So let's get
concrete. The plain fact is that you graduating seniors do not yet have
any clue what "day in, day out" really means. There happen to be
whole large parts of adult American life that nobody talks about in
commencement speeches. One such part involves boredom, routine,
and petty frustration. The parents and older folks here will know all
too well what I'm talking about. By way of example, let's say it's an average adult day, and you get up in the morning, go to your challenging
white-collar college-graduate job, and you work hard for nine or ten
hours, and at the end of the day you're tired, and you're stressed out,
and all you want is to go home and have a good supper and maybe unwind for a couple of hours and then hit the rack early because you
have to get up the next day and do it all again. But then you remember
that there's no food at home — you haven't had time to shop this
week because of your challenging job — and so now after work you
have to get in your car and drive to the supermarket. It's the end of the
workday, and the traffic's very bad, so getting to the store takes way
longer than it should, and when you finally get there the supermarket
is very crowded, because of course it's the time of day when all the
other people with jobs also try to squeeze in some grocery shopping,
and the store's hideously, fluorescently lit, and infused with soul-kill-
ing Muzak or corporate pop, and it's pretty much the last place you
want to be, but you can't just get in and quickly go out: you have to
wander all over the huge, overlit store's crowded aisles to find the
stuff you want, and you have to maneuver your junk cart through all
these other tired, hurried people with carts, and of course there are
also the glacially slow old people and the spacy people and ADHD
kids who all block the aisle and you have to grit your teeth and try to
be polite as you ask them to let you by, and eventually, finally, you
get all your supper supplies, except now it turns out there aren't
enough checkout lanes open even though it's the end-of-the-day rush,
so the checkout line is incredibly long, which is stupid and infuriat-
ing, but you can't take your fury out on the frantic lady working the
register, who is overworked at a job whose daily tedium and meaning-
lessness surpasses the imagination of any of us here at a prestigious

college . . . but anyway you finally get to the checkout line's front, and pay for your food, and wait to get your check or card authenticated by a machine, and then get told to "have a nice day" in a voice that is the absolute voice of *death*, and then you have to take your creepy flimsy plastic bags of groceries in your cart with the one crazy wheel that pulls maddeningly to the left all the way out through the crowded, bumpy, littery parking lot, and try to load the bags in your car in such a way that everything doesn't fall out of the bags and roll around in the trunk on the way home, and then you have to drive all the way home through slow, heavy, SUV-intensive rush-hour traffic, etcetera, etcetera. Everyone here has done this, of course — but it hasn't yet been part of you graduates' actual life routine, day after week after month after year. But it will be, and many more dreary, annoying, time-consuming, seemingly meaningless routines besides.

Except that's not the point. The point is that petty, frustrating crap like this is exactly where the work of choosing comes in. Because the traffic jams and crowded aisles and long checkout lines give me time to think, and if I don't make a conscious decision about how to think and what to pay attention to, I'm going to be pissed and miserable every time I have to food-shop, because my natural default setting is the certainty that situations like this are really all about *me*, about my hungriness and my fatigue and my desire to just get home, and it's going to seem, for all the world, like everybody else is just *in my way*, and who the fuck are all these people in my way? And look at how repulsive most of them are and how stupid and cow-like and dead-eyed and nonhuman they seem here in the checkout line, or at how annoying and rude it is that people are talking loudly on cell phones in the middle of the line, and look at how deeply unfair this is: I've worked really hard all day and I'm starved and tired and I can't even get home to eat and unwind because of all these stupid goddamn *people*. Or, of course, if I'm in a more socially conscious, liberal arts form of the default setting, I can spend time in the end-of-the-day traffic jam being angry and disgusted at all the huge, stupid, lane-blocking SUVs and Hummers and V-12 pickup trucks burning their wasteful, selfish, forty-gallon tanks of gas, and I can dwell on the fact that the patriotic or religious bumper stickers always seem to be on the biggest, most disgustingly selfish vehicles driven by the ugliest, most inconsiderate and aggressive drivers, who are usually talking on cell phones as they cut people off in order to get just twenty stupid feet ahead in the traffic jam, and I can think about how our children's children will despise us for wasting all the future's fuel and probably screwing up the climate, and how spoiled and stupid and selfish and disgusting we all are, and how it all just *sucks,* and so on and so forth.

Look, if I choose to think this way, fine, lots of us do — except that thinking this way tends to be so easy and automatic it doesn't *have* to be a choice. Thinking this way is my natural default setting. It's the automatic, unconscious way that I experience the boring, frustrating, crowded parts of adult life when I'm operating on the automatic, unconscious belief that I am the center of the world and that my immediate needs and feelings are what should determine the world's priorities. The thing is that there are obviously different ways to think about these kinds of situations. In this traffic, all these vehicles stuck and idling in my way: it's not impossible that some of these people in SUVs have been in horrible auto accidents in the past and now find driving so traumatic that their therapists have all but ordered them to get a huge, heavy SUV so they can feel safe enough to drive; or that the Hummer that just cut me off is maybe being driven by a father whose little child is hurt or sick in the seat next to him, and he's trying to rush to the hospital, and he's in a way bigger, more legitimate hurry than I am — it is actually *I* who am in *his* way. Or I can choose to force myself to consider the likelihood that everyone else in the supermarket checkout line is probably just as bored and frustrated as I am, and that some of these people actually have much harder, more tedious or painful lives than I do, overall. And so on. Again, please don't think that I'm giving you moral advice, or that I'm saying you're "supposed to" think this way, or that anyone expects you to just automatically do it, because it's hard, it takes will and mental effort, and if you're like me, some days you won't be able to do it, or else you just flat-out won't want to. But most days, if you're aware enough to give yourself a choice, you can choose to look differently at this fat, dead-eyes, over-made-up lady who just screamed at her little child in the checkout line — maybe she's not usually like this; maybe she's been up three straight nights holding the hand of her husband who's dying of bone cancer, or maybe this very lady is the low-wage clerk at the motor vehicles department who just yesterday helped your spouse resolve a nightmarish red-tape problem through some small act of bureaucratic kindness. Of course none of this is likely, but it's also not impossible — it just depends what you want to consider. If you're automatically sure that you know what reality is and who and what is really important — if you want to operate on your default setting — then you, like me, probably will not consider possibilities that aren't pointless and annoying. But if you've really learned how to think, how to pay attention, then you will know you have other options. It will actually be within your power to experience a crowded, loud, slow, consumer-hell-type situation as not only meaningful but sacred, on fire with the same force that lit the stars — compassion, love, the subsurface unity of all things. Not that that mystical stuff's necessarily true: the only thing that's capital-T True is that you get to *decide* how you're going to try to see it. This, I submit, is the freedom of real education, of learning how to be well adjusted: you get to consciously decide what has meaning and what doesn't. You get to decide what to worship.

Because here's something else that's true. In the day-to-day trenches of adult life, there is actually no such thing as atheism. There is no such thing as not worshiping. Everybody worships. The only choice we get is *what* to worship. And an outstanding reason for choosing some sort of God or spiritual-type thing to worship — be it J. C. or Allah, be it Yahweh or the Wiccan mother goddess or the Four Noble Truths or some infrangible set of ethical principles — is that pretty much anything else you worship will eat you alive. If you worship money and things — if they are where you tap real meaning in life — then you will never have enough. Never feel you have enough. It's the truth. Worship your own body and beauty and sexual allure and you will always feel ugly, and when time and age start showing, you will die a million deaths before they finally plant you. On one level we all know this stuff already — it's been codified as myths, proverbs, clichés, bromides, epigrams, parables: the skeleton of every great story. The trick is keeping the truth up front in daily consciousness. Worship power — you will feel weak and afraid, and you will need ever more power over others to keep the fear at bay. Worship your intellect, being seen as smart — you will end up feeling stupid, afraid, always on the verge of being found out. And so on.

Look, the insidious thing about these forms of worship is not that they're evil or sinful; it is that they are *unconscious*. They are default settings. They're the kind of worship you just gradually slip into, day after day, getting more and more selective about what you see and how you measure value without ever being fully aware that that's what you're doing. And the so-called real world will not discourage you from operating on your default settings, because the so-called real world of men and money and power hums along quite nicely on the fuel of fear and contempt and frustration and craving and the worship of self. Our own present culture has harnessed these forces in ways that have yielded extraordinary wealth and comfort and personal freedom. The freedom all to be lords of our own tiny skull-size kingdoms, alone at the center of all creation. This kind of freedom has much to recommend it. But of course there are all different kinds of freedom, and the kind that is most precious you will not hear talked about much in the great outside world of winning and achieving and displaying. The really important kind of freedom involves attention, and awareness, and discipline, and effort, and being able truly to care about other people and to sacrifice for them, over and over, in myriad petty little unsexy ways, every day. That is real freedom. That is being taught how to think. The alternative is unconscious, the default setting, the rat race — the constant, gnawing sense of having had and lost some infinite thing.

I know that this stuff probably doesn't sound fun and breezy or grandly inspirational the way a commencement speech's central stuff should sound. What it is, so far as I can see, is the truth with a whole lot of rhetorical bullshit pared away. Obviously, you can think of it whatever you wish. But please don't dismiss it as some finger-wagging Dr. Laura sermon. None of this is about morality, or religion, or dogma, or big fancy questions of life after death. The capital-T Truth is about life *before* death. It is about making it to thirty, or maybe even fifty, without wanting to shoot yourself in the head. It is about the real value of a real education, which has nothing to do with grades or degrees and everything to do with simple awareness — awareness of what is so real and essential, so hidden in plain sight all around us, that we have to keep reminding ourselves, over and over: "This is water, this is water; these Eskimos might be much more than they seem." It is unimaginably hard to do this — to live consciously, adultly, day in and day out. Which means yet another cliché is true: your education really *is* the job of a lifetime, and it commences — now. I wish you way more than luck.

"Shipwreck" is **Cat Bohannon**'s first published piece. She's doing an MFA at Columbia University and is nearing completion of her first book. Tell her what you think at stillrising@hotmail.com.

Judy Budnitz is the author of two story collections, *Nice Big American Baby* and *Flying Leap*, and a novel, *If I Told You Once*. Her stories have appeared in *The New Yorker*, *Harper's Magazine*, *Story*, the *Paris Review*, *McSweeney's*, and elsewhere.

Born in Quebec City in 1966, **Guy Delisle** now lives in the South of France with his wife and son. Delisle has spent ten years, mostly in Europe, working in animation, which has allowed him to learn about movement and drawing. The majority of animation is now done in Asia, so Delisle is currently focusing on his cartooning. In addition to contributing to *Drawn & Quarterly*, Delisle is published by Éditions de l'Association and Éditions Dargaud in France, and Éditions de la Pastèque in Montreal.

Tom Downey hails from New York and is the author of *The Last Men Out: Life on the Edge at Rescue 2 Firehouse*. After a couple of years spent researching that book in the borough of Brooklyn, he now ventures out into the rest of the world to write about politics, travel, or anything else that strikes his fancy for publications including *Rolling Stone*, *Condé Nast Traveler*, *Men's Journal*, and the *New York Times*.

Gipi, whose real name is Gianni Pacinotti, was born in Pisa in 1963. After working as an advertising and book illustrator, he began writing and drawing comics in 1992. He has published his work in several magazines, such as *Cuore, Blue, Il Clandestino*, and *Lo Straniero*.

▪ In January 2000 he founded Santa Maria Video, a company under which he produces live and animated short films.

▪ His main publisher is Coconino Press, which published his first anthology, *Esterno notte;* it was released in several European countries and won the Micheluzzi Award and the Gran Premio Romics, both in 2004. Coconino also released the graphic novel *Appunti per una storia di guerra*, published both in Italy and in France, where he was a huge success, winning two awards: the Goscinny Award and the Grand Prix of the Angoulême International Comics Festival.

▪ His latest graphic novel is *Questa è la stanza*. Currently, he's begun working on the third volume of his Ignatz title (*Wish You Were Here*) and he continues to work as a magazine illustrator.

Miranda July makes movies and performances and writes fiction. She wrote, directed, and starred in her first feature film, *Me and You and Everyone We Know*, which won a special jury prize at Sundance and the Camera d'Or at Cannes in 2005. *No One Belongs Here More Than You*, a collection of short stories, is forthcoming. She lives in Los Angeles.

Michael Lewis grew up in New Orleans and lives in Berkeley, California, with his wife, Tabitha Soren, and their two daughters. He is the author of several books, including *Liar's Poker, Moneyball*, and most recently, *The Blind Side*.

Naguib Mahfouz was born in 1911 in the crowded Cairo district of Gamaliya. He has written nearly forty novel-length works, hundreds of short stories, and numerous movie plots and scenarios. He was awarded the Nobel Prize in literature in 1988. He lives in the Cairo suburb of Agouza with his wife and two daughters.

Rick Moody is the author, most recently, of *The Black Veil*, a memoir, and *The Diviners*, a novel.

Haruki Murakami was born in Kyoto in 1949 and now lives near Tokyo. His work has been translated into thirty-four languages, and the most recent of his many honors is the Yomiuri Literary Prize, whose previous recipients include Yukio Mishima, Kenzaburo Oe, and Kobo Abe.

Stories by **Jeff Parker** have appeared in *Ploughshares, Tin House,* and other journals. "False Cognate" first appeared in *Hobart* and in the anthology *Stumbling and Raging: More Politically Inspired Fiction.* His novel *Ovenman* will be published in summer 2007.

David Rakoff is the author of *Fraud* and *Don't Get Too Comfortable.* He is a regular contributor to *GQ, Outside,* the *New York Times Magazine,* and Public Radio International's *This American Life,* and his writing has also appeared in *Salon, Slate, Vogue, Wired,* the *New York Observer, Gourmet,* and *Seed,* among other magazines. He can be seen (fleetingly) in the film *Capote,* and also (fleetingly, mutely) in *Strangers with Candy.* He lives in New York City.

Joe Sacco was born in Malta in 1960. He studied journalism at the University of Oregon and has been working as a cartoonist since the mid-1980s. His books of comic journalism include *Palestine, Safe Area Gorazde, The Fixer,* and *War's End. Trauma on Loan* was nominated in 2006 for an Amnesty International Media Award.

George Saunders is the author of the short story collections *Pastorulia, CivilWarLand in Bad Decline,* and most recently, *In Persuasion Nation.* He is also the author of the novella-length illustrated fable *The Brief and Frightening Reign of Phil* and the *New York Times* bestselling children's book *The Very Persistent Gappers of Frip* (illustrated by Lane Smith), which has won major children's literature prizes in Italy and the Netherlands. He teaches in the creative writing program at Syracuse University.

Sam Shaw supplied the voice of a talking orangutan in a television commercial for Hi-C Fruit Drink, circa 1991. A graduate of the Iowa Writers' Workshop, he lives in Brooklyn, New York, where he is working on a novel about aviation, hard rock mining, and tropical birds.

His fiction has appeared in *The Best American Mystery Stories 2005*, *StoryQuarterly*, and *Open City*.

Julia Sweeney is best known for her androgynous character Pat on *Saturday Night Live* and for her critically acclaimed one-woman monologue, *God Said, Ha!*, which played on Broadway, at the Lyceum Theater, in 1996. Miramax released the film version of the show in 1998, which was produced by Quentin Tarantino. The CD version of the show was nominated for a Grammy. More recently, Sweeney has been a consultant for the HBO series *Sex and the City* and has written and performed two other monologues. She has appeared as a guest star on several TV shows and has had small parts in a few movies.

Kurt Vonnegut is among the few grandmasters of contemporary American letters, without whom the very term "American literature" would mean less than it does. He was born in Indianapolis, Indiana, on November 11, 1922. He lives in New York City and Bridgehampton, New York, with his wife, the author and photographer Jill Krementz.

David Foster Wallace is the author of two essay collections, *Consider the Lobster* and *A Supposedly Fun Thing I'll Never Do Again*, the bestselling novel *Infinite Jest*, and several story collections. He lives in California.

The Best American Nonrequired Reading is compiled with the help of many people, some who are in high school and some who have finished high school and even college. Each week, the students of the *Best American Nonrequired Reading* Committee meet at 826 Valencia, in San Francisco, and they discuss what they've read and what they like. Aiding in all this are the hundreds of publications, large and small, that have been kind enough to keep us on their subscription lists. We dearly wish we could include more pieces in this collection; we always have an exceedingly difficult time narrowing down the list to twenty-five or thereabouts. Especially difficult this year was casting a net around the increased scope of what *BANR* could republish. Because we sought to include screenplays, propaganda, constitutions, commencement speeches, and the like, we sought help from a group of adults who work as tutors for 826 Valencia and/or as interns for *McSweeney's*. The following people were very enthusiastic and helpful, and in some cases tracked down hard-to-find pieces: Dan Sanders, Lisa Amick, Ian Brill, Jim Fingal, Rebecca Winterer, Caitlin Van Dusen, Monique Wells, Sona Avakian, Patrick Knowles, Holly Griggspall, and Matt Werner.

Acting as a sort of managing editor, helping in a hundred ways and inspiring the respect and affection of the student committee, was Kevin Collier. He helped organize the list and brought us a great bounty, from which we selected a smaller bounty.

About the students on the committee:

Rachel Bolten's current nature is the product of seven fantastic and occasionally hilarious years of single-sex education at Castilleja School in Palo Alto, where, among other things, she has cultivated an enduring passion for the three R's: reading, (w)riting, and ritual sacrifice. Next year Rachel will leave all that she knows and loves to do one of two things: (1) go to college, or (2) tour the world giving motivational speeches, based on experiences from her already brilliant career as an avid enthusiast.

Alison Cagle just finished her senior year of high school in Pacifica. Having finished her whirlwind safari adventure with *Best American Nonrequired,* she plans to attend a four-year university while studiously using the existence of *Futurama* as her alibi for procrastination. She joyfully endures a long-term addiction to the written word, especially if that word happens to be in Russian, and constantly preaches that we neglect the earth's obvious warnings only at our peril. When not actively advocating for equal rights or singing along to Labyrinth, Alison devotes herself to writing, editing, and promoting the "Free Alexander T. (Wolf)" campaign. When she is a rich sugarmamma, Alison (also known as Santiago) intends to send 150 roses to Stephen Gaghan, for doing her the honor of existing beautifully.

 At the time of this writing, **Kimberly Chua** was a senior at Lowell High School in San Francisco, and by the time you read this she will be attending San Francisco State University, which can be seen from the Lowell football field. As a newbie on the *Best American* staff, she has raised numerous eyebrows with her weekly snacks, a.k.a. puppies.

Lia Mezzio is an eighteen-year-old dual native of Oakland and Berkeley. She spent the better half of her infancy flipping through the pages of paperback novels for amusement, later developing into a chronic writer and excellent pasta chef. She enjoys opening scrunched wads of paper to reveal their mistakes, beat poetry, punk rock, and the concept that sound can be burned into plastic. One day she was late for work at 826 Valencia because a dancing man obstructed the subway tracks for several minutes while simultaneously evading the police. She currently is waiting out high school graduation, drinking too much coffee, and sometimes laughing for no apparent reason. When she grows up she wants to be the president of the United

States, an ancient Greek philosopher, or a dinosaur (triceratops). Good luck, cheaters!

Emily Vo Nguyen, a graduate of Lick-Wilmerding High School, is not afraid to work with her hands and think with her heart. She will remember her many Tuesday-night adventures with the *BANR* All-Stars, which include: reading tales about dismembered body parts, lobbying for *BANR* tattoos, and exploring the underground dens of the *McSweeney's* office. She would like to give big shout-outs to the Bay Area and Vietnam.

At the time of this writing, **Kerry Tiedeman** has absolutely no idea what university she will be attending next year. However, she does know she will be missing *BANR* greatly. Kerry will be remembered for her friendly yet vulgar nature, her witty anecdotes, her affinity for Steve Gaghan, and her disgusting tan slippers. Now, before leaving, she would like to clear up one thing: she absolutely adores French people!

Matt Wagstaffe just graduated from high school in San Jose. In his free time he helps teach a painting class and rows under the tutelage of a former Polish Olympian who has not done much by way of assimilating into American culture. He does not know what he wants to do with the rest of his life, except eventually to become an adult without outgrowing his current penchant for bubblegum ice cream, Push-Ups (the Flintstones sherbet variety), and hot chocolate instead of coffee.

Emily Winter has lived in the same house in San Francisco for her entire life. By the time you read this, she will no longer be in high school. She will have happily graduated and moved to Wyoming for the summer. Then she will go to college somewhere where it snows. This year was her first on the *Best American* committee, and boy, did she love it. Tuesday nights have never been so action-packed!

Next year, as a senior at the School of the Arts, **Felicia Wong** will play the opening lines of "Pomp and Circumstance" on a melodica every morning before entering class. This is her second year at *BANR* and she has learned some very important life lessons. (1) It is never polite to gawk. (2) Neutral Milk Hotel is a very vintage and secret band. (3) Saving all your hair clippings in a fancy hatbox will provide hours of amusement at other people's expense. (4) Being obsessed with a certain Mr. Stevens is never a bad thing. (5) Beard-growing contests are filled with fun, but determining the winner is always difficult. Felicia wishes she could grow a beard. (6) Adding mail-order brides to your story can make it more literary. (7) Bill Haverchuck for president!

Adrienne Formentos, a spring 2006 graduate of Thurgood Marshall High School, has thankfully matured in the two years since she first joined the *Best American* committee. She is looking forward to attending college and gaining the projected fifteen pounds this fall. When time allows, she attempts to write poetry and has failed many times, but she has not given up the idea that writing is her niche. She is both a liberal San Franciscan and a devout Catholic. She believes every day is a blessing.

Born and raised in San Francisco, **Roz LaBean** attends Wallenberg High School in San Francisco and hopes one day to be a lawyer or an interior designer. She loves spending time with her boyfriend, Eddie, listening to Johnny Cash, and performing the spoken word. Her role model is her great-grandmother, who encouraged her to always pursue her interests and never give up. After volunteering at an animal shelter, Roz produced the most memorable quote in the *BANR* committee's hundreds of hours together: "I thought it was gonna be all bunnies and puppies, but the next thing I knew, I was squeezing anal glands."

Christopher Bernard lives in the Fillmore district of San Francisco and is a senior at Wallenberg High School. A voracious reader, Chris hopes to go to law school and become a prosecutor or a state senator; in either case, he wants to change the way laws are written. He considers himself a cool and collected person who on weekends spends a lot of time on his homework and even some time enjoying himself.

At press time, **Teresa Cotsirilos** was temporarily hobbled due to a renegade extra bone in her left foot. Though this picture may suggest otherwise, she is thrilled by her recently discovered mutant status and recently acquired a special parking permit. She is also relieved that the anomaly is not more extensive, considering the gene pool of pyromaniacs, spontaneous tap dancers, and lawyers whence she came. A native of Berkeley, Teresa enjoys eating hummus and galvanizing revolution.

All photos by **Felicia Wong**

Additional help provided by **Adrianna Kandell**

826 Valencia is a network of six nonprofit writing and publishing centers for young people, ages eight to eighteen. The centers have at their core a belief that one-on-one tutoring can make an enormous difference in the lives of students, and to that end, 826 has recruited and trained thousands of volunteer tutors, who work with students at our centers and, more often, in public schools. This concentrated attention, which helps both the students and their teachers, has a lasting effect on student self-esteem, on students' understanding of concepts, and on their overall enjoyment of and success in school.

Because the tutor base is so diverse and talented, 826 is able to offer workshops every evening and field trips almost every day. In these classes, all of them free, students can learn more about writing-related arts, from haiku to filmmaking to writing short stories for their pets. These classes, and the programs in schools, lead to a wide array of student publications and other productions, from monthly newspapers to quarterly journals to chapbooks to digital films to radio shows. (This book is edited by a group of students at 826 Valencia in San Francisco, as part of a year-round class that meets once a week.)

With so many students working with so many volunteers on so many projects, the communities in which 826 centers exist are strengthened and the load on students, teachers, parents, and schools becomes just a little lighter. To learn more:

826 Valencia in San Francisco, CA
www.826valencia.org <http://www.826valencia.org>

826NYC in Brooklyn, NY
www.826NYC.org <http://www.826NYC.org>

826LA in Venice, CA
www.826LA.org <http://www.826LA.org>

826CHI in Chicago, IL
www.826CHI.org <http://www.826CHI.org>

826Michigan in Ann Arbor, MI
www.826michigan.org <http://www.826michigan.org>

826Seattle in Seattle, WA
www.826seattle.org

NOTABLE
NONREQUIRED READING
OF 2005

SAMMY HARKHAM
Somersaulting, *Drawn & Quarterly*
ELEANOR HENDERSON
Thanks for Festooning Me Through the Heart, *Indiana Review*
DON HERTZFELD
Dance of the Sugar Plums; or, Last Month on Earth, *Flight*
BOB HICOK
Watchglow, *Swink*

ROLIN JONES
The Intelligent Design of Jenny Chow: An Instant Message with Excitable Music (play)
MIRANDA JULY
The Shared Patio, *Zoetrope: All-Story*

JESSICA LAMB-SHAPIRO
We Need Heart-Touching Soul-Penetrating Stories!, *The Believer*
EVAN LAUENDER-SMITH
Appalachian Spring, *Land-Grant College Review*
MARK LEWANDOWSKI
The Silent Fall, *Florida Review*
KELLY LINK
The Great Divorce, *One Story*

CHARLES MCLEOD
The Individual Altimetry of Stripes, *Iowa Review*
RICK MOODY
Grocery List, *Salmagundi*
RYU MURAKAMI
I Am a Novelist, *The New Yorker*

CHUCK PALAHNIUK
"Guts," from the novel *Haunted*
FRANCES DE PONTES PEEBLES
The Disappearance of Luisa Porto, *Zoetrope: All-Story*
LUCIA PERILLO
Medicine, *Michigan Quarterly Review*
TOM PRICE
Exiles of the Kalahari, *Mother Jones*

ELIZABETH ROLLINS
Joint Custody, *New England Review*

KAREN RUSSELL
   Haunting Olivia, *The New Yorker*
MARK RUSSELL
   Make Your Love an Adventure, *Eye~ Rhyme: Journal of New Literature*

MATT ST. AMAND
   Continental Divide, *Hobart*
SHAHAN SANOSSIAN
   The Man with the Hairy Back, *Speakeasy*
DAVID SEDARIS
   Turbulence, *The New Yorker*
TOM SINCLAIR
   School's Out, *Spin*
GEORGE SINGLETON
   The Lickers, *Kenyon Review*

JUSTIN TUSSING
   The Laser Age, *The New Yorker*

BINYAVANGA WAINAINA
   Ships in High Transit, *Virginia Quarterly Review*
MARGARET WEATHERFORD
   East of the 5, South of the 10, *Waterstone Review*
HANNAH WILSON
   Thieves, *Other Voices*
MATTHEW WOODSON
   Tendergrass, *Flight*
G. K. WUORI
   Naked Circus, *StoryQuarterly*

THE B·E·S·T AMERICAN SERIES®

Introducing our newest addition to the BEST AMERICAN *series*

THE BEST AMERICAN COMICS 2006. Harvey Pekar, guest editor, Anne Elizabeth Moore, series editor. This newcomer to the best-selling series — the first Best American annual dedicated to the finest in graphic storytelling and literary comics — includes stories culled from graphic novels, pamphlet comics, newspapers, magazines, mini-comics, and the Web. Edited by the subject of the Oscar-nominated film *American Splendor,* Harvey Pekar, the collection features pieces by Robert Crumb, Chris Ware, Kim Deitch, Jaime Hernandez, Alison Bechdel, Joe Sacco, Lilli Carré, and Lynda Barry, among others.

ISBN-10: 0-618-71874-5 / ISBN-13: 978-0-618-71874-0 $22.00 POB

Alongside our perennial favorites

THE BEST AMERICAN SHORT STORIES® 2006. Ann Patchett, guest editor, Katrina Kenison, series editor. This year's most beloved short fiction anthology is edited by Ann Patchett, author of *Bel Canto,* a 2002 PEN/Faulkner Award winner and a National Book Critics Circle Award finalist. The collection features stories by Tobias Wolff, Donna Tartt, Thomas McGuane, Mary Gaitskill, Nathan Englander, and others. "Story for story, readers can't beat the *Best American Short Stories* series" (*Chicago Tribune*).

ISBN-10: 0-618-54351-1 / ISBN-13: 978-0-618-54351-9 $28.00 CL
ISBN-10: 0-618-54352-X / ISBN-13: 978-0-618-54352-6 $14.00 PA

THE BEST AMERICAN NONREQUIRED READING 2006. Edited by Dave Eggers, introduction by Matt Groening. This "enticing . . . funny, and wrenching" (*Cleveland Plain Dealer*) collection highlights a bold mix of fiction, nonfiction, screenplays, alternative comics, and more from publications large, small, and online. With an introduction by Matt Groening, creator of *The Simpsons* and *Futurama,* this volume features writing from *The Onion, The Daily Show, This American Life,* Judy Budnitz, Joe Sacco, and others.

ISBN-10: 0-618-57050-0 / ISBN-13: 978-0-618-57050-8 $28.00 CL
ISBN-10: 0-618-57051-9 / ISBN-13: 978-0-618-57051-5 $14.00 PA

THE BEST AMERICAN ESSAYS® 2006. Lauren Slater, guest editor, Robert Atwan, series editor. Since 1986, *The Best American Essays* has annually gathered outstanding nonfiction writing, establishing itself as the premier anthology of its kind. Edited by the best-selling author of *Prozac Diary,* Lauren Slater, this year's "delightful collection" (*Miami Herald*) highlights provocative, lively writing by Adam Gopnik, Scott Turow, Marjorie Williams, Poe Ballantine, and others.

ISBN-10: 0-618-70531-7 / ISBN-13: 978-0-618-70531-3 $28.00 CL
ISBN-10: 0-618-70529-5 / ISBN-13: 978-0-618-70529-0 $14.00 PA

THE BEST AMERICAN MYSTERY STORIES™ 2006. Scott Turow, guest editor, Otto Penzler, series editor. This perennially popular anthology is sure to appeal to mystery fans of every variety. The 2006 volume, edited by Scott Turow, author of the critically acclaimed *Ordinary Heroes* and *Presumed Innocent,* features both mystery veterans and new talents, offering stories by Elmore Leonard, Ed McBain, James Lee Burke, Joyce Carol Oates, Walter Mosley, and others.

ISBN-10: 0-618-51746-4 / ISBN-13: 978-0-618-51746-6 $28.00 CL
ISBN-10: 0-618-51747-2 / ISBN-13: 978-0-618-51747-3 $14.00 PA

THE B·E·S·T AMERICAN SERIES®

THE BEST AMERICAN SPORTS WRITING™ 2006. Michael Lewis, guest editor, Glenn Stout, series editor. "An ongoing centerpiece for all sports collections" (*Booklist*), this series stands in high regard for its extraordinary sports writing and top-notch editors. This year's guest editor, Michael Lewis, the acclaimed author of the bestseller *Moneyball*, brings together pieces by Gary Smith, Pat Jordan, Paul Solotaroff, Linda Robertson, L. Jon Wertheim, and others.

> ISBN-10: 0-618-47021-2 / ISBN-13: 978-0-618-47021-1 $28.00 CL
> ISBN-10: 0-618-47022-0 / ISBN-13: 978-0-618-47022-8 $14.00 PA

THE BEST AMERICAN TRAVEL WRITING 2006. Tim Cahill, guest editor, Jason Wilson, series editor. Tim Cahill is the founding editor of *Outside* magazine and a frequent contributor to *National Geographic Adventure*. This year's collection captures the traveler's wandering spirit and ever-present quest for adventure. Giving new life to armchair journeys are Alain de Botton, Pico Iyer, David Sedaris, Gary Shteyngart, George Saunders, and others.

> ISBN-10: 0-618-58212-6 / ISBN-13: 978-0-618-58212-9 $28.00 CL
> ISBN-10: 0-618-58215-0 / ISBN-13: 978-0-618-58215-0 $14.00 PA

THE BEST AMERICAN SCIENCE AND NATURE WRITING 2006. Brian Greene, guest editor, Tim Folger, series editor. Brian Greene, the best-selling author of *The Elegant Universe* and the first physicist to edit this prestigious series, offers a fresh take on the year's best science and nature writing. Featuring such authors as John Horgan, Daniel C. Dennett, and Dennis Overbye, among others, this collection "surprises us into caring about subjects we had not thought to examine" (*Cleveland Plain Dealer*).

> ISBN-10: 0-618-72221-1 / ISBN-13: 978-0-618-72221-1 $28.00 CL
> ISBN-10: 0-618-72222-X / ISBN-13: 978-0-618-72222-8 $14.00 PA

THE BEST AMERICAN SPIRITUAL WRITING 2006. Edited by Philip Zaleski, introduction by Peter J. Gomes. Featuring an introduction by Peter J. Gomes, a best-selling author, respected minister, and the Plummer Professor of Christian Morals at Harvard University, this year's edition of this "excellent annual" (*America*) gathers pieces from diverse faiths and denominations and includes writing by Michael Chabon, Malcolm Gladwell, Mary Gordon, John Updike, and others.

> ISBN-10: 0-618-58644-X / ISBN-13: 978-0-618-58644-8 $28.00 CL
> ISBN-10: 0-618-58645-8 / ISBN-13: 978-0-618-58645-5 $14.00 PA

THE BEST AMERICAN GOLD GIFT BOX 2006. Boxed in rich gold metallic, this set includes *The Best American Short Stories 2006*, *The Best American Mystery Stories 2006*, and *The Best American Sports Writing 2006*.

> ISBN-10: 0-618-80126-X / ISBN-13: 978-0-618-80126-8 $40.00 PA

THE BEST AMERICAN SILVER GIFT BOX 2006. Packaged in a lavish silver metallic box, this set features *The Best American Short Stories 2006*, *The Best American Travel Writing 2006*, and *The Best American Spiritual Writing 2006*.

> ISBN-10: 0-618-80127-8 / ISBN-13: 978-0-618-80127-5 $40.00 PA

 HOUGHTON MIFFLIN COMPANY www.houghtonmifflinbooks.com